JOHN SEALEY

GW00480833

A YOUNG MAN'S AWAKENING

To PHILLP MY (BEST)
FRIEND. I TRULY HOPE
you RECOVER SOON.
Very Best Wishes

John

In the nineteenth century
masturbation was the primary
activity of men and women and
looked upon as a disease.
But now in the twenty first century
it is considered a cure.

Thomas Szasz

Part I

Ireland
The Beginning

Chapter 1

The schoolhouse was a simple stone cottage a little larger than the others in the small communal cluster. The walls and roof covered with mud and grass to add to the structure's weatherproofing. It was windowless with the only light coming through the gaps in the cracked panels of the ill-fitted door.

Outside, stacked in piles, were as many chunks of peat as there were children, each having brought a piece as a tribute and remuneration to Mrs Talbot the teacher.

The children that is those whose parents could barely afford to let them go to school, would squat on the cold earthen floor wrapped in their tattered clothing and holding their little books as high as possible so they could catch the light. Mrs Talbot would sit on the only chair, placed in the middle of the room, so that everyone could see and hear her as she taught them the alphabet and rudiments of the English language.

Mrs Talbot appeared to have a stern-looking face, put on more to intimidate the children into being frightened and more obedient, but it hid a gentler, more passionate nature that she was careful never to show. She wore a dress with low-sloping shoulders, a pointed waist, and a voluminous bell-shaped skirt. Her hair parted in the centre with ringlets at the sides of her head and was pulled into a bun at the back. On her feet she wore black brogue shoes.

Michael Flanagan was one of her pupils, aged fifteen with a strong, lean muscular body standing five feet eight. He had a mop of dark unruly hair covering his head, and his rugged weather-beaten face showed the early pain and the wear and tear that he, his family, and the rest of the community suffered given the hardship of their impoverished lives.

Michael lived with his parents on a small plot of land in

one of the small communal clusters in the rural countryside outside Dublin. The family were barely able to feed themselves, existing on the meagre amount of potatoes they were able to grow on the small stone-walled plot they had alongside the cottage, struggling to pay the rent with the pitiful wages Michael's father earned as a farm labourer.

He was growing up like any other boy in the poverty-stricken areas, too young to understand the bleakness of his parents' life and yet old enough to know the rigours of having to go without food, so that his father could have enough to eat to be able to work.

Mrs Talbot had taken a particular liking to Michael. Although he was of a good build, he appeared a little reserved, quiet, and very sensitive. Nevertheless he seemed brighter than the rest of the class. She by chance discovered he had a love for music when she happened to notice him standing outside the schoolhouse one evening listening to her playing the violin and decided that if he was really that interested, she would teach him about music, even how to play the violin. It would also be good for her as it would help to fill the lonely nights as she did not mix readily with the local farmers and their wives, many of whom did not approve of their children being taught, particularly by a woman, about things that they themselves had never been taught.

Although excited by the offer, Michael was reluctant at first, but he became more interested when she told him that the violin is one of the most rewarding and beautiful instruments to play and that Michael William O'Rourke, the son of a Dublin tradesman, born in South Great George's Street, had learned to play the violin at an early age and went on to become a great musician and composer, later being appointed chorus master and deputy leader of the orchestra at Crow Street Theatre. It was there that he composed his first opera, *Amilie*.

Michael began to enjoy the evenings with Mrs Talbot, who was surprised by how quickly he was learning the basic fundamentals of playing the violin.

"Very good, Michael," she said encouragingly one day during his lesson. "That was much better. But your arm movement needs to be much tighter so that the chord is more vibrant. And try to make your strokes smoother. Remember, the down bows should always start at the frog. Relax and feel the balance of the body in your stance, feet firm on the floor with the upper body flexible yet firm, and learn to breathe between the phrases. Play it cantabile."

"Cantabile?" Michael repeated, looking at her, puzzled by the strange word.

"Sorry, I'm running ahead of myself. Cantabile simply means playing it smooth, flowing, and melodious, just as if you were singing, making it sound more natural," she explained.

"I will try my best," he said, letting a pleased smile spread across his face as he looked at her, a little apprehensive.

"I know it is a lot for you to take in, but I want you to keep practising every chance you get, because I believe you could become an accomplished violinist, if not a great one. But as Michael O'Rourke, and every great musician will tell you, it takes practice, practice, and more practice."

"But I can only practise here with you until I manage to have my own violin," he said, a bit of sadness sounding in his voice.

She smiled. There was gentleness in her eyes and a deep understanding on her face. "I'll tell you what I will do, Michael. I will let you borrow the violin so that you can practise in your spare time. And who knows, maybe one day you'll be famous like Michael O'Rourke," she said, her words so unexpected that it left him speechless, not sure how to respond.

"Thank you, Mrs Talbot. I will practise as much as I can, I promise. And thank you for trusting me with the violin. I will take great care of it," he said, taking the violin from her and carefully placing it back in its case, along with the bow.

"Make sure you do. Now off you go. I don't expect to see you until you can play that piece we've been practising perfectly. Treat that instrument with the same love and care you have for music," she said, as a shadow of a smile touched her lips.

"I will, Mrs Talbot, I promise you," Michael assured her as he picked up the violin case and made his way out, feeling that this was the beginning of fulfilling his new-found ambition to become a great and famous musician.

Chapter 2

Patrick sat with his mates in the schoolroom, his mind solely on hoping for the lesson to end so that he could do what he had planned.

Mrs Talbot was teaching them the English alphabet. But Patrick wasn't interested whether *B* followed *A*, or *E* followed *D*, for his mind was set on Michael and the lesson they were going to teach him about what it means to be a proper boy, not a sissy playing a stupid fiddle.

Patrick was the same age, dressed a little scruffier than Michael, with unruly hair that was in need of a good combing and cutting. He had a dirty face with dark rings around his eyes that gave him menacing look. His trousers were baggy, his socks were slumped around his ankles, and the toes of his boots were badly scuffed. He was uncaring about his appearance other than to show he was tough and not to be messed with. Patrick was a bully who bullied because he enjoyed it and loved the power he thought it gave him.

As soon as Mrs Talbot announced the end of the day's lessons, Patrick was on his feet and the first out of the schoolroom, quickly followed by his mates, who already knew what he was planning.

"Is it all right if I stay and practise, Miss?" Michael asked as soon as all the other children had gone.

"Of course, Michael. I'm pleased you want to practise. Unfortunately I can't stay with you as I have to be somewhere else, but stay as long as you like," Mrs Talbot told him with her usual encouraging smile. "And I will see how well you've progressed tomorrow," she added as further encouragement before she left.

Michael, full of enthusiasm, set up the music stand, placed the sheet music on it, then took out the violin from its case and stroked it devotedly. Next he removed the bow. Mrs Talbot had impressed upon him that the tension on the bow hair must always be loosened before putting the bow back in its case, very important to keeping the hairs in the best condition. He carefully turned the screw at the end of the bow to tighten the hair and slid his tiny finger between the stick and the hairs as she had taught him to gauge the right tension. He then took the little tin of rosin and rubbed it into the bow hair, moving his hand gently up and down repeatedly.

Now ready, he tucked the violin under his chin, took up the perfect hand positions, and began practising the open strings, G, D, A, and E, from top to bottom string.

"Silly bugger can't even play it properly. Sounds like he's strangling a cat," Patrick said with a short scathing laugh, standing with his mates outside and listening, not having any idea of what Michael was playing, only that it didn't sound like a tune he recognised. But that didn't matter; it was not the music Patrick and his friends were interested in.

Patrick was becoming restless as he stood listening to Michael, not understanding anything he was playing, and not caring for that matter, only wanting him to pack up and come out.

Eventually the music stopped. A few minutes later Michael came out into the playground and was surprised to find fourteen pairs of eyes staring at him expectantly.

"So, sissy boy, we've been waiting for you. We want you to show us how good you can be with your hands apart from playing that stupid fiddle," Patrick said menacingly as he stepped forward.

Michael's chest tightened with fear; he knew what Patrick and his gang were capable of. "Why are you picking on me? Why can't you just leave me alone? I've done nothing to upset any of you," he said forlornly.

"We don't care for sissies in our school," Patrick said spitefully.

"Why do you call me a sissy?"

"Because only sissies play with fiddles."

"That doesn't make me a sissy, just because I like to play

the violin."

"So, OK, if you don't want us to think you're a sissy, show us how tough you are with your fists," Patrick challenged.

"No, I don't want to fight. I don't like fighting," Michael said, the naked fear in his voice beginning to show on his face.

"He doesn't want to fight because he's scared," one of the other boys cried out.

"Scary, scary, monkey," the rest of the boys started to chant.

Suddenly the boys surged forward and began to attack Michael. It was an unprovoked savage attack, giving Michael no chance to defend himself. Patrick just looked on smiling as his cronies continued to beat and kick Michael until he was lying on the ground bloodied and bruised, curling his body up in an effort to protect himself from the continuing blows and kicks being inflicted on him.

Patrick then stepped in and kicked Michael for good measure as he spat out, "Sissy, bloody sissy. Only Ivy boys play with fiddles," giving him another kick for good measure, before picking up the case and wrenching the violin from it.

Michael looked up, horror written all over his face, as he pleaded. "Please don't. It doesn't belong to me. It belongs to—"

Patrick kicked him again to silence him then leisurely walked over and smashed the violin against the stone wall, feeling almost saint like in his devotion to seeing Michael suffering.

"Come on, lads, the only music he's going to hear for a while is the ringing in his ears," he said malevolently as he tossed the broken violin at Michel's feet. The boys laughed, joining in the joke as they walked off, following Patrick.

* * * *

Confused and in great pain, Michael eventually found enough strength to drag himself to his knees. He looked inconsolably at the broken violin, the neck snapped completely off from the body with only the strings connecting the two pieces together.

He struggled to his feet and limped across to where the case was lying. A sharp pain shot through his body as he bent down to pick it up. *What am I going to say to Mrs Talbot? How am I going to be able to tell her, her lovely violin has been ruined?* he thought apprehensively as he carried the case back to where the broken violin was lying. He carefully gathered up the two pieces and placed them carefully in the case, snapping it shut.

* * * *

The Flanagans lived in a small single-room cottage built with a mixture of local stone and turf. It had a stone fireplace which provided heat for cooking and helped to keep the room warm, particularly as the ill-fitting wooden door that opened out to the elements was no barrier against the bitter conditions during the cold nights and harsh winters. The single room was barely furnished with a wooden table and four chairs, which were moved close to the fire during mealtimes and then moved to one side so that the bedding made up of rags and animal skins stuffed with straw could be spread out on the bare stone floor for everybody to sleep on.

"What on earth has happened to you?" Beatrice, Michael's mother, cried out in anguish, her face wrought with concern as she stared at Michael as he stumbled in, his badly bruised face splashed with blood, his clothes muddy and torn, and his hand clutching the battered violin case.

Beatrice Flanagan was in her midthirties, her hard life having taken its toll on her once pretty face, her straggly hair covered in a linen headscarf. She had on a long woollen black skirt, over which she wore an apron. The blouse was low-cut at the neck with a kerchief tucked into the top. Thick woollen stockings covered her legs, and on her feet she wore brogue shoes, the same type as the men wore.

She rushed forward, taking his face between her hands and looking into his eyes that were full of pain. His swollen mouth trembled worryingly. "My son, what has happened to you?"

"The other boys, they …" His voice quavered as he fought to find the words, his face straining as he looked at her, but there could be no doubt of the pain he was trying to hold back.

She felt his pain, clasping at her heart. "Have you been fighting?" she asked, her voice a little brittle.

"Yes. I mean no. I was set upon. They called me a sissy because I like music and playing the violin," he said, his face consumed with uncertainty. "Why would they want to do that?"

"Because they are ignorant and bullies. Let me have a look at your face," she said, taking his free hand by the wrist and leading him over to the warmth of the fire.

"You said they attacked you?" she asked as she tore off a piece of rag and dipped it into the iron pot of water that was heating on the fire. He winced as she began to dab his face.

"Stop being a nanny; I'm not hurting you," she said irritably. "Why did you argue with them. Why didn't you simply walk away and let them get on with it?"

"I couldn't. They wouldn't let me. There were a lot of them. They had been waiting for me, wanting to pick a fight. I didn't want to fight. I don't like fighting."

"Quite right too. Only fools and bullies fight."

"Bullies? What the blazes has been going on?" Luke Flanagan, Michael's father, asked as he walked in, a gush of cold air rushing in before he had a chance to close the door, his sudden appearance filling the room like a heavy cloud.

Luke Flanagan was a tall, heavily built man with an unshaven face set hard with a jutting chin. His yellow tobacco-stained teeth showed whenever he smiled, more so when he snarled. He had broad shoulders and muscular arms, developed from his work as a farmworker digging potatoes and humping heavy loads of them on and off the carts. Luke had grown up in a world where you were only respected if you could hold your own—with your fists if necessary.

"Michael's been in a fight," his mother said offhandedly

as she continued bathing his face.

"I hope you gave as good as you got," his father said laconically.

"I couldn't. There was—"

"There were a bunch of them, who just set about him," his mother answered for him.

"Why would they do that?" his father asked.

"They called me a sissy because I'm learning to play the violin. It's not fair. Why can't they just leave me alone?" Michael replied, his swollen lips making it hard for him to speak.

"Anyone who expects fairness in this life has a lot to learn," his father said caustically. "You know what I think about you wasting your time with that sort of thing. A fat lot of good playing a violin is going to be for you after you finish whatever it is that woman is teaching you at that school."

"Mrs Talbot is teaching us the ABC and how to read and write."

"She should be teaching you how to plant and reap potatoes, because that's the only thing that's going to keep a roof over your head and buy food and clothes," his father said bad-temperedly.

"No, he has a chance to be a musician, a good one. And who knows, one day he could play in one of the big orchestras. Mrs Talbot told me she thinks he has great potential," his mother said. There was an element of pride in her voice.

"So when did she tell you that?"

"When I bumped into her while I was out trying to buy some fish."

"You're just as daft as he is," Luke said, motioning towards his son. "Who the blazes is going to want to employ someone who plays the violin?" Turning to Michael, he said, "What are you going to do, serenade the workers as they pick potatoes, hoping they'll toss you a few?" A flash of irritation crossed his face as he clenched his fist and pressed it close to Michael's face, exclaiming, "This, Son, is the only thing people understand and respect. Be good with these, and no one will dare to call you a sissy."

His mother angrily pushed his fist away, saying, "Don't you think he's seen enough violence for one day?"

Michael looked a picture of puzzled innocence but could feel the growing tension between them.

"If the boy doesn't start to stand up for himself, he's going to be seeing a lot more of that," Luke said, talking to his wife but still waving his clenched fist in Michael's face. "How do you think I've managed to keep working all this time? I'm a contract labourer guaranteed work three days a week at ten pence a day, plus we get to live here free and have a small plot to grow our own potatoes. I can tell you, there are many willing to fight me for it. Make no mistake about that. If I hadn't stood up for myself, where do you think we would be now? I'll tell you where, out in the streets with nothing but the clothes we stand up in. Ask your mother about the times the bailiffs came to try to force us out of the cottage. I had to fight them off as I had to fight those who tried to stop me from getting the contract. They wanted the contract and were prepared to beat the shit out of me to get it. If you don't turn up for work, then they give your contract to someone else and you lose the house and the plot of land in the bargain. So the sooner you learn how to take care of yourself, the better chance you'll have of making something of yourself."

Michael looked across at his father. "Would you teach me?" he said, seeing the conflicting emotions on his father's face.

Beatrice watched them look at each other and said, "Oh no, I don't want my son being taught to fight and becoming a hooligan just when he's doing so well at music."

"He'll do better than music once he knows how to defend himself," his father said, his voice sharp.

"How do you make that out?" she asked, the harsh edge of strain showing in the lines around her eyes.

"Simple. If he can take care of himself, the bullies will leave him alone."

"The trouble with you and people like you is that you think

violence is the answer to everything," Beatrice said scornfully.

"It's kept a roof over our heads, fed us, and put clothes on our backs. And talking about clothes, look at the state of his. So you tell me where we're going to get the money to buy him some new second-hand clothes. You tell me that?"

Beatrice looked at them both and rolled her eyes in frustration, not sure what to say.

"Are you telling me it's better we should suffer the troubles and stand by and do nothing?"

"No, but …" she began, not sure what to answer.

"Dad's right, I have to do something. I have to learn to stand up for myself, or else they'll keep doing it to me. And I still don't know how I am going to tell Mrs Talbot they smashed her violin," Michael said with an air of despondency.

"I'll tell you what. When you've learned how to handle your fists, then you can make those bullies pay for a new violin for Mrs Talbot," his father said with an air of triumph.

"Yes, you're right. So when can we start?"

"Not until his bruises go down; he's been badly hurt," his mother asserted, her heart heavy with apprehension.

"Never again. I'll make sure of that," his father said. "Always remember, life is the most precious thing we have, and we must be willing to do anything to preserve it."

"What, by risking your own life, you mean?" his mother said sardonically.

"If necessary, yes."

"It makes me wonder whether the pain comes from giving in and surrendering or from fighting back. No wonder we have so many wars. It seems people just don't want to live in peace," Beatrice said, depression sweeping over her like a dark cloud.

Both Luke and Michael stared at her, flummoxed at the profundity of what she had said, neither of them having any idea of what to reply.

Luke's mouth turned down in a frown. "You talk in such riddles sometimes. I don't know where you get those silly ideas from," he said, his natural antagonism coming to the fore.

Michael stared up at his father, a look of determination beginning to spread across his face.

Chapter 3

It was a warm summer evening as they walked along the muddy road to the barn where the potatoes were bagged and stored.

"Right, do you think you're ready to start learning?" his father asked, noticing Michael's pace seemed to be slowing.

"As ready as I'm ever going to be, I suppose," Michael replied, sounding a little apprehensive at what his father was planning.

"Good," his father said, ignoring his nervousness. He quickened his pace, anxious to get on with things before Michael could change his mind and chicken out.

Michael picked up on his look and quickened his pace to catch up with his father to show he wasn't scared.

Once inside the barn, his father took off his coat and hung it on the nearest nail sticking out from the wooden struts. As Michael started to remove his jacket, his father moved swiftly across and struck him on the jaw, not hard enough to knock him out, but hard enough for it to hurt.

Michael, very surprised, cowered back and began to rub his sore chin. "What did you do that for?" he asked, blinking and trying to focus, shaking his head as if to shake the pain away, confusion and uncertainty spreading across his face.

His father smiled, making no apology as he began to explain: "Be that your first lesson: always be prepared, for when it comes to a fight, the rule is there are no rules, so you have to be prepared. Your opponent will attack when you least expect it, particularly at a time like that, when you're slipping your coat off. For a brief moment your arms were trapped in the sleeves, and you couldn't offer any defence. If I had wanted to, I could have done you some real damage."

Michael looked at his father while still rubbing his sore

chin. "Why couldn't you have explained it to me as you just have, instead of hitting me?"

"Because the message would not have got home. The best lessons are the ones learned the hard way, and I bet that will be a lesson you'll never forget," his father said, coming across to embrace him. "Now that we've got that over with, we can start with teaching you how to fight with skill, using your feet and body as well as your fists.

His father began to demonstrate by taking a rigid upright stance with his fists held high, just below his chin. "This is commonly the stance most fighters take when preparing for a fight - you see it in all the photos - but it's too rigid and restricts body movement," his father explained. He then lowered his arms to a more relaxed position and bent his body into a slight crouching stance with his knees also slightly bent to allow for easier movement with his feet. "You see, this way you can move easier and faster to hit your opponent. It also makes it harder for him to hit you. Now you try it."

Michael tried to copy his father's stance, but he looked awkward—even more so when he tried to move around.

"You look like a fart in a colander trying to find a way out," his father said mockingly. "You're too tense. Your body's too taut. Relax and loosen up."

"It's all right for you to say that. I've never done anything like this before."

"That's exactly the problem. The way you're standing, anyone could knock two kinds of shit out of you."

"Look, I don't think I'm cut out for this. I don't like the idea of fighting anyway. It's not what people should be doing. Why can't we all live together without having to fight each other? Why can't we just live in peace like Mother says?" Michael said dolefully.

"That's exactly the point. We fight so that we can live in peace," his father said with a brittle edge to his voice.

Michael looked at him, puzzled by the remark. "That doesn't make sense. Fighting and peace don't go together."

His father could see the confusion on his face. "Every man

has the right to defend what is his when someone threatens to take it away or when he simply wants to prove he's the strongest or the best. Or if he is simply out to make trouble."

"But trouble only makes trouble, so what good does that do?"

"It sorts the men from the boys."

"You mean the bullies from the bullies?"

"Yes, if you like."

"But there will always be one bully much stronger who will then bully the other bullies, so what good will that do?" Michael asked despairingly.

A flash of irritation crossed his father's face as he said, "Bullies bully because they are bullies and know no better, but you will find all bullies are real cowards when it comes to taking it. And the time will come when you can dish it out to the bullies who attacked you, that's for sure. But you've got a lot to learn before that can happen. So, do you want to learn how to fight, or do you want to let them keep calling you a sissy?" His father challenged him with an unwavering stare.

The words fell heavy. Michael could see the challenging expression on his father's face and knew he had to make a decision, but too many thoughts were colliding in his brain. What his father was telling him was right, yet what he was telling him was also wrong. But somehow one thought powered through his brain, the thought that he never wanted anyone ever to call him a sissy again. "Yes, I want to learn to fight," he said, with finality sounding in his voice.

"Right, let's get to it. But I don't want you to learn to fight," his father said with a quizzical look.

"But you just told me …" Michael said. There was confusion in his shocked expression.

"I don't want you to learn to fight; I want you to learn to box. I want you to be a clever boxer. It's no good just learning how to punch your opponent. You've got to learn how to avoid being punched, and that means being light on your feet, able to move around, making you a more difficult target to hit, which means strengthening your legs and body so you're more agile and able to move around the ring. And when you throw a punch, the power will surge all the way up from your legs."

Michael looked at his father and could see the ruthless lines of experience on his face. He knew that what he was saying was good advice. "I want to learn all the skills because I want to be the best and make you proud of me when I take my revenge on that bully Patrick."

"As I said, all in good time."

* * * *

As they walked back home after their first gruelling session, his father, feeling a new sense of pride in his son, put his arm around his shoulder and said, "Have you ever heard of Simon Byrne?"

"No, I don't think so. Why?"

"Tomorrow we're going to the cemetery at the Old Cobh Church in Cork. I want to show you something," his father said with a mischievous grin.

* * * *

At the cemetery Michael watched as his father began to search around the graves.

"What are we looking for?" Michael asked ponderously.

"I'll tell you when I find it," his father said as he continued searching around, gradually moving over to the sadly overgrown and neglected area, brushing away the long grass and tall weeds in an effort to find what he was looking for.

"Can I help?" Michael offered, watching his father grapple his way through the maze of broken tombstones.

"Ah, here it is," he exclaimed jubilantly, waving at Michael to join him. "This is what I wanted to show you," he said, pointing down at a grave nestling under a canopy of trees. "This is where Simon Byrne is buried, the last great bare-knuckle champion of Ireland. He was nicknamed the Emerald Gem, born in eighteen hundred and six. He had his first fight in eighteen twenty-five, when he lost to Mike Larking, the fight lasting an incredible hundred and thirty-eight rounds spread over two and a half hours. His second fight was a draw against Jack Manning in eighteen twenty-six, earning Byrne one hundred pounds."

"One hundred pounds? That's a lot of money!" Michael exclaimed.

"It was his fight against Alexander McKay, champion of Scotland, that was to be his first brush with notoriety. The fight lasted forty-seven rounds before McKay was beaten into submission. He collapsed and was carried to his corner, where he slowly regained consciousness. But he died at a local inn some thirty hours later. Incredibly Byrne was accused of manslaughter and was arrested three days later on his way back to Ireland. He was brought back in chains to face trial, and if found guilty he faced the possibility of the death sentence."

"And was he found guilty? Is that how he comes to be buried here?" Michael asked, shocked at what he was being told.

"No, he was cleared of any blame for McKay's death and was allowed to collect his two hundred pounds prize money and permitted to continue fighting. He challenged Jem Ward, the English heavyweight champion, but the bout only lasted thirty-three rounds before Simon Byrne was forced to retire. Everyone believed it to be the strain of the trial and his imprisonment."

"I'm not surprised. What a way to treat someone. I never knew someone could earn that kind of money fighting," Michael added.

"That fight was soon followed by a win against Bob Avery, earning him a further fifty pounds."

"Hang on a minute, you're telling me he'd earned two hundred pounds, then suddenly he earned only fifty pounds. Why is that?" Michael asked, a little confused.

"I don't know the answer, but his next fight against Phil Samson earned him another two hundred pounds."

"You seem to know a lot about him. Did you ever see him fight?"

"No, I was never lucky enough, but I followed his career. And I wanted you to see his grave because it was the fact that someone had tried to bully him that started his career. Sadly his final fight was against James Burke, who had the nickname the Deaf Un.

"The Deaf Un?"

"Yes, because he was deaf. He was tall and round, about six feet two inches, weighing around two hundred pounds, and was the champion of England. The match took place in May eighteen thirty-three in a field somewhere in Hertfordshire. The newspapers reported it was a very bloody fight, lasting an incredible ninety-nine rounds, taking over three hours. The newspaper reports said Byrne seemed to be on top for most of the fight until Burke caught him with a vicious punch to the forehead, knocking Byrne unconscious. Still in an unconscious state, he was carried from the ring to the Woolpack Inn in nearby St Albans. During the following two days he seemed to be making a slow recovery, but suddenly he had a relapse and died on Sunday, the second of June. His body was brought back to Ireland and buried here," his father said, bowing his head in reverence to his great hero.

"It's surprising how quickly people are forgotten," Michael said with an air of sadness.

"It's the way of life. At least he achieved something, which is more than I've managed to do," his father said with an air of atonement.

"Maybe if you had the chance, you could have been as great as him," Michael said empathetically.

"Maybe, who knows? But one thing life has taught me is that we must learn from yesterday, live for today, and hope for tomorrow. As your mother tells us, the Bible says that the journey of life begins when you take your first step. You've just taken your first step. And I am going to make sure you're the best fighter there is around here. So come on. Let's get ourselves home."

Chapter 4

With encouragement from his father, Michael was soon putting what he had learned from Simon Byrne's training methods into practice.

Michael would get up at dawn and run six miles round trip, three miles out and three miles back. Then he would tuck into a hearty breakfast before going to school. After school he would go to the barn with his father and work out, lifting the heavy sacks of potatoes then running around the barn with a sack of potatoes on each shoulder.

His father toughened his hands by wrapping them in cloth soaked in vinegar so that he could work on the punch bag he had made by filling one of the sacks with earth and rotten potatoes. He made him do sit-up exercises, holding a sack of potatoes to his chest to strengthen his stomach muscles so as to be able to absorb punishment.

Running in the mornings before school and again after school gave Michael no time to bother with music lessons, much to the dismay and disappointment of Mrs Talbot, who also still felt anger over the loss of her treasured violin and having to go to the expense of buying a replacement.

But Michael had a determined purpose in his perseverance as Patrick and the other members of his gang, he hoped, would soon discover.

Luke was pleased with the way Michael had developed and was confident he was now a match for anyone of his age and size. It made Michael feel that every day was a new day. The past was the past, nothing to do with the way he felt now. He had stopped feeling a victim and had started taking action towards the life he now wanted to lead. He had the power and determination to shape his life in a way he had never expected. He was now able to break free from the poisonous victim mentality and embrace the skills his father had given him. It was time to settle the score with Patrick and his bullies.

* * * *

This time Michael made sure he was the first out of the schoolroom as soon as the day's lessons had ended, much to the annoyance of Mrs Talbot.

He waited, remembering how they had waited for him, and he called out to Patrick as soon as he stepped outside.

"You told me last time you would like to see what else I can do with my hands besides play the violin. Well, now's your chance. Or are you going to turn chicken and be called a sissy as you dared to call me?" he challenged, confronting Patrick as he approached.

Patrick stopped in his tracks and stared at Michael, his gaze disconcerting as he said, "Some people never learn. I would have thought you had had enough. At least you haven't got a stupid fiddle to play with any more."

"Yes, you made sure of that. But now you and your mates are going to pay to have it repaired or replaced," Michael said. He could hear his own breathing as he made the threat.

"Oh yeah, and who is going to make us do that? You?" Patrick said contemptuously.

"Me. You see, you not only upset me but also, more important, you upset Mrs Talbot when you smashed her violin. So as I said, you are going to have to pay for it to be repaired. I suggest you start collecting the money as quick as you can."

"Let me give him a thrashing," Tom, one of the gang members, said with a little bravado as they all began to surge forward.

Michael stood firm with his eyes fixed on Tom's hands, watching for the slightest movement. And when it came, Michael moved with such lightning speed that Tom never saw the punch coming. It hit him full in the face. He dropped like a stone, his nose spouting blood.

Full of anger, Patrick rushed forward and swung a wild

punch, which Michael easily brushed aside, countering with a straight left, catching him square on the forehead. Patrick stumbled back, stunned by the blow, and before he could recover himself, Michael caught him with a right hook to the chin, breaking his jaw.

As Patrick's knees buckled and he collapsed to the ground, the rest of the gang shuffled back in fear of who was going to be next.

"Right, like I said, you are all going to pay to have the violin you smashed repaired."

"But we didn't smash it; Patrick did," one of the gang called out nervously.

Michael's face flushed with anger as he stepped closer to that gang member and said, "You're all as guilty as he is. You did nothing to stop him. In fact, you all cheered at his arrogant stupidity. Now this is what I want you to do. Take your pathetic leader and the other one and clean them up, then set about gathering the money together. And understand this: if I don't get it by next week, I will set about teaching you all a lesson none of you will ever forget."

"You're a hard man," one of the gang members said.

"It's bullies like you that have made me so. I was happy the way I was until you lot came along to spoil it," Michael retorted.

The gang shuffled over to where Patrick and Tom were still lying on the ground. They pulled them to their feet and helped them walk off.

"Remember what I said," Michael called after them.

* * * *

Michael went home that night feeling triumphant. He felt he was someone to be reckoned with. He hoped his father would be proud that he had taught the bullies a lesson.

"I will never play the violin again," he told his mother, raising his clenched fist to emphasise the point as he came in through the door. "These are my instruments now. Like Dad said, no one will ever call me a sissy again."

His mother gazed at him distantly, the breath slipping from her lungs in a low gasp of consternation. It was not what she wanted to hear. It seemed Michael was suddenly bereft of normal reasoning, unable to see beyond his immediate wants and desires, which she felt was changing him from a gentle, loving boy into someone she no longer recognised. "What is happening to you? I don't know what your father has done to you, but violence is not the answer. It causes more troubles than it solves, and it has no place in a Christian society."

"Christian society? So where was God when I was being beaten up?"

"God is always there. 'Vengeance is mine, sayeth the Lord.'

"Just remember, anger and resentment doesn't change the mind of others; it only changes yours. The best revenge is not to turn into the one you are seeking revenge on. It saddens me you have so wantonly abandoned your music, which had so much promise," she said with an air of despondency.

He looked at her with genuine sadness, which allowed her to drop her guard for a moment. He said, "Father told me that life is about making the right decisions and moving on."

"Moving on is a simple thing, but what you leave behind is never that simple."

"It's only by letting go of what I was that I can become the person I want to be. As Dad said, it's not whether you get knocked down; it's whether you are strong enough to get up."

Chapter 5

The summer of 1846 gave the farmers high hopes of a good harvest. The climate was mild with the winter having passed without snow. However, with the unusually cool, moist weather came the ideal conditions for what was to become known as the potato blight.

The disease travelled from the United States and Canada to Europe on trade ships, spreading to England. Winds from southern England then carried the fungus to Ireland.

The blight rapidly spread throughout the fields as fungal spores, settling on the leaves of healthy potato plants, were able to thrive and spread with such savagery that the blight not only devastated local crops but also spread across the entire country with ferocity, ultimately destroying every crop in its path.

The first sign of the infection was brown freckles appearing on the surface of the leaves, which spread to form large dark brown patches. These dark brown patches became surrounded by a light green halo. Dark brown lesions also developed on the stems and spread downwards, causing them to weaken and collapse. The potatoes themselves became shrunken on the outside and rotting on the inside, producing an odour that reeked to high heavens.

Adding to the disaster of the winter of 1846 and making it the worst in living memory, bitter cold gales of snow, sleet, and hail moved in as one blizzard after another buried homes up to their roofs in snow.

As a consequence, the men were unable to earn enough money to feed themselves and their families, the children sometimes having to go without food so the parents could stay healthy enough to go out and try to find work. In the meantime the children were forced to live off anything they could find:

nettles, turnips, old cabbage leaves, edible seaweed, shellfish, roots, roadside weeds, even grass. The parents pawned anything they could, including their clothing, to pay the rent to avoid eviction.

But in the end all the desperate efforts and sacrifices were not enough. Luke Flanagan, like so many others, fell into arrears on the rent, but he was not a man to give up easily. Determining that the potato famine was a countywide problem and that evicting him and his family would only add to the problem, he decided he would resist any attempts to evict his family.

Having made the decision, he started to prepare to repel the evictors by gathering up every heavy wooden plank he could find from the cottages that had already been repossessed and demolished, so that the moment word came, he could barricade the front door, the only point of access.

With no work, people spent their time foraging for anything to eat and keeping a lookout for any strange group approaching. Word had gone around that the landlords had hired a group of heavies with no respect for people's plight to enforce the eviction of tenants by whatever means. It wasn't long before Michael came running back to the cottage at breakneck speed to tell his father a gang of men, known as "the crowbar brigade", whom everyone feared, was heading their way.

Once Michael was back inside, Luke immediately began to board up the front door by nailing the wooden planks to the supporting timber around the door frame.

"What happens when they've broken down the door?" Michael asked, holding up the planks as his dad hammered in the nails.

"Then we beat them off with these," Luke told him, clenching his hand into a fist and holding it up for him to see.

"But there are six of them," Michael protested.

"Yes, but the difference is that we're desperate and they're not. So how much do you think they will want to risk serious injury just to get us out of this miserable place?

"Well, we're about to find out," Luke said as he heard the heavy footsteps come ever closer.

"I am Sean O'Brien, a bailiff, and I have an order to repossess this cottage. You are thereby ordered to vacate the property. You will be given time to gather your possessions together and then leave, never to return," he called out in a very authoritative voice.

"We have nowhere else to go, so we are not leaving," Luke answered back.

"Then you leave me with no choice but to force entry and evict you bodily with no time allowed to gather up your belongings," Sean O'Brien replied.

"It will take more than you lot to break down this door. And even if you manage to do so, you will have to deal with me and my son. And I can promise you, you won't escape without a good hiding."

Sean O'Brien looked pensively around at the men with him and said, "What do you think? You lot up for it?"

"I know Luke, and I wouldn't want to go up against him at the best of times. In the mood, he makes it sound like some of us could get badly hurt. And his son, I hear, is pretty handy with his fists, so to my mind it's not worth getting our teeth knocked in for the sake of a tight-fisted landlord who wants to repossess this miserable place," one of the gang argued.

"That's what I and you are being paid to do," Sean O'Brien countered.

"I'm not being paid to take a beating. I've got my family to feed and look after, and I'm not going to be able to do that if I've got a broken jaw," another of the gang spoke up.

"Cowards, the lot of you," Sean O'Brien said accusingly.

"Yeah, well, since you feel so brave, we'll break down the door and you can go in and haul them out. After all, you're getting paid a lot more than we are," another of the gang spoke out.

"We'll be back," Sean O'Brien called out as he and the others turned around and walked off.

"There. What did I tell you? They've given up and

walked away," Luke said jubilantly.

"All very well, but they will come back with even more men, so what happens then?" Beatrice cut in.

"We'll deal with it when and if the time comes. There are a lot of others they will be able to evict much easier than us, so let's hope they decide to stay away," he said as he began to remove the planking from the door.

Beatrice was right, of course. The following day the gang were back, in force now, armed with pickaxes, crowbars, and wrenches and carrying ladders, ready to deal with the occupants in any way necessary.

"Luke, it's no use. We can't fight them. There are too many. And it will only result in you and Michael getting hurt. And then what will we do?" Beatrice pleaded as Luke and Michael boarded up the door.

"You mean you want us to just let them walk in and throw us out?" Luke retorted angrily.

"What else can we do? The law is on their side."

"Law! If there was any law, it would be here to protect us, not to throw us out into the streets like beggars."

"This is your last chance," Sean O'Brien called out. "If you come out peacefully, you will not be harmed and will be allowed to take your belongings with you, but if you continue to resist, then we will have no choice but to break the door down and remove you forcibly. I will give you some time to collect your things together and open the door, but don't be too long about it."

"What are you doing now?" Luke asked as Beatrice began to rush around, gathering up her meagre possessions.

"You heard what he said, so stop being silly and gather up what you and Michael can carry before they break the door down," Beatrice said, not stopping in her task.

"She's right, Father. We don't stand a chance against them. And we could get badly hurt," Michael reasoned.

"I thought I'd taught you to be strong to stand and fight for what you believed in," his father said in a disparaging tone.

"Oh, I'll fight for what I believe in, but it has to be a fight

32

where we have a chance of winning. With this one we have no chance," Michael told him, feeling the sweat begin to creep down his neck, fearing what his father might do next.

Sean O'Brien glanced up at the small chimney stack on the roof and noticed the smoke drifting out. "Right. We've waited long enough. One of you get a ladder, climb onto the roof, and block the chimney. That will soon smoke them out."

"Put that damn fire out," Luke shouted as the room began to fill with smoke.

"Your time is up," they heard Sean O'Brien call out at the same time as they heard the crunching noise of crowbars hacking at the corner of one of the walls.

"They're not even bothering to break the door down; they're going to come in through the wall," Beatrice said, stating the obvious. "We're coming out," she shouted, clutching her possessions tightly to her chest, fearful the house would collapse around them.

Luke gave her a cold forbidding look, screwing up his face in exasperation, his chest becoming so tight that he could hardly breathe as he watched Michael begin to lever the planks off the door.

"The sooner it's over, the better," Michael's voice of reason echoed as the first plank crashed to the ground.

"I never, ever thought we would give in without a fight," his father said laconically.

As they removed the last plank, they heard a sudden movement outside. The door burst open and the gang charged in, propelling Luke and Michael back across the room.

Luke sprang to his feet and lashed out at the nearest man, catching him with a powerful punch to the jaw, sending the man reeling backwards. But at Luke went to attack the next man, he was hit over the head by one of the other men wielding a shovel, and he sank to the floor.

"I am a bailiff acting on behalf of Lord Blamfont. I hereby serve you notice of eviction," Sean O'Brien announced, bending over to hand Luke the notice.

"Who the blazes is he?" Luke asked angrily.

"He is the landlord who owns most of the land around here," O'Brien told him.

"Never seen or heard of him," Luke remarked lugubriously.

"You wouldn't have. He lives somewhere in England. Now let's try to do this in a civilised manner without any further violence," O'Brien added, his voice sounding loud in the confined space. "So quickly gather up your belongings and quietly leave."

Luke glared at him, his face flushed with outrage as he struggled to his feet, tossing the notice away. "Sean O'Brien. I'll remember that name. And if I ever come across you again, I will remind you of this day in a way you won't forget."

"Idle threats won't get you anywhere, so in the meantime just be on your way out of here," O'Brien told him, gazing at him distantly as the gang started to remove the little furniture the Flanagan family had.

"And where do you expect us to go?" Beatrice asked, a cloud of concern darkening her eyes as she brushed past O'Brien, making her way to the door, clutching her possessions.

"That's not my problem," O'Brien snorted contemptuously. "I suggest you make for the workhouse in town," he said as an afterthought.

"What the hell are they doing now?" Michael called out as the men started hacking at the four walls with their crowbars and pickaxes.

"We're knocking the cottage down so that you or anyone else can't move back in," O'Brien said abrasively.

Luke stood looking as the crowbars and pickaxes cut easily into the stone and turf walls. He was slowly coming to terms with the realisation the he had spent years of his life completely misunderstanding the world around him. It was as though he had lived his life in a cocoon. He had felt that nothing would ever change, that things would go on forever, and that there would always be an abundance of potatoes. They had had a roof over their heads, as tiny as it was. It was a place to live. And he believed most people were good, decent individuals whom one could trust when times were hard. He knew that like other people he had his flaws, but they were never a serious threat to anybody unless he or his family was threatened.

There was a sudden pounding noise as the walls crumbled, bringing the roof down in a cloud of dust.

"What's the point in knocking it down? The landlord won't earn anything from it now," Luke said, bemused at what they were doing.

"The landlord can get a higher income by returning the land to pasture," O'Brien explained.

"But he can't grow any potatoes. They are still blighted."

"Precisely the point. There are other crops that can be cultivated instead of relying on the potato," Sean said as the last of the furniture was carried out and unceremoniously dumped on the ground. "You must leave. You are not allowed to remain on the land or linger about the area. Nor may you attempt to erect any form of shelter out of the remains of the cottage," O'Brien instructed them. "If you attempt to return, you will arrested and imprisoned."

Beatrice, overwhelmed by what was happening, fell to her knees, letting everything she was clutching fall to the ground. She began to pray:

> O Christ, our only king, co-eternal Son of
> the gracious Father, have mercy on us.
> You saved lost humanity, restoring all from
> death to life.
> Have mercy on us.
> Jesus, Good Shepherd, so the sheep of Your
> pasture will not perish, have mercy on us.
> O Spirit, Comforter, we Your people pray.
> Have mercy on us.
> O Lord, our strength and our eternal
> salvation,
> have mercy on us.

The few seconds of silence seemed to stretch into eternity before Beatrice finally clambered to her feet and asked, "What are we going to do about the furniture?"

"What the blazes *can* we do with it? We can't carry it on our backs. And even if we could, where would we carry it to?" Luke retorted, his voice thick with anger.

"Maybe they'll buy it off us," Michael suggested.

"Who the blazes do you think would want to buy this rubbish?" one of the gang said, smashing his crowbar across the table, splitting it in two.

"Now be on your way before there is any more trouble," O'Brien ordered them.

Michael, seeing his father's hands clenching into fists with every muscle strained, quickly put a restraining hand on his arm. "Father, it's not worth it. With the weapons they're carrying, we stand no chance," he cautioned.

"Maybe, but I'd take a few with me," his father said, his hands clenching even tighter.

"And what good would that do? You still have a wife to take care of. She won't survive any of this without you and me."

As grief suddenly overwhelmed him, he grudgingly relaxed his hands and looked across at his wife, confirming or denying nothing. She met his eyes squarely. He could see the hurt in her eyes.

"Why is there so much evil in the world?" she asked as a strange sense of despair filled her soul.

Luke turned his head away in shame. He didn't know what to say; there was nothing he could say or do to try to make it right, because there was nothing there any more. But he knew he had to carry on, however tough it was going to be.

"You had better start moving if you're going to try to make the workhouse in Dublin. It's going to take you at least three days, and you'll need to find shelter somewhere for the night as the weather doesn't look too promising," O'Brien told them, his voice void of any emotion.

"I hope God can find it in His heart to forgive you, because I can't," Beatrice said with acquiescence.

Chapter 6

The one thing O'Brien was right about was the weather. Heavy clouds began to darken the sky.

"We must try to find somewhere to take cover before it pours, or else everything will get soaked," Beatrice said wearily.

They had been walking practically all the time, carrying their meagre belongings between them since they'd been evicted. Beatrice was exhausted and needed to rest; otherwise she feared she'd collapse. The night was drawing in. Luke knew they had to find shelter somewhere soon, before they were totally exposed to the freezing cold the night would bring.

There were no streets, just trodden paths that had turned muddy after the heavy rain, making their progress much slower.

As they trudged through the increasingly mucky area, the mud tugging at their feet, Beatrice was finding it increasingly arduous to walk. Grief suddenly overwhelmed her, and she felt a darkness rise up in her as she looked across at a woman and child lying on the muddy wayside, both dead, the woman with bits of grass sticking out of her gaping mouth.

There were other families collapsed along the wayside, lying huddled together, their ragged, worn-out boots and shoes sticking out from under a single filthy blanket that barely covered them. Their emaciated bodies had become too weak to walk any further. The gaunt faces held sunken eyes which stared out at nothing, knowing there wasn't anything they could do, or that anyone else could do, to save them.

Beatrice found the energy from somewhere to rush over to these people with no idea of what she could do to help. She couldn't offer them food as she had none for herself; she couldn't offer them clothing because her family only had the clothes they were wearing, plus a few blankets, which they were going to need for themselves.

"You poor souls," she said as she knelt down beside one family and took hold of the woman's hand. "May God have mercy on you," she prayed.

The woman stared up at her with her sunken eyes but said nothing as by now she was unable to speak, every last drop of strength having been long drawn from her.

"I know how you must be feeling, dear, but we can do nothing for them. We must find somewhere to shelter, or we'll be in the same state as them," Luke said, coming over to help Beatrice to her feet. He looked at her. Tears were beginning to roll down her cheeks. "Why is God so cruel? Why does he allow so much suffering?" he asked. He felt an oppressive gloom gathering about him.

"God? There is no God. There are only landlords and governments, and neither give a damn about the likes of us," Michael retorted angrily.

"That is not true. God bestowed on us free will. But we have abused that free will, and by rejecting Him we have allowed all kinds of evil to come into our world and try to take His place," Beatrice proclaimed. There was firmness, yet reverence, in her voice.

Michael was amazed at her words. It showed on his face as he said, "Are you saying evil is responsible for what happened to the potatoes?"

"Yes. It's what the church calls natural evils, things like wildfires and earthquakes, which they say are the result of sin being allowed into our world," she explained.

"Look, we can't stand and argue about God. As far as I'm concerned, the only thing I'm praying for is somewhere we can shelter for the night and get something to eat," Luke said, pulling an agonised face.

The scene they had witnessed weighed heavily on Beatrice, making her efforts to stay on her feet and keep walking even more difficult. She had to rely on Michael and

Luke to support her as well as carry to their meagre belongings, which meant their pace was reduced to a crawl.

As they emerged from a wooded area, Luke spotted some tall rocks and what looked like an entrance to a cave. "At least we might be able to shelter there for the night," Michael said with an air of enthusiasm.

On hearing the news, Beatrice managed to find the strength to quicken her pace as they made their way towards the cave.

Another shock hit them as they cautiously entered the cave: it was full of people lying huddled together in the same way the Flanagans had seen the families earlier.

The atmosphere and smell was nauseating, a mixture of human excrement and sweaty unwashed bodies, added to which was a cacophony of people coughing and groaning and children crying from hunger. It was a pitiful sight.

Beatrice immediately fell to her knees in total despair. "Have we all sinned that badly that we are made to suffer in this way?" she cried out.

"It will only be for the night. You have to rest. We all have to rest. And tomorrow, with luck, we'll get to the workhouse," Luke said in a desperate effort to offer some kind of comfort as he led his wife and son into the cave, looking for a space with enough room for them to lie down together.

"Wait, I think I can hear water running. You go and find a place while I'll go and find out where it's coming from. I'll bring some back," Michael said, taking two of the tin mugs from the belongings he was carrying.

There was a little waterfall running down from the rocks which formed into a small lake at the bottom. The lake was dirty, coloured brown from the human excrement, rotten food, and rubbish that had been recklessly thrown into it. It amazed Michael to see a woman squatting at the edge with her skirts tucked up around her waist and her drawers around her ankles, relieving herself, her immediate needs outweighing any sense of privacy.

Michael realised that if he was to get some clean water

fit to drink, he would have to climb up the rocks to where the water was flowing clear and uncontaminated.

As soon as he reached the place where the water was running clear, he filled one of the mugs and drank it down without pausing for breath, savouring every mouthful.

"Can you get some for me? I haven't got the strength to climb up there any more," the woman called up to him, hitching up her drawers.

Michael refilled the mug, scrambled back down, and handed it to the woman, who grabbed it voraciously, almost gulping the water down in one swallow.

"Thank you," she said with a satisfied gasp. "I haven't had a drink of anything for over a day, and I'm getting stomach cramps. And I've got the runs," she added, handing back the mug.

Holding tightly onto the two mugs, Michael filled them with clean water and made his way back to the cave. It was getting dark, causing the inside of the cave to become duskier and making it more difficult to see where his dad had managed to find a space.

"Over here, Son," he heard his dad call out from somewhere he couldn't yet make out. "Keep coming, Son. Over here," he heard his dad call out again.

Squinting desperately, trying to see where his parents were, Michael tripped over a pair of outstretched legs, causing him to lose his grip on the two mugs, which spilled out the water as they clattered to the ground.

As Michael frantically looked around for the mugs he was shocked to see bodies suddenly scramble on their hands and knees, shoving each other out of the way in a desperate attempt to lick the droplets of water before it soaked into the ground.

"You bloody idiot," his father called out, angry at what had happened.

"I'll get some more when I find the mugs," Michael said. He continued to feel around for the mugs, but he soon realised somebody had already gotten their hands on them and he was never going to find them.

As he crawled over to where his mother and father were, he heard a voice say, "I will give you one of the mugs back if you get me some clean water for me and my wife."

Michael stopped and looked around to work out where the voice had come from. He realised it was the man's leg he must have tripped over, which the man had deliberately stuck out.

"You bastard!" Michael screamed. "I could kill you. My mother and father desperately need a drink."

"And so do we," came a chorus of rasping voices.

Michael, now getting used to the dark, began to look around at the mass of bodies huddled together in rows along either side of the cave. The sight sent a cold shiver down his spine.

"OK, I'll tell you what. Let me bring some water to my mother and father, and then I will bring as much water as I can for all of you," Michael offered. He knew that without the mugs, their chances of survival would be as low as the others'.

"I'll help you, Son," his father said, getting to his feet.

"And I'll help," another voice spoke up.

"Then let's get to it before it gets too dark and we won't be able to see at all," Michael said, taking back the mugs that were offered up.

Michael climbed back up the rocks. He filled the first mug and handed it to his father. "Here, drink this. Then I will refill it so you can take it to Mother. If anyone tries to steal it from you, tell them no one will get any water, because I will stay here and fight anyone who tries to climb up here all night if I have to."

"You're a good lad, so like your mother. Neither one of you deserves to be suffering like this," Luke said, looking at his son with pride. Then he drank the water.

"No one deserves this, and whoever believes there is a God when they see all this suffering is a blind fool," Michael said, seized with momentary anger.

"Don't let your mother hear you say that," his father

rebuked him.

Remarkably, with a little help, Michael managed to provide everyone with a mug of clean water before he collapsed beside his mother and father and fell into a deep sleep before his mother could thank him and wish him good night, although she did pray for him, thanking God for guiding him to help others.

> Maker of the world, King eternal, have
> mercy on us.
> Fount of boundless pity, have mercy on us.
> Drive away from us all that is harmful. Have
> mercy on us.
> Christ, the Light of the world, giver of life,
> have mercy on us.
> Look on those wounded by the craft of the
> Devil;
> have mercy on us.

Chapter 7

The following morning Michael was awakened from his exhausted sleep by the commotion going on around him.

"What's going on?" he asked as he tried to focus his eyes on his surroundings, the morning light having lifted the darkness.

"We have to get going and get to the city and try to find work and food before all these other buggers get there before us," his father said, roughly pulling him to his feet.

"Where is Mother?"

"She's out front waiting for us. One of the men has borrowed our mugs and climbed up the rocks to get fresh water for people to drink. Your mother is holding a cup for you," Luke told him.

Once Michael had been refreshed with the water, they gathered up their belongings, retrieved the mugs, and made their way back onto the road, heading for the city. They were accompanied by the many others who were emerging from the cave with the same intention.

The trek was becoming even more arduous because, although they had managed to find water, they had not found food. Their stomachs were beginning to churn with hunger and their bodies were beginning to lose their strength, making the effort of walking painful and much slower.

Even more harrowing was the sight of families who had lost the strength to go any further and had collapsed by the roadside with gaunt looks of hopelessness on their hunger-stricken faces with their hands held out, begging for anything. But there was nothing they could give them because they had nothing themselves, except for a bottle they had managed to scavenge from the pile of rubbish by the cave and fill with clean water. That was now far too precious to share with anyone.

As they made their agonising way along the uneven road, the scene became even more harrowing when they realised some had not just merely collapsed but had died. Corpses, whole families, sons and daughters, all huddled together in what looked like a last desperate attempt to ward off the freezing cold of the nights.

Suddenly a woman carrying a child in her arms approached Beatrice, begging for help.

Beatrice looked sorrowfully at her, saying, "Sorry, but we have no food even to feed ourselves."

"I'm not begging for food. I need money to buy a coffin to bury my child," the woman said, holding up the corpse she was clutching to her chest.

Beatrice was so overcome with sorrow that she fell to her knees and prayed:

Kindling fire, proceeding from the Father and the Son, fountain of life,
purifying force, have mercy on them.
Purger of sin, most excellent bestower of pardon, blot out their offences, enlighten them with
Your holy gifts.
O gracious Spirit, have mercy on them.

As she tried to get to her feet, the weakness in her legs made her wobble. Luke had to rush to her to stop her from falling over. "There is nothing we can do for them. We have to think about ourselves and get to the workhouse before something happens to us," he said, carefully holding onto her.

"But what about the dead? Are they just going to be left here to rot?"

"That is up to the authorities. As I said, there is nothing we can do about it.

"Come on, Mother. I know how painful it is for you. You prayed for them, and I reckon that is more than most people have done who have passed this way, but as Dad says, we have to get to the workhouse," Michael said in an effort to console her.

"Authorities! Where were they when we were thrown out of our house? They didn't care then, and they don't care now. The Lord bring shame on them," she cried out in anguish.

* * * *

Their faces brightened up as they saw a mass of people gathered around a small building, ravenously eating from little wooden bowls they were clutching tightly, careful not to spill a morsel.

"Food!" Michael called out excitedly. "They're eating food."

The mention of the word *food* gave them impetus, and they managed to quicken their pace.

As they got close, they looked around at all the people shovelling the food into their mouths as fast as they could to ease the pangs of hunger. Others were queuing to get inside, while another group were standing away from the entrance, not seeming to want to join the queue.

"I wouldn't go in there unless you want to be branded a souper," a man said, standing by the doorway.

"A souper? What the blazes is that?" Luke asked, bewildered, as his nose sensed the aroma of some kind of stew or whatever it was. But that didn't matter. It was food, and that was all that concerned him.

"They are Quakers, and they won't serve you unless you are prepared to convert from Catholicism," he told him.

Luke and Michael looked at each other, wondering what to do and say. Michael, sensing his father's indecision, said, "There is food there, and if we don't eat, we'll die, so let me go and see what I can find out. We don't know for sure whether what that man said is true."

"OK, Son, you go in, and I'll stay here with Mother," Luke told him.

Michael cautiously entered, not sure what to expect.

Against the far wall there was a large cauldron standing on a heavy table with steam rising from it. A few women with long-handled ladles were scooping the soup from it, pouring a measure into a small wooden cup, handing it out progressively to the next person in the long queue.

"Are you ready to convert?" a man standing by the door asked.

Michael stared at him, realising that what he'd been told outside was true. "I need to check with my family," he replied, hurrying back out.

"We have to be willing to convert if we want any food," he told his mother and father as soon as he got back to them.

"How can they be so uncaring with so many starving? It's an affront to God," Beatrice exclaimed, seized by a sense of outrage.

"Affront or not, we're starving, and I'll convert to anything to get some food in my belly," Michael asserted.

"You mean to tell me that you are prepared to sell your soul to the Devil? How could you? All our family have been brought up as devout Catholics as the only true faith and I will never surrender to other such unchristian forces," Beatrice said, and there was a renewed determination in her voice.

"Mother, we have to eat," Michael protested.

"I cannot go to my Maker knowing I betrayed Him for a piece of bread," Beatrice said, white with fear as she turned her back and started walking on.

"Mother," Michael called out.

Luke stared at Michael, his face full of doubt and confusion. "You won't change her mind. She would rather die than accept food from them. We just have to hope we find another soup kitchen that is more generous in its help," his father said as they hurried off and caught up with her.

As they reached the edge of the town, they spotted a large warehouse with masses of people surrounding it. Some were sitting at tables or on the ground, tucking into bowls of soup, while others were queuing in a long line that stretched around the building, anxiously awaiting their turn to be given some soup.

"Let's pray to heaven they are not Quakers," Luke said as he headed for the building.

"If they are demanding we convert, then I want none of their false generosity," Beatrice called out to him, her voice firm, but Luke was determined that whatever was demanded, he was going to get them some food. It was either that or else they would, like so many they had seen on the way, die of starvation.

He went to the entrance. As he stepped in, someone shoved him forcefully. "Get to the back of the queue and take your turn like everyone else. We're all starving here," the scrawny man told him. Luke looked at him, thinking, *I could flatten him with one simple punch,* but then he thought, *I'm not sure I could given the way I feel.*

He looked around the warehouse with people pushing past him in a desperate hurry to get to the food.

Along the far wall was a row of six very large boilers with steam spewing out of them in which he guessed the soup was being cooked. Several men were attending the boilers. When they felt the soup was cooked enough, they ladled the mixture into metal buckets and carried the buckets across to where there was a line of six small tables. They emptied the contents into large iron pots, from which the women standing at the tables ladled it into the small wooden bowls and handed them out to the next hunger-stricken person in the queue.

A great smile of relief began to spread across Luke's face as he realised there was no one guarding or making demands on anyone, just people making sure everybody behaved in an orderly manner.

He hurried back. "It's all right. No one is making any demands about converting. It is free to everyone," he told Beatrice as he grabbed her arm. He held tightly onto her as he guided her to the building.

The Flanagans joined the long queue, which seemed to be ever increasing, and patiently moved forward, hoping there would still be some soup left by the time they got there.

They were lucky; each of them was given a bowl of the hot steaming soup. They made their way outside to find a space where they could sit down and relish the first meal they had eaten since they were evicted.

But their joy was quickly soured for the soup tasted like nothing they had ever tasted before. It was a mixture of odd bits of meat, vegetables, and Indian corn all boiled together.

"This is vile. Don't any of them in there know how to cook?" Beatrice exclaimed, spitting the soup onto the ground.

"For God's sake, Mother, eat it. Just look around you. We queued long enough, and it's the only food we're likely to get for some time, so whatever it tastes like, be grateful," Luke said. There was an angry edge to his voice.

Beatrice glared at him as she forced herself to take another mouthful.

The problem was that their diet was based solely on the potato and their stomachs were not used to meat or particularly the corn, Indian corn. It was a completely new taste. It wasn't long before their stomachs began to react, adding to the discomforts they were already suffering.

* * * *

As the Flanagans continued on their way, their problems got even worse as all of them began to suffer problems with their bowels. They were reduced to finding anywhere they could to relieve themselves.

Finally with a huge sigh of relief they could see the large workhouse building with the high walls surrounding it and crowds of hungry and destitute families massed around the large wooden entry gates, begging to be let in.

Beatrice breathed another sigh as she appeared to be getting worse by the minute. It seemed dysentery had set in, caused by starvation and the odd bits of meat, vegetables, and

49

Indian corn they were not used to but, were forced to eat.

"We're never going to get in there," Luke said in exasperation.

"We have to try. There is nowhere else to go. We are starving, and I can't go on any further," Beatrice said, exhausted, her body drained of energy. She fainted and slumped to the ground.

"If we don't get her in there, she is going to die," Luke said, falling to his knees and taking her head into his arms.

"Let's pick her up and carry her to the gate. They will have to let us in when they see her," Michael suggested, crouching down to tuck his arms under his mother's frail body.

"It's our only hope, I suppose," Luke said, tucking his arms under her legs so that he and his son could lift the body together.

It was hard work trying to push their way through the mass of people, all trying to do the same and get to the gate.

"Please let us pass. This woman is dying," Michael kept shouting out as he and Luke carried Beatrice, pushing and shoving their way to the gate. It had some effect. To their surprise, some people stepped back and allowed them through.

By now Beatrice was groaning in pain, her eyes staring wildly and her hands rubbing her swollen stomach to try to ease the pain.

The gatekeeper took pity on her and allowed them to enter, much to the anger of those immediately surrounding the gate, who shouted abuse and tried to stop them from entering. It was only with a heavy punch delivered to the nearest man who tried to grab him that Michael managed to get his family through the gate.

Once safely inside, they soon discovered that the workhouse was not a haven, not the friendly, caring place they had expected it to be. It was harsh, an institution where conditions were deliberately made hard so as not to encourage people to come and stay for any length of time. The staff appeared uncaring, generally made up of ex-policemen or ex-army who had been dismissed for being cruel, incompetent, or dishonest.

One of the harshest aspects was that the family were forced to split up. Only children up to two years old were allowed to stay with their mothers. Beatrice was taken off to the women's quarters without being given much chance to say goodbye to her husband and son, albeit she seemed to be drifting in and out of consciousness. Luke and Michael were moved off to the men's quarters.

The system was already at the breaking point. The facility could not cope with the overcrowding. Unsanitary conditions were becoming a serious problem, together with people unable to wash themselves or their filthy and tattered clothing, providing the perfect breeding ground for lice.

Typhus was nicknamed black fever because of the way it blackened the skin. Typhus was caused by lice invading the body through cuts and scratches in the skin, through the eyes, or by way of inhalation, which in itself added to the dysentery and diarrhoea they were already suffering from.

The food was monotonous and basic, known as a stirabout, a watery gruel which tasted of nothing, but it was food—and for the moment that was all that mattered. It seemed everyone was starving, frustrated, and badly treated and had lost the will to live. Luke and Michael were horrified to see the dead being unceremoniously dumped on carts, wheeled out, and dropped into large burial pits dug into the grounds of the workhouse.

It was rumoured that some of the men had become so desperate that they left the workhouse and deliberately committed a crime so they would be arrested and sent to prison, where it was rumoured the food was much better and the regime not as strict.

It was a strict rule of the workhouse that all inmates were expected to wear a uniform. And all those considered able, both men and women, were expected to work to help pay for their keep. The work was hard and monotonous. Women and children, several hundred of them, walked around in a circle pushing a big heavy wheel for grinding corn, or else they worked in the laundry, scrubbing tirelessly, trying to get the dirt out of the filthy clothes. It was hot, steamy work, and they had to work with their bare hands using carbolic soap, washboards, and flat irons heated over a hot stove. Or they were assigned to sewing and mending dresses, petticoats, and shirts and the repair of the house mattresses, as well as cleaning the dormitory block, including the matron's quarters, the nursery, the women's workroom, and the laundry.

Some women not as fit as others were given domestic jobs such as cleaning, helping in the kitchen, looking after the sick, or spinning wool.

The men were given the tedious task of breaking tough old ship ropes apart, which involved separating out the strands so that the rope could be reused, causing blisters and cuts to the hands.

Luke and Michael were selected to work at a quarry, where they had to break up large rocks for road building with a heavy hammer until the pieces were small enough to pass through a one-and-a-half-inch heavyweight sieve.

After a few weeks they were reassigned, along with some of the very fit women, to building the roads. The broken stones were placed in baskets and carried by the women to the place where the men were working. The women would empty the basket and walk back to collect another. The men then laboriously laid out the stone to build up the road surface.

Many of the workers, poorly clothed, undernourished, and weakened by fever, fainted or simply dropped dead. Those who died were carried back on the cart to be buried with the rest in the communal burial pit.

In the haste to find work for the men, little thought had gone into the planning for the building of the roads other than to provide jobs for the vast number of unemployed.

As the area was very remote and rural, the road seemed to be going from nowhere to nowhere with no obvious need for such a road to be built there in the first place.

"When we finish today, I'm going to go and see Mother whether they like or not. We haven't seen her since we've been here, and that's not right," Michael said, watching one of the women bringing over another basket of stones.

"As long as you don't get us into trouble," Luke said, looking up at him from where he was kneeling and carefully laying stones into place.

"What's the matter with you? Don't you care what is happening to your wife?" Michael responded angrily.

"Of course I care. It's just that, well, the fight has gone out of me and I don't have the energy any more. In fact, I'm not sure I can carry on with this work much longer," Luke said, gazing up at his son distantly.

"Are you all right?" Michael asked, looking down at his dad, slowly absorbing what he had said, his eyes screwing up in exasperation.

"No, Son, I'm not. My muscles are really aching. I'm getting a lot of headaches and stomach pains, and I've got a sort of rash coming up around my waist," his father told him.

"Right. I'm taking you to the medical room just as soon as we get back, and then I'll go and see Mother," Michael told him, a cloud of fear darkening his face.

The medical room was a mass of people, all sitting or standing with blank expressions, and there was an acrid smell of sweaty unwashed bodies that made Michael want to be sick, but he managed to hold it down as he rushed to the first woman he saw. She was wearing a long heavy gown with a white apron and cap. "Excuse me, my dad's—"

"You'll have to wait your turn," she said without paying much attention as she continued to treat the scabs on an elderly woman's face.

"But he's not well," Michael protested.

"Neither is any of them here," the nurse retorted, although she wasn't actually a qualified nurse as no qualifications were required for nurses in workhouses, which meant the level of care was limited. "Someone will see to him if we get time," she added dismissively.

"You have to stay here and make sure someone sees to you while I go and try to find Mother, OK?" Michael told his father, who responded with a nod.

* * * *

The women's dormitory was a large block laid out with a mixture of two-tier and three-tier bunks.

"Where do you think you're going?" the matron called out as Michael entered the dormitory.

"I would like to see my mother," he said nervously.

"We do not allow males into the female dormitory as you know very well."

"But I have not seen her since we arrived, and I want to know how she is," Michael persisted.

"What is her name?" the matron asked sternly.

"Flanagan, Mrs Flanagan."

She took a long measured look at his face at the mention of the name. Her face creased into a worried frown as she said, "I think you have just come in time. I will let you in for a brief moment."

Michael followed her into the dormitory, which was as quiet as it could be, except for the hollow sounds of women coughing and groaning as they lay helplessly in their bunks. Michael sighed in the semidarkness as the matron led him across to one of the three-tier bunks.

He felt a shadow fall across his face as he looked down at his mother, her face gaunt, her eyes staring straight up at nothing, her mouth gaping as though wanting to say something but not having the energy or the will to say it.

"She's not long to live," the matron said, her voice cold, devoid of emotion.

"Then why wasn't my father told about this?" Michael said angrily. He fell to his knees and took hold of his mother's hand. He noticed the skin had changed colour and the hand felt cold.

"It's an impossible task. We don't have access to all records or the staff to know who and where everybody is," she explained in the same wearied, toneless voice.

"Mother, it's me, Michael," he whispered to her.

Her eyes slowly lowered and turned to look at him. Her mouth closed to form a half smile. "Hello, Son," she said, her mouth twisting in an effort to say the words.

"How are you, Mother?" he asked stupidly, for he could see all too clearly how ill she was.

"She has typhus," the matron answered for her.

Michael's head spun to look up at the matron, the shock of what she had said showing on his face. "Typhus?" he asked.

"Yes, typhus. And it's at an advanced stage. I'm afraid it won't too be long," she said, her voice having a little emotion in it this time.

"I am empty, and it seems pointless to live. Why does God seem so distant when you need him most?" his mother suddenly said, surprising him.

A few more minutes of silence passed. Michael realised he was crying. "What do I do now?" he asked, trying to control his emotions.

"There is nothing you can do, nothing any of us can do. It's all in the hands of God," the matron said. There was now a hint of softness in her voice.

There was another brief silence and then a breathless cough as his mother quietly said a prayer, which he had to lower his head closer to her face to be able to hear:

> O Lord, I pray that the fiery and sweet
> strength of Your love
> may draw my soul to You from all things
> that are under heaven,
> that I may die for love of Your love
> as You did die for the love of my love.
> Amen.

At the end of the prayer, Beatrice looked at Michael. "He is taking me from this darkness to His brightness," she said. Her eyes closed and her face relaxed, and at that moment she looked more peaceful than he had ever seen her.

"She's gone," the matron said, putting a comforting hand on his shoulder. "Don't," the matron said, restraining him as he lowered his head to kiss his mother. "She had typhus. It could still be infectious."

Their eyes met. The matron could see Michael's sorrow. "She will be buried today," she told him, back to her matter-of-fact voice.

"And my dad will never have a chance to see her or to have said goodbye to her. Why is there so much evil in the world? Why do we have to suffer and die of hunger or disease?"

"There is much in life we don't understand, and as much as we'd like to know why, we will never know the answer. Only God knows why, and no one else can speak for Him," the matron said in a tone that made Michael think that maybe she was not as hard as he had thought she was.

"I'm afraid you have to go now. I shouldn't really have allowed you in here," she said in a gentle but firm voice.

Michael turned and followed her out, taking one last look over his shoulder at the lifeless body of his mother, knowing he and his father would never see her again.

* * * *

His dad was still sitting in the medical room waiting to be seen. He seemed to look worse than when Michael had left him. "Are you all right?" Michael asked.

"Not really, Son. It seems to be getting worse. I had to go and relieve myself twice, and I found I'd lost my place when I got back. How is your mother?" he asked. The pain he was suffering clearly showed as he gripped his stomach.

Michael took a long, deep breath, pausing to think of the best way to tell his father.

"What's the matter? She ill too?" his dad cut in, seeing the worried expression on his face.

"She's dead. She died while I was there. She had typhus, and I watched her die. I think she recognised me, I'm not sure, but I had a feeling she was only waiting for one of us to come and see her before she passed away. The last thing she said to me was that she was empty and there was no point in living any longer—that she wanted to die."

Luke began coughing. His body began to shake as he loudly exclaimed, "She's dead?! Why the hell didn't they tell us she was dying?"

Everyone in the room looked around at the raised voice as Luke continued to cough uncontrollably and began to spit up blood.

"Help. Help!" Michael called out, seeing the state his father was now in, but it seemed to fall on deaf ears as there was only one so-called medical attendant, who was busy with someone over on the far side of the room.

"I've got to go again. I've got the runs," Luke said, hurrying for the door.

"OK, while you're gone I'll try to get the attention of someone who can help," Michael said as he watched his father hurry out.

"I think my father is very ill and needs attention," Michael told the medical attendant when he eventually got his attention.

The medical attendant looked at him somewhat surprised. "So does everyone else in here," he said with a hapless shrug as he continued to bathe the sores on the man's body.

A chill swept over Michael at the thought of what the man had said. He realised there was very little, if anything, he could do for his father.

"Tell him I will get to him when I can," the medical attendant said casually, but Michael sensed there was little hope in his voice and decided to go and find his father, bring him back, and take him over to the medical attendant.

The condition of the toilets was indescribable, the set-up consisting of a concrete cubicle with a hole in the middle of the floor with the object being the men could crouch over the hole to relieve themselves. But as often as not, many failed to make the hole before they were forced to relieve themselves, with the result being that excrement was everywhere, making it almost impossible to avoid treading in it. The smell was sickening. Michael was glad he had made sure to relieve himself when they were out in the fields building the roads.

Michael suddenly froze as he looked down at his father's body, which was slumped on the floor amidst all the filth. He sprang into action as he rushed to him and knelt down, feeling the slimy mixture beginning to seep into the knee of his ragged trousers.

"Dad, come on. You can't lie here in this filth," he cried out, but there was no movement from his father. Luke was dead, having collapsed as soon as he'd gotten there, coughing violently, his face pressed into the filthy layer covering the floor as he swallowed gulps of it and fought for breath.

Michael let out one almighty scream as he said, "If God loved us, why didn't He protect us instead of letting this happen? It's not fair. My mother worshipped You. Even through all that she suffered, she stayed faithful to You. Why did You desert her and my father? Look at him. Does anyone deserve to die this way? He was a good man, and You deserted him as I'm now going to desert You."

Slowly Michael got to his knees. He got hold of his dad's feet and dragged him out, which was made easy by the wet, slimy mixture. Then he searched in his pockets for any money he may have had concealed. He surprisingly found a little money and wondered why his father had not used it to pay the rent, before slipping it into his trouser pocket as he looked around, wondering what to do with the body.

"Put him in the cart over there," he heard a man speak up. "Here, I'll give you hand," the body collector offered, the lower half of his face covered with a cloth in an attempt to avoid breathing the germs. "Dropping like flies they are. Been another busy day," he said in a matter-of-fact voice, undaunted by the dead and dying. "Here, you had better put this on, or you'll end up like him," the body collector said, offering Michael a piece of rag to cover his face.

Michael wrapped the rag around the lower half of his face. He bent and grabbed hold of his dad's shoulders while the body collector took hold of the legs, and together they carried him to the cart and placed him in it without further ceremony.

"What's his name?" the body collector asked as he started to wheel the cart away.

"Flanagan, Luke Flanagan," Michael called out as he stared at the departing body of his father.

"Got another Flanagan here, female. Any relation?"

"Yes, that's my mother."

"You poor devil."

"None of it makes any sense."

"It never does," the body collector said irreverently as he pushed the cart ahead of him.

Michael turned away slowly, the muscles in his chest tightening as he suddenly felt abandoned. He was unable to understand what was happening or why it had happened. His world, such as it had been, seemed secure and happy, but now it was falling apart—and none of it made any sense.

The trauma was too much for Michael. Having managed to clean himself up as much as he could with the cold water from the hosepipe in the garden, he walked out of the workhouse, determined to get away and never return, although having no idea of where he was going to go.

Chapter 8

Michael managed to find another soup kitchen on the way, further into the city, where he began to hear rumours about ships that were taking people to new lands like the United States and Canada. He decided that he should try to find out how to get on one of those ships wherever it was going, for anywhere had to be better than here, he resolved.

As he got closer to the harbour, his eyes lit up at the sight of the big ships bustling with activity, with goods being loaded and unloaded.

"How do you get to sail on one of those ships to the United States?" he asked the first man he saw who looked like a sailor.

"You look as though you could do with a good meal and a change of clothes before you think about going anywhere," the man quipped, studying Michael's gaunt and shabby appearance. "Go to that building over there," he said, indicating the direction with his arm. "They deal with all those wanting to emigrate," he added disparagingly.

Michael made his way to the building and nervously entered. He was surprised to see the reception area packed with families, pale and gaunt, their eyes wild and hollow and their movements feeble, barely able to support themselves, their threadbare garments hanging loosely from their bodies, all shoving each other in a desperate attempt to get to the counter.

He stood there amongst the melee, realising that like the rest of them he was going to have to fight his way to the counter. He started to weave through the heaving crowd to get to speak to someone.

"I want to go to America," he called out as he got to the counter.

The man behind the counter looked at him with a sneer

as he said, "And so do thousands of others. Where are your parents?"

"They are dead. They died in the workhouse," Michael said mournfully.

"Got any money?" the man asked bluntly, offering no sympathy for his loss.

"Very little, sir," Michael answered, his face showing his resentment, not wanting to part with the little money he had taken from his father.

"Then you won't be going anywhere," the man said facetiously as he turned his attention to a family hustling for his attention.

Michael turned and fought his way back out. "You know, there is one way you can get on a ship and sail for nothing," he heard a voice say as he stood outside gazing around, wondering what to do next.

Michael spun around to look at the stranger who had just spoken to him. "What did you say?" he asked, not sure he had heard correctly.

"I said, there is a way you can get on a ship and sail for free," the stranger repeated.

"You mean sneak on board?"

"No, you don't need to do that. You can sail to Liverpool for nothing."

"How do I do that?" Michael asked, not sure he believed him.

"Find your way over to where they unload the coal and other goods and talk to them," the stranger told him.

Still not sure whether to believe the stranger, Michael made his way around the harbour until he spotted a tall-masted paddle steamer with black smoke belching from the tall funnel. As he got closer, he could see it was unloading coal. Reading the name *Athlone* blazoned on the side of the giant paddle wheels, he wondered how it was possible to travel free on such a magnificent and beautiful ship like that.

Well, there is only one way to find out, and that is to ask one of the workers unloading the coal, he told himself as he hurried to the ship.

"Excuse me, sir," he said meekly.

"Why, what you have done?" the heavily built docker asked jokingly.

"Nothing, sir. I was wondering how I might be able to get a free lift on this boat?"

The dock worker stopped what he was doing and looked at the bedraggled Michael. He shook his head, not sure whether to feel sorry for him or tell him to get lost, but he was so used to seeing people in Michael's state or worse that he felt a little compassion. "Go over to that office and ask in there. And by the way, it's a ship, not a boat," he said reproachfully, indicating the direction with a sweep of his arm.

The office, unlike the first one Michael had gone into, was quiet with one man sitting at a desk, busy entering figures into a large ledger.

"Excuse me, sir," Michael spoke up gingerly.

The man looked up and stared hard at Michael. "Yes?" he said, his face showing his annoyance at being interrupted.

"I was told," Michael began hesitantly. "I was told you can sail free on your ship."

"Where are you trying to get to?" the man asked, the irritation of being interrupted still showing on his face.

"Anywhere. I just want to get away from here. I've just lost my mother and my father, and I have little money and nowhere to go."

The man's face softened. "This ship goes to Liverpool. You can travel as ballast."

"Ballast? What does that mean?" Michael asked.

"You travel in the hold along with the others who want a free ride, as well as the animals, to make up the weight the ship has when it is loaded with coal," the man explained. "So hang around with the others, and you'll be told when the ship is to sail. Then you can come aboard, OK?"

"Where are the others?" Michael asked, surprised.

"They're all bunched together at the back of the building."

"Thank you, sir." Michael hurried out the office with a feeling of great excitement that he was going to get away from this place and start a new life in a new country.

The man was right, there were hundreds standing or sitting wherever there was a space, most of them in the same decrepit state as he was. Some even looked worse, which made Michael wonder whether they were fit enough to get on the ship, but he resolved that this wasn't his problem and concentrated his mind on what the accommodation would be for ballast. Totally exhausted, he settled himself down on the hard ground and quickly fell into a deep sleep.

Chapter 9

Michael was suddenly awakened by raised voices as people, excited by what was happening, were busy gathering their things together and hurrying off. He struggled to his feet, trying to shake off the drowsiness as he attempted to work out what was happening.

"The ship's leaving, so you'd better hurry up," someone called out as a group rushed past him.

Michael turned and simply followed them. He was taken aback to see so many massed around the boarding ramp, pushing, shoving, and elbowing each other to make sure they got themselves and their families on the ship. He began to wonder whether there would be room for him at the end of it.

Amazingly he managed to get on board. He felt a great sense of relief that he was going somewhere away from all the wretchedness that had caused him to lose his mother and father, leaving him abandoned with little money and only the ragged clothes that hung loosely over his emaciated body.

That sense of relief drained away as he was ordered to follow the others and climb down the metal ladder into the dark hold.

To his bewilderment, the hold was filled not only with the mass of men, women, and children but also with cattle. Although tethered, the cattle were unsettled by the bodies beginning to crowd in on them.

Even in an uncrowded situation, movement would have been a little restricted, but with the addition of the animals, movement was almost totally restricted. Michael had to ease someone away just to be able to get off the ladder and find somewhere to stand. Finding somewhere to sit, he quickly realised it was never going to be possible and might even be precarious.

One woman Michael noticed had forced herself into a corner, where she had managed to sit with her two small children tucked under her skirts for safety.

At least this won't be for long, Michael thought as he heard the crew rushing about, preparing to set sail with the captain or whoever it was shouting out orders. He began to relax a little as he felt the vibrations of the engines as they started to turn the big paddle wheels. He could hear the splashes as the blades ploughed in to the water to move the ship.

The hold was filthy. As the ship got under way, the hatches were battened down, plunging the hold into darkness, which caused many to start to panic and cry out in protest. With no fresh air, they were left to breathe a toxic mixture of coal fumes, animal odour and the odour from the mass of unwashed sweaty human bodies.

The average length of the journey from Dublin to Liverpool was about twelve to fourteen hours, but in bad weather the journey could take much longer.

With the hatches closed, it was impossible to know what the weather conditions were like, but Michael could sense the sea was rough as the ship was heaving on the swells. It wasn't long before some began to feel seasick, their uncontrolled vomiting splashing over those unfortunate enough to be standing close to them before the bile spattered onto the floor.

With no sanitary provision whatsoever, the situation was becoming increasingly worse with everyone forced to indiscriminately relieve themselves where they stood. The same held true for the animals. The floor was soon covered in a quagmire of vomit and human and animal waste.

By the time they were halfway through the journey, the situation was becoming unbearable with the wind picking up and the waves lapping against the hull, the sound combining with the sounds of moans and groans of those no longer able to bear the horrendous conditions with some of the older men and women fainting and falling to the floor amidst the quagmire of filth with no one offering to help, more concerned with their own plight.

Some of the men began hammering on the side of the hull with their fists and screaming, "Open the hatches. Let us out. … Let us out!" But it seemed no one was listening, or if they were, they were not taking any notice.

The nightmarish journey came to an end when the hatches were finally opened and the light and fresh air rushed in, making everyone gasp. They raised their heads so as to suck in as much fresh air as they could with every gulp. What had been a subdued crowd a moment ago was now starting to push and shove with each person making an effort to be the first up the ladder.

Michael stood back, deciding it was better to wait and let the others go as there was plenty of time. The ship wasn't going anywhere in a hurry, and neither was he as he had nowhere to rush to and no idea of what he was going to do once he got off the ship.

The most able scrambled up the ladder first, one after the other, leaving the mothers, who were forced to wait for someone to kindly hoist up their screaming children after they had managed to climb up the ladder.

Michael was disturbed as he continued to watch the antics of those who had no care for anybody but themselves, completely ignoring those who were still lying on the filthy floor and groaning in obvious in pain, trying to get to their feet, and those who were not moving at all.

"Is somebody going to come down and help these poor people?" Michael shouted up.

"When we've got everybody off, we'll come down and deal with them," he heard someone call out in a strange accent he didn't quite recognise. "You get your Irish arse up here and leave everything to us," the voice shouted down at him.

Michael reluctantly made his way to the ladder and scrambled up.

As he walked along the deck, the sea air hit his nostrils. He stopped and stood breathing deeply, letting the air fill his lungs, wondering where he was going to go from here.

"Move on, lad. You can't stand there all day. Move on to where you're going to, and get a bath and a change of clothes while you're at it. You stink," one of the sailors said deprecatingly.

"But I have nowhere to go to and very little money," Michael said despondently.

"That's the trouble with you bleeding Irish. You come over here and expect us to take care of you," the sailor said acrimoniously. "Just follow the others. They're all penniless and looking for somewhere, just like you," he added, the acrimony still in his voice.

Michael hurried off to catch up with the other bewildered immigrants to find out where they were heading.

Part II

Liverpool, England

The Awakening

Chapter 10

Liverpool began as a tidal pool off the River Mersey, originally called the Lifer Pol, meaning muddy pool.

By the mid-nineteenth century, Liverpool was becoming a great port city, the gateway to the world, able to harbour large ships that could cross the Atlantic, sailing to New York, Boston, and Canada, as well as the ships transporting slaves from Africa and the Caribbean.

It was a lively city with the port being central to its prosperity. Extreme wealth and extreme poverty lived alongside each other. As a result, crime was rampant with murders, muggings, crimps exploiting sailors and the newly arrived, and prostitutes fleecing their clients for whatever they could get.

Many young women dreaming of a new life believed Liverpool to be a staging post on their way to the United States, the New World, the land of opportunity, but sadly for many they were only a few steps away from a new kind of misery in one of the downtown whorehouses, finding themselves easy prey for those who were raking in a fortune by running the brothels.

The conditions in Liverpool were generally unsanitary. In 1832 there had been a cholera epidemic. Although during the early part of the nineteenth century, the supply of fresh water began to improve with private companies starting to supply piped water to the upmarket houses, it was expensive with only the well-off being able to afford. The poor still had to rely on barrels or collect water from wells. With the massive influx of the Irish, Liverpool was bulging at the seams with people living in crowded cellars that had no sanitation of any kind.

Whatever the conditions, it is a deliverance from hell,

not to mention the privations of a long and miserable sea journey, Michael thought to himself as he meekly followed the others, still not knowing where they were all heading. He looked around, amazed at Liverpool's size. A series of granite docks and warehouses spread out over a vast area in both directions along the banks of the Mersey. He was astonished by the number of large ships being loaded or unloaded with goods, and he made a mental note that this would be a good place to try to find work once he got himself settled somewhere.

As they all progressed along the way leading out of the port, Michael noticed some strange healthy-looking types starting to mingle in with the crowd. It seemed rather strange. The more he looked at them, the more he noticed one of the younger strangers sidle up to a frail old man, dip his hand into his back pocket, and remove what looked like a wallet.

"Hey, you!" Michael shouted, but the young stranger was quick and moved off fast. Angered by what he had seen, Michael chased after him, surprising himself that he still had the energy to do it.

The young stranger seemed to panic. He dropped the wallet as he ran off. Michael picked up the wallet and looked around for the man it had been taken from, but he couldn't see him anywhere, realising he didn't have any idea what the man looked like as he had only seen the back of him.

He looked into the wallet and was surprised to see how much money was in there: three pounds, and two shillings and sixpence in coins. He quickly closed the wallet and hurried on, hoping he would still catch up with the man and give the wallet back, but before he had a chance to put it in his pocket, another crimp—as the pickpockets, runners, and thieves were called—snatched it from him.

Michael stared after him, but in his feeble state he knew he had no chance of catching him. And even if he could, he would have been no match for him.

Three pounds, two shillings, and sixpence was a fortune. He had never held so much money in his hands before, and he felt at the moment that he never would again.

"You looking for lodgings?" he heard a voice ask as they came to the exit gates of the port.

Michael looked at the man who had spoken and had a strange feeling he had seen him before. *Is he one of the immigrants like me?* he thought. *Or is he one of the thieves who stole the wallet?* He wasn't sure.

"Well, does yer?" the young man asked, an impatient tone in his voice.

"Yes, but I have little money, so I can't afford much."

"Don't worry, it's only a sixpence a week. But you'll have to pay a week's deposit plus sixpence for me troubles. Follow me and I'll get you settled."

Michael trudged along on what seemed like an endless walk through a tough, uncompromising neighbourhood, the narrow streets littered with discarded newspapers, rubbish, and rotting vegetables, the surface covered with the slime of human and animal waste. The narrow alleyways were crammed with men and women leaning out of doorways, drinking alcohol, smoking, and shouting obscenities in various accents. Prostitutes approached any man who passed them. The buildings seemed to close in on Michael. Many of them were divided into several dwellings, some derelict, while others had broken windows or no windows at all, the gaping frames covered with filthy rotten rags, making Michael nervous. It was becoming overwhelming to him as he never seen anything like this before. He had the uncomfortable feeling that this was not a place he would like to venture to on his own, even during the day, for fear of being attacked by someone.

"Here we are," the young man announced encouragingly as they at last came to a large house. Michael breathed a sigh of relief as he looked at the house. It appeared a lot better than the other houses. He guessed the rooms would be better, although he was still worried about the amount of money he was having to pay out, which would leave him with just a shilling and a few pence of the money he had taken from his dad. The worry deepened as they descended the uneven stone steps to the basement.

"In yer go then," the young man said as he opened a heavy wooden door and shoved Michael in ahead of him. The acrid smell of sweaty bodies and tobacco immediately hit Michael's nostrils. His eyes burned in the suffocating atmosphere of so many people crowded together into the cellar with no apparent ventilation.

"Give me the money and I'll pay the landlord while yer finds yerself a space and some bedding if yer lucky."

"Oh, I don't know." Michael hesitated, looking around the cellar, with people seeming to be aimlessly moving around or lying on makeshift bedding, some of them groaning.

"Well, if yer think you can find anywhere better than this for sixpence a week, then go ahead. The place is already overflowing with yer bloody Irish, so make yer mind up fast as there'll be others wanting somewhere to stay."

"Well, maybe for week while I look for somewhere else and-"

"Please yerself, but yer'll still have to pay me and the deposit. But if yer decide to leave, yer'll get the deposit back."

"OK," Michael said with a hapless shrug as he handed over the money.

"Good luck," the young man said as he turned and hurried out.

Michael looked around to see where he could find a spot that he could make his own, but the place was crowded. And above all else, at that moment he was desperate to relieve himself.

"Excuse me," he said to the nearest man, who was rolling up his bedding. "I need to have a pee. Where do I go?"

The man looked at him suspiciously. "Another bloody one. How many more are they going to let in here? There's no bloody room as it is. There are a couple of buckets behind those curtains over there, that's if they're not already overflowing." The man snorted contemptuously.

Michael moved through the crowd over to the curtains.

He pushed one aside enough to slip in and was surprised to see a woman with her skirts hitched up, squatting over one of the buckets.

"Sorry, I didn't know. I, er …"

"Don't worry, love, this happens all the time," the woman said, straightening herself up and stepping away from the bucket as she pulled up her drawers and smoothed her skirt down. "It's too crowded for any modesty in this place," she said, disappearing out through the curtains.

The smell was terrible, but Michael had to relieve himself now or else the situation would become even worse, so reluctantly dropped his trousers, squatted over the bucket and relieved himself trying not to make any noise in the process.

Back in the main cellar, Michael started look around again. He could see in the far corner that there was a washbasin with a single tap, which several people were lining up to use.

"If you're looking for somewhere to lie down, there's some bedding over there that's going begging as the poor sod who had it died this morning, so I'd grab it before some other bugger does," the voice said. As Michael turned and looked at her, he realised it was the woman he had seen squatting over the bucket.

"Thank you," he replied meekly. The whole situation had become overpowering, making him wish he had stayed in Ireland.

He crossed over to where the woman had indicated the bedding was and examined it. It was in pretty bad shape, covered with stains and in need of a good wash, but even so, it had to be better than sleeping on the bare hard concrete floor.

"Where can I get some food around here?" he asked the woman as his stomach started to rumble with hunger.

"Food? The rats eat better than we do," she replied. "The landlord will sell you some grub, but make sure you eat it outside, cos if you bring it in here, some bugger will try to steal it from you as we're all bloody starving in here," the woman told him.

"What do you want?" the landlord asked gruffly, after having opened the front door of the main house to find Michael standing there. He was dressed rather smartly in that his clothes, although not expensive, were clean and in relatively good condition.

"I understand I can buy some food from you," Michael said nervously.

"Who told you that?" the landlord snapped.

"A lady down in the cellar told me."

"What are you doing down in the cellar?" the landlord asked, his voice becoming even more gruff.

"I'm renting a space. Didn't the man tell you about me and give you my rent and deposit?"

"Man? What man? You bloody Irish are all the same. You come over here with your thieving ways and expect us to take care of you. 'Man gave me the rent.' That one's been tried so many times."

"But he gave you a week's rent and a deposit," Michael persisted.

"Week's rent and deposit? You buggers don't half try to pull a fast one, but not with me, so clear off and find someone else to scrounge off," the landlord said, slamming the door in his face.

Chapter 11

Walking back along Hope Street with his head down, Michael had his shoulders drooped. He was feeling utterly dejected, having been cheated out of most of his precious money.

As he continued along, two men suddenly appeared from the shadows in one of the narrow alleyways.

With his head still bowed, Michael carried on, not taking much notice, until one of the men pulled out a pistol, cocked it, and pointed it at Michael's head, bringing him to an abrupt stop.

"Give us all you've got," the man demanded.

"I haven't got much, and what I have got I'm going to need to survive. I've already been cheated out of most of my money," Michael protested.

"Most of your money, which means you still have some left. It's amazing how you Irish somehow manage to come over here with money tucked away in your trousers, so give us what you've got," the other man cut in.

"I'm not giving you anything," Michael said angrily, his eyebrows furrowed and his lips pressed together. Their aggressive attitude was beginning to stroke his nerves.

The two men looked at each other, surprised by his defiance. "You want me to blow your fucking head off?" the man aiming the pistol said. He didn't get a chance to finish as Michael shot out a fist and hit him full in the face, causing the man to drop the pistol and put his hands to his head. Blood began to gush from his nose. As Michael went to punch the other man, he pulled a cudgel from the inside of his coat and struck Michael over the head, giving the other man a chance to pick up the pistol, which he used to hit Michael repeatedly with the butt.

It was too much for Michael in his frail condition. He buckled under the onslaught and fell unconscious to the ground. The two men then quickly riffled through his pockets, found what money he had, and hurried off.

* * * *

"Are you all right?" Michael heard an echoing voice ask. He looked up through bleary eyes, not sure what he was seeing as the face seemed very dark.

He continued to blink as the voice asked again if he was all right.

"If you mean being robbed twice in one day is being all right, then the answer is no, I'm bloody not all right," Michael snapped, staring up at the man.

"Let's get you on your feet. I saw the two men run off, and it looked like you had given one of them a good hiding," the man said, bending down to help haul Michael to his feet.

As Michael stood up, still feeling a little dizzy from the beating, he stared strangely at the dark features of the man. "I would have beaten both of them if I were not so weak from the lack of food. Where did you come from?" he blurted out, having never seen anyone with black skin before or heard anyone talk in such a strange voice.

"I was just out for a stroll. My name is Leon Boxer."

"Leon Boxer, you look different from everybody else," Michael said, uncertainly.

"That's because I came here from America, although I'm originally from Africa."

"I see," Michael uttered, still a little hazy and unsteady on his feet and no idea of where Africa was. What surprised him was the way the man was dressed smartly in a tight-fitting double-breasted calf-length frock coat which fell over his broad shoulders and wide chest. He had blunt handsome features which were alive with aggressive energy. The front of the coat was cut up to the waistband of his light-coloured breeches. Underneath he wore a white linen shirt, the collar

76

turned down with a patterned wide cravat neatly knotted around the neck, which complemented the very decorative single-breasted waistcoat. On his head he was wearing a wide-brimmed hat, and his feet were encased in highly polished tall-fitted boots. The only time Michael had ever seen anyone dressed like that was when the English lords occasionally came to visit their farms before the famine.

"I think you had better come with me," Leon said, looking at Michael compassionately.

"Come with you to where?" Michael asked, his brain still in turmoil.

"To where I work. You look as though you're in need of a good meal and somewhere to stay. You just come off the ship?"

"Yeah, and I got robbed of all the money I had, so I don't know what to do. I can't even afford the fare back to Ireland as you have to pay as the ship is loaded with coal. And of all things, it's my birthday today."

"And how old does that make you?"

"Sixteen," Michael said proudly.

"Well, this could be your lucky birthday as Madame is looking for someone to assist me."

"Madame! Doing what?" Michael asked, his brain clearing at last.

"You'll find that out when we get there. You able to walk?"

"Yeah, I'm OK, except my head is hurting," Michael said, rubbing his head to make the point.

* * * *

Michael began to feel a little relieved as he followed Leon out of the slum area and into a more respectable area of Everton to the north-east of the city, which was surrounded by open spaces of fields and trees where the elite and wealthier merchants looked for more space to live and build their luxury houses, which gave them a commanding view over the landscape.

They stopped in front of a tall elegant three-storey house with a large bay window and white lacy curtains draped across the inside.

"Is this where you live?" Michael asked, somewhat surprised.

"It's where I work. Come with me," Leon said as he opened the small iron gate and stepped down the cast-iron steps that led to the basement. Michael followed him around to the back of the house. Leon pulled open the rear door and indicated for Michael to enter.

As he followed Leon through a narrow passage past several storerooms, the smell of food being cooked began to assail his nostrils. It made his stomach churn.

As they entered the kitchen, Michael looked around in total amazement. The kitchen was large like nothing he had ever seen before. There was a large table in the middle of the room with a variety of cooking utensils spread out on it with two women standing around it busily preparing food. The kitchen had a high ceiling with high windows cut into the whitewashed walls, which had a scrubbable wainscot covering the bottom half. At the far end wall, where the fireplace would normally have been, was a large cast-iron oven. Michael stared in wonderment at the large array pots on it with steam rising from them. Around the other walls were large cupboards and dressers filled with copper pots and pans, crockery, and utensils.

Leon looked at Michael, whose mouth was now drooling. "I guess you're hungry. Wait there. I'll have a word with Mrs Baxter. She is the head cook."

Michael continued to stare around as Leon went over to Mrs Baxter, a woman well into her fifties with a well-rounded plump figure. She was wearing a long black dress with a white apron over the top. On her head she wore a white cap with lace edging, covering most of her dark hair.

"Who's that you brought in with you?" Mrs Baxter asked disgruntledly as soon as Leon got close to her. "Get him out of my kitchen. He's filthy, and he stinks."

"He's someone I came across in the street. He has been beaten up and robbed and is in desperate need of food. Can you find him something?"

Mrs Baxter looked begrudgingly across at Michael. "He looks like he could eat a horse. I'll make him a sandwich, but you'll have to take him outside. I can't have him eating in here. He looks like he needs a good bath apart from anything else."

"Thanks, Mrs Baxter. I'll—"

"What the devil is this?" Madame Rosita demanded as she walked into the kitchen and saw the bedraggled Michael standing there.

Madame Rosita ran the most exclusive brothel in Liverpool, catering to aristocrats, politicians, businessmen, and the nobility. There was no form of sexual service which she was not willing to provide for her clients. Always elegantly dressed in the finest of clothes adorned with a rich selection of gold and diamond jewellery that displayed her wealth, most of which she had obtained by a little blackmail, extorting money and jewels from her wealthy clientele, she was in her late forties and still relatively attractive. Her face was made up with a touch of rouge to the cheeks and the lips painted a daring bright red. Her hair, coiled and curled with a braided tail, folded around her head. It was secured in a bun and decorated with a light blue ribbon.

"Er, sorry, Madame. I—"

"Not as sorry as you will be. What is the meaning of this, bringing a ruffian into this establishment?" she asked, her face flushed with outrage, the atmosphere suddenly becoming like a heavy cloud.

"I'm sorry, Madame. I found this young man lying in the street. He'd been set upon by some crimps who stole what little money he had. He told me on the way here that he had just arrived from Ireland and found a room to rent, but he gave the rent money to a man to pay the landlord. The man was obviously another crimp, who ran off with the money. So he is penniless with nowhere to go."

"Well, he can't stay here, that's for sure. Give him some

food, Mrs Baxter, and send him on his way," Madame Rosita instructed her.

"Excuse me, Madame, but one of the reasons I brought him back here was because I watched him put up a good fight against the crimps. And I reckon that if he had been in a much fitter state, he would have easily dealt with them."

"So?"

"Well, Madame, you said that I should look for another man to help with security. It is my view that this man, when back to his true fitness, could be such a man to assist me," Leon explained.

"What makes you so sure you can trust him?"

"Well, on the walk back I gave him every opportunity to try to rob me, but he didn't attempt anything."

"But he wouldn't have stood a chance against you with your boxing skills."

"True, but he didn't know that. Particularly given the way I'm dressed, he could have tried to pick my pocket. If he was a ruffian, he certainly would have tried."

"I see. So what are you proposing?"

"With your permission, I propose I take him into my care, get him cleaned up and into some decent clothes, and then instruct him in what his duties will be."

"Very well. But I warn you, if he tries anything untoward, then not only he but also you will be thrown out. Do you understand?"

"Yes, Madame, I understand," Leon said. She turned and stormed off.

"I hope you know what you're doing," Mrs Baxter said to Leon as she started to prepare a beef sandwich.

* * * *

"I don't understand. What was all that about?" Michael asked as he sat in the garden with Leon, hungrily devouring the layers of beef sandwiched between two thick slices of bread.

"If you're what I think you are, you have just landed

80

yourself a job," Leon told him.

"Doing what?"

"Security. Taking care of this place and the girls. It's the house policy to call them girls, even though some of them are older than me."

"The girls," Michael exclaimed, almost choking on the last mouthful of the sandwich.

"Right, let me explain. This is a brothel, one of the best in town."

"A brothel? What exactly is a brothel?"

Leon looked at Michael, astonished he didn't know what a brothel was. "A brothel is where men, in this case men of wealth and nobility, come to be entertained by women. And Madame Rosita, whom you saw in the kitchen, owns this one. I work for her. It is my job to protect her and the girls from the men who sometimes become drunk and start to act violently towards them. Such men need to be restrained and barred from being allowed back until they've sobered up."

"I see. I heard her say you were good at boxing."

"Yes I am, which is why she employs me."

"My father taught me to box. Did your father teach you?"

"My parents were from West Africa. They were captured, transported to America in a British slave ship, and sold to a plantation owner in a place called Georgetown County, South Carolina, where my father met up with a woman called Monifor, which ironically in Yoruba means 'I am lucky,' which as a slave she certainly wasn't. As a result of their liaison, I was born. My father was forced to fight with other slaves to entertain the plantation owners. He was good and earned Eugene Trompson, the plantation owner, a lot of money by winning the fights he had bet on him winning. When I had grown up and my father was no longer able to win fights, the owner forced my dad to teach me to fight so I could take his place. I was successful in winning the owner a greater fortune, but of course nothing for me as I was his property, a slave."

"So how did you get away?"

"More of that another time," he said evasively. "The

important thing right now is for you to have a good wash and get into some decent clothes."

"But I don't have any money to buy clothes," Michael said anxiously.

"Don't worry about that. Madame Rosita will pay for them and take it out of your salary."

"How much am I going to be paid?"

"That is up to Madame Rosita. Not a lot to begin with, but a lot more than you could earn anywhere else. And if you prove yourself, you can earn even more. Right, now that you've filled your belly, let's get you out of those filthy rags so I can take you to my room, where you can have a good wash. But first I'll have to use the bucket out here to get the worst off."

Michael looked at him, horrified. "I'm not taking my clothes off out here or anywhere else for that matter."

"You will not be allowed back into the house unless you let me clean you up. It's up to you. You can either get up and leave or grab the opportunity that is being offered. With the state you're in and having no money, your chances back out on the streets aren't good, I don't think."

Michael knew that what Leon was saying was true, and he had just eaten the best meal he had ever had in the whole of his life, but taking his clothes off in front of someone else was another matter. He had never completely taken his clothes off in front of anyone. The only time he had ever stripped down to his underwear was when he went for a bath and a swim with his mates in the local stream during the hot summers.

"OK, I don't know what your background is, but let me make it clear. You get cleaned up and into some new clothes or you're out."

"What about the girls you talked about? I don't want them seeing me …"

"Don't worry about them. They've seen it all. And once you start working here, you'll be seeing naked bodies all over the place. So hurry up while I go and fill a bucket."

Michael didn't understand what Leon meant by seeing naked bodies all over the place. He shrugged, concerned with his own body being naked, and hesitated a while longer before he slowly began to remove his clothes, the ragged garments almost falling apart from having been stuck to his unwashed body for so long.

Leon looked down at Michael's feet. They were black, the nails long, uncut, and yellow, infected with fungus. "I think you're going to need more than one bucket of water judging by the state of you. I'll get you a bathrobe so you'll be able to cover yourself when you're finished," Leon said, hurrying off.

* * * *

"Mind your head as you move around," Leon warned as they entered his room. The room was in the attic. One had to climb several flights of stairs at the back of the house to get there. It was well kept, clean, and comfortably furnished. The ceiling sloped steeply on one side of the room with a small window bay cut into the sloping roof.

There was a single bedstead with a pretty eiderdown spread over it. On the opposite wall was a handbasin fitted into a decorative marble-topped cabinet on which stood a large pretty porcelain water jug.

"Right, I'll go and fetch some hot water, and then I'll find you some clean underwear and decent clothes," Leon told Michael, picking up the jug and hurrying out.

Michael stood there looking around the room. He noted the pretty curtains in the window and the luxury patterned carpet on the floor. He was beginning to feel nervous about being there, not able yet to comprehend how he'd come to be there.

"Right, having got the worst off, you can now have a proper wash," Leon told him as he filled the basin with hot water from the jug.

As Michael removed the bathrobe, Leon studied his

naked body. He could see even in his emaciated state that there was strength enough in his body to be able to put up a fight after being without food for so long. He was barrel-chested and had broad shoulders. There was certain solidity to him.

"When was the last time you had a good wash?"

"Only when we used to go down to the stream, but that was only in the summer months as the water was far too cold in the winter," Michael told him as he picked up the bar of Pears soap and stared at the translucent amber colour. He sniffed the soap, surprised that it smelt of what he thought was flowers. As he dipped his hands in the warm water and began to rub the soap, it felt soft and began to foam, the sweet aroma becoming stronger. The only luxury with soap he had ever experienced was when one of his neighbours had lent him a bar of carbolic soap to take to the stream with him.

"I'll go and get some more water," Leon said, leaving him to carry on washing himself.

"You said your father taught you to box. Was he a boxer too?" Leon asked as soon as he returned with another jug of hot water.

"He could take care of himself. He had to because there were always those around who wanted his job and were prepared to do him harm so he wouldn't be able to work and they could then take his job and the cottage and the little bit of land that went with it where we could grow our own potatoes. I hated the way we lived, always seeming to struggle just to stay alive and have some food to eat and a roof over our heads. Our schoolteacher seemed to take a liking to me and encouraged me to learn to play the violin so I could better myself, but the other kids thought anybody playing the violin was a sissy. One day the local bully and his gang set about me and smashed up the violin the teacher had loaned me to practise on. That was when my father told me the only way to survive in this world is to be good with your fists. So he taught me to box."

"Where is your father now, still in Ireland?"

"Yes, but not alive. He and my mother died as a result of

the potato crops failing. We were thrown out of the cottage with nothing and nowhere to go. We were starving and were forced to make our way on foot to the nearest town to try to get food and shelter like so many others. We eventually made it to the workhouse, where first my mum died of typhus and then my dad. Somehow I was lucky not to catch it, and I managed to make my way here."

"I'd better get you some more clean water so you can shave. Then I'll cut your hair and sort out some clothes for you to wear," Leon said, hurrying out.

* * * *

Once Michael had thoroughly washed his body, Leon fitted him out with a shirt made of linen worn with a wide cravat, a waistcoat, breeches with a fly front, a calf-length frock coat, and high lace-up boots.

"Now you look much better. And always remember, if you look the part, you will be treated accordingly. We can now go and see Madame Rosita and see if she approves, but be careful what you say. Let her do the talking."

Leon knocked gently on the highly polished solid oak door and waited until he heard the voice call out "Enter."

Michael's eyes widened in wonderment as he entered the room. It was richly furnished. Heavily carved and plumped-up sofas and armchairs, and an ottoman, filled the room. The floor was covered with a thick-piled carpet woven with a fleur-de-lis motif. The walls were adorned in rich ruby-red decorative wallpaper. A large ornate marble fireplace with inserted patterned tiles dominated the room, illuminated by an array of oil lamps, two of which were placed on the mantel shelf in front of a large mirror, reflecting the light across the room.

Madame Rosita rested back on the ottoman, elegantly dressed in the finest full-skirted dress, festooned with a selection of gold and diamond jewellery. She stared at Michael's impassive face enquiringly.

Michael stared nervously back at her.

"Well, you don't look anything like the ruffian I saw earlier," she eventually said. "Has Leon told you what your work will be and what will be expected of you?" she continued, her voice warm, but the warmth tinged with a touch of hardness.

"No. Er, Leon hasn't, and I—"

"I thought it would be better coming from you, Madame," Leon cut in, before Michael had a chance to say anything else.

"I see. What is your name?"

"Michael. Michael Flanagan."

"Well, Michael, you will address me as Madame at all times. Your job will be to protect the property and the girls from unwanted attention or violence of any kind. Sometimes our clients may inadvertently act unruly because they have had a little too much to drink or are on drugs, but they must at all times be treated with the respect their position demands," she began to explain. Michael continued to stare at her, not sure of what sense to make of what she was saying.

"Oh, and one more thing. The girls are strictly off limits, and you are not to have anything to do with them socially or otherwise. If you do, then you will be instantly dismissed. Is that understood?"

"Er, yes, Madame," Michael answered meekly, still trying to take it all in.

"You will be paid ten shillings a week, all your meals and accommodation provided, for which I expect total loyalty and hard work," she added. "And if you prove satisfactory, you will be rewarded with an increase in your pay."

He was amazed at her words, and it showed. *Ten shillings a week.* The thought resounded in his head. *It would have taken my father something like four months to earn anything like that kind of money.*

"Right, he is in your hands, Leon, and your responsibility. Show him around and introduce him to the girls so they know who he is."

"Yes, Madame," Leon said, guiding Michael out.

Leon began to lead him around the house, taking him first into a large room decorated in the same opulent style as Madame Rosita's room. What surprised Michael to the point of embarrassment was the array of females lounging on sofas and ottomans, scantily dressed in corsets and black stockings, their heaving breasts seeming to threaten to free themselves from the tight confines of the corsets.

"Girls, may I introduce Michael," Leon announced with a flourish, completely unabashed by the scantily clad females.

"Hi, Michael," the women responded with a wave of their hands.

"Michael is joining me and will be helping in looking after you lovely girls, so be nice to him as he has a lot to learn."

"Want me to teach him a few tricks?" Mary, one of the older women, called out jokingly.

"You know the rules better than anyone, Mary, so don't tease him," Leon chastised her.

"Looks like he's never seen a near-naked woman," Bridgit, one of the younger women, cut in.

"Bet he's never had a good fuck either," Maisie blurted out, causing them all to laugh, which made Michael blush bright red and turn to rush back out.

Leon grabbed his arm. "Don't take any notice of Maisie. She's just joking. That's something you're going to have to get used to. Right, let's move on and show you the other rooms before it starts to get busy. See you later, girls," Leon said. He and Michael left the room.

"I see that shocked you," Leon said as they walked along the corridor. Haven't you seen a half-naked female before?"

"No, never. Why are they all sitting around so unashamedly like that? Doesn't it embarrass them and you?"

"Course not. I see them every day, a lot of the time with no clothes on at all. And you will too when you've got into the swing of things.

"They're very pretty," Michael reflected, beginning to feel a strange sensation in his loins at the thought of seeing them naked.

"Yes they are, because Madame provides them with personal hairstylists and dressmakers, ensuring they are amongst the most elegantly dressed whores in Liverpool."

"Whores, so that's what they are. I've heard talk of them. I remember my father calling a woman a whore, but I had no idea what it meant."

"Well, now you know."

"This is the mirror room," Leon explained as he opened the door and entered, followed by Michael, who stared around the room aghast at the mirrors covering all four walls. The ceiling had an expansive crystal chandelier suspended directly over the king-size bed in the centre of the room, and the floor was covered with a rich white deep-pile carpet.

"I can see why they call it the mirror room," Michael said, his eyebrows furrowing and his lips pressed together as he looked aimlessly at his different reflections in the various mirrors.

"Gets a lot of use, this room," Leon said, amused at Michael with his head tilted all the way back to study his reflection in the mirrored ceiling.

"We've only ever had a small handheld mirror that my mother wouldn't let anyone else use, frightened it would be broken and bring us seven years' bad luck. I reckon it must have been broken when we were thrown out of our cottage as we had nothing but back luck from that moment on," he said, his voice low and strained.

"Right. I'll show you the gold room next," Leon said, leading him off.

The gold room took its name from the large shiny bronze bath encased in a highly polished veneered wooden frame with inlaid gold motifs set in the centre of the room. The head of the bath had a cushion woven with gold thread. The ceiling and walls were draped in exotic gold-threaded curtains, and the ceiling had a tent like roof with a crystal chandelier at its peak that gave the feeling of being in an Arabian tent. The was floor covered in a rich, deep-piled, gold-coloured oriental carpet.

"It'll take several buckets to fill that," Michael said, gazing at the bath, having never seen a bath of any sort before, never mind one of that size.

"It certainly does, but the girls are expert at it and have it filled in no time. Right, the next room is called the blue room," Leon told him as they moved along the corridor. Once again Michael's eyes widened as he stepped into the room. It was completely done out in blue. The walls were covered in a blue flock paper, and the matching blue curtains were laced with a white silk edging. A large bed occupied one end of the room with matching blue silk quilt and pillows. The floor was covered with a thick-piled matching blue carpet.

"And this is the Kama Sutra room," Leon explained as they entered yet another room farther along the corridor. The room was plain compared to the others with a large square bed against the far wall. The bed just had a mattress with no sheets or eiderdown. On the walls were hung a series of explicit Kama Sutra drawings depicting couples in various sexual acts and positions. Michael gazed disconcertedly at them, his mouth turned down in a frown, not sure what to make of the drawings.

"Kama Sutra is the world's oldest book on the pleasures of sensual living, originally compiled in the third century by the Indian sage Vātsyāyana. *Kama Sutra* literally means 'a treatise of pleasure'," Leon explained knowledgeably.

"One more room and we've finished," Leon said, dragging Michael away from the drawings.

"This is called the flagellation room," Leon told him as they stepped inside. It was fitted out like a torture chamber with rings fixed to the ceiling for suspending clients by their wrists and a stretcher on which the client could be strapped, unable to move, subjected to whatever was his pleasure. There were also various instruments hanging around on the walls, including canes, leather straps, birches, whips, holy branches, and wire-thonged cat-of-nine tails.

"What in the devil is flager or whatever it is you said?" Michael exclaimed in horror, giving Leon a cold, forbidding look.

"The flagellation room is where men and women come to satisfy their peculiar sexual desires."

"Men and women?" Michael asked.

"Yes, men and women. You see, some men like to be flagellated by women, and some women by men, which means we have to have female and male flagellants to service them. The flagellants, as they are called, have had to learn to gracefully and effectively administer the flagellation to satisfy the peculiar demands of their clients," Leon explained.

"I don't understand. It is against all things Godly," Michael exclaimed, again rather loudly.

"Depends on your, or rather other people's, point of view. Sodomy is still illegal and punishable by death, although it's mainly a heavy fine or imprisonment these days, but as long as it is kept under cover, nobody gets to know or care about it."

"But men and women were brought together for procreation, my mother said the Bible teaches us."

"Procreation? My word, you have a lot to learn about what the Bible says and how much people take notice of it when it comes to seeking out their secret desires."

"I'm not sure I'll ever understand any of this, and I'm not sure I want to either. It's all the work of the Devil, and I don't want to be part of any of that."

"Well, the Devil or not, you had better make your mind up quickly, because it's either this or back out on the streets in your old rags," Leon said sternly. "What's it to be?"

Michael stood hesitantly. He said nothing as he looked around him, the blood draining from his face.

"I'll take that as a yes. I need to show you the reception area, and then we're finished until tonight, when it all starts," Leon said, leading a reluctant Michael off.

The reception area was even more lavishly furnished with elegant tables and chairs. The walls were covered in opera house heavy-textured floral wallpaper in stark black and scarlet colours. The thick-piled carpet matched the garish red of the wallpaper. The ceiling was painted a mauve that matched the plain heavy velvet curtains covering the entire end wall opposite the door where a magnificent Louis XIV baroque table stood acting as a bar, offering a varied selection of liquor. To the right of the desk was a grand piano. The area left of the desk was curtained off with heavy, highly decorated curtains which allowed entrance to the inner sanctum.

"I've never seen anything like this in my life," Michael said, his stare so intent that it began to raise the hairs on the back on his neck.

"You'll see a lot more before you're through," Leon said with an indulgent smile. "So now you've seen it all. You stick with me and follow me wherever I go unless I or Madame Rosita tells you otherwise, OK?" Leon added as they walked back to his room.

"OK, but you still haven't told me how you escaped and got here," Michael asked, keen to know more about Leon once they were back in his room.

"It all started as I said, when Gene Trompson, the owner, along with other plantation owners in Georgetown County, started to argue about who had the toughest and strongest slaves. They decided to arrange boxing contests to entertain themselves to see who had the best fighter. As the competitions grew in rivalry, the money increased too, with the owners placing heavier bets on who they thought would win. There were virtually no rules; it was a fight to the finish. The only break allowed was to give the one knocked down time to recover so he could continue to fight. The winner was declared when his opponent could no longer stand on his feet."

"Your father was a good boxer, was he?"

"Yes, he was very good."

"Is that how you got the name Boxer?"

"Yes. As I said, my dad taught me well. I was good, winning all my fights, and was declared champion of the plantations, which resulted in me travelling around South America, eating and living well."

"So how did you finally get away?"

"I was not earning any money as I was still a slave, the property of Gene Trompson. My dad by then had died from the terrible beatings he had received towards the end of his boxing time, and my mother died of a broken heart, distraught at her loss, soon after."

"So you lost your parents just like me?"

"Yes. So with no ties, and safe in the knowledge that Gene could not exact punishment on them, I decided to make plans to escape. The chance came when out of the ordinary I was, or rather Mr Trompson was, challenged to put me up against a white man for the championship of America, but I refused to fight unless I was paid this time."

"And were you?"

"Gene was so keen on the fight, knowing he could make a killing if I won, that he agreed."

"And did you win?"

"Yes, I won fairly easy as the white American was not as toughened or as experienced as I was from the brutal fights I'd had. As a result, Mr Trompson made a killing and paid me handsomely. Of course what he didn't realise in his enthusiasm to make money was that he had given me enough money to buy my freedom, which is exactly what I did. Even though I was a freeman, it wasn't that easy as I could still be mistaken as a runaway slave and sent back to where I had come from or, worse, beaten and sold to another plantation owner, but I was lucky to find out about the Underground Railroad and—"

"Underground Railroad?" Michael exclaimed in bewilderment, not knowing much about railways, not even the new Liverpool-to-Manchester railway.

"Actually it wasn't underground—or overground—or a railroad for that matter," Leon said, looking at Michael's puzzled face. "It got the name because of its secret activities. There were various stopping places on the escape routes which they called stations, which were often located in barns, under church floors, or in caves or hollowed-out riverbanks. And the people operating them were called conductors. Anyone trying to escape was called a package. The organisation was made up of Northern abolitionists, church leaders, and former slaves. It was a long, perilous journey as there were always bounty hunters known as slave catchers on the lookout for runaway slaves. They could earn good money returning the slaves to their owners or simply selling them back into slavery. They didn't care if those they captured had free papers; they would simply tear them up. And once they got a suspected slave back to the Southern States, they could do what they liked with them. Anyway, I managed to make it through and bought a passage to England," he explained, the memories coming back with appalling vividness. Talking about it seemed to help control his emotions.

"That must have been frightening. I can't imagine what it must have been like to be a slave."

"Slave life varied greatly depending on how cruel the plantation owners chose to be. You worked from sunup to sundown six days a week and lived on a diet of fatty meat and cornbread. We lived in small shacks with a dirt floor and little or no furniture. We would be given one pair of shoes and three items of underwear a year. Although these and other clothing would be provided by the owner, they were often ill-fitting and made of coarse material.

"Some slaves who worked in the plantation house generally had slightly better housing nearer to the house and were given better food and clothing than those who worked in the fields. We were lucky and were treated with better food and clothing because of my dad's boxing skills, but we were still slaves.

"You should read the book Mary Prince wrote about her experience as a slave, suffering many floggings and forced to stand for hours in salt ponds that left her flesh deformed with boils and deeply scarred."

"I would like to, but I can't read. I know my ABC, but not enough to read a book," Michael said, lowering his eyes to the ground in embarrassment.

"You need to learn to read to get anywhere in this world.

I will teach you to read," Leon offered.

"Thank you. I would like that. I'm amazed you can read. My father said reading wasn't as important as learning to plant and take care of the potato crops."

"The owners believed that to maintain their control of their slaves, they could not rely on physical threats as they knew knowledge was power. Therefore, they made it illegal to teach slaves to read or write. I learned to read and write with the help of the slaves who helped me escape because I had to be able to read the directions to get to the next station.

"There is a saying that says it is much easier to educate the uneducated than it is to reeducate the miseducated."

"I wish I could be as clever as you. You talk so clever."

"Like you, I came up the hard way. And the one thing I learned is that if you want to achieve something in life, you must first believe you can achieve it."

"I want to achieve something with my life."

"Like what?"

"I don't know, except I never want to dig another potato. I suppose I would like to become a great violin payer as my schoolteacher wanted me to."

"There's no reason why you can't. As they say, you will achieve something better than what you've known if you're determined enough."

"At least you were determined and got here and got a job."

"It wasn't that easy. Don't forget, there was slavery here in England, as well as the transport of slaves to America, until slavery was abolished, but even then, many who had managed to escape like me were still frightened of being discovered because the former owners were being paid compensation by the government for every slave they had owned considered to have been a valuable part of the company's assets. So the companies continued to search, offering rewards for the capture of any of the runaway slaves so as to increase their claims for compensation. So there are still many forced to hide out in overcrowded lodging houses with stinking courtyards, surrounded by brothels and thieves' and sailors' dens, having to live out an illicit, subterranean existence by doing whatever they can to stay alive, some going to sea, which is some cases is no better than slavery, or robbing, pickpocketing, or even begging, pretending to be blind."

"But that didn't happen to you?"

"No, I was a freeman, and I still had some money left after giving money to the Underground Railroad for helping me, but I was continuously stopped, suspected of being a runaway slave. Fortunately I had my free paper and could prove I wasn't, but I was black and not generally liked, which is also the case with the Irish Catholics as you will find out, if you haven't already."

"Yes, I am beginning to find that out. So how did you get to be here?" Michael asked, his eyes alive with curiosity.

"There was Abu, another black slave who had run away and was hiding in one of the stinking lodging houses where the landlord didn't ask too many questions as long as the rent was paid on time. I used to take Abu food and pay his rent, that is until I went to see him and discovered someone had split on him, hoping to claim the reward, and he had been captured. I never saw him again. As I was making my way back to my lodgings, I was attacked by a couple of crimps. Unfortunately for them, they picked the wrong man. I soon flattened them both. What I didn't know at the time was that the incident had been witnessed by Madame Rosita, who was so impressed with the way I had handled myself that she found out where I was staying and offered me the job here."

"Is that why you offered me the job, because you thought I could handle myself?"

"Yes, and the fact that you looked like you had had a tough time, the same as me, and needed help."

"Thank you. I don't know what I would have done. Lucky you found me."

"Yes, because the crimps or runners as they're called are amongst the most hated of the Liverpool parasites. As soon as a ship docks, they push their way forward on the pretence of wanting to offer help to the confused newcomers with their bundles or cases, telling them they can get them cheap lodgings and tickets for those who want to immigrate to America. Having got possession of their luggage, they only return it if the person pays them a large fee or else find themselves destitute, left with nothing and nowhere to go, as the crimps seem to have left you."

"Why doesn't someone do something about it?"

"That is what everyone is asking. There seem to be more criminals than police with many of the policemen being sacked for being drunk on duty, asleep on duty, absent from their beat, or taking bribes, so it's no wonder the criminals get away with it. Anyway, you'd better have a rest before it all starts, because it goes on until the early hours of the morning. Unfortunately you will have to sleep on the floor until we can organise a bed for you."

"Don't worry about that. I've slept on the floor all my life and probably wouldn't know how to sleep on a bed."

"OK, I'll make a bed up for you."

"Thank you. Can you explain something to me while you're doing that? I was taught that whoring or prostitution, as you call it, is a sin against God and is against the law and must be punished."

"Prostitution is not against the law. It is not illegal, but the laws are confusing because women can be arrested and treated like criminals if they are suspected of being a prostitute and—"

"But you've just said prostitution is not against the law."

"Yes, a little bewildering. The reasoning for this is that there is an increase in people contracting venereal diseases, particularly amongst the military. Enlisted men are not allowed to marry, so they search out prostitutes for their sexual gratification."

"So they come here?"

"Oh no, not here. They can't afford to come to a place like this, nor would they be allowed entrance. They pick prostitutes up off the streets or in public houses, but the girls are poor and can't get or afford condoms, whereas the girls here are supplied with condoms to—"

"Condoms? What are condoms?"

"Condoms are a way of protecting the girls from catching or transmitting venereal diseases and preventing them from getting pregnant. Condoms are made of rubber and are soaked with scented oil to make them easier to use. After use, they are washed, oiled and put away in special wooden boxes, ready to be used again."

"But what about Madame Rosita. Couldn't she be arrested?"

"No. Why should she be arrested? Prostitution is not illegal. And anyway, she has little fear of being arrested, not with the clientele who frequent this place."

"How do you mean?"

"The elite clientele know only too well that if she were ever arrested, their names and activities could be exposed, so they make sure no law enforcement officers come anywhere near this place, except of course for a few of the high-ranking police officers, which is another reason I'm allowed to walk around as freely as I do. And while we're on the subject, any names or titles you happen to hear, you keep to yourself. If you dare mention them outside these walls, your life will come to an abrupt and unpleasant end. Make no mistake about that. Understand?"

Chapter 12

Right. The first duty of the night is to stand by the entrance and politely welcome the clients while at the same time keeping an eye out for anyone whom Madame Rosita would not consider acceptable in this establishment and those whom Madame has barred. So just stand on the other side of the door and bow gracefully as they come in," Leon instructed Michael as he adjusted the black bow tie against his crisp white linen shirt, part of his uniform of a black frock coat, black waistcoat, black creased trousers, and highly polished ankle-high boots.

The night began slowly with the clients mingling and enjoying a variety of drinks served by a young woman acting as barmaid, dressed in an elaborate costume that displayed an ample amount of heaving bosom full of promise.

A smartly dressed man was seated at the piano, playing soft melodic music as the women demurely swept into the reception in their alluring costumes, spreading themselves out as they moved evocatively around the tables, awaiting a client to invite them to sit and drink with them. The women were instructed to order only champagne whenever they were offered a drink, The barmaid would serve them a nonalcoholic champagne so the women could drink as much as they liked and pretend to be the worse for wear from drink, but still remain sober and in control of what they were doing. Madame Rosita had made it very clear that the women were there to please the clientele, not to get drunk, behave recklessly, or fail in their tasks, for if they did, she would send them packing. The nonalcoholic champagne also produced an additional profit for the establishment.

"Good evening, my lord," Leon greeted the rather short, podgy, expensively dressed man who thrust his hat and cane for Leon to take as soon as he entered, immediately ignoring him as he hurried past to one of the tables.

Michael watched the man settle down at one of the tables and start to look around at the women, finally deciding on one, indicating with his finger for her to join him. The barmaid hurried over to take his order. Michael smiled, knowing the woman he'd chosen would be ordering fake champagne.

"Be careful of him," Leon warned after he returned, having taken the hat and cane to the cloakroom. That is Lord Blamfont, very rich and very powerful, a man not to be crossed."

Michael was seized with momentary weakness as the name reverberated in his brain. He seemed to remember he had heard the name somewhere, but he could not remember how, where, or why.

"What's the matter?" Leon asked, seeing his worried expression. "Do you know him?"

"I don't know," Michael said with a puzzled shake of his head.

"Well, just make sure you're always polite and subservient to him. And make sure you don't ever mention his name anywhere, OK?"

"OK," Michael readily agreed, the name still perplexing his brain as he watched Lord Blamfont get up from the table and walk off with the young woman, the two of them disappearing together through the heavy curtains.

The night passed peacefully with nothing untoward happening that required Michael and Leon's services other than to remain at the entrance checking all those who came and went.

"I will fetch your hat and cane, my lord," Leon said, springing into action as Lord Blamfont came out through the curtains and strolled towards them.

"Thank you, my man," Lord Blamfont acknowledged, handing him a half-crown tip.

"Thank you, my lord. May you have a safe journey home," Leon said, giving a light bow as he pocketed the half-crown.

"You see what you get for being polite?" Leon told Michael, taking the half-crown back out of his pocket to show him.

"How much is that?"

"Half a crown—two shillings and sixpence."

"That's a quarter of what I'm going to earn a week," Michael said, giving him an unsmiling look.

"Yes, but you'll get tips as well once they know who you are and you treat them with respect."

Suddenly screams for help were heard coming from outside. Leon immediately dashed out with Michael following him. They were immediately confronted with Lord Blamfont, who was trying to make it to the entrance while being pursued by three crimps.

Leon was the first to step in to protect Lord Blamfont, delivering a straight hard right to the jaw. The first crimp's knees buckled and he dropped to the ground. Michael followed up with a swinging left hook to the jaw, which stopped the second crimp in his tracks, leaving him staring in disbelief at what had just happened, before his knees gave way and he sank to the ground. The third crimp spun on his heels and ran away as fast as he could.

Leon took hold of the dazed Lord Blamfont and helped him back into the reception, where he sat him down at one of the tables. "Pour my lord a brandy," he called over to the barmaid.

"Thank you," Lord Blamfont said after taking a large sip of the brandy, his chest so tight that he could hardly breathe. "I don't know what would have happened if you hadn't come out when you did. They would have robbed me of everything. I think the one who ran away had my wallet and gold watch. They must have been waiting for me," he added, his eyes flickering with the first hint of fear.

"My goodness, what happened?" Madame Rosita exclaimed as she came rushing into the reception, holding her hands up in exaggerated concern.

"I was attacked, but thanks to the quick action of your

man and his assistant," Lord Blamfont told her, waving an almost dismissive finger in Michael's direction, "I was saved from being completely robbed or worse."

"Well, that's what I pay them for," Madame Rosita said, wanting to take some of the credit.

"Indeed. However, I would like to reward these two valiant men, but without my wallet I am unable to. So, Madame, would you be so kind as to give them a fiver and put it on my account?"

"Of course, my lord. I shall see to it."

"That is for your assistance. You deserve it. I would have lost a lot more had you not been as expert as you were. I have to say, you are both handy with your fists. Have either of you ever boxed?"

"We both have, my lord."

"Hmm, interesting," Lord Blamfont replied, taking another large gulp of brandy.

"Would you like one the girls to give you some relaxing treatment, on the house of course, my lord?" Madame Rosita invited.

"Yes, I think that might help to calm me," he said, finishing the rest of the brandy before getting to his feet and following Madame Rosita out without any further acknowledgement of Leon or Michael.

"There you are. You just earned five weeks' wages in one day," Leon told Michael as soon as Madame Rosita and Lord Blamfont had disappeared behind the curtains.

"Well, we sure knocked the shit out of those thugs," Michael said proudly.

"Yes we did."

"And just one managed to get away—"

"To fight another day. Just remember, some gangs don't like it when they're beaten, and they never forget when they are, so be on your guard that they don't come back."

"And they'll get the same next time."

"If there is a next time, they'll come armed with knives,

sticks, and iron bars, and we might be the ones who have to run."

"You two did well," Madame Rosita told them as she came back into reception with a broad smile on her face. "And I am pleased with the way Leon has turned you out and how you have conducted yourself," she said, turning to Michael. "Keep up the good work," she added, her smile broadening as she turned and walked away.

* * * *

Lord Blamfont thought it quite a delightful sight as he sat in the flagellation room watching intensely as Mary, the flagellant dressed in a tight black corset and black stockings, removed all of Maisie's clothing, laid her face down, and strapped her legs and wrists to the stretcher. After gently stroking her bare buttocks, she showered them with a series of smart slaps.

With his urges increasing, Lord Blamfont got up and crossed to one of the walls, from which he took down a leather whip. "I want to see you whip her hard, no part of her body to be spared, particularly her thighs," he said, grinning wickedly as he handed the whip to Mary.

Mary began flicking the leather whip on Maisie's left buttock, then the right buttock, letting the tips of the whip trickle over her skin down to her thighs.

Maisie twitched at the sensation, her buttocks moving together then apart as Mary increased the pressure of the whip, the skin beginning to redden, adding to his sexual excitement as he listened to the sound of the whip swishing through the air. Soon her buttocks were crisscrossed with crimson streaks.

"Oh, my bottom, my legs. It hurts," Maisie cried out in pain.

"Whip her hard," he called out, his voice trembling with excitement. "Give that bottom a good whipping."

Maisie didn't enjoy having this done to her. It didn't give her any sexual pleasure. Not that she enjoyed sex, especially after working in the brothel as long as she had. To her it was just part of the job, a commodity she was selling. There was no feeling to it; it was simply a means to an end.

She knew just how much pain she would be in by the end of the session. The only reason she allowed herself to be subjected to such physical abuse was that the money was more than the other women were earning for allowing themselves to just lie back and be fucked.

Mary slowly moved the whip around, making the strokes harder, starting at the soles of Maisie's feet then moving up her legs and striking the thighs, causing Maisie to twitch and writhe within the restrictions of her bounds and involuntarily raise her buttocks, which were now covered in red welts.

Lord Blamfont winced with perverted pleasure, his hand going to his manhood to feel the swelling as he listened to Maisie's groans.

Realising he was about to reach an orgasm, he leapt from his chair and rushed to Mary. "Roll her onto her back and bind her with her legs spread," he ordered.

Mary undid the bounds, shifted Maisie onto her back, and strapped her down with her legs fastened wide apart.

"Now whip the insides of Maisie's thighs," he said. He watched lasciviously as Mary began to gently whip the insides of her thighs.

Maisie began twisting her body, straining at the bounds which held her, as she felt the first strokes at the top of her thighs.

Feeling his body pulsating with raw energy and unable to control his high state of arousal, he pushed Mary aside. "You've done a great job," he said, turning to Mary, "as you always do. And I may want to fuck you afterwards," he added, taking out his penis to show it was ready for her to roll on the condom she had kept warm and oiled by tucking in the top of her corset.

"Now, you little slut, it's time for you to admit what a whore you really are and to prove to me that you deserve being treated this way by your betters," he said as he knelt down behind Maisie, who was already on all fours.

As he thrust into her, she let out a loud gasp, not of pleasure but of pain, as it was really hurting her, which only inspired him to thrust harder and deeper into her, knowing it was causing her pain. This was no pretence at passion; this was an exercise in pure male dominance, hard, shattering, and real. The more she groaned, the more ecstatic he became, until he erupted in a violent explosion, his body trembling in a throbbing orgasm as he came inside her.

Chapter 13

Although the work and the environment was still a little strange to Michael, he had proved satisfactory to Madame Rosita, and true to her word, she increased his wages by five shillings to fifteen shillings a week, not counting the occasional tip. He was beginning to build up a nice little nest egg.

It was a bright sunny morning. The sky was a bright blue. He felt happy walking along with a slight skip in his step past the row of expensive houses on his first day off since Leon had picked him up off the streets. He smiled, thinking how lucky he was to be clean and well-clothed and to have money to spend if he wanted to treat himself.

He had no idea where to go as this was the first time in his life he could walk around freely, not having to worry where he might find somewhere to sleep or where his next meal was coming from. Indeed he could now walk into a restaurant and buy a meal or into a pub and buy a beer.

Hope and confidence began to slip away as he approached the city, worried about the fact that he had never been into either a restaurant or a pub, wishing Leon was with him to guide him. *What do you do, just walk in and sit at a table? And how and what do you order, and how much does it cost?* The thought made him nervous.

But as he arrived in the centre of the city and moved amongst the crowd, all thoughts of a meal or a beer began to drain away as he looked at the poorly clad and ill-fed children, mere girls and boys, their clothes ragged, careless, and uncared for, a look of hopelessness on their faces as they reached out their hands in a begging gesture, desperate for anything. Drunkard men and women brushed past them with no sign of taking any notice of the children's plight, more concerned with trying to find their way home or worrying where to get the money to keep drinking. There were prostitutes on every corner offering their services, some as young as ten.

It was a sight that appalled him. He instinctively dipped his hand into the pocket of his breeches to feel for the loose coins. He pulled them out and studied the amount. He had four farthings, two halfpennies, five pennies, two threepenny pieces, three sixpences, two shillings, and half a crown, making a total of seven shillings and four pence.

He looked up as the children moved closer to him in the hope that he was going to give them something. His thoughts went back to when he had first come here and he was starving, his clothes ragged with no money in his pocket. Someone had reached out to him then, and if it hadn't been for Leon, he would still be on the streets begging like these children were now.

Michael decided he wanted to give the money to them, but the problem was how to share the money amongst them. It was easy to give out the small change, but he wondered whom he could give the large coins to. He looked around frantically and spotted what looked like a mother with two children huddled against a wall, her clothes just as ragged as the children's. She looked haggard, but he could see as he got closer that she was not as old as her scruffy face suggested.

Michael walked up to her and handed her the half-crown. "Here, please take this and buy some food for you and the children."

The woman looked up in surprise at the man standing over her dressed in smart clothes, holding out his hand with the shiny coin in it.

"Here, please take it. I want you to have it," Michael told her, proffering the coin closer to her.

She took the coin from him and held it close to her face to study it, having never seen or held a coin of that size in her hand before. She put it to her mouth and bit on it as a way of checking it was real.

"It's half a crown—two shillings and sixpence," he

explained, offering a smile. "You can feed yourself and the children for a week with that money and find a place to rent until you find work. Here is another two shillings," he added, realising that if she was lucky to find any kind of work, she would still need money for clothes and food.

The woman looked up. He could see her sorrow as tears began to roll down her cheeks, making streak marks in the dirt patches on her face.

He handed out the rest of the money amongst the other children and, feeling pleased with what he had done, happily turned on his heels, but as he started to walk off, he heard the woman scream. He spun around and was horrified to see two crimps trying to steal the money from her.

"Oi! You two," he called out as he rushed over.

The two crimps turned their attention to him. "Piss off, unless you want your head bashed in, Ivy boy," one of the crimps threatened, narrowing his eyes, his mouth opening to reveal a row of chipped yellow teeth.

"It will take more than you two to do that," Michael said with a quiet anger.

"Oh yeah?" the other crimp cut in, giving him a cold, forbidding look.

Michael studied them squarely, annoyance flickering in his eyes. They looked like they could cut up rough in an instant. "I don't want any trouble. She is starving and has two children to feed, so just leave her alone."

"Please let them have the money. They'll only come back for it later," the woman pleaded in anguish.

"Not if I have anything to do with it," Michael retorted, fury simmering at the back of his mind as he wondered whether it would be better to back off and walk away because, as the woman said, they will only come back again.

But his mind was jerked back as one of the crimps said menacingly, "Why don't you piss off, before I stick this in you?" His stare was intense. A tiny spark of fear flared up in Michael.

The unease was mounting, and Michael knew he had to do something. The pulse in his body seemed to be speeding up as the man kept looking at him with hostile eyes, waving a knife in his face. But before Michael could do anything, the two crimps attacked, grabbing hold of his clothes and swinging wild punches to every part of his head and body.

"Leave him alone!" the woman screamed.

Michael backed away, raising his arms in an attempt to protect his face while he awaited his opportunity. It came when one of the crimps stopped and said, "Right, you Irish piece of shit. That's just to begin with. Just give us all the money you've got and we'll leave you alone. We'll deal with the old hag after we—"

He didn't get a chance to finish the sentence as Michael shot out his left fist, catching the crimp full in the mouth, his lips exploding with blood and his teeth bursting out before his body fell backwards and buckled to the ground.

The other crimp reached into his coat and pulled out a knife with practiced ease, the shiny metal reflecting in the sunlight as he moved threateningly forward, slashing wildly at Michael's coat, slitting it in several places.

Michael stepped back, swiftly removed his coat, and wrapped it around his left wrist and hand to protect himself for when the chance came to make a grab for the knife.

The crimp, thinking he had the advantage, waved the knife menacingly, his voice thick with rage, his lips curling into a snarl as he said, "You're going to pay heavily for what you did to my friend. I'm going to slit your fucking throat, you fucking Irish Catholic git. There are too many of you Irish bastards here already. You should all fuck off back to where you came from."

The words shook Michael as no one had ever called him a fucking Irish Catholic git. *What is wrong with being Irish, and what is wrong with being a Catholic? Catholicism is the true religion of God as my mother had always told me,* he thought, his whole body now bristling with frustration and anger. He rushed forward to try to get a grip on the knife with his guarded left hand while swinging his right hand at the crimp, catching him with a square cut to the jaw, stunning him and allowing Michael to get a firm grip on the hand holding the knife.

With a firm grip on the crimp's wrist, Michael pulled him closer while at the same time delivering another right hook to the jaw, causing the crimp's legs to fold under him, the knife flying out of his hand and hitting the ground with a clatter as he collapsed to the ground.

Michael stood over the two crimps and looked down at them, blood oozing from their faces as they stared, dazed, back up at him. "Don't ever let me hear you call me an Irish Catholic git again. Now what I want you two pieces of shit to do is empty your pockets of all the money you've stolen and then remove your clothes as there are many around here in desperate need of some good clothing and shoes."

The two crimps remained looking up at him. They were motionless, not believing what he was telling them. "Don't think about it too long. I promise you, I will beat the living shit out of the pair you, and I promise that you will never want to rob anyone, or for that matter be able to, again."

The two crimps began to empty their pockets. Michael was surprised by not only how much money they were carrying but also the expensive gold watches and rich leather wallets, one emblazoned with gold initials, which they had on them, all obviously stolen.

"I'll take those," Michael said, bending down to pick up the watches and wallets. "I might even be able to return them to their rightful owners. Now remove your clothes," he ordered.

"No, we're not removing our clothes. We're not getting naked here in front of everyone," one of the crimps protested.

Michael looked around, not realising a crowd had gathered and were now looking on in anticipation that they might get some of the money or some of the clothing. "Right, since you're not keen to do it yourselves, maybe you people would like to help them," Michael said, turning to the crowd.

The crowd didn't need any encouragement. They pounced on the two crimps, some grabbing for the money while others started removing their clothes. It wasn't long before they were lying there naked, stripped of all their clothes.

Michael walked away, feeling the day had not turned out as he had planned, although he reminded himself it was his first day out and he hadn't actually planned anything. But he felt happy that he had done some good and in a way had gotten some kind of revenge on the crimps who had ripped him off.

"You were very brave," he heard a gentle voice call out to him, causing him to stop and turn around. He was surprised to see a very pretty young woman smiling at him. She was dressed smartly in a voluminous red dress with a bell-shaped skirt and a pretty bonnet on her light auburn hair.

"I think you're a very brave man," she repeated in a soft demure tone.

"Thank you," he said, staring at her awkwardly.

"I heard about your other act of bravery, but I never thought I would actually see you in action. You really know how to take care of yourself. Wait till I tell the other girls," she said, a look of wry amusement around the corners of her eyes.

"Other girls? What other girls?" he asked, but she had seen the question in his eyes before he spoke.

"I'm Mary. I work at the brothel. You see me every day—well, almost every day."

"Mary," he repeated, eyeing her sharply, the recognition coming slowly. His eyes were still calculating as he started to back away. She had an intelligent face. He reckoned she was a little bit older than he, maybe two years or so, and it unnerved him.

"I'm not allowed to talk to you. Madame has forbidden it," he said sorrowfully.

"That's at work, but we are not at work now, so we are not breaking the rules. Why don't you join me for a coffee? I know a nice little coffee shop just a short walk from here," she suggested with a flirtatious smile.

He smiled back, but the smile on his face did not match the anxiety in his eyes as he thought of what would happen if they were found out. He pursed his lips with worry as he said, "Are you sure it will be all right?"

"Of course, but I don't care anyway. I just want to sit and talk to you, find out about you. I see you every day but have no idea who you are."

"I don't know anything about you either."

"Then this is a chance for us to get to know each other," she said, taking hold of his hand. She was about to lead him off when she stopped. "On second thought, I don't think they would allow you in with your coat in tatters. Why don't we just go for a walk?"

* * * *

There was a light breeze coming off the water, which was shimmering with the bright sunlight reflecting off it.

"So how did you get to work for Madame?" Mary asked, looking into his eyes enquiringly.

"It's a long story," he said with a pensive expression.

"You're obviously Irish. There's no mistaking that accent around here."

"What's wrong with being Irish, or a Catholic for that matter?" he snapped, spinning around to face her, the words sounding more heated than he intended.

The smile went from her face and was replaced by shock. She gave a sharp intake of breath, surprised by his reaction. She could see a deep underlying sadness on his face. "I didn't mean anything by it. I was just making the point you are Irish," she said apologetically.

"Sorry, it's just that it isn't a pretty story. If it hadn't been for Leon, I don't know what would have happened to me. I came off the boat from Ireland having lost both my parents with the little money I had taken by the likes of those thieves I beat up. All I wanted to do was give that poor woman with the kids, as well as the other poor kids, some money."

"Yes, I know. I was watching you."

"Watching me? You mean you were there all the time?"

"I was walking past when I heard the commotion and recognised you. I became terrified when I saw that one crimp pull the knife. I thought he was going to kill you, but you were brilliant in the way you dealt with them both. You wait till I tell the girls," she said in admiration. "You said you lost both your parents. How did that happen?"

"The potato crops failed. We had no food to feed ourselves and no work, so we were unable to pay the rent. We were thrown out of our cottage and left to starve with no money and nowhere to go. Desperate, we walked all the way to Dublin, passing people who were starving and dying where they lay on the streets. We finally made it to the workhouse, where first my mother and then my father died."

"But what kind of landlord would be that uncaring?"

"The landlords didn't care. They were rich and lived in England. They rarely ever came to see us and just sent their henchmen to do their …" He stopped as a dreadful grief welled up inside him.

"What's the matter?"

The name Blamfont, which had been worrying him, suddenly came into focus as fragments of the nightmare flooded into his head, the memory coming fresh to his mind as though it were yesterday. He could even remember the words of Sean O'Brien, the bailiff, telling them he was acting on behalf of the landlord, Lord Blamfont. It sent a cold shiver down Michael's spine. His hands began to shake, and a thin trickle of sweat started to run down the back of his neck at the realisation that the man he was being so polite to at the brothel was the same man who had ordered his family to be thrown out of their cottage and caused his mother's and father's deaths.

"You've gone white. Whatever is the matter?" Mary asked, her face creasing in a worried frown.

"Sorry," he said, shaking his head as if to get rid of the

thought. "Something just went through my mind. Tell me about you. How did you come to work in the brothel?" he asked, desperately wanting to put his mind to something else, anger beginning to gnaw at him.

He saw a sadness come into her face, making her look away in embarrassment as she said, "Just as bad as yours, I suppose. I lost my parents." This last she delivered in a soothing voice in an attempt to ease his pain. "There was an outbreak of cholera caused by the filthy drinking water, killing thousands, my parents among them. I cared for them, watching them suffer from dehydration, diarrhoea, vomiting, and stomach cramps. It was terrible to watch."

A few more minutes passed before he realised she was crying. "We couldn't afford a coffin, and they were both carried away on a cart with other dead bodies of people who had died that day. Their death in the end was a great release, but it left me, like you, homeless with nowhere to go."

"So what happened to you?"

"Luckily I got a job as an under housemaid in a very large mansion. It was drudgery from morning to night. By the time you had finished cleaning the rooms and preparing the fires, it was almost time to start all over again. I had to sleep in a room no bigger than a cupboard with a mattress on the floor. Mind you, I was so knackered by the time I'd finished, I could have slept on anything."

"That must have been awful."

"It was, but for some reason which I didn't know at the time, I was promoted to lady's maid, which meant looking after all the mistress's dresses. Amazingly she would change for a morning meeting, change for lunch, change for an afternoon meeting, and then change yet again for dinner. It was a job in itself, that is until I got sacked."

"Why did you get sacked?"

"Lord Blamfont took a—"

"Lord Blamfont? You worked for Lord Blamfont? You mean the one who comes to the brothel?"

"Yes, the one you saved from being robbed. He seemed very impressed with you."

"But I don't understand. Do you, er, entertain him there?"

"Yes, as do the other girls. You see, the reason I was fired, as I was about to explain before you interrupted, was that he had taken a fancy to me and used to chase me around, trying to touch me up when his wife was out on one of her regular visits, but I was frightened and knew very little about sex except what my dear mother had always told me: 'Don't let a man put his cock in you as you will get pregnant and he will just walk away, leaving you holding the baby.' So I resisted, and then he started to offer me money if I would let him touch my breasts. Well, I knew I couldn't get pregnant from him doing that, so I said OK as I could do with the extra money, determined one day I would not have to be a servant. It was fun really, watching him get excited as he fondled my breasts. He then said he would like to feel my pussy, and I said he could if he paid me more money. I used to lie on the mistress's bed and let him put his hand up my petticoats and feel around. It was quite thrilling really. I started to relax and enjoy it, feeling he really liked me. He then of course wanted to fuck me, but I said no, remembering what my mother had told me. So he came up with the idea of me baring my breasts, removing my pantaloons, and lying back on the bed, spreading my legs wide, so he could look at my breasts and my pussy while he wanked."

"Wanked?"

"Yes, you know, played with himself until he spent his load."

"Spent his load?"

"You don't know what spent means? No, I suppose you wouldn't. You see, men of the so-called elite of society in their perverse attitudes towards sex liken a woman's vagina to a purse, the attraction being that it is offered for sale with no complications. In other words, the man who pays for sex literally spends his money putting his penis into the woman's

114

purse and ejaculating. So the man's ejaculating into the women's purse, her vagina, means he's spent his load."

Michael looked at her, his jaws clenching at the thought of what she was telling him. "So he sacked you for doing that?"

"No, of course not. We were lucky, doing fine, until his wife came home unexpectedly. The trouble with luck is, it eventually runs out. And mine ran out when she caught me rushing out of the bedroom with my clothes in disarray," she explained. "You have to understand, in so-called high society, the men have mistresses as long as their wives don't know about them, yet they still expect their wives and mistresses to be faithful whatever their own wrongdoings. Of course if the wife took a lover and it became public knowledge, she would be ostracised by society, while the man can amble along to one of his favourite brothels and be guaranteed a warm welcome. There have been many cases of a client visiting a brothel to be confronted by one of his parlour maids, one of his cooks, or his children's nanny. The children's nanny also have the opportunity of earning extra while out with the children, pushing them in their perambulators around the parks, dolly mopping as it is called, attracting the attention of admirers who are willing to make some illicit arrangement."

Michael smiled, but his face revealed nothing as he continued to listen to what Mary was saying.

"Anyway, suddenly I was back where I started, except this time I had quite a bit of money saved up from his antics, so I was able to rent a nice comfortable dwelling. And I was free from the drudgery of that house, where you were ignored as though you didn't matter, where you were made to think you were useless and looked down on. It was then that I suddenly realised I was on my own, that nobody cared what happened to me, and that the only person I could rely on was myself. You either accept your fate or make up your mind to take a chance to try to improve your situation. It was Lord

Blamfont who gave me that chance."

"Lord Blamfont," he repeated, irritation creeping into his voice.

"Yes, he found out where I was living. He came to visit me and asked me if I would continue doing what we did before. I told him I would, but as I was no longer an employee of his, it would cost him more. He agreed, but he said he was fed up with wanking and wanted to fuck me. I still refused, explaining I didn't want to risk getting pregnant. It was then that he came up with the suggestion of me meeting a woman who he said would be interested in me and—"

"Madame Rosita?"

"Yes, when I met her and she told me what she did, or rather what the establishment did, I thought, *Why not?* It wasn't so different from what I was already doing with Lord Blamfont, except that she said the clients, as she called them, would expect to fuck me. I wasn't happy about that until she explained that all her girls were supplied with rubbers."

"Rubbers?"

"Condoms."

"Oh yes, Leon explained them to me." Then a cloud of concern darkened his eyes at the explicit language she was using, his never having heard anyone talk like that, let alone a female. "You don't seem shamed by any of it."

"Why should I? I earn four times a day as much as I earned in a year slaving away in that big house."

Michael said nothing. He just continued to stare at her, not sure what to say or whether to say anything.

"What about you? Do you have a girlfriend?" she asked, surprising him.

"No," he said, his mind still reeling from what she had been telling him.

She stopped walking. She turned around, placed her hand under his chin, and raised his head as she said, "You should have. You're a handsome fellow. Would you like me to be your girlfriend?"

The question stunned him. Her gaze was disconcerting. Uncertainty flickered in his eyes. He was not sure what to reply.

"You're really weird. You showed no fear against those thieves, yet you seem nervous with me. Have you never been with a woman?" she asked, taking a long measured look at his face.

"No," he answered, trying to avoid her eyes. She saw sadness come into his face, causing him lower his eyes to the ground in embarrassment.

"I think you need taking in hand. Would you like to have sex with me?" she asked unashamedly.

Courage was deserting him by the second. "Look, I think we had better get back or we'll both be in trouble," he told her, a hint of panic showing in his shocked expression.

"No, I don't have to get back. I have the next three nights off because I have the curse and—"

"The curse?"

"My periods. My God, you've got a lot to learn. Why don't you come back to my place and have a drink? I have a nice bottle of gin there."

"Er, no, thank you," he replied, more out of fear than anything else. "I have to get back and get my coat repaired," he said, looking positively stricken.

"That coat is beyond repair, but never mind, maybe another time," she said. To his surprise, she lightly kissed him on the cheek before smiling and walking away.

Michael stood watching her walk off. Putting his finger to the spot on his cheek where she had kissed him, he smiled.

* * * *

"What the devil have you been up to? Just look at the state of you. Look at your coat. It's all crumpled and torn. How dare you treat the clothes I buy you with such contempt," Madame Rosita said angrily the moment she spotted Michael coming into the kitchen.

"Sorry, Madame. I went to help some poor people, and I was attacked by a couple of thieving crimps. One had a knife and slashed my coat, but I managed to beat them off. I took these from them, which they had obviously stolen from some wealthy gentlemen," he explained, handing her the wallets and watches.

Madame Rosita took hold of the wallets and watches. Her eyebrows flew upwards in surprise. "Oh my goodness," she exclaimed after closely examining the initials on one of the wallets. "T. B. Could that be Theodor Blamfont—Lord Blamfont if I'm not mistaken?" she pondered.

"I do remember him saying that the one who had run away had got his wallet and his watch," Michael told her.

"If this is his wallet and gold watch, then you have done well, and no one will be more pleased than him," she said. "So go and get changed into your duty clothes, and don't worry about the damage to your coat. I will order you a new one at my expense. I'm glad Leon found you," she added with a smile as she turned and walked out of the kitchen.

"You're beginning to look like the ragamuffin who walked in here not so long ago," Mrs Baxter said, looking at Michael's torn coat.

Michael sneaked a freshly baked biscuit from the cooling tray on the table. Popping it into his mouth and chewing on it thoughtfully, he said, "Yes, and I feel a bit like him at the moment."

"None of that thieving around here," she quipped, lightly slapping his hand away as he tried to sneak another biscuit.

Chapter 14

Fortune knocks but once, but misfortune has much more patience—something Michael would find out in time. He was riding high and his nest egg was steadily building up, particularly with the ten pounds Lord Blamfont had instructed Madame Rosita to give him for recovering his wallet and gold watch.

Michael was grateful, but he couldn't stop the growing resentment for what Lord Blamfont had done to him and his family. He determined that one day he would get his revenge.

"We are being sent on a mission today," Leon announced as he sauntered into Michael's room.

Michael had now been given his own room, albeit a small one. It was reasonably comfortable. The only problem was that it was next to the women's room, and their noise and antics often gave him sleepless nights.

"What mission is that?"

"There is a boat coming in today, and Madame has asked me to go down to the docks and see if there is anyone I think Madame would like, so you're coming with me."

"Why do you need me?" Michael asked innocently.

"Just in case there's trouble."

* * * *

"What are we actually looking for?" Michael asked as he and Leon watched the immigrants coming off the boat, all of them looking weary and confused, still suffering from the privations of a long and arduous sea journey, feeling the same as Michael had when he stepped off the *Athlone*.

"Young females, preferably on their own. Madame wants some fresh girls, especially virgins."

Michael looked around at the girls and young women standing on the strange quayside, as he had once done, hoping for a new life somewhere far away from the miseries of Ireland, surrounded by a babble of strangers, not knowing where to go or whom to talk to with no relatives or friends to greet them upon arrival.

"How many girls does she want?" Michael asked, looking at Leon, studying the young women closely.

"Only one or two, but they have to be young, be very pretty, and have good figures. If you spot one, point her out to me," Leon told him.

Michael looked around and spotted two rough and hard-faced youths, obviously runners. Whatever they were planning, he knew they were up to no good with their hands stuffed into their pockets as they leaned against a wall, eyeing the crowd for someone they could con or steal from. Suddenly they spotted something, pushed themselves off the wall, and moved with speed towards a young woman with a bundle under her arm who was seeming to be wandering around aimlessly.

"There's a couple of crimps approaching a pretty girl over there who doesn't seem to be with anyone and who looks a bit too young to be on her own," Michael told Leon, indicating where the runners were with his hand.

"The bastards, I know what they're up to!" Leon exclaimed.

"She doesn't look like she's got anything worth stealing."

"She's got something worth much more than anything they could steal," Leon said, hurrying off in the direction Michael had indicated.

Michael watched as Leon barged his way through the crowd. He managed to reach the young woman just as the crimps got to her. The crimps took one look at Leon and decided to turn their attentions elsewhere. They moved off. Michael became more curious because whatever Leon was saying to the young woman, she did not appear to be frightened of him. Indeed, as the conversation continued, he was surprised to see Leon take hold of the small bundle she was clutching and guide her back to where he was standing.

"She would like to come and see what Madame Rosita can offer her," Leon said. "This is Holly," he said by way of introduction.

"Hello," she said, her voice soft and lilting.

"Hello, Holly," Michael replied, unsure of what else to say as he studied her. She was pretty, prettier than he'd first thought. Young with milky white skin, she was wearing a simple white dress that was very grubby, caked in dirt. Her long, straggly auburn hair fell untidily over her chest and shoulders. She had taunting blue eyes that shone out from her unwashed face. He thought she was the most beautiful young woman he'd ever seen. "Where are your parents?" he finally asked with a genuine sense of care.

"My mother died on the way over. I didn't know what to do. They told me I had to leave the ship and they would deal with her body. We got free travel, but we were put in a huge hold, I think they call it, in the bottom of the ship along with everyone else. I don't know how many there were, but it was packed with animals too. It was dark, smelly, and stinking of everything. The floor was filthy with the mess from the animals and people. My mother was very ill. She hoped she would get better medical treatment in Liverpool so we could go to America. I would like to go to America."

A look of sympathy flashed across Michael's face. "I'm sorry. My parents died too, not on the boat, but back home in Ireland in the workhouse," he said remorsefully, the misery vivid in his eyes.

"I'm sorry," Holly said ruefully. He could see tears pricking at her eyes.

"Right. Back to the house," Leon said, handing the bundle to Michael to carry before taking the young woman by the hand and leading her off, fearing that if he delayed any longer, she might change her mind.

* * * *

121

"Beautiful," Madame Rosita exclaimed with an expansive gesture of her hands as she walked around surveying the young woman from every angle as the she stood motionless before her. "The clients will love you when we've got you cleaned up and trained, but first things first. You look like you could do with a good meal, then a good scrub-up and some decent clothing. I'll get Mary to look after you. Come with me," she said, grabbing Holly's hand and dragging the bewildered young woman out of the room.

"What do you think she's going to train her for? She's so young," Michael asked as he and Leon walked back to their rooms.

"I wouldn't worry your head about that. Let them get on with it, because we've got another job Madame Rosita wants us to do."

"What's that?"

"There's a client who owes her a considerable sum of money and doesn't seem able or keen to pay up. It never surprises me that some of the wealthiest are so mean with their money, but I suppose that's how they become rich in the first place," Leon explained.

"But what does she want us to do about it?"

"You'll find out. I just want you there for backup."

"You expect trouble?"

"You never know."

* * * *

The manor was like nothing Michael had ever seen before, much larger and more grandiose than the brothel. It was set in its own grounds, surrounded by a high red brick wall.

"Here we go," Michael said. He and Leon opened the tall black wrought-iron gates with their boots, which crunched as they stepped onto the long gravel pathway that led up to the house.

There was a pitch-roofed porch with a red quarry-tiled

floor at the entrance. On entering the porch, they reached the heavy oak front door.

"Be prepared for anything," Leon warned Michael as he pulled on the black iron bell crank.

Nothing seemed to happen for a while, then they heard the hollow sound of footsteps approaching and the noise of metal bolts moving. The door finally opened.

"Yes," Stevens, the butler, said brusquely, his face implacable as he stared at Leon's black face. "Servants to the rear," he said surely as he went to shut the door, but Leon stepped forward, stopping him from closing it.

"I am here to see Sir Richard Fernwright," Leon informed him, holding the door firmly open with his body.

"Do you have an appointment?" Stevens asked, giving him a scornful look.

"Kindly tell Sir Richard I am calling on behalf of Madame Rosita," Leon said, his eyes challenging defiantly.

"Wait here. I will inform Sir Richard," Stevens said, his face a mask of indulgent compliance as he eased Leon back from the door frame and closed the door.

"Do you think he will see us?" Michael asked as they waited.

They didn't have to wait long before the door was opened and the butler ushered them in. "Sir Richard will see you in the reception room," Stevens announced as they stepped into the large, impressive entrance hall with its high archway ceiling and mouldings. The floor was covered with decorative tiles.

"Please take a seat. Sir Richard will be with you shortly," Stevens informed them in a detached manner as they entered the reception room. Then he abruptly turned and walked back out of the room.

Michael's eyes widened at the opulence of the room. The large bay sash windows were covered with heavy gold-embroidered curtains. The walls were covered in a flower-patterned wallpaper in rich, dark colours. The floor was covered with a vibrantly coloured deep-pile carpet. The room itself filled with expensive overstuffed furniture. The ornate tables were set in various corners, displaying a variety of expensive delicate ornaments.

"What is the meaning of this?" Sir Richard demanded as he burst into the room, his voice thick with indignation.

Sir Richard was in his fifties with a rather rotund figure. The bulge made more apparent by his tight-fitting clothes.

"I have been instructed by Madame Rosita to—"

"For what purpose Madame Rosita would be sending the likes of you to see me?" he demanded in a derogatory manner.

"I am instructed, Sir Richard, to personally hand you this letter," Leon answered with quiet dignity.

Sir Richard's eyes narrowed in disguised malice. "Why could she not have simply waited until the next time I called upon her?"

"Sir Richard, I have also been instructed to inform you that your presence will not be welcome until you have satisfactorily dealt with the matters detailed in the envelope. Her hope is that you will be able to deal with it now."

Sir Richard angrily tore at the envelope, ripping it open. He pulled out the sheet of paper and read it, giving a sharp intake of breath as he exclaimed, "Three thousand pounds! The woman's mad. Does she think I would entrust that kind of money to the likes of you? Never mind the fact that I don't keep large amounts of money in the house. Tell that whoremongering woman that I will settle the account when I am good and ready. You can also tell her that there are plenty more whorehouses around that would welcome my custom."

"I will convey your comments to Madame Rosita, Sir Richard," Leon said as he prepared to take his leave.

"Yes, you do that. Now get out of my house. And don't ever come back, or I'll have you arrested."

"I am only carrying out the instructions of my employer and do not see that as an arrestable offence," Leon said with a hint of defiance.

"Arrestable? If I had my way, you would be back in chains, flogged, and shipped off somewhere along with your friend here, who has said nothing. Who are you anyway?"

"I'm Michael Flanagan from Ireland. I also work for Madame Rosita."

"Well, it would seem she is becoming impudent in whom she employs. They should send all you bloody Irish back where you came from. We have had enough of you coming over here and turning our streets into slums and spreading disease everywhere."

A flare of anger rose up in Michael. His eyes were hard as he stared back at Sir Richard. "It was you people who caused our suffering in the first place. I lost my mother and father because of your greed and …"

Leon stretched out a restraining hand to stop him from saying more.

"How dare you? The potato famine was caused by your people's inability to farm properly. It cost me a fortune. I lost thousands, so I don't have time for your problems. You brought those on yourself," he said dispassionately as he walked over and pulled the bell tag to summon Stevens.

"Show these two out, and do not permit them to enter again," he instructed Stevens as he hurried into the room.

* * * *

"What a nasty man. What was that all about? Does he actually owe Madame Rosita three thousand pounds?" Michael remarked as they made their way back.

"Yes. Wasn't very pleasant, was he? More embarrassed than anything."

"But he said he's not going to pay her."

"Oh, she'll make him pay one way or another. That you can be sure of. She'll probably take him to court and have him thrown in the debtors' prison."

"In the what?"

"Debtors' prison. If you can't pay your bills, you can be sent there and not be released until you are able to clear your debt. And if you have no money to pay for your food and keep, then it can be worse than hell, I'm told."

"But lords and sirs like him don't get sent to prison; they're the privileged class. It's only the poor who get sent to prison."

"In most cases, yes, but if anyone, whatever their status, can't pay their bills, the people they owe money to can apply to the courts to have them sent to debtors' prison," Leon explained. "So make sure you never owe money."

* * * *

On the long walk back, as they turned into Bisham Street, they were confronted by a Protestant mob attacking a Catholic chapel. The mob were hurling bricks and whatever else they could lay their hands on at the windows, shattering them, as they shouted abuse at the occupants sheltering inside, who were being hit by whatever was being thrown at them through the broken windows.

"Why are they doing this?" Michael asked.

"Catholics are not popular here. In fact, in most places they are hated, accused of being cheap labour and taking all the jobs on the docks. There are fights like this all the time."

"Well, I'm not going to let them get away with it," Michael said, about to rush forward as Leon grabbed his arm.

"Don't. There are too many of them."

"I have to do something."

"There's nothing you can do. And if you get into a fight and get your clothes ripped, then Madame Rosita will not be pleased. So let's move on before we get dragged into it."

* * * *

"So how did it go?" Madame Rosita asked as soon as they both walked into the reception.

"Not very well, Madame. He was angry that you had sent me and said he would settle the account when he was good and ready. He threatened to have us arrested, and he forbade us from ever visiting his house again."

"I see. Well, lord or not, we can't let him get away with that, can we?"

"Will you send him to debtors' prison?" Michael asked.

"No, we don't need that kind of publicity, although that's exactly what he deserves. No, something a little more subtle, I think."

"He did say there were plenty of other whorehouses that would be happy to have his custom," Leon told her.

"Did he indeed? Well, then the first thing to do is to spread the word to the other houses that he doesn't honour his debts. That will certainly cramp his style. Right. I will give you a list of the other houses I want you to visit. Tell them about how much he owes and refuses to pay. The only flagellation he'll get now is if he beats himself," she said with a satisfied smile.

* * * *

"Get out of my way!" Sir Richard Fernwright shouted as he attempted to barge past Leon and Michael as they stood on duty at the door. Following on the heels of Sir Richard were two heavily built, smartly dressed gentlemen.

"You are not permitted to enter these premises, Sir Richard," Leon addressed him, attempting to block his way.

"I should advise you that these two gentlemen are members of the fight club and will not hesitate to protect me should you offer any further resistance to my entering this establishment."

"With respect, Sir Richard, my instructions are to not allow you to enter," Leon informed him, still blocking his way.

"I have little time to waste, so will you deal with these two and show them their place while I sort out Madame?" Sir Richard ordered the two men as he attempted to shove his way past.

Leon instinctively pushed Sir Richard backwards, causing him to crash against the wall, as one of the men advanced towards him, holding his fists up in a gentlemanly fashion. Leon shot out a straight left, catching the man on the chin, followed up with a right hook to the jaw. The man dropped to the floor.

At the same time, the other man went for Michael, who caught him with a heavy punch to the solar plexus that bent him double, allowing Michael to deliver a right uppercut that forced his head back and his knees to buckle.

Sir Richard, slowly recovering his dignity, looked down in disgust at the two near-unconscious men.

"I must ask you to leave, Sir Richard," Leon said firmly.

"Not until I have seen Madame Rosita. Would you kindly inform her I'm here?" he said, his voice having lost some of its arrogance.

"I will, Sir Richard, providing you remain here and ask those two gentlemen to leave," Leon told him, as the two men began to recover and struggle to their feet.

"They may as well go. A fat lot of use they've turned out to be against ruffians like you," he said disparagingly.

"I hope the reason you are here, Sir Richard, is to settle your account," Madame Rosita said as she walked purposefully into the reception.

"Can we talk privately?" he asked, his voice a little acquiescent.

"No, we talk here. You are not to be trusted after what Leon has told me."

"Very well. As you wish. I have to inform you that I am taking out writ against you for libel as it appears you have been spreading malicious rumours about my ability to honour my debts and—"

"No more than is the truth."

"Not in your case, because my refusal to pay your excessive bill is because of the quality of the services you provide. And I could have you shut down. I know a lot of influential people and—"

"As do I, Sir Richard, people who don't like a scoundrel, whatever his rank. And I don't think you would wish that to go public, so I suggest you pay up and let the matter be closed," she said, watching his eyes. She saw him thinking.

"I will pay what you ask, but I assure you, Madame, this is not the end of the matter. I will get my revenge; of that you can be assured. In the meantime I am going to have your two ruffians here charged with assault of my person. Good day to you, Madame," Sir Richard said, his face brimming with resentment.

"That would be unwise, Sir Richard."

"You forget, Madame. I have two witnesses who were also assaulted."

"We were only carrying out your instructions," Michael said to Madame as soon as Sir Richard had left.

"You did well and averted what could have been a nasty situation. Don't worry about it. He knows better than to do anything like that."

Chapter 15

Help me, help me!" Michael heard a female voice screaming as he came out of his room and descended the stairs. "Please help me," the young woman pleaded, her voice hysterical.

"What on earth is the matter?" Michael asked, surprised as she ran at him and threw her arms around his neck, her body shaking with fear. "Please help me. They are trying to force me to be a prostitute."

"Who is?" he asked. A chill swept over him as he thought over what she had just said.

"Mary. She's been beating me, telling me I have to have sex with men who come to this place. I can't. I won't. Please help me," she pleaded, looking at him through tearful eyes. "She says I have to go with some important lord who likes young virgins. She and that black man, the one who spoke to me when I got off the boat, stripped me and tied me to a ladder and then beat me with a whip to make me agree to have sex with whomever they chose. She threatened that the black man would rape me if I didn't agree to go with this lord or whoever he is. They said they wanted to keep me as a virgin for him, so they would keep beating me until I agreed."

Michael grabbed her hands from behind his neck, lowered them, and held them tightly, looking into her eyes as he said sadly, "No one should make you do anything you don't want to do. I will have a word with Leon."

"Let go of her, Michael," he heard Leon call out.

"Please don't let him get near me," she pleaded. He saw fear creeping back into her eyes at the sound of Leon's voice.

"I said let go of her, Michael. It's none of your business. Just get on with what you were doing and leave this to me," Leon said. There was a savage tone in his voice which had not been there before.

Michael had not expected this reaction from Leon. He could see the hatred in Holly's eyes as she looked at him.

Michael looked into Leon's face. Something was wrong, very wrong. It was in his voice, in his eyes, in his whole expression. Michael was looking at him in a new light.

"No, I'm not letting go of her until I know what's going on. I thought you said she would be getting a job as a maid or something."

"It's not for me or you to decide what happens to any of the girls here. That's not our job. We do what Madame Rosita tells us to do and nothing more. So be sensible and let go of the girl."

Michael could barely contain the anger he felt building up inside him. "No. I'm taking her out of here."

"No, Michael, I can't let you do that," Leon told him. There was firmness in his voice.

"Why, you going to stop me?" Michael challenged defiantly.

"If I have to. And your days will be finished here, have no doubt about that."

"What the fuck is happening?" Mary exclaimed as she rushed out of the flagellation room.

"This idiot here wants to be a hero."

"Michael, please don't get involved. Stay out of it. It's nothing to do with you. I was really beginning to like you," she said, her voice wavering.

Michael lived by a moral code that was only he alone understood, given to him by his mother, who had her own way of doing things, ways that she believed were laid down by God. "My mother always told me the golden rule was 'Do not do unto others what you would not have them do unto you.'"

"Fine words, Michael, but they have no place here. So I will ask you one more time. Let go of the girl."

"Please, Michael, let her go. We are only trying to help her so she can have a better life," Mary pleaded, her face sullen and resentful.

"What, by being a prostitute like you?"

"We all have a choice. She has a choice. She can make her life fun or miserable. What else would her future be, scrubbing floors, polishing the fire grates, and being at the mercy of an unscrupulous master, who would try to bed her anyway. At least this way she'll earn a lot more money. The smart ones end up getting paid, not pregnant."

Michael shook his head seriously. "I'll tell you what I think: we took advantage of her. Yes we did, and I was part of it, at least in assuring her she was coming to someplace that would take care of her and give her a job and a safe place to lay her head. Which is all she wanted, having managed to have got away from the misery of Ireland, losing her mother in the process. And what do we do, force her into something she doesn't want to do, something against her religion and all that she believes in? No, I'm taking her somewhere away from here and—"

"You have nowhere to go, Michael, except back on the streets where I found you, so be sensible and stop the nonsense before it's too late," Leon told him.

"Please listen to him, Michael," Mary again pleaded.

"It's already too late. I can't stay in a place that treats girls like this. It's a sin and against God."

"Everything can be a sin if you want it to be. Just look in the Bible," Leon said deprecatingly.

"That's blasphemy, and I'll have no part of it," Michael said, determination in his eyes as he moved to the stairs, pulling Holly with him.

Leon rushed at Michael as he turned. With his free hand, Michael landed a solid punch on Leon's face, temporarily stunning him, giving Michael the chance to make it down the stairs to reception.

The clients and the women sitting in reception looked up, surprised, as Michael charged in, dragging Holly with him. As he made it to the door, Leon managed to catch up. He hurled himself at Michael.

Michael let go of his grip on Holly as he was hurtled

backwards through the main door onto the street. Quickly springing to his feet, he lashed out at Leon, catching him with a right hand to the head.

"You're a fool, Michael. You've ruined everything. After all I've done for you! So take my advice and get the hell away from here before Madame gets the law on you."

"There can be no law that allows a young girl to be forced into prostitution. I'm going, and I'm taking Holly with me."

"What nonsense is this?" Madame Rosita demanded as she rushed outside to see what the commotion was.

The two men were exchanging blows, so they couldn't hear what she way saying. "Stop this at once! Grab the girl and take her back inside," she shouted to Mary at the top of her voice.

"No, Madame, I won't. Michael is right: we shouldn't be doing this," Mary said with surprising dignity, but there was a tremor of uncertainty in her voice as she felt the coldness behind Madame Rosita's words. Seeing her lips curling into a snarl, her voice thick with rage, Mary heard her say, "Lord Blamfont won't be pleased with you."

"I don't give a fuck about Lord Blamfont. He's a fucking disgrace to society. His obsession with wanting to deflower young virgins is disgusting, and your willingness to be part of it is also disgusting. Girls willing to fuck for money is one thing, but forcing a young innocent girl to be fucked against her will is another, and I no longer want any part of it. I'm leaving with Michael and the girl," Mary said, her words simmering with resentment.

"I've had enough of this! Leon, stop fighting with that ruffian. Grab the girl and take her back inside," Madame Rosita ordered as he'd managed to get a strong hold on Michael, whose concentration had momentarily lapsed.

"No, she's coming with me and Mary if she wants to," Michael said, breaking the hold Leon had on him.

"You and Mary can do what you like as neither of you have a place here any longer."

133

"What about my things?" Mary asked.

"All the things in your room were paid for by me and therefore belong to me. That goes for the ruffian too. So be on your way, the both of you, before I call the law," Madame Rosita said vindictively.

"No, there are some things that are mine. I will collect them and then be on my way," Mary said rebelliously.

"Yes, and I have some things that belong to me, so I will gather them up and leave," Michael said, moving off before Madame Rosita had a chance to stop him.

"Right, let's go," Mary said, a sense of foreboding tightening in her chest as they both got back down to reception.

"What about Holly?" Michael asked.

"We can't do anything about her," she said as she looked at Leon holding tightly onto her.

"Take her inside and let them go. They're not worth the trouble," Madame Rosita said in her derogatory manner.

* * * *

"So where to now, my hero?" Mary asked after she and Michael had hurried off together.

"I don't know. I had no idea this was going to happen," Michael said, his face consumed with uncertainty. "What are we going to do about Holly?"

"There's nothing we can do at the moment, but maybe we can think of something to rescue her."

"I hope so. I won't rest until we do."

"You're a good man, Michael. That's what I like about you. You care about people."

"A fat lot of good it did me. I'm now out of a job. How the hell did this suddenly happen?"

"I shouldn't have allowed Madame Fucking Rosita to bully me into trying to turn Holly into a whore."

"She mentioned Lord Blamfont. Was Holly being groomed for that bastard?" Michael asked, his expression as much puzzled as angry.

"That was the plan. He got bored of every other kind of perversion and had told Madame he wanted to deflower a young virgin as he had me."

"He did it to you?" he asked, surprised.

"Except it wasn't rape. I let him do it because he offered me money. He's been paying me and fucking me ever since, or has been I should say, since I won't be there any more. Anyway, at least I've got somewhere we can go to."

"You've got a place?"

"Oh yes, I've been clever with the money I've earned and rented a little apartment."

"Well, I managed to rescue my money, so I can help with the rent until I find someplace to rent myself," Michael offered.

"Good. I'm sure we can work something out between us," she said with an encouraging smile.

"I don't understand Leon and the way he acted. I thought we were friends." Michael sighed wearily.

"Yes, I must admit I was a little surprised at that. He has always been there for the girls, making sure no one did anything untoward against us, but I reckon Madame must have some kind of hold over him," Mary suggested.

Chapter 16

"Well, this is it," Mary said as she guided Michael into the apartment.

"Wow, this is nice," Michael said approvingly as he looked around. "This is actually yours?"

"Yes, actually mine. That is, until the money runs out or I find another brothel to work at."

Mary's apartment was reasonable given the money she had been earning. It had three rooms: a lounge with a small cast-iron stove fitted into the fireplace, a bedroom with a small-size bed, and a kitchen-cum-washroom that contained a small iron bathtub. It was clean. The walls were papered with a bright flowery pattern, and the floors all carpeted, except the kitchen-cum-washroom, which had a wooden floor. The toilet was situated outside in the back yard and which consisted of a row of four wooden seats with holes cut in the middle. The seats were raised on a wall of bricks. The toilet was shared with the neighbouring houses.

"Don't worry. We'll manage somehow," she said as she flopped down in the chair by the fire and kicked off her boots. "Thank God for that; they were killing me. I only bought them last week, or rather Madame did, but she's never getting them back," she added as she began to rub her stockinged feet.

"Right. The first thing is to light the stove so we can heat up the water and make ourselves a nice pot of tea," Mary said, getting to her feet and going to the bedroom to get her slippers.

"You've certainly done well for yourself," Michael said as she came back from the bedroom."

"So far, so good, but now everything's changed. And unless, as I said, I can find another way of earning the same money, all this will disappear."

"I'm sorry I caused all this. And poor Holly is still trapped there."

"It's not your fault. You were dragged into this as we all were. I should not have let Madame use me to try to force Holly. You showed courage and a decency I never thought I'd ever see in a man. I'm proud of you."

The words made him shift uneasily on his feet as he looked down at her, his face flushing red with embarrassment.

"You're a good man, Michael," she said. There was a glint of admiration in her eyes.

"I only did what I felt was right," he said sheepishly. "Anyone would have done the same."

"Not anyone. Leon didn't, for a start, and I don't know of anyone else who would have. There's a little grocer's store not far from here. Go get us a loaf of bread and some cheese. Here's some money," she said, dipping her hand into her purse and taking out a few coins.

"No, it's OK. I've got money."

"OK. And while you're doing that, I'll get the oven going. It won't take me long as I had plenty of experience with it in the past," she said jokingly.

* * * *

"Hey, you there!" Michael heard a voice call out as he made his way along the pavement. Thinking it had nothing to do with him, he continued walking.

"Hey, you there," he heard the voice call out again. There was something in the voice that made him stop and turn around to see where it was coming from. Once he did so, he was surprised to see a hansom cab wheeling around in the street and heading in his direction.

The driver reined in the horse and pulled up beside him

"Just the man I've been looking for," Sir Richard Fernwright said as he flung open the folding half doors and stepped out.

"I have nothing more to do with Madame Rosita," Michael said nervously.

"I know all about what happened, which is why I want

137

to talk to you. I have seen for myself your abilities as a fighter, and I have an offer I wish to make to you," he said, pausing to assess Michael's reaction, which was one of relief. He was glad this wasn't about the visit he made with Leon regarding the money Sir Fernwright owed to Madame Rosita.

"What offer would that be, sir?" Michael heard himself ask.

"To be my champion."

"Champion of what, sir?"

"Fighting, bare knuckle fighting. As I said, I have seen how good you are with your fists, and I am prepared to be your patron and have you trained to become the best fighter and challenge for the championship. How say you to that?"

It took Michael a moment to absorb what he was saying. "I don't know, sir. It's all a bit sudden. I have to find work and a place to stay before I can think about anything like that."

"That you need have no worry of," he assured him as he paused to take a puff on his large cigar, gently blowing the smoke out so it formed a small cloud above his head. "You will enter into a contract with me, and I will provide you with a place to train and with accommodation. I'll even pay you a wage."

"I don't know what to say. Can I think about it as—"

"What is there to think about? Offers like this don't come around that often. And—"

"I don't like fighting. I don't want to hurt—"

"You don't like fighting? I'm told you fight like a tiger and that you gave some crimps a real good hiding."

"That's because I had no choice. The crimps were trying to steal money from me. And I fought your men because that was my job. I fought Leon because of what they were trying to do to a young girl against her will."

"Very noble. That is exactly the fighting spirit I want in my man. You do this right and you'll earn more money than you can working on the docks, which is where I guess you will end up earning a pittance if you don't grab this opportunity," Sir Richard said. He turned and climbed back in the hansom cab. "I expect you to call at my manor tomorrow. You know where it is, of course," he added, banging on the roof with his cane to signal the driver to move on.

Michael stood watching the cab drive off, his mind swirling around with what he had been offered.

* * * *

"Why did it take you so long?" Mary asked as soon as Michael walked in and dumped the bread and cheese on the table.

"You're not going to believe this, but as I was walking along to the grocer's, I was suddenly approached by Sir Richard Fernwright and—"

"Fernwright!" Mary exclaimed with an audible gasp. "You mean that old reprobate?"

"You know him?"

"Oh, I know him all right. I've serviced him enough times, and he owes Madame Rosita for my and the other girls' services. So why would he approach you?"

"Yes, I know about his debt. Leon and I were sent to his house to collect it."

"So what did he want with you?" Mary asked, becoming ever more curious.

"He offered me a job as a boxer. He wants me to become his champion. Says he will provide a place for me to train, provide my accommodation, and pay me a wage."

"Can you trust a man like him?" she asked, eyeing him sharply.

"I don't know. He said he would draw up a contract, whatever that means."

"That means you will be tied to him. He'll own you."

"It seems whomever you work for seems to think they own you."

"Yes, that's true, I suppose. So what are you going to do?"

"I don't know. I really don't know what to do. He says I would make more money than I could earn working in the

139

docks or anywhere else for that matter."

"When do you have to let him know?"

"Tomorrow. He told me to call at the manor tomorrow."

"Right. Well, we've got some time to think about it. I've got the stove going, so let's eat. And I've got a nice bottle of wine we can relax with while we discuss what you should do," she said encouragingly.

* * * *

The bread and cheese went down well, as did the wine, as Michael and Mary sat together on the floor in front of the blazing stove.

"You know, I always wanted to invite you here, since the first time I met you, when you beat up those nasty men. I'll tell you one thing: Sir Richard is right. You would make a good boxer. You've got the body for it," she said, looking at him admiringly over the rim of her glass.

The look made him begin to shift uncomfortably. He was nervous as he had never sat this close to a woman before, particularly given the way she was sitting with her long skirt hiked up over her knee with one leg stretched out, revealing the top of her black stocking.

She placed her glass down on the floor beside her and placed her hand on his thigh as she said, "You know, I really fancy you. Would you like to have sex with me?" She invitingly looked into his eyes and thought for a moment he was angered by the suggestion, then she saw him relax as a soft smile broke out on his face.

"Does that mean a yes?" she asked tantalisingly. She leaned over and kissed his brow before lowering her chin to brush his lips with her own, the touch sending a tingling sensation down his spine.

She moaned softly, smiling with her lovely blue eyes. Placing a soft hand on his face and looking at him intently, she asked in a gentle voice, "Have you never made love to a woman?"

140

He shook his head, still unnerved by her frankness. "No I haven't. I've never … My mother always told me sex outside of marriage is a mortal sin," he said, attempting to turn his head away in embarrassment.

She silenced him. Sensing his embarrassment, she took his face in her hands. Looking into his eyes, she said, "Sex is not a sin, just a necessary part of life. And I want to teach you everything a young man should know about pleasuring a woman. I want you to learn how to pleasure me in a way no man has ever managed to. I want to experiment with you."

A shudder of fear shot through him at his sense of inadequacy. He did not know what he should do or say.

"Come, I want to feel loved, be loved, live for the moment, and cherish it," she said, getting to her feet, taking hold of his hand, helping him up, and leading him off to the bedroom.

"I've had a fantasy about you since I first saw you fighting those crimps," she said as she sat him on the bed and began to unbutton his frock coat. "It's nice and warm in here, so you won't need that on," she added as she got to her feet and pushed the coat back over his shoulders. He could feel the firmness of her breasts pressing against him as she pulled it down so that he could slip his arms out and let it fall to the floor.

"Right, now just sit there," she told him as she slowly eased the straps of her long-sleeved dress with its dipped neckline down over her shoulders and then shuffled the dress down over the curves of her body, revealing a pretty embroidered camisole.

Michael began to shift uncomfortably. This was something completely new, something he had never experienced. He had never seen a woman, even his mother, without being fully clothed. His mother had always impressed on him that nakedness was ungodly. He remembered that every time she needed to wash herself and remove some of her clothes, she would order him and his father out of the cottage and would not allow them back in until she had finished and was fully dressed again.

Kicking the dress to one side, Mary removed the camisole in one swift movement, revealing a tight corset strengthened with whalebone that pulled her in at the waist and pushed up her voluptuous bust. Her black stockings, held up by pretty patterned garters, reached halfway up the thigh.

Provocatively she began to unhook the corset, which was fastened at the front, leaving her wearing just her cotton drawers and sleeveless knee-length chemise, which she quickly removed.

Michael stared at her standing there in just her black stockings, arranging her body into a sensuous pose, completely comfortable in her nakedness. His eyes admired the polished smoothness of her skin. The nipples on the two round brown patches of her breasts were proud. As he continued to stare, he felt a stirring in his loins that he had never experienced before. Then his eyes lowered to the neat triangle of dark hair at the lower part of her body, making him feel even more uneasy.

Realising her nakedness was beginning to have its desired effect as he remained staring, mesmerised, too shy to do more than continue to stare, Mary decided she would have to lead the way. The prospect excited her. It was different from the men she usually had sex with, who were only interested in a quick shag, spending their load and thanking her as they tucked their limp members back in their trousers, giving her a tip as they left.

"Right," she said, getting down on her knees and shuffling up to him. "Just lie back and enjoy the experience," she said, her voice filled with urgency as she reached her hands up and started to undo his breeches.

Instinctively he pulled her hands away, although she had managed to feel the beginnings of a swelling, giving her confidence she was making progress.

"Just relax. Let's not waste a precious moment of this." She sighed, tugging at the buttons of his fly. It wasn't long before she had managed to undo them all. Then she reached in and took out his now semierect penis.

She looked at it admiringly, although it didn't look quite as hard as she had expected it to be. She knew she still had to do some work on it.

Mary touched herself, excitement brushing the surface of her skin as she provocatively caressed her breasts. Then she took hold of his hands, inviting him to touch her breasts. She let out a gasp as she felt him nervously take the fullness of them in his hands. She sensed a tremble of exhilaration, feeling her nipples harden at the gentleness of his fingers caressing them, causing goosebumps to surface on her skin and a huge flood of warmth to wash over her, so different from the insensitive and sometimes brutal manner of the men who paid her for sex.

"You are the most beautiful woman I have ever seen," Michael murmured, running his thumbs over her firm, pert nipples.

"Thank you, kind sir," she said with a smile, admiring the solid chiselled beauty of his features, before stretching out her hand to his penis and beginning to gently stroke it, emitting a little squeal of pleasure as she felt it start to stiffen once she closed her fingers around it, tightening her grip.

Michael timidly lowered his hand from her breast and ran it across the flat of her stomach, reaching down until his fingers felt the dark triangle. He began to stroke the soft, silky hair.

Her body trembled as his fingers involuntary sought and found her now moist opening. She shuffled on her knees to ease her legs apart so that he could explore her more. She felt his fingers gently begin to probe inside her.

She reached up and took hold of his penis and, as if in slow motion, guided it to the moist lips of her mouth tantalisingly flicking her tongue over the tip. She heard him emit a gasp as he felt the sensation of her lips closing around his penis, now glistening with her juices, before taking him fully into her gaping mouth.

Slowly, using long and deep strokes, she began to suck on it while her hands took hold of his buttocks to draw him in even deeper. He let out another gasp, louder this time, as he felt the tip of his penis brush against the back of her throat.

Suddenly his movements became quicker and quicker. He arched his body up to match her downward movements as she began to suck harder. It wasn't long before he began to shake uncontrollably.

Nothing could stop him now. The thrusting was becoming faster. Michael reached an uncontrollable orgasmic state as he exploded. He kept cumming, ramming into her as she continued to suck. Even though she was prepared, the force of his warm semen splashing against the back of her throat took her by surprise, causing her to gasp as she continued to suck, wanting to take in every last drop.

Finally she raised her head to look up at him, letting his member slip from between her lips as she wiped the semen from her chin with her finger. "That was quite something. I've never had a man cum like that before," she said with a contented smile on her face.

After a while, Michael looked down at Mary, who was still on her knees, his mouth trying to shape the words he wanted to say, but he was too nervous to say them.

"It's all right. You don't have to say anything," she said soothingly, standing up to brush his lips with a gentle kiss. "I enjoyed that just as much as I guess you did. I think we should have a glass of wine," she suggested. The sight of her standing naked began to arouse him again.

"Fuck the wine," she said. "Don't move. I'm just going to get a rubber," she told him as she moved to a small chest of drawers on the other side of the bed. She opened the top drawer, took out a small wooden box, removed the rubber condom, and hurried back to where Michael was still lying back, his penis beginning to lose some of its firmness.

"Don't let me down now," she said, taking him between her lips. She was relieved as she felt his penis begin to stiffen. Satisfied, she pulled her head away. He looked down, staring curiously at the unfamiliar thing she was rolling onto his rigid member. It looked and felt strange. He began to slacken, full of apprehension about what was going to happen next. It was only when Mary started to rub some kind of scented oil over the rubber condom that he became rigid again.

"I don't want to get preggers," she said, climbing onto the bed and straddling him, letting out a painful cry as she gently guided him into her, surprised by how big he felt. As she began to move slowly up and down on him, the thrusting penetrated deeper into her. Abandoned pleasure took over. Moans began to escape from her mouth. Before she realised what was happening, her movements became quicker and her thrusting faster. She felt that at any moment her body was going to explode. She spiralled uncontrollably to an orgasmic state that made her scream out at the top of her voice: "I'm cumming. I'm really fucking cumming!"

Michael tried to muffle her screams by placing his hand over her mouth, fearing someone might hear them.

Feeling the full length of him deep inside her with his movements becoming quicker, she began to move in rhythm with him. "Come on," she screamed. "Cum with me. I want to cum again, and I want you to cum with me," she screamed. He didn't attempt to stop her this time as nothing could stop this moment. The most extraordinary things were happening to both of them. She was about to have a second orgasm. In the whole of her life she had never experienced a single orgasm, let alone two, something she'd never believed possible with a man. *This is how sex should be,* she moaned to herself, the thought heightening the sensations as she pressed down hard on him.

"Cum with me," she screamed again as she approached another agonising orgasm. She got her wish as Michael's breathing became heavy. He gripped her bare buttocks and held on tightly as he came inside her, his shuddering body heralding the end of his climax.

"And I thought I was going to teach you something," she said breathlessly. "I think I'm going to need more than a glass of wine after that. I don't know about you, but a glass of brandy is what I need right now." She sighed as she clambered off him and slumped to the floor, her body still aching with orgasm.

Chapter 17

Mary stirred, slowly opening one eye and then the other. She blinked at the morning light, which was streaking in through the half-closed curtains.

She sat up. A big yawn creased her face as she stretched her arms and looked down at Michael, lying on his side in a deep sleep. She smiled, thinking of last night. The thought made her touch her bare breasts, the nipples immediately responding to her touch.

Silently she slipped out of the bed and put on a dressing gown she had hanging on a hook on the back of the bedroom door. She gave a laugh as she walked to the lounge, realising she was still wearing her black stockings.

Balancing alternatively on each leg, she gently unrolled the stockings, pulled them off, and tucked them into the pocket of her dressing gown.

"Right, let's get the stove going so I can make us some breakfast," she murmured happily to herself. She got to her knees and set about the task.

"Can I help?" she heard Michael's voice behind her ask as she put a match to the paper to get the stove alight.

"No, it's nearly all done. Once the flames get going, I'll put on the coal, and we can have some breakfast. Did you sleep all right?" she asked. There was an air of vitality and happiness to her as she smiled.

"Yes, fine, thank you," he said sheepishly, standing there bare-chested, dressed only in his crumpled breeches.

The urge to grab him and drag him back to the bedroom was overwhelming to Mary. She had to control her feelings as she went to get to her feet.

He held out his hand to help her, and she grabbed it willingly. This was something new. The touch of his hand was making her heart beat fast. The urge to go ahead and do what she wanted to do, consequences be damned, was overpowering. It gave her an exhilarating feeling she had never felt before.

"So have you decided what you're going to do about Sir Richard?" she asked in a desperate attempt to shake off the thoughts of seducing him again.

He studied her lips, the same lips that had done such extraordinary things to him the night before. "No, I haven't thought about it since we ..." He stopped, too shy to say the words.

"Had sex," she cut in, finishing the sentence for him.

"Yes, and I don't know what to do."

"Well, after you had fallen asleep, I got to thinking, and I remembered reading something about a fighter in the Times. Bendigo, I think his name was. Bendigo, that's right, Bendigo Thompson. He got into the fight game to earn money for his family. Apparently when he was just fifteen, after his father had died, he and his mother were sent to the Nottingham workhouse. After leaving the workhouse, he got odd jobs selling fish around the streets of Nottingham, before obtaining a job as an iron turner, but it wasn't enough. At the age of eighteen, he had his first fight against the champion of another town called Bingham. He was very agile, earning the name Bendy because of his constant bobbing and weaving around the ring. His nickname evolved, and Bendy Abednego became Bendigo. He won the fight and earned himself twenty-five pounds. As a result he took up boxing as a living, becoming famous and earning a lot of money."

"How do you know all this?"

"I told you, I read it in the paper. He went on to become champion of England. Just think, with the right help you could become a champion just like him."

"I remember my father taking me to a graveyard to see where Simon Byrne, the last great champion of Ireland, was buried. He told me how he was earning something like two hundred pounds a fight. Do you think I could earn that sort of money?"

"I think you can. You've got the build," she said, admiring his muscular body. "And you've got the ability. I've seen you fight twice now. You're not afraid. I reckon you can beat anybody."

"But what about you? I said I would help you out with the rent until—"

"I thought about that too. He said he would provide you with accommodation, so he can pay the rent here, and that takes care of both of us. I quite like the idea of us being together," she said, bristling with excitement.

"You mean you want us to live together? But we're not-

"Married," she said, finishing his sentence for him again. "I lost my innocence a long time ago. I'm a whore and not ashamed of it," she said, her eyes sparkling with fury as she looked at his face, noticing he seemed shocked by her words.

"Look, I've never had any involvement with a man before. I've always just gone to Madame Rosita's, done the business, and come home to my flat to be by myself and enjoy a bit of peace and quiet. And then you came along."

"If you want me to leave …"

"No, I didn't mean that. I don't want you to leave. Don't you understand what I'm trying to say? I want you to stay. I've never felt this way about anybody before."

"I would like to stay, but do you think Sir Richard would pay the rent for a place like this?"

"Don't worry, I can always find another brothel to work at. There are plenty of good ones around that would take me like a shot, and—"

"You mean you'd still…" He hesitated, sensing the first pangs of jealousy.

"Look, it's just a job like anything else. It's not sex like we had last night. I don't have any feelings for those who come to have a quick shag and go back home to their adoring wives—or not so adoring as the case maybe. Do you know last night was the first time I've ever had an orgasm? And that's saying something with the number of men I've serviced."

He was looking at her with hostile eyes, his cheeks an angry colour, as he thought, *Was last night a cruel illusion?* He suddenly felt cheated and angry. "I don't understand. I thought ..."

She felt the whole weight of his anger like a physical blow, and she knew she had to hold herself together. This wasn't going the way she had intended. "There's some hot water now. Why don't you go and have a wash while I make the breakfast. Here, take the kettle. Fill the bowl in the washroom and bring the kettle back so I can make the tea."

The warm soapy water felt nice. Michael rubbed it gently on his face as he looked at himself in the small round mirror hanging on the wall above the washbasin. *I'm not going to let life happen to me. She's right, I'm going to have to go out there and get it for myself.*

Chapter 18

So you've decided to accept my offer," Sir Richard Fernwright said, giving Michael a hard, silent stare as he raised the big fat cigar to his mouth, struck a match, and put the flame to the end of it, drawing in the smoke and letting it roll around his mouth, savouring the aroma while his bleak cold eyes continued to assess Michael.

The intensity of his gaze was beginning to make Michael feel uncomfortable. "Yes, sir," he said hesitantly.

"You are sure now? Because once you sign that contract, there is no going back," Sir Richard told him, blowing out a large cloud of smoke.

"Yes, I'm sure, sir," Michael replied, sounding a little more positive. "Providing you will, as you said, pay for my accommodation and pay me a wage."

"Of course. I am a man of my word. And you needn't let that incident with Madame Rosita concern you, although it's of no consequence now that you have left her. I will arrange accommodation for you in one of the properties I own—"

"I want to stay in the flat where I am now," Michael interrupted, surprised by the sudden firmness in his voice.

"You mean where you're sleeping with that whore? You seriously expect me to keep both of you?" Sir Richard said, jamming the cigar angrily back into his mouth.

"I don't like her being called a whore, Sir Richard."

He gave Michael a peculiar twisted smile as he said, "She's a prostitute; I've fucked her enough times to know."

Michael's jaw tightened as he sprang to his feet, barely able to contain the anger that was welling up inside him. "I knew it was a mistake coming here. And it was the prostitute, as you call her, who persuaded me to accept the offer. I will not trouble you any more," he said, turning to leave.

"*Sit down!*" Sir Richard shouted. "I'm sorry. I should not have said that. In fact I have always considered Mary to be a fine girl. Look, I'm really interested in you as a boxer, and I see great things for you, for both of us. So let us start again. I will pay the rent on the flat, but it is more expensive than I had planned, so the cost will be deducted from your purse money once you start earning. Agreed?"

"Agreed."

"I will set up a training camp here in the grounds, and you will come here and train every day. Is that understood?"

"Yes, sir."

"Good, then we start tomorrow. I will have the contract drawn up. And I have someone good to train you. His name is Owen Fitzgerald, but everybody calls him Fisty Fitzy because of his prowess with his fists. He was a great fighter, learning his skills when travelling with the fairs that had boxing booths. They would challenge anyone in the crowd to take on their man, offering a prize of a few pounds to anyone who beat him. Fisty was never beaten. He became a local champion. That's when I took him on. I had great hopes for him until success went to his head and sadly he started drinking, so much so that when he came up to the scratch, he was in no condition to fight."

"And you think he can train me?"

"Oh yes. He doesn't drink now, having seen the error of his ways—too late, unfortunately, to make it to the top—but he still has the skills to pass onto you. So listen and learn from him and don't make the mistakes he made. I want a champion, and I'm giving you that chance, so don't waste it. If you do, I will hound you into the ground."

* * * *

"How did it go?" Mary asked when Michael arrived back at the flat.

"I've taken up the offer, but I nearly walked out when he called you a prostitute and said he had had sex with you many

152

times."

"No, Michael, he fucked me. He didn't have sex with me. You had sex with me, and that's the difference. Can't you understand that?"

"No I can't," he said, looking at her dubiously.

"My God, you've still got a lot to learn. Look, Michael, I'm happy for you to move in with me, but you have to accept that I am a prostitute and have always been. And I'm not ashamed of it. Although I like to think of myself more as a courtesan as it is in those oriental countries, rather than as a whore. I work at the high end of the business. I don't walk the streets. They say it is the oldest profession in the world, and to me that's exactly what it is, a profession like any other business, an exchange of services for money. The word *prostitute* or *whore* was created by men out of blind ignorance and bigotry, the men responsible for all the wars being fought around the world, for degrading religion, using it only when it suits their purposes and ignoring it when it doesn't. Condemning women as witches and sentencing them to be burned at the stake, as well as perpetrating every conceivable atrocity known to humankind—these things are done by the same men who come to Madame Rosita's in the day or night for a quick bunk-up with a prostitute, but then they condemn her the next day for what she is."

He looked at her, his eyes hiding the confused thoughts behind them. "I never thought about it in that way."

"That's because you come from a strict Catholic background," she said, regretting the words as soon as she'd spoken them. "Women are just the chattel of men. We have no rights, and we are not allowed to own property. We're not allowed to do the same work as men. We can't vote or have any say in politics. Women are expected to remain chaste without any sexual feelings of any kind until they marry, and then they are expected only to have sex when the master demands it, more like rape when he comes home drunk and demands that his wife lie on her back while he fucks her without giving and without caring whether she has any sexual or emotional satisfaction, while he of course, being a man, can go and fuck around with his animalistic attitudes as much as he likes. Why do you think Madame Rosita employed you and Leon?"

"To make sure the wrong people were not allowed in."

"That was part of it, but the main reason was to protect us from clients who thought they could do anything they liked to us because in their minds we are just usable pieces of flesh, whores, a necessary evil. You have no idea what some of them want to do to us or have done to us. Some of the noises you must have heard coming from the flagellation room should have given you some idea."

She looked at him, watching him think about what she had said, and held out her hands for him to come to her, not sure whether he was angry. But then saw a smile break out on his face.

As he took hold of her hands, she could not stop her eyes from straying to his hard biceps and forearms and the muscled neck under his mop of hair. She drew him to her, feeling the power of his body as she kissed his hair and his brow and raised his chin to brush her lips against his, the kiss filling her with a heady passion.

"Come, take me to bed. I want you to make love to me," she said, intoxicated by the intensity of her emotions. Being with someone had never felt so right. She loved the way he stood, his hair, his smile, his vitality, his spirit, his smell, and how his skin felt firm under her touch.

Chapter 19

"The first thing we're going to have to do is toughen up your hands," Owen Fitzgerald said as he took hold of Michael's hands and closely examined them.

Owen was a stocky man with broad muscular arms and shoulders. Five feet eight inches in height, he had a face covered with a beard matching the silver-grey colour of the curly mop of hair on his head. He was dressed in a sleeveless vest, tight woollen breeches, and canvas shoes.

Michael and Owen were at the rear end of Sir Richard's large garden in an area that had been set aside for their training purposes, partitioned off by a neatly trimmed hedge. It had a roped ring squared off by a stake driven into the ground at each corner, and a heavy punchbag covered in leather suspended from an iron frame with a pile of sandbags packed around the base.

"They seem pretty tough to me. My dad used to toughen my hands by wrapping them in cloth soaked in vinegar," Michael told him, a little upset by the remark.

"That helps, but it's the skin we need to toughen, because with repetitive punching the skin will start splitting and become very painful. Not very long after you wouldn't be able to keep punching, so you could lose the fight."

"So how do we toughen the skin?"

"You soak your hands daily in a mixture of brine, green vitriol, copper, whisky, gunpowder, and horseradish until they become as hard as iron. It's a mixture all boxers use. There are some other methods too that we'll come to later, but in the meantime you take the mixture home and soak your hands in it for an hour every night, OK?"

"Sir Richard told me that you were once a fighter."

"A boxer, I prefer to think, but I somehow managed to

throw it all away. If you don't make the same mistakes, you'll probably succeed where I failed. For blessed are the ones who persevere under trial, because having stood the test, they will receive the crown of life that the Lord has promised to those who love Him."

Michael gazed at him distantly, surprised by the sudden religious outburst. "I didn't know you were religious."

"The temptations were there, and I immersed myself in a reckless life of pleasure and excesses. I had it all—at least I thought I did—but soon there was nothing left. I was stripped of everything, not only my possessions but also my self-respect. Nobody wanted to know me. All those whom I had bought drinks for were no longer interested in me."

"So what did you do?"

"I was desperate for help, forced to live in filthy hovels or on the streets, sorrow swelling up in my heart, praying the pain would go away. Over and over I prayed, saying, 'If there's a God, then please help me.' Just as I had given up all hope, a silent alarm went off inside me and a calmness swept over me, and I felt a great release as the pain eased and left me. That same night, the Lord came to me, or rather I should say I came to the Lord in a prayer of repentance. I felt humbled, undeserving. I began to cry, not understanding how or why it had happened, but I knew I was emerging from the darkness that had enveloped and controlled me for so long. I felt lighter, the heaviness of guilt lifting from me. After some time in prayer that night, I decided or was told, I don't know which, to get a Bible—and it has been my guide ever since."

"That's quite a story. But why then do you still want to be involved in boxing?"

"Boxing is a noble sport, and I'm determined you will be the noblest of all."

Uncertainty tugged at Michael's sleeve. "I'm not sure I'm the right person. I'm a Catholic, but I keep asking myself whether there is a God, and if there is, why He let my mother, my father, and all those others be thrown out of their homes, left to starve and die in the horrible way they did."

"There is something in every believer wanting to doubt and in every disbeliever wanting to believe."

"I don't know what to believe. Why is there so much evil in the world? Why are good people made to suffer?" Michael said thoughtfully.

"Whatever your beliefs, there is no denying that religion is a powerful motivator, for we learn something from everyone who passes through our lives. Some lessons are painful and some are painless, but all are priceless. I may not yet be where I want to be, but thanks to the good Lord, I am no longer where I used to be."

This isn't about you, Michael told himself. Although he'd been poor and desperate like Owen, he had resolved he'd never be either poor or desperate again. "So what are we going to be doing today?" he asked, wanting to change the subject.

"Simple exercises to strengthen the body. Press-ups and road running to begin with, then onto harder stuff."

* * * *

"What's that you've got with you?" Mary asked, looking up at Michael as he walked in carrying a large stone jug.

"It's a mixture the trainer has given me to soak my hands in for an hour every night to get them toughened up."

"So what's this trainer like?"

"Bit strange really," he said, placing the stone jug down against the wall.

"Strange in what way?"

"Strange in that the man Sir Richard's got to train me is an ex-fighter. Sir Richard had told me the trainer had blown his chances as a boxer by resorting to drink, but what he didn't tell me was that the man has become some kind of religious nut. And I'm not sure what to make of it."

"You should be pleased he's not a hardened drinker any

more and has been able to reach inside himself and find an inner strength that motivates him and gives a whole new meaning to his life," she said, the words catching him by surprise.

"You talk so well for a—"

"Prostitute," she cut in, her tone becoming irritable. "You think because I'm a whore, I'm ignorant? The one thing that being a whore has given me is the chance to learn to read and write. And strangely enough, now that I've had a little more time to myself, I've been reading *Oliver Twist*, a book written by a man called Charles Dickens. There's woman in it called Nancy, who's a prostitute controlled by an evil man called Bill Sikes. Bill has got a vicious dog called Bull's-eye, which he uses to frighten her and other people. And there's another man called Fagin, who's got all these kids under his control, making them go out and steal from people. You should read it when I've finished with it."

"Yes. I will, if I have the time," he said half-heartedly, not wanting to admit he could barely read.

"Anyway, I've cooked us a nice steak and kidney pie. That is another thing I've learned to do. Mrs Baxter used to give me cooking lessons when we had nothing else to do."

"That sounds nice. I'm starving. Fisty is already working me hard, and—"

"Fisty? Is that his name?"

"His name is Owen Fitzgerald. He got the name of Fisty Fitzy because of his boxing. I think he could still make a good show of himself if he had a mind to, but he'd rather preach the Bible at someone than throw punches at them."

"He sounds a good man to me. Go clean yourself up, and we can have dinner."

* * * *

"Have you decided what you're going to do?" Michael asked after they had finished eating.

"Not yet, but I need to be doing something. I don't like

the idea of being stuck indoors all day. I'll look after you, but I don't like the idea of being a housewife or being treated like one. I've seen too many of them being abused and treated like slaves, and—"

"I would never treat you like that," Michael cut in, an indignant look of panic on his face, worried she might be thinking he would behave like that. "I have no respect for a man who treats a woman badly. That's why I tried to rescue Holly. I often think about what might have happened to her."

"Maybe I should try to find out. I know you wouldn't behave like that; otherwise I wouldn't let you move in. But when you look around and you read *Oliver Twist*, it makes you think that something should be done to better the conditions of women who have been abandoned by their husbands, left to fend for themselves and their children, having to resort to begging, stealing, or selling their bodies on the streets to anyone willing to pay."

"I've never seen you as serious as this. Sounds like you really care."

"I do care. Another book I've been reading is *Plea for Women* by Marion Reid. Here, listen to this," she said, reaching for the book on the side table and opening it to the place where the corner of the page had been folded over. "She writes about the want of equal civil rights for women and the removal of the unjust laws oppressing married women to give them some form of economic independence. She also urges that girls should be given the same education opportunities as given to boys."

"All a bit too much for me. I'd better get my hands soaking in that stuff or I'll be in trouble tomorrow," he said, his expression unreadable.

* * * *

"Did you soak your hands for an hour last night?" Fisty asked, already in the training area awaiting Michael's arrival.

"Yes, sir, I did."

"Don't mess with the sir crap. Call me Fisty. Everybody else does. Right, today we're going to get to know how to use the punchbag. We'll start with fairly light pounding then gradually build up to heavier punching. Once you're able to throw solid punches without hurting your hands, we'll start working on techniques I learned during my boxing days. They say I could have been a great champion. Anyway, your hands won't be tough enough yet, so we are going to have to wrap them in canvas to protect the skin."

Fisty, true to his word, had told Michael his training would be vigorous. Having wrapped his hands in canvas, he started to teach him the correct stance to be able to move around the ring more easily so as to avoid being hit while at the same time remaining able to throw punches.

As Michael took up the stance, Fisty adjusted the position of his feet, bending his knees and the top half of his body forward so that he wasn't standing awkwardly and straight.

"When you punch the bag, make sure your knuckles are flat so that the punch has greater impact when you hit the bag. But always remember to keep both hands loose when you're in a defensive stance, only tightening them when you're about to punch."

Michael clenched his fists as he was told and started punching the bag.

"Hit the bag with sharp, crisp punches. Pull each punch away from the bag just as quickly as you deliver it. It is not only strength that counts; it's also making sure you hit your target. Keep your arm as straight as you can when you hit the bag."

Fisty allowed himself to smile as he watched Michael go through his paces. He could see the gradual improvement and felt Sir Richard would be pleased that Michael had all the makings of a good fighter.

"Keep that up for a while, and then we'll try some dead lifts."

* * * *

Mary listened to the echoing silence of the flat all around her. She felt her eyes fill with tears. She was beginning to get bored with nothing much to do after having finished reading *Oliver Twist* and the book by Marion Reid, and she had to admit to herself that she missed the excitement of working at Madame Rosita's. She began to think whether she would like to go back to work there, that is, of course, if Madame would ever allow her back.

The thought had intrigued her for days, as had the thought of what had happened to Holly. Mary decided to take the risk and visit Madame Rosita.

"You've got some nerve turning up here," Madame Rosita said, glaring angrily at her.

"Yes it took some courage to come here," Mary said, her voice wavering.

"So why have you come?"

"I wondered whether you'd take me back."

"Why should I, after what you and that ruffian tried to pull, who I'm told is shacked up with you now. They say people get the friends they deserve," she said vindictively.

"Yes," she confirmed, ignoring the hurtful remark. "And he's training to be a fighter, and Sir Richard Fernwright is his patron."

"Oh really?" she responded, her face flushing angrily at the thought. "Sir Richard Fernwright of all people. So why do you want to come back and work for me if your fancy man has got Sir Richard taking care of him? Not paying him enough, I suspect, knowing that miserly bastard."

"Michael will earn good money when he's trained and begins fighting."

"Yes, but for whom, you have to ask yourself. Because Sir Richard is a skinflint and, like I said, hates to give his money away. He expects everything for nothing as I have found out to my cost, but I'll get the money back one day, that's for sure. You're a good worker. The clients like you, and

161

I've never had any trouble with you up until that moment. Let me think about it. I'll let you know."

"Thank you, Madame. Is Holly still here?" Mary asked, the words spilling out of her mouth before she had a chance to decide whether she should ask her or not.

Madame Rosita fixed her with a meaningful look. "No, she was too much trouble, so I passed her off to a client who was looking for a young servant."

Mary felt her blood run cold at Madame Rosita's callous attitude towards such a young innocent woman and her own role in her plight, but she knew she couldn't do or say anything. "Thank you for seeing me," she said, turning around and walking out of the reception.

* * * *

"Right now we're going to do some dead lifts, lifting and carrying sandbags and other heavy objects, which will do a lot to strengthen the hand and grip," Fisty told Michael after the latter had finished a hard session punching the bag with blood beginning to seep through the bandaging.

* * * *

As Mary walked home, she began to reflect on what Madame Rosita had casually told her about Holly. She could feel the heartbreak coming off her in waves. It made her think about what was more important in her life. Was it a case of necessity over morality, her own well-being uppermost in the grand scheme of things, and to hell with anything or anyone else? Was it that life was just a series of events that she had no control over? She really liked Michael and loved the idea of them living in sin together. It excited her, yet she felt there was something missing in her day-to-day life. Was it Holly and young women like her that was worrying Mary? The thought saddened her.

With her shoulders hunched, deep in her troubled

thoughts as she strolled along, Mary was suddenly surprised to hear someone calling out her name. She stopped and turned around. Her stomach tightened as she stared at the young woman hurrying awkwardly towards her.

"Oh my God," she exclaimed, looking at the bruised and battered face of the young woman. "Please help me, Mary. Please help me," the young woman pleaded as she flung her arms around Mary's neck to stop herself from collapsing.

"Do I know you?"

"It's me, Holly. Please help me," she said, raising her head to look at Mary.

Mary looked at the almost unrecognisable features of her bloodied face, the lips cracked and swollen. Holly's eyes were set back and blackened, her hair was scraggy with streaks of blood running down the strands, and she bruise marks around her neck.

"Holly, whatever has happened to you?"

"Please help me. I've run away. Please take me somewhere safe before he catches up with me and drags me back."

"Before who drags you back?"

"Please help me get me away from here. I'm frightened they'll come after me."

"Right, let's get you home, and you can tell me all about it," Mary said, wrapping her arms around Holly to give her support.

* * * *

"So tell me what happened?" Mary asked, after she had settled Holly into a chair and began to bathe her face, gently dabbing the cotton wool over the cuts and bruises.

"I still refused to do what Madame Rosita wanted, so she locked me in a cupboard, telling me she would only let me out when I had changed my mind. It was dark and horrible, and she only gave me food and water once a day. I only had a small pot for doing my business, which made the small cupboard

163

stink even more."

"How long did she keep you there?"

"Several days, until she unlocked the door, hauled me out, and told me I was of no use to her and she wasn't going to waste any more time on me. She said she had sold me to-"

"Sold you?"

"Yes, to a Lord Blamfont."

"Oh my God, he was the one she wanted you groomed for in the first place. So he was determined to get you one way or another. So what happened?"

"I didn't know I was being sold. She told me Lord Blamfont was looking for a maid, and as she didn't want me, she said I could go and work for him. I was happy, relieved, thinking I wasn't going to be working as a prostitute, but once I was in his mansion, it quickly became clear he wanted me not only to work as a maid but also to be his personal sex slave."

"The bastard. What an evil man."

"I refused, and he started to beat me, saying he'd paid good money for me and he was determined he was going to get his money's worth. The more I refused, the more violent he became. He finally lost his temper and beat me to the point that I almost lost consciousness. And then he undid the front of his breeches, took out his, er, thing, and forced it into me. It hurt. It was horrible. I cried out all the time he was doing it, but he wouldn't stop. Afterwards, he got off me and stood there, saying it's what I'd been asking for all along, and now that he'd done it, it would be better the next time and I would get to enjoy it. After he'd left, I lay there in pain. There was a lot of blood running between my legs. I was crying my eyes out and knew I had to get away before he did it again. I was in such a panic that I just made a dash for it. Luckily I got away before anyone heard or noticed I'd gone. And that's when I saw you walking along the street. I hoped you would help me, remembering how you had tried to help me before."

"I should never have let them keep you there. I should have taken you with us."

"I wish you had, but you couldn't …"

"What the blazes?" Michael exclaimed as he walked in and took in the scene, a hint of panic in his shocked expression.

Michael was feeling totally exhausted as he made his way home. It had been a tough day, a very tough day with no let-up. Fisty had driven him hard, and he could feel it in every muscle of his body. His hands were hurting the most and were bleeding even though they had been bandaged. But he had a smile on his face, knowing that when he got home, as he now looked upon Mary's apartment as being his home, both her and a nice meal would be waiting for him.

"Don't be angry, Michael. This is Holly, and she's in a terrible state. She's been beaten and raped."

"What kind of man would do a thing like that?" he asked, looking across at Holly, who was sitting in the chair with Mary carefully cleaning the wounds on her face.

"Lord Blamfont in this case," Mary said solemnly.

"Lord Blamfont." He nodded slowly. "Why does that man's name keep haunting me? It's about time someone sorted him out. He bullies because he enjoys it and loves the power it gives him."

"They will in time," Mary said assuredly.

"Who? They are still the power in the land and no one can touch them."

"It won't be like that forever. Things will change. People are already calling for change."

"Yes, but nobody seems to be listening." Michael snorted contemptuously.

"Anyway, we have to take care of Holly. We can't let her roam the streets as they're sure to be out looking for her," Mary told him, concern shadowing the contours of her face.

"I suppose so. There is nowhere else for her to go, and there's no way she's ever going back to that bastard. I swear, one day I'll do him some damage."

"I haven't cooked us any dinner because of what's happened."

"How did Holly get here?" he asked Mary, curious to

know how Holly knew where they were living.

"She found me in the street. I was just walking back from Madame Rosita's when—"

"You went to Madame Rosita's? Why?" he asked, confusion flickering in his eyes.

"Because I was thinking of going back to work," she said, meeting his eyes squarely.

Holly turned her head to look at Mary, surprised by the announcement. "How could you think of wanting to go back there?"

"I need to work. I'm not the sort to hang around the house all day doing the daily chores. I'm not used to it, and I feel bored."

An ugly thought rolled to the front of Michael's mind, and he tried to shut it out. "You mean you want to go back to being a prostitute?"

"I *am* a prostitute, in case you've forgotten, and I was only thinking the extra money would help with the food and other things. Clothes, women's things, cleaning materials, coal—they all have to be paid for."

She could see the hurt on his face as she said, "We'll talk about it later. In the meantime, I must see to Holly's wounds, give her some laudanum, and make her comfortable. Then I'll find something for us to eat."

"Laudanum? What's that?"

"It's what Madame Rosita gave us for the curse."

"The curse?"

"Periods. When we have them, it helps take the pain away."

"I see," he said sheepishly, not really understanding what she was telling him.

Chapter 20

Today we're going to do the farmer's walk," Fisty told Michael as soon as he'd arrived for another day's training.

"What's the farmer's walk?"

"You grab a sandbag in each hand, hold yourself straight, and try to walk as far as you can without dropping them. I have half-filled them to begin with, and I'll gradually fill them with more sand to increase the weight and see if you can still walk the same distance. It helps to strengthen the back, arms, wrists, and legs."

"You don't let up, do you?" Michael said, trying to keep a note of despair out of his voice.

"What's the matter, Michael?" Fisty asked, sensing the unfamiliar edge to his voice.

"Nothing," he said, his tone becoming sharp.

"Michael, let's get something clear: I don't want any secrets between us. I know all about secrets and not wanting tell someone what is worrying you. If I had spoken out about my problems, I wouldn't have finished up where I did."

"It's Holly."

"Who's Holly, and what is it that's bothering you about her?"

"It's a long story."

"We have plenty of time, so pick up the sandbags and you can tell me as you do the farmer's walk."

Michael bent down and picked the bags, one in each hand. He straightened up, took a long deep breath, and let it out slowly as he began to walk around the squared-off area. "Holly was badly beaten and raped by Lord Blamfont, whom she was working for as a maid."

"How do you know this Holly?"

This was the difficult part he didn't want to tell Fisty, but he knew deep down he had to. "She had come off one of the boats from Ireland, her mother having died on the voyage over because of the filthy conditions of the hold they were forced to travel in. I know because that's the same way I came across. Anyway, Leon and I, that's when I worked for Madame Rosita, and—"

"Madame Rosita, that evil woman. A curse upon her house! She will have to give account of her actions on the Day of Judgement," Fisty said in a reverent tone. "What did she have to do with it?" he asked.

"Leon and I were sent to the docks to look for what I believed were girls looking for work as domestic servants. Holly was the girl we found. It was only later when I heard screaming that I learned they were trying to force her to become a prostitute. I and Mary tried to rescue her."

"And who is Mary?"

"The girl I'm living with."

"You're living in sin?"

"Yes. She was thrown out the same time as I was for trying to help Holly. Mary kindly took me in; otherwise, I don't where I would have ended up. She's the best thing that's happened to me, and I don't care what anybody thinks," he said with a hint of defiance in his voice.

"Who was the rapist?" Fisty asked, not wanting to pursue the matter of Michael's living in sin any further, knowing it would affect their relationship if he did.

"Lord Blamfont, the same man who threw us out of our cottage in Ireland," he told him, the anger he felt giving his legs strength despite the weight he was carrying. "I've sworn one day I will get my revenge on that bastard if it's the last thing I do, for causing the death of my mother and father."

"Revenge is mine, sayeth the Lord," Fisty reminded him.

"Well, I don't see the Lord doing anything about it. Where was He when the whole of Ireland was starving and people were dying?"

"Is it possible the reason you feel as if God doesn't see you or your problems or care about you is because you are focused on yourself instead of Him, as I was at one time? The Lord works in mysterious ways. You mustn't blame the good Lord for all the wrongs that happen. It is the work of the Devil. The Devil is just as much an actual being as God Himself. The Bible tells us of God's good work. It also tells of the Devil's evil doings and says that he should not be underestimated for he is cunning, clever, and an opportunist."

"Then Lord Blamfont is surely the Devil."

"Not the Devil himself, but one who serves the Devil and will forever be with the Devil and perish with him, for God declared that all who side with him will surely die, both physically and spiritually."

Michael came to a stop and dropped the sandbags, exhausted and breathing heavily.

"Right, that's not bad for the first attempt, but I expect you to carry them farther tomorrow. Have a rest and some refreshment, and then I want to try you on a traditional Chinese method of strengthening the grip by thrusting your hand in a bucket of sand and squeezing handfuls of the sand as hard as you can."

* * * *

Mary walked to the grocer's to get some fresh food, amongst others things, including bandages and some soothing cream for Holly's pain, but as she turned the corner into the main street, she heard a commotion with one voice sounding louder above the rest. Curious, she crossed over to where a group of women were crowded around a woman standing on a wooden box talking to them. She moved closer, eager to hear what the woman was saying.

"When will the government listen to us? Year after year we keep complaining, but it seems no one wants to listen to our plight. We are scorned by the rich, who say a woman's place is in the home and that she has no place in politics. But I ask you, what is so wrong with women wanting rights, the right to own property, the right to think, and the right to divorce a husband who treats her as his slave? What is wrong with women wanting freedom and justice to eradicate poverty and ignorance, for our children to be given an education so they have a better chance in life, which has been denied them for so long? So, my friends, come and join us. Because the more we come together, the more we can help the cause of freedom, justice, honesty, and truth and bring about a true religion, a righteous government, and good laws to protect women."

At the end of her speech, the crowd of women broke into loud applause, cheering her words.

As Mary turned away, the words the woman had spoken about eradicating poverty and ignorance were racing around in her head and made her think that she should embrace the cause for women's rights and stop the abuse women suffer because men think women are their property and have the right to do with them as they please. Like Lord Blamfont thinking he had the right to do to Holly whatever he wanted. It made Mary angry. She quickened her step to the grocery as an idea began to form in her mind.

"We're going to take Lord Fucking Blamfont to court. You are going to accuse him of beating and raping you," Mary told Holly excitedly once she'd hurried into the apartment and plonked the groceries down on the table.

Holly looked up ponderously. "But how do we do that? And who would believe me?"

"The jury, if we get the right solicitor."

"I can't afford a solicitor," Holly exclaimed, a hint of panic in her shocked expression.

Mary looked at her anguished face. "No, but I can. It will cost about a guinea, and it will be money well spent to get that bastard."

"Do you know a solicitor?"

"Yes, as a matter of fact I do. And I think I might be able to get him to do it for nothing," she said with a quirky smile.

* * * *

170

Mr Makepiece was a balding man in his fifties with a beer belly and a rounded jovial face. His office was comfortably furnished with a solid oak desk set against the curtained window overlooking the street. The walls on either side of the desk were lined with bookcases filled with leather-bound volumes on various aspects of law.

He looked up at Mary over the top of his spectacles, a mixture of surprise and embarrassment spreading across his face as he saw her walk into his office. She felt his eyes sliding over her legs, hips, waist, and breasts as he awkwardly got to his feet and shuffled around from behind his desk and proffered his hand.

"Sorry if I looked surprised. I didn't recognise the name Bagley when you made the appointment."

"Why should you? You've only ever known me as Mary since you've been coming to Madame Rosita's to fuck me and the other girls," Mary reminded him. She saw him wince, shame filling his face as he walked back behind his desk and plopped down on his leather chair.

"So what is it I can do for you?" he asked with a petulant tone in his voice, not sure why she was there, fearful she was going to attempt some kind of blackmail.

"I want you to prosecute a case of a savage beating and rape," she said, her face brimming with anxiety.

His face matched her anxiety as he looked gravely at her. "Am I to presume it is you who is the victim of the alleged rape?" he asked, feeling a stirring in his groin at the thought of her being raped.

"No, it is a young innocent girl beaten and raped by her master," Mary snapped, giving him a narrowed look, angry at his assumption.

"I see. And who is her master, the alleged perpetrator of this crime?" he asked solemnly.

"Lord Blamfont."

The shock on his face widened. A sense of foreboding tightened in his chest as he repeated the name. "Lord Blamfont, you say?" The shock turned to a look of bewilderment.

"Yes, the bastard. And I'm determined to get him for what he did."

He shot her a wary look. "It is not going to be that easy. You are accusing one of the landed gentry, and—"

"I don't give a flying fuck. Landed gentry or not, he beat and raped a young girl, a virgin, and he must pay for it. That's the law of the land."

"The law of the land, Miss Bagley, is not as you think or wish it to be. It is money that makes the law, and the law protects money. And the courts tend to protect the people with money."

"But that's unfair."

"Fairness is decided not by some divine being but by those in authority," Mr Makepiece said gravely.

Mary took a deep breath as she wondered what he was going to say next. "Does that mean you won't take the case?"

"It depends," he said, thinking of what to answer.

"On what?" she asked irritably.

"The thing is, men are capable of many things, but that does not mean men do what they are capable of. Proving he beat and raped this girl could be difficult, very difficult," he said, experiencing a twinge of guilt. "Rape is generally considered by the courts to be an attack on a woman defined as respectable by a complete stranger of a lower social class, leaving her with severe physical injuries besides the actual rape. Respectable men, however, who sexually harass, molest, or rape a domestic servant seem to be regarded as incapable of such a crime, defined as the acts of a bestial subhuman underclass. The courts generally consider women of the lower class as capricious. Their moments of rationality, as far as their employers are concerned, are selective and untrustworthy."

"So what you're saying is the courts will let him get away with it?"

"The problem is, the rules of evidence tend to help the men to defend themselves against charges of rape. Evidentiary rules govern what information can be made available to the jury during a trial and what weight the jury may assign to that information. Juries aren't sophisticated; they're just ordinary people, some bored and some wishing they weren't there at all. Usually they don't really understand what's going on, so they look for things they can understand. For example, do they like the look of the accused? Is he the type capable of such violence? Does he look guilty? What would they themselves have felt if the victim had been their daughter? Any trial is an ordeal, but a woman making an accusation of rape can be expected to be questioned in great detail about her personal life, particularly her sex life, and—"

"But Holly has never had a sex life. She was still a virgin when that bastard raped her," Mary angrily interrupted him.

"A man can only be found guilty of rape if his victim can demonstrate that she had physically attempted to resist but had been overpowered. If she was not physically bruised in the attempt to protect herself, then she would have little chance of proving her case."

"Holly was beaten black and blue for resisting, for fuck's sake."

"So you say, but if a woman does not promptly make a complaint, then there is little chance of her complaint being heard, because a delayed complaint is more likely to be considered by the courts to have been fabricated, either because the woman was ashamed of having consented to sexual intercourse or because she had been rejected by her lover and wanted revenge. Or she had simply fantasised about being raped. Judges play a major role in conducting trials. They are allowed to examine witnesses and the accused, and in their summing up of the case they often state their views on what the potential outcome of the trial should be. Sometimes judges place pressure on jurors, asking them how they had reached their verdict and sometimes asking them to reconsider it."

"Holly would have no idea how to make a complaint. All she was concerned with was getting away from that man. It was me who had the idea of charging him. So you reckon we don't stand a cat in hell's chance?"

"Not necessarily, but the law, particularly in this case, doesn't come cheap. My initial fee will be one guinea. Can you afford that?"

"Yes, I can afford that and whatever else it takes to get the bastard."

"Well, you'll be pleased to know the courts are allowed to reimburse a prosecutor's fees and expenses if the person making the allegation is poor and a conviction is obtained. There is a risk, of course, in that if you are not successful, you will be ordered to pay the defendant's, the court's, and your own costs."

"Holly is poor for sure, jobless and homeless," Mary said, forcing herself to perk up.

"And where is she now?"

"At my place, where I'm taking care of her and her injuries."

"I see. Well, I'd better come and have a look at her injuries and take a statement. When would be a good time?"

"Now, before the wounds start to heal up," she invited him.

"Are you certain about this? After all I've said, do you really want to go ahead with this case?"

"You fucking bet I do, because if nothing else, it'll scare the shit out of him, and the public will get to know what an evil bastard he really is."

"That is assuming you win, because if you lose, the public will believe you and Holly are the real evil ones. And he could countersue for libel. So I urge caution. I will need a doctor with me to carry out the actual examination as it will be his evidence that will count in court."

Chapter 21

Most of the old prize fighters prefer to aim for the solar plexus instead of the face; that's because they want to protect their hands. But I learned the head is a better target, and for that you need to keep the elbow bent at an angle of ninety degrees. The benefit of that is that the punch is faster and you can be certain you are going to hit what you're aiming at," Fisty explained as he and Michael began another intensive day of training.

Sir Richard had come down to watch them training and was becoming a little impatient with Michael. He was anxious to see him fight, having gotten tired of just parading him in front of his dinner guests. It used to amuse him to watch the women's reaction as they stared at him stripped to the waist in his tight breeches, his muscles bulging, particularly as the perception was that respectable women felt little or no sexual arousal, and if they did, they did everything possible not show it. Only those of the lower class, abnormal and pathological loose women, were perceived to feel or display any sexual desire.

Sir Richard knew that a man who patronised a fighter gained status among his peers because it showed he was willing to lose and could afford to risk losing in an effort to win big. Patronage of this kind was seen as a mark of courage, so he needed his protégé to have a real fight to prove he had been astute in choosing Michael. He decided he would have to look around for a potential challenger.

Incredibly he didn't have to look around for long as the opportunity came a few days later in a way he could never have expected, when a travelling fair enquired whether they could pitch in one of the fields he owned on the outskirts of the city.

Sir Richard happily agreed, welcoming the extra income this would produce as the field was fallow, awaiting cultivation.

On the first day of the fair, he decided to go and have a look around to make sure they were not doing anything to damage his field. He was surprised to see the varied number of sideshows, waxworks, freak shows, menageries, peep shows, glass-blowing acts, sword swallowers, and tattooists, but what excited him most was when he came across the boxing booth. It had an elaborately painted wooden facade with a platform, on which stood three heavy-set boxers stripped to the waist with a man holding a loud hailer, challenging anyone to take on any one of the boxers and go three rounds to win a cash prize.

As Sir Richard stood watching, becoming more intrigued, a local hardman, a little worse for drink, was being coaxed to have a go by his distraught wife, obviously desperate for them to win some money.

He paid the admission fee and followed the crowd inside to what was a fairly large tent that could, he reckoned, hold eighty to a hundred people.

He smiled as the drunken man, unsteady on his feet, struggled to strip off his jacket and shirt to the amusement of the crowd. Then he ducked to enter the roped-off square at the end of the tent, where the professional boxer was waiting for him.

"Right. Come up to the scratch, shake hands, go back to your corners, and come out fighting when you hear the bell," the booth owner instructed them, acting as referee.

As soon as the bell sounded, the drunken man came out of his corner and started swinging wild punches, all of them missing their target, the professional easily dodging them.

The crowd kept cheering on the drunken man while the professional kept the fight going by dancing around, inviting the drunken man to hit him.

Sir Richard allowed himself to smile at the one-sided fight, knowing it would take only one solid punch from the professional to end it. The punch came quicker than expected. The drunken man's knees buckled and he fell unconscious.

The crowd reacted with a mixture of boos and cheers as they sauntered back out of the tent, clearly having enjoyed the spectacle. It made Sir Richard think this could be the perfect opportunity to test his protégé.

Excited at the thought, he went over and introduced himself to the owner, suggesting he would like to challenge his best fighter with his own fighter whom he was training.

Sam Bicket, the owner, looked at him suspiciously, as he did with everyone. He thought he might be trying to get one over on him.

"I'm prepared to put up the stake money," Sir Richard offered.

"How much?" Sam asked, suspicion still showing on his face.

"Twenty-five pounds, winner takes all."

Sam had never had a challenge like this before, one in which he didn't have to risk his own money, so he readily accepted.

"In order to make the fight more interesting, we should let everyone know about the fight and the stake money. In fact, I will increase the stake to thirty pounds to make it more exciting."

* * * *

On the night of the fight, a large crowd had already gathered. It was getting bigger by the minute as Michael and his opponent were paraded on the platform in front of the booth, both stripped to the waist, displaying their muscular bodies.
"This is crazy. We'll never get all those people into the tent. They'll wreck the place in no time," Sam said, becoming increasingly worried.

Sir Richard, quick to see the potential as more and more people gathered, keen to see a real fight, replied, "I have an idea that could benefit both of us."

"Anything to stop the numbers. At this rate there is no way we can stage the fight."

"Why don't we arrange the fight for tomorrow night in the next field?"

"We'd have to get the owner's permission. What happens if we don't?"

"I own it. We can accommodate as many as want to come and see a good fight. And I will increase the stake to fifty pounds."

Sam's eyes lit up at the thought. "That would be fantastic. But I have to ask, is your man any good? Because if he's anything like the ones who come to the booth, we'll have a riot on our hands."

"I rather think it's your man you have to worry about. Just make sure you pick the best you have, for as you say, if he goes down at the first hard punch, then there will be a riot."

"You think your man is better than mine? Perhaps I should remind you that my fighters are all professionals and have never lost a fight."

"That's because they've only been fighting drunken idiots like the one I saw, but this time whoever you choose will be up against a real fighter, sober and determined to win."

"My man, the one I'm going to choose, has been up against some of the best-known champions of the area and has beaten them all," Sam said with an air of confidence.

"In that case, it promises to be one hell of a fight," Sir Richard countered, showing the same amount of confidence.

"You're offering to put up the stake money, but what about the gate money? We're surely not going to let them in for free."

"No, of course not. We split it equally. Unless you would like to gamble. Winner takes all?"

Sam looked at him, uncertainty spreading across his face. "That's one hell of a wager. I'm not sure …"

"If you're not sure of your man, then maybe we should forget the idea. As you said, the crowd could turn nasty if it looks like a fix," Sir Richard taunted him.

"No, that won't happen. You're on," Sam agreed, offering his hand to seal the deal.

"Right, then you had better explain things to the crowd before it's too late."

Sam swallowed hard. "I hope they like the idea, but I'd rather you speak to them. They're more likely to listen to you than to me, I mean, you being a gentleman like."

Sir Richard climbed up onto the platform. "Ladies and gentlemen," he shouted as loud as he could in order to get their attention. "As you will have all noticed, there is lot of you, far too many to accommodate in the small tent, which means many of you would not be able to get in and consequently would miss the fight. So what we are planning is to arrange the fight for tomorrow, to be held in the neighbouring field, where we can accommodate everyone."

"What about those of us who have already paid to see the fight?" one of the crowd shouted out.

"All those who have bought tickets will be given free entry. So bring your tickets with you, and tell your friends and everyone else. I promise this is going to be one hell of a fight. You won't want to miss it."

* * * *

"How's Holly?" Michael asked as he ambled in after another day of intensive training.

"That man is going to wear you out," Mary said, looking at the exhausted state of him.

"That's because I've got my first fight coming up," he told her, slumping down on the nearest chair.

"You mean a real fight?" she responded, excited and worried at the same time.

"Yes, a real fight. You know the fair that's come to town? Well, they have a boxing booth, and Sir Richard has challenged that I can beat their champion. Sir Richard has put up a stake of fifty pounds, and if I win, we will be fifty pounds better off."

"That's fantastic. It will help towards the legal costs."

Michael looked at her, stunned by the remark. "Legal costs? What legal costs?"

"Holly is suing Lord Blamfont for rape."

"Blamfont," he repeated disparagingly. "You seriously think you can take on a man who is shrewd, resourceful, and totally unscrupulous, who considers bending the law to be part of everything he does?"

"Someone has got to stop the bastard. He can't be allowed to get away with it," Mary said, a wave of anger engulfing her.

"No, he can't be allowed to get away with it, but I don't know anything about the law except that it seems to be only for the rich."

"I'm paying for it and have got a good solicitor."

"Well, you'd better watch your back, because you're threatening his reputation. And when he finds out, if he hasn't already, he'll come after you, court or no court."

"Let him try," Mary said defiantly.

"He will. You can be certain of that. My advice is, stop it before it gets out of hand."

"So what about Holly? Do we just do nothing?"

"She'll suffer a damn sight more if you continue with it. We'll get our revenge on that bastard one day in a way he'll never expect."

"How?"

"I don't know, but I'll find a way. I haven't forgotten what he did to my parents, and I never will. I'll make him pay for it one way or another."

"OK, I'll talk to the solicitor," Mary reluctantly agreed.

Chapter 22

It was a cold evening with a clear blue cloudless sky, the perfect weather for a gathering. Word of the upcoming fight had spread widely throughout the city, and the crowd was already building up, hustling and bustling in the queues to get into the field with some clambering over fences or scrambling through hedges to get in without paying, very much to the consternation of the Sam Bicket, who knew there was very little he could do to stop them but who was still confident he was going to make a lot of money, having set up a number of betting stands around the field.

Sir Richard arrived with Michael and Fisty and was delighted to see the ever-increasing crowd, many of them already well imbibed with alcohol, which made him wish he had set up a marquee with a bar, something he would remember for the next time. He was also delighted to see many of his peers arriving in their coaches, all dressed in their finery, keen to see the fight.

Sam's eyes widened and a wicked smile flittered across his face as he saw Sir Richard approaching with Fisty and two others he didn't recognise.

"Well, well, Fisty Fitzgerald, what a nice surprise. So this is the man you think can beat my man. The only thing Fisty could win these days is a drinking contest. The way you spoke, Sir Richard, I thought you were going to come up with some real tough guy, not a washed-up has-been," Sam said derisively.

Sir Richard looked at him wryly. "Michael Flanagan here is the one who is going to beat your man."

Sam's confident smile drained from his face as he looked at the powerful muscular body of the man. "You are full of surprises. But muscle is not enough. Boxing is a skill. It takes experience, which my man has plenty of, so it looks like being an interesting fight," Sam said, adopting a more consolatory expression.

"Indeed it does. And may the best man win."

"Let me explain the rules in case your man doesn't understand them," Sam continued, ignoring the remark while giving Michael another once-over. "Kicking, biting, and gouging are not allowed, and neither is hitting or grabbing below the belt, but anything else is. The opponent can be knocked or thrown to the ground either by picking him up or by grabbing him around the waist. Once an opponent has been knocked or thrown to the ground, it is permitted to drop on him, but it is not permitted to punch or inflict damage while he is on the ground. There will be a thirty-second break to allow the floored opponent to recover and get to his feet, although the rounds themselves can last any length of time, until one of the contestants falls or is unable to continue. Each opponent is allowed a second and a bottleman if he wishes. I will act as referee, but generally we rely on the spectators to be the guardians of fair play."

Sir Richard looked at Fisty for confirmation. Fisty nodded his approval.

"Right, then let's get the show on the road," Sir Richard said excitedly.

"Just one more thing: you realise a fight of this nature is illegal. Should the police arrive, they will stop the fight and we'll have no winner. And we could possibly face prosecution," Sam warned.

"Have no worries on that score. The chief constable is a personal friend and has already laid a bet on my man, as have many others, including the local Justice of the Peace," Sir Richard assured him.

"That is very reassuring news. I have erected a tent over there for your man to change in. As soon as we've got the crowd organised, we'll get them to the ring, which is staked out with a rope. We'll parade the fighters as you tie the money to the stake so that people can see it, encouraging those who as yet haven't had a chance to lay a bet," Sam explained, feeling a little more confident.

"Right, this is how it works. I will be acting as your second, and Charlie boy here will be your bottleman. And—" Fisty began to explain to Michael.

"What does being my second mean?"

"The second is there to look after you and take care of your injuries and get you back in the ring. Most seconds are fighters themselves. Should your fight end very quickly, then traditionally the seconds, hence the term, are expected to step into the ring to keep the crowd happy and cause them to feel that they're getting their money's worth."

"Fuck me, I didn't think there'd be this many," Mary exclaimed as she and Holly joined the queue at the gate.

Holly was feeling better, but her face was still showing the bruises. She had covered her head with a hood to hide them. "I don't like seeing men fight. What if Michael gets hurt?" Holly said worriedly to Mary.

"Badly hurt. He's going to get his head bashed in. He don't stand a bleedin' chance. I should know," a drunken voice behind her spoke out.

"It's the other guy who's going to get his head bashed in, just you wait and see," Mary told him, turning on him angrily.

"Well, he sure as hell flattened me, and I'm considered a good fighter," the drunken man countered.

"Well, you obviously weren't that good, were you?" she retorted, not knowing he was the drunkard who had made the stupid challenge in the booth a few days ago.

The field was filling up fast with the motley crowd known as the fancy. They were pressing forward, pushing and shoving for space, with little fights breaking out as people sought to get the best spots closest to the ring. Mixing amongst them were thieves, pickpockets, prostitutes, professional gamblers, and purveyors of pornographic pictures known as French postcards, all out to make a score.

The ring was a rope, squared off by four stakes, one at each corner, driven hard into the ground with a line scratched across the middle, known as the scratch. There were no stools. Between rounds, the fighters were to sit on the bent knee of the bottleman while the second attended to the fighter's injuries.

A great cheer went up as the two fighters approached and threw their hats into the ring as a traditional acknowledgement that they both had accepted the challenge.

"Here is the stake money, the sum of fifty pounds for the winner," Sir Richard announced, tying the bag containing the fifty pounds to one of the stakes so that everyone could see it and nobody could run off with it. The crowd roared their approval.

"And I bleedin' challenged him for a miserly guinea," the drunken man moaned to the man next to him.

"Then you must have been more pissed than you are now," the man next to him replied.

Michael was the first to get into the ring. Now stripped to the waist, he was wearing tight-fitting knee-length breeches and canvas boots. He walked to his corner and sat down on the bottleman's knee as Fisty spoke to him. "You've been training for several months now, and you've come on spectacularly well. Just remember all the things I've taught you. Place each punch accurately, being careful not to strain your wrist and break your thumbs. Be light on your feet and keep moving so as to make yourself a harder target to hit. Now have a good swig of water and go out there and show me all my efforts have been in vain," Fisty said, taking the bottle from the bottleman.

Tom Dyer, Sam's man, was next into the ring, followed by Sam himself, who raised his hands for silence from the boisterous and noisy crowd. "My lords and ladies, gentlemen and fancies, you are about to see a great fight between two of the best fighters you'll see anywhere. In the corner to my right is the challenger, all the way from Ireland, Michael Flanagan, weighing in at eleven stone, eight pounds.

There was a mixture of cheers and boos—cheers from the Irish and boos from the Geordies. "Ádh mór ort," the large section of the Irish crowd shouted out.

"Defending the challenger is the one and only Tom Dyer, the current champion of Liverpool and surrounding areas, weighing in at twelve stone, six pounds."

The betting stands were crowded with people frantically trying to get their bets on before the fight started. The odds started at ten to one against Michael as the underdog.

Sir Richard was pleased with the way the odds were going, thinking that if Michael won, he was going to make a killing.

Sam gave a loud blast on his whistle to announce the fight was about to begin and to summon the fighters to the middle of the ring. "You know the rules, so let's have a clean fight. Go back to your corners. When I blow the whistle, come up to the scratch and start fighting. May the best man win."

As the fight began, those closest to the ring watched with delight as Michael took up his stance and started to move around the ring, easily avoiding the short, sharp jabs Tom was throwing, but others became worried as it seemed Michael was making no attempt to throw any punches himself.

"Come on, show us you can punch too," a group of the Irish crowd shouted out.

"Nah, too frightened to 'urt his 'ands 'e is," one of the Geordies shouted across.

But Michael ignored them. He was carefully putting all the lessons he had been taught by Fisty into practice. *Be patient, size up your opponent, try not to be hit, and watch how he moves, how quick he is on his feet, and how hard he punches. And when you're sure of his every move, then you can start to attack.*

It was about eight minutes into the fight with the crowd beginning to boo Michael and shout all kinds of abuse, encouraging Tom to keep jabbing. Tom was thinking he was onto an easy win and that it was only a matter of time before he would catch Michael with a solid punch and the fight would be over. But Michael, knowing Tom was already beginning to slow, threw out a right, his arm rigid. It shot through Tom's guard, striking him full in the face.

To everyone's surprise Tom went down. His second and his bottleman rushed in and dragged him to his corner with his supporters beginning to boo him, shouting, "He's got no bottom."

"Do you hear them? You'd better get out there and show them you've got plenty of bottom," Sam said, rushing over. As Tom's second, Sam set about trying to revive him, as well as trying to stop the blood that was oozing from his broken nose, as he sat on the bottleman's knee.

"That was perfect," Fisty told Michael, giving him a swig of beer as he sat on the bottleman's knee. "Take it steady. Don't go in for the kill. Let him come at you, but don't get into a slogging match, because that's when he'll try to wrestle you and use dirty tricks. I trained you as a boxer. A few more punches like the one you gave him and you'll soon finish him as he's obviously not the fighter he once was."

Amongst the crowd the betting was changing dramatically with the odds narrowing on Michael from 6 to 1, to 5 to 1, down to 4 to 1.

After the thirty seconds allowed, Sam blew the whistle for the second round. Tom was much slower coming up to the scratch. As Michael took up his stance, Tom lowered his head and rushed forward, trying to grab Michael around the waist, but Michael saw it coming. He stepped back and brought up an uppercut that caught Tom smack under the chin, jerking his head back, sending him reeling across the ring and hitting the rope. The fancies nearest the ring shoved him violently back into the centre, where Michael was waiting. Michael started to pummel him with a series of punches to the head and body, culminating with a perfect right hook to the side of the head. Tom's knees buckled, and he dropped to the ground.

His second and his bottleman rushed in and dragged him to their corner, his body now badly bruised and his face spattered and streaming with blood.

The odds now switched to 2 to 1 against.

"You can go in for the kill now. Another rally of punches

and he'll be finished. I've taught you better than I thought," Fisty said with a satisfied grin.

Sir Richard was grinning even more, realising he was going to make a killing.

Sam blew the whistle for the third round, and Tom's second hauled him off the bottleman's knee and shoved him forward to make sure he came up to the scratch in time, or else he would be counted out.

Tom was wary this time, trying his best to keep out of range so as to give himself time to recover, but he was still slow, allowing Michael to pick him off with carefully aimed punches to the stomach to knock the wind out of him. Then he launched a series of blows to the head and body.

Tom, having little defence against the influx of blows that were pounding into his body, finally telescoped to the ground. This caused a great cheer to erupt from the Irish, mixed with boos from the Geordies, who started to shout, "Fix, fix. It's a stitch-up. *Fix, fix.*"

In that split second, the Irish turned on the Geordies, shouting, "No fix. No fix. He won cos he's better than your excuse for a fighter," causing a fight to break out that quickly spread amongst the crowd with all kinds of weapons suddenly being produced—sticks, pickaxes, iron bars, cudgels, and anything else the crowd could lay their hands on.

"Let's get the hell out of here," Fisty said, grabbing the stake money as the intensity of the fighting increased.

"Get him out of here before they turn on us," Sam said in panic as he, the second, and the bottleman dragged the semiconscious Tom out of the ring.

Fortunately the crowd were not only fighting amongst themselves but also were now turning on the bookies and professional gamblers, taking no notice of what was happening in the ring, allowing the bookies and gamblers to escape to the adjoining field and hide in the boxing booth.

Mary and Holly had managed to get clear of the fighting by scrambling through a hedge into the next field, catching their clothes and stockings on the prickly brambles.

"How could they think it was a fix? Michael beat him fair and square," Mary said once they were clear of the fighting. "I hope he's all right. I couldn't see what happened with all that was going on. He won't be looking for us as I didn't tell him we were coming."

"Why didn't you tell him we were coming?"

"I know he wouldn't have liked the idea of us being here. I think he thought he was going to lose."

"I did see him running off with the others, but where they were going I couldn't see with all the fighting," Holly said with a hapless shrug of her shoulders.

"The best thing we can do is go home and wait for him there," Mary said, taking Holly's hand and leading her off.

* * * *

"I'm ruined," Sam uttered, looking positively stricken.

Sir Richard took a deep calming breath before he said, "Sympathy is something I don't have time for. You know the game and the pitfalls better than anyone, and you know the people you're dealing with, so you should be able to see trouble before it arrives. And I don't need to remind you, you owe me two grand."

Sam's body began bristling with anger and frustration. "I know. And I took other bets. I was so sure Tom would win. He has never been beaten before and is known to have gone twenty rounds lasting three hours, but your man took him down in no time. Where the hell did you find him? I have to say, Fitzy certainly trained him well. I'd be happy to take him off your hands. He'd do well in the booth," Sam offered.

"No way. He is going to go on and become a champion," Sir Richard told him, his voice full of confidence.

"I suppose you wouldn't consider buying the booth?"

"You suppose right. And if you don't honour your debt, I will have you thrown into debtors' prison, and then I could take the booth for nothing," Sir Richard told him without any sense of compassion.

The thought changed his face. "You are a hard man," Sam said accusingly, his tone laced with sarcasm. "You will have to give me time. I can't just lay my hands on that kind of money right away," Sam pleaded.

"I will give you until close of business tomorrow, no longer. And if you have not paid the debt in full, I will foreclose on your business, and you will end up in court and debtors' prison," Sir Richard told him, his tone firm and definite. "Right. Now that we have got that settled, I think we can safely make our way out of here," he added, indicating to Michael, Fisty, and the lad that they should leave.

Chapter 23

I'm afraid to have to tell you, Lord Blamfont has engaged Sir Peter Rushington, QC, as his barrister. And, I should advise you, he is one of the most formidable barristers in the country. He will tear Holly to threads when he gets her in the witness box—and you too. So my advice is to tell Holly to lick her wounds and forget about everything," Mr Makepiece explained to Mary.

He was afraid for her. She could sense the genuine concern in his voice and could see it in his eyes. Her face tightened with worry. "I see," she said, letting the words hang for a moment. "Then are you saying there is nothing we can do? The clever bastard hires a smart lawyer and gets away with it?"

"Unfortunately a clever lawyer uses the law rather they obeys it, and Sir Peter, as I said, is one hell of a smart lawyer, or barrister I should say. To my knowledge, I don't think he's ever lost a case."

"Well, maybe this will be the first time," Mary said with an air of defiance.

"You mean you still want to go ahead, despite what I've just told you?" Mr Makepiece asked with a look of incredulity.

"Yes, because the bastard is guilty and should pay for what he did. We have my, your, and the doctor's testimony, and the fact that Blamfont bought Holly from Madame Rosita."

"We can't prove that, and Madame Rosita, I'm sure, if asked, will testify that Holly was already working at her establishment as a prostitute, that Lord Blamfont in his compassionate manner took pity on the girl and offered her a job in his household as a maid, and that she continued to offer

190

her services while in his employ."

"But that isn't true."

"You know that and I know that, but just imagine what the jury will think when Sir Peter tells them how it was. Once a whore, always a whore; that is how he will portray Holly."

"Whose fucking side is the law on?" Mary said angrily.

"That is a matter of conjecture. What I'm trying to do is stop you from making a big mistake. The law is loaded against you, and unfortunately barristers sometimes do worse things within the law than most villains dare to do outside of it. The truth depends on which way it is presented, whether as your truth or someone else's lies. In my opinion, you have no chance of winning but every chance of having your life ruined because, as I said, he'll come after you and won't stop until he's ruined you. And I'm worried he might still take some kind of action even after you've dropped the case, because men of his standing don't like to be humiliated and never forget if they are."

"I will have to discuss it with Holly, and I will let you know. Thank you, Mr Makepiece, for your time and your frankness."

"Very well. I will take no further action until I have heard from you," he said, standing up and holding out his hand to shake.

Mary got up from her chair, took his hand and shook it, turned, and walked out, her face scrunched in anger.

* * * *

"The law is an ass as Mr Bumble said. He's right: the law is a fucking ass," Mary exclaimed the moment she walked back into the apartment.

"Mr Bumble? Who's Mr Bumble?" Holly asked, looking up, surprised.

"Mr Bumble in *Oliver Twist*, when told that a husband bears legal responsibility for his wife's actions, replied, 'If the law supposes that, then the law is an ass.'"

"I don't understand. It didn't have anything to do with his wife," Holly said, a pensive frown creasing her forehead.

"I know, but the point is, I have just come from the solicitor, and he says the odds are stacked against us and we have no chance of winning. He said that if we pursue the case, Lord Fucking Blamfont will come after us and try to destroy us. He might do that anyway if he knows what we're up to, which I guess by now he probably does."

"So what are you going to do?"

"I started thinking on the way back. There are several ways to skin a rabbit as they say. So if we can't beat him one way, then we'll try another," Mary said, her face framed in concentration as the thought took a firm hold on her.

"So what are you thinking of doing?"

"We are going to form a group to help girls keep from being sexually abused."

"How are we going to do that?"

"We will patrol the docks when the boats come in and look for young girls all on their own and get to them before the pimps and brothel keepers get their hands on them. We won't be able to save them all, but we'll save quite a few. And the more people know what we are doing, the more girls we can save. I am going to talk to someone at the *Weekly Star* and tell them about what we are going to be doing, also dropping little hints about what happened to you."

"I don't want my name in the papers," Holly said in panic.

"Your name won't be mentioned, but I will, when the timing is right, drop Lord Fucking Blamfont's name. That'll scare the shit out of him."

"Won't that get us into more trouble?"

"I learned some time ago that some things are worth being afraid of and some things are not, and I'm not afraid of that bastard," Mary said vehemently. "And I've thought of a name for the group: HARASA," she announced proudly.

"HARASA? What's that mean?"

"Help against Rape and Sexual Abuse. Like it?"

"Love it," Holly said, joining in Mary's enthusiasm.

"Good. I'll go to the newspaper later today."

* * * *

"Well, have you got my money?" Sir Richard demanded after storming into the boxing booth with Fisty as backup.

Sam felt the muscles in his chest tighten as sweat started to trickle down his face. "It's a lot of money …"

"I know how much it is. What I want to know is, have you got it?"

"I'm still trying to get it together. I hope to have it by—"

"The end of today, I expect you at the manor not later than six o'clock. Otherwise I will have you arrested. A bet is a bet, and it must be honoured. If you fail to honour that debt, you will most certainly end up in debtors' prison."

"What would you think about a return match, double or quits?" Sam ventured as a desperate last-ditch thought.

"You mean if my man wins again, you pay me double?"

"Exactly."

Sir Richard's eyebrows went up. "But if you can't pay what you owe me now, how the devil are you going to be able to pay me double? No, I've got much bigger plans for my man. Just make sure you are at my place by six o'clock," Sir Richard said hard-heartedly. Then he turned and walked out with Fisty following.

* * * *

"So what's so different about what your group is doing that other female organisations aren't doing already? They all seem to have different aspirations and expectations for the work they do," Stewart Matthews asked with a hint of cynicism as he sat at his desk in the editorial office of the *Weekly Star* newspaper, a pencil poised over his notepad, ready to write down anything worthy of note.

"Helping poor young girls landing on our shores and being lured by false promises into sexual slavery and prostitution by unscrupulous pimps and the landed gentry," Mary answered, studying his appearance.

Stewart Matthews was aged around thirty, she reckoned. He was dressed in a smart but not overtly expensive suit. He had an intelligent face with inquisitive eyes. He had a mop of curly reddish hair and sported a moustache.

"The landed gentry?" Stewart asked, immediately interested. "And what do you know about the landed gentry?"

"You would be surprised. I wanted to charge one of them with rape, but you know the courts, run by the privileged for the privileged. The ordinary person has little chance against them."

"So you were raped?" Stewart said, already excitedly writing the word down on his notepad.

"No, not me. Her name's Holly ..." She stopped, instantly regretting having said the name as she saw him write it down.

"And who is the man alleged to have raped her?" he asked without looking up from his notepad, ready to write down her answer.

"I can't tell you that."

"Can't or won't?"

"Both, but that's not what I came to talk to you about. I want the paper's help by writing a story of what happens to these lonely unsuspecting women who are tricked into becoming sex slaves."

"So how do you know this Holly? Is she your sister, daughter?" he asked reading the name off his notepad.

"No, she was brought into Madame Rosita's and—"

"That whorehouse?" he exclaimed, writing it down. "What is your connection with Madame Rosita?"

"I worked there."

"Interesting. You said you worked there. What as?"

"A prostitute."

"I see," he said, looking at her squarely, but her eyes

didn't waver.

"She threw me out when I tried to save Holly."

"A prostitute wanting to save someone from becoming a prostitute. What made you want to do that? Is it because you are ashamed of being a prostitute?"

"No, I'm not ashamed. And that's the difference. I chose to be a prostitute—nobody forced me—but they tried to force her. She refused, so they started to beat her. Unfortunately I was a part of that until I was shaken out of it by Michael, who tried to rescue her."

"Michael? Who's he?"

She was about to lie, but she thought, *He's a boxing champion now, so why not mention his name?* "Michael Flanagan. He's a fighter."

"You mean the one who knocked out Tom Dyer the other day?"

"Yes, him."

"This is getting more and more intriguing by the minute," Matthews said. "So you and this Michael tried to save the girl Holly from becoming a prostitute working for Madame Rosita?"

"Yes, but we failed, and they kept hold of her. There was nothing we could do, until one day she came running up the street after me, having managed to escape from the bastard who beat and raped her."

"And who was that?" he asked surreptitiously.

"I told you, I can't give you his name," she said firmly.

Matthews put down his pencil. His mouth tightened in a curious expression. "Look, this is an incredible story, but I can't run with it unless I know the name of the rapist. You don't have to worry, a journalist never reveals his sources," he quickly assured her.

"You wouldn't have to. He would know immediately where his name came from."

"Well, you've already told me he's from the landed gentry."

"If you mention that, I'm sure it will stir things up with

them all beginning to panic, wondering amongst themselves which member of the landed gentry is the rapist," she said, adopting a more calculated expression.

"Yes, I can imagine it would. And I'm sure a lot of them will be coming to the office to protest their innocence and complain to the editor, that is, of course, if he allows me to write the story."

She could see the conflicting emotions on his face. "He will, and if I know that bastard as well as I think I do, then he will be the first to come banging on your door."

"You sound like you know him well."

"Oh, I know him well. He's fucked me enough times. But it's his antics in the flagellation room that amused me the most, or should I say horrified me the most."

"Tell me about the flagellation room," he said eagerly, snatching up his pencil, ready to write.

"You're sounding a little naive. Have you never been to a brothel?"

"No, I haven't."

"Really? You surprise me."

"Why do I surprise you?"

"Because I don't know of any man who hasn't at one time or another visited a brothel to get rid of his urges in a way he can't with his wife—or in the stupid belief that as a respectable woman she can't display any sexual feelings."

"That's cynical."

"Maybe, but it's a fact, a case of supply and demand. There would be no whorehouses or prostitutes if there weren't a demand. And you have no idea how perverted the so-called landed gentry can be in their demands."

"I'm beginning to learn. So tell me more about flagellation and our alleged rapist," he said, trying to put some emotion in his voice, but it still sounded lascivious.

"You really want to know?" she asked, arching a disdainful eyebrow.

"Like any journalist, I—"

"Want to know about the evils of sex. I bet the thought

is giving you a hard-on," she said provocatively.

Stewart Matthews shifted uncomfortably in his seat, sensing her looking down at his crotch.

"If I'm to learn and understand more of the character of the alleged rapist, then you need to tell me everything," he said with a slight tone of irreverence.

"Not if you write it from the point of view of what we are going to be doing in trying to save other girls from the same fate," she said encouragingly.

She told him everything and watched his expressions with curious amusement as she explained the details of the flagellation room.

"Very interesting. Watch this space, as they say," he said, offering his hand. "Thank you for coming in."

"My pleasure. You print the story, and he'll be flushed out without your having to name him," she said, shaking his hand vigorously.

Chapter 24

There is a Madame Rosita here to see you, sir," Stevens, the butler, rather disdainfully informed Sir Richard, who was seated at his desk in the study, calculating how much money he'd made from the boxing match, his face ebullient until he heard the name.

"What the blazes is she doing here?"

"Come to collect the three grand you owe me," Madame Rosita announced as she charged into the study, not waiting for the butler to show her in. "I heard you scored big with the boxing match you set up, so I'm here to collect my money."

He waved for Stevens to leave before he said, "Under normal circumstances I would acquiesce, but since you banned me from visiting your establishment, I—"

"What did you expect me to do, allow you to continue running up your account?" she said, interrupting him. There was real antagonism in her voice.

"Yes, because I would have paid you, but when you sent your henchmen to threaten me—"

"One of whom is now your prize fighter, earning you good money," she cut in scornfully. "I could have you sent you to debtors' prison," she added to make her point.

"No, I don't think so, because, one, you don't want the bad publicity a case like this would bring, which would inevitably scare many of your clients away, and two, I could prolong the court action for a very long time, which would in the end cost you more than I owe," he said. There was a hard scoff in his tone.

"As it happens, I've been thinking, and there may be another way of settling the debt," she offered, her voice beginning to quiver with excitement.

"And what is that?" he asked in a dull, flat voice.

"Well, you stole my man Michael, whom I clothed and trained, and—"

"I didn't steal him; you kicked him out," he countered.

"Anyway," she said, waving her hand dismissively. "Since you seem to be able to organise these things, I would like to take a wager on my man beating your man in a boxing match," she challenged, her voice measured and relaxed.

The challenge caught him by surprise, causing him to hesitate. She could see the indecision in his eyes as he drummed his fingers on the desk. "You're really serious?" he finally asked.

"Yes, deadly serious. You see, you forget Leon beat your boy up when he tried to interfere in my business, so I'm confident he can do it again."

"Interesting. So what's the wager?"

"If your man loses, then you pay me double what you owe. If my man loses, I will wipe off your debt and pay you three thousand."

He studied her impassive face. He knew she was a shrewd by nature, but this was something new. *Can she be trusted with a deal like this?* he wondered.

"You're taking a long time to make up your mind. Perhaps the challenge is too much for you. So pay the debt and we'll talk no more of it," she said, turning on her heel and starting to walk out.

"No, wait. You're on. It will take a bit of time to arrange, but I'll sort it out and let you know where and when."

"Then may the best man, or in this case may the best woman, win," she said in a jubilant tone as she strolled out of the study.

* * * *

"Have you read the paper?" Mary asked Holly, handing her a copy of the *Weekly Star*.

"Why, what does it say? You know I can't read, Mary."

"It writes about me, an ex-prostitute ashamed of what

happens in the brothels, wanting to save young girls from being lured into prostitution and to save women in general from all forms of sexual abuse. Then it goes on to write about you and-"

"Me!"

"No, it doesn't mention you by name. He just mentions a servant maid having been hired by a member of the landed gentry who had been in his employ for only a few days when he is alleged to have sexually abused, beaten, and raped her. 'The victim, who cannot be named at this stage, is consulting with solicitors about bringing charges of rape and sexual assault against the alleged assailant,'" Mary read out, refolding the newspaper and placing it back on the table. "It goes on a bit more, but that's the gist of it. It's going to be interesting to see what happens next."

"What do you think will happen next?" Holly asked pensively.

"Oh, I'm pretty sure Lord Fucking Blamfont will be straight down to the newspaper offices, knowing full well the article is referring to him, and demanding they publish some kind of assurance that the article is in no way connected to him."

"What will the papers tell him if he does?"

"They won't tell him anything. They dare not as they could find themselves being sued for libel and—"

"How can he sue for libel? He raped me."

"The problem has always been proving it, and that, as we have found out, is very difficult, if not impossible. The only hope is for the bastard to shoot himself in the foot as they say."

* * * *

"Try to remember, don't try to take his head off, because you can injure yourself if you keep hitting the hardest parts of his skull. Just try to open him up with jabs as you started doing in your last fight. That way you weaken your opponent and make him ready for the killer punch to the jaw," Fisty explained as he and Michael started the day's training.

"Can't we relax a bit? I mean, I've proved how good I am, and—"

"No time to relax. I've got to get you ready for your next fight."

"Next fight?"

"Didn't Sir Richard tell you? He's arranged a match between you and the guy who works at that den of iniquity. The work of Satan is to blind the minds of men to the wickedness they are tempted to, especially the unbelievers who so willingly submit themselves to fornication," Fisty told him in his reverent manner.

"Madame Rosita's brothel?" Michael queried, ignoring his reverent remarks.

"Yes, that woman, evil personified," he said caustically.

"Oh no, not Leon. There's no way I will fight him."

"You have no choice. You fight who Sir Richard tells you to fight."

"No, you don't understand. OK, I had a fight with Leon over trying to rescue Holly, but when I was on the streets, having been beaten up and robbed of the little money I had, Leon came to my rescue and got me a job with Madame Rosita. Had he not found me, I don't know what would have happened to me. I will always owe him that."

Michael was telling Fisty something he had known since they'd first met but had not allowed himself to accept. He had allowed himself to believe that everybody lived by the same rules as he did, but deep down he knew that wasn't the case.

"Respect, honour, and loyalty are good, and I respect you for it, but I don't know how you can get out of this one," Fisty said worriedly.

"Well, one thing is for certain: I will not fight him. I'll fight anybody else, but not Leon."

"Then that is something you are going to have to tell Sir Richard yourself."

* * * *

"You sent for me, Madame?" Leon said politely as soon as he entered her luxuriously furnished private lounge.

Madame Rosita was looking happy. She was relaxing on her chaise lounge, elegantly dressed in a gown, the fullness of her lengthened skirt now increased with the addition of a horsehair crinoline, which had lately become a status symbol of wealth.

She smiled up at Leon and indicated for him to sit. "As of now I would like you to go into strict training," she began. It was said as a suggestion but was clearly meant as an order.

"Training for what, Madame?" he asked subserviently.

"To be the best boxer, for you're going to be fighting that little shit you stopped from taking Holly from us."

"You mean Michael!" he exclaimed, shocked at the revelation.

"Yes, that son of a bitch. And I want you to teach him a lesson he'll never forget, after all I and you did for him, the ungrateful ruffian."

The thought was making him feel unhappy, particularly given the way she was looking at him, studying his reaction.

This was something he wasn't expecting. He began to feel the iron grip of fear constricting his chest. He needed to think, still looking at her, waiting for her to say more.

"Well?" she said.

"Well what?" he replied, not knowing what else to say.

"Aren't you excited at the thought?" she asked, looking at him curiously.

"I don't know. He's the last person I want to fight."

Her eyes narrowed. "Don't tell me you're scared of him?"

"I'm not scared of anyone, but he was a friend, I mean is, and—"

"Exactly, *was* a friend," she said, cutting in. "But not any more. And I've got a lot riding on this, so you've got to train hard, so you don't let me down. Beat him into oblivion, and you will be handsomely rewarded. I happened to mention it to Lord Blamfont, and he's so enthusiastic about the idea of you getting the chance to beat the living daylights out of that ruffian for trying to take Holly away from us that he has offered to put up five hundred pounds' stake money."

Leon inhaled deeply, still wishing he knew what to do or say. "I don't think I—"

"That's right," she said, cutting across him. "You don't think. I do the thinking, and you do what I tell you to do."

Chapter 25

What exactly are we looking for?" Holly asked as she stood with Mary in the docks, waiting for the immigrants to pour off the ship, which was already tied up at the quay.

"Keep your eyes skinned and look for any young girl who appears to be on her own, looking around bewildered, not certain what to do with herself, like you when you came off the ship."

"I was only on my own because my mother had died on the ship," Holly said, fighting to control her emotions at the thought.

"So what actually happened?"

"We were starving and penniless, with no money to buy food, and the only way we were able to get away from the poverty was by travelling free in that great big horrible chamber on the ship. It was dark, smelly, and filthy, covered in coal dust. There were animals packed in with us too and nowhere for anyone to do their, um, you know, business. My mother was already sick, and she suddenly collapsed. I cried out for help, but nobody seemed to care or came to help. She was left lying in the filth. I tried to lift her up, but I was also weak from not having eaten for some time, so I knelt down in the muck and cradled her head as she looked up at me. Then she smiled, closed her eyes, and died. I stayed there holding her head, crying my heart out, until we reached land. I tried to get help to bring her body up, but I was told to get off the ship and they would take care of her body."

Mary wrapped her arms around Holly. "I'm sorry. That's pretty much what Michael had told me it was like. Lucky you were found when you were," she said, hugging Holly tighter.

"Lucky? First you tried to force me into becoming a

prostitute, and then I'm raped by that bastard. How can you say I was lucky?"

Mary let go of Holly as she felt her blood run cold at the thought of what she had done. "I'm so sorry, Holly. It was wrong of me. I should never have done it."

"It's OK, Mary. You did your best to save me in the end, and you've taken care of me otherwise. I don't know where I would have ended up—probably back with that evil man."

"That's why I want to try to make good, by trying to help young girls and women before they are tricked like you were."

"Is that one over there?" Holly said, pointing in the direction of a young woman seemingly walking around on her own, a stranger in a strange place, looking around, not sure what to do or where to go.

"Great, let's get to her before anyone else does," Mary said, grabbing Holly's hand and rushing off. Unfortunately, just as they got close, two young men appeared and got to the young woman before they did.

"We're too late," Holly said despondently.

"No we're not," Mary said, barging her way between the two young men.

"What the fuck do you think you're doing?" one of the young men said angrily.

"Hello, Jean. Sorry we couldn't get here earlier," Mary said, taking hold of the young woman's hand and pulling her closer.

The young woman looked puzzled as she stared in bewilderment at Mary. "Do I know you?"

"Your mother asked us to come and pick you up."

"My mother? But my mother's—"

"Yes, I know, which is why she asked us to come and collect you."

The two young men looked on curiously. "Hang on. You don't know this chick. You're trying to steal her for your own ends. We got here first, so she belongs to us. Piss off before you get hurt, the pair of you," the other man threatened.

"Hang on, looks like we might finish up with three," his

mate said, looking eagerly at Holly.

"The trouble with idiots like you two is that you think you rule the docks and can do what you like, with whom you like. Well, your games are over, so it's time for you two to piss off," Mary said with as much venom as she could muster.

"Listen to the stupid bitch," the other young man chipped in. "If you only had balls, I might start to be afraid, but …"

Those were the last words he uttered as Mary brought her knee up squarely between his legs. Then all he could utter was "Shit" as he doubled up in agony.

"Why, you fucking cow," his mate swore as he lunged at Mary, who neatly stepped aside and kicked him hard in the shin with the pointed toe of her boot, causing him to start hobbling around.

"Like I said, your days are over, so fuck off. And don't come back or else you might be reading your story in the *Weekly Star*," she said, watching them amble off.

"Right. You had better come with us before some other crimps come along trying to lure you," Mary said to the young woman.

"Lure me into what?"

"We'll explain everything to you when we we get you home."

"I don't understand what's going on. Why do you want to take me home?"

"For your own safety. It isn't safe for you to be hanging around here all on your own. How did you manage to get here anyway?"

Her eyes darkened, and her lips pressed together. "The weather had suddenly changed as winter set in with bitter cold gales, with some of the cottages buried up to their roofs in snow. The potato crop was ruined and we had no way of feeding ourselves, and Dad had no way of earning money to buy food, so Mother and I went without food so that Dad could eat to be strong enough to go out and find work to earn money. And while he was away, these terrible men suddenly appeared and threw us out of our little cottage. I screamed at them, asking what they thought they were doing. One of the men, who said his name was O'Brien—yes, that's right, Sean O'Brien—said he was a bailiff and had orders to repossess the cottage on behalf of a lord something or other, I can't remember his name, and—"

"Lord Blamfont?" Mary suggested.

"Yes, that was the name, Lord Blamfont. But what I didn't understand was, although O'Brien said he was there to repossess the cottage, his men started to knock it down. We had to watch as they demolished the cottage and our furniture and …" The hurt of remembering what had happened seemed to flood up in her throat, almost choking her, as she tried to blink away the tears that were threatening.

Mary wrapped her arms around her and hugged her tightly in an effort to comfort her, her head resting on her shoulder as she began to shake.

"My mother, who was already very weak from us both having gone without food, collapsed at the shock of watching what was happening. I cried out for help, but the wreckers took no notice and just carried on smashing up the place. I knelt down beside her. And I will never forget her dying words as she looked up smiling at me: 'My darling daughter, God is about to call me to a better place, but I want you to trust that our gracious Lord will take care of you and lead you to a safer and happier place. And as the good Lord Jesus said, "Father, forgive them, for they do not know what they do.' I knelt there, unable to move, as she gave a little cough and her eyes slowly closed."

A chill swept over Holly at what the young woman was telling them. She could feel the hurt, but she kept to herself, her own thoughts of what happened to her, which were torturing her brain. "I watched my mother die on the boat coming over," she said, her face darkening a little as a cloud of sadness fell over her.

"The wreckers just picked up one of our old blankets they had thrown on the ground with the rest of the broken furniture and placed it over her body and told me to go away or else they would take me to the workhouse. I didn't know what a workhouse was, but the way they said it, it didn't sound nice, so I just ran away."

"So how did you get here?"

"I don't remember much of it. I was in a daze for most of the time, but a family I didn't know took pity on me and told me that if I went with them to Dublin, they could get a free ride on a boat to Liverpool, from where they said they could get a boat to the United States. When I got off the boat, I was looking around for them when those two men and you came over to me. I have no idea where the family are now," she said, her face pale and anxious.

"Let's have a look around and see if we can find them," Mary suggested.

They moved amongst the mass of people, some still seeming to be wandering around aimlessly, when they suddenly heard a voice calling the name Brianna.

"That's them," Brianna said excitedly, rushing over to where they were standing with Mary and Holly quickly following behind her.

"We've been looking everywhere for you. What happened? And who are these people?" the man asked, looking suspiciously at Mary.

"Oh, this kind lady saved me from some men trying to talk to me. I don't know what it was all about, but she had to deal violently with them before they would go away. She offered to take me home and—"

"Yes, well, we've heard about you kind of people luring young girls into wickedness, so we'll take care of her now, thank you very much," the man said sternly, taking Brianna firmly by the hand and leading her off.

"Fuck me, and that's the thanks we get for trying to save someone."

"At least she's with a family, so she's safe. And you did save her from those evil men," Holly told Mary. "And I'm amazed at how you managed to deal with those two the way you did."

"When you've been around men as much as I have, you soon learn how to deal with the difficult ones. Come on, let's go home."

* * * *

As they reached the front of the house where her apartment was, Mary was shocked to see Leon standing there.

"What the fuck are you doing here?" she asked, her face clouding over, an uneasy frown creasing her brow.

"Has he come to take me back?" Holly exclaimed, a wave of fear engulfing her as she moved behind Mary for protection.

There was a brooding intensity about Leon as he said, "No, I've not come to take you back. I need to talk to Michael. Is he with you?"

"No, he's training. He's a boxer now, and he'll be a champion soon. Sir Richard Fernwright, his patron, is already planning his next fight," Mary said with an air of pride.

"That's what I want to talk to Michael about. He is living with you, isn't he?"

"What the fuck has that got to do with you or that fucking cow you work for? Has she sent you to nose around?" Mary said, her face as puzzled as much as it was angry.

Leon raised a reassuring hand. "No, that's not why I'm here. It has nothing to do with her. Well, actually it has, which is why I need to speak to Michael urgently. When will he be home?"

"Usually around six. Can you tell me what it's about?"

"I'd rather discuss it with Michael and let him tell you," Leon said, his face giving nothing away.

"I hope this has nothing to do with Holly here, because no way is she ever going back there or anywhere near that fucking pervert."

"No, it's not about her. Not directly anyway."

"What the fuck does that mean?" Mary asked angrily. He could see the conflicting emotions on her face.

"Look, Mary, I'd rather discuss it with Michael first and then let him tell you. Unfortunately I can't make six. As you know, I will be on duty then. Can I suggest we meet early tomorrow morning before he goes off to his training?"

"OK, I'll tell him, but I'll be there since I don't trust you or her," she told him as she swept past him. She entered the house, pushing Holly ahead of her, firmly slamming the door shut behind her.

* * * *

"So what's this all about? The last person I expected to see again after the last fracas," Michael said as he let Leon into the apartment.

"Me too, I suppose, but something has happened that-"

"I know, they're planning for us to fight each other and-"

"They're planning what?" Mary interrupted, her voice quivering at the news.

"I don't how you feel, but I'll tell you how I feel. We were friends once, and although we had that fracas, I still have respect for you and don't want to fight you," Leon said. There was genuine warmth in his voice.

"Funny, I said the same when Fisty told me about what they were planning. I told him I didn't want to fight you either."

"Hang on, let me try to get my head around this," Mary interrupted. "Who's planning what?"

Leon and Michael looked at each other, trying to decide which one of them should tell her. "Apparently Madame Rosita went to see Sir Richard to try to collect the money he owes, and somehow they decided to set up a fight between the two of us, making a wager on which one of us is the best. I don't know the exact terms, but Madame Rosita told me Lord Blamfont has put up five hundred pounds' stake money," Leon explained.

"That man again. So what do we do about it?" Michael asked.

"Tell them to go fuck themselves," Mary said angrily.

"Not as easy as that. There's too much at stake on both sides, so they certainly won't accept that we don't want to fight each other," Leon explained.

Michael said to Leon, "The thing is, we've got some time, as the date hasn't been fixed yet, to think of a way around this. I hope nobody saw you coming here, because we can't let anyone know we're talking. We'll find a way out of this. I'm not sure what, but we'll find some way. We have to. Thank you for coming. I appreciate it. Just make sure nobody sees you leaving." Michael embraced Leon.

"I'm sorry I was hard on you, Leon, but I had no idea."

"It's OK, Mary. If only there were more like you, the world would be a better place. And I can tell you, Madame Rosita's is not the same place since you left. The clients still keep asking after you."

"Maybe I should open my own place?" Mary quipped.

"If you did, I'd certainly come and work for you," Leon volunteered.

* * * *

"I'm worried about the story that's building up in the newspaper about the girl being raped by her employer, a member of the landed gentry, and I'm concerned it won't take long for people to put two and two together. Before we know it, they'll be banging on our doors and—"

"By that, Madame, are you implying that you think it is me they are referring to?" Lord Blamfont said, indignation brimming in his voice.

"Let's not play games with each other. I know it was you. You couldn't wait to get your hands on that girl. But I don't care about that. What I care about is whether it will get to the courts."

"No, it will never get that far," he interrupted to assure her. "And even if it did, no court would convict someone of

211

my stature," he asserted in righteous anger.

"Let us hope you are right. The other worry I have is the big fight coming up with you putting up the stake money, which means you are going to have a high profile. Just think of the money we can make with the betting amongst my rich clientele. Do you seriously want to risk all that?"

"So what do you suggest I do, not that I'm admitting to anything?"

"What all sensible people do to avoid a scandal: pay her off."

"No way," he said stubbornly, indignation still in his voice.

"OK, be as stubborn as you like, but I'll tell you this: when the story breaks, as it eventually will, and they come knocking on my door and the place is forced to close, my clients, your friends and associates, will turn on you and have nothing further to do with you. And not to put too fine a point on it, you could end up in prison or worse. Rape is a capital offence."

Lord Blamfont looked at her gravely, a haunting expression filling his face. "But if I were to do what you say, it could be taken as an admission."

"No, you don't do anything yourself. You get someone to negotiate on your behalf."

"I can't possibly get my lawyers to do something like that."

"Of course not. You get someone you can trust."

"I don't know anyone outside my circle I can trust."

"Then may I suggest someone?"

"Yes, if you're sure you can trust them."

"How about Leon?"

"Leon? Then he'll know everything."

She considered his words. "Leon reads the papers like everybody else, and if I know Leon, he'll have already worked it out for himself."

"Very well, get him to offer her twenty-five pounds," he agreed begrudgingly.

Her face suffused with anger. "Are you completely stupid as well as miserly? She'll, or Mary, whom she is staying with, will—"

"She is shacked up with Mary?"

"Yes, and it seems Mary has turned into some sort of do-gooder. And, it may interest you to know, I nearly had a new virgin for you until she and Holly turned up at the docks and somehow managed to stop the two lads I'd hired from bringing back a young girl they'd spotted coming off the boat."

"Then let us just go and get the fucking bitch and take care of her—and Mary too, while we're at it."

"Oh no, Mary is shacked up with that ruffian Michael. You would have to find a couple of really tough guys to overcome him. So be sensible and offer some real money, and then the matter can be over quickly. And remember this: when Leon has destroyed the ruffian, we will have a champion on our hands. What you pay Holly will be a mere pittance compared to what we can make," she explained, her voice filled with excitement at the thought.

He looked at her, turning the idea over in his mind. "You've had this all worked out?"

"Of course," she said, letting the words hang for a moment. "Do you think I was going to let you throw it all away just because you raped some stupid little girl who ought to have known better? She'll probably finish up on the streets as a whore anyway. Offer her two hundred."

"Two hundred?" he exploded.

"Yes. And knowing Mary, who I'm sure will be advising her, you'll probably have to settle for three hundred."

"This is getting worse by the minute." He sighed, shaking his head in frustration.

"This is something you started which I'm trying to help put an end to."

"Very well, you arrange it," he said with an air of reluctance.

Chapter 26

"Are you all right?" Mary asked as Holly came back into the house looking rather pale. "I thought you got the runs the way you charged out to the shithouse."

"I've been starting to feel sick in the mornings, and I don't know why," Holly said, grabbing a handkerchief to wipe her face.

Mary's eyebrows went up as she looked at Holly, waiting for her to say more. "You're telling me you're starting to feel sick every morning?"

"Yes. Strange. I thought it must be something I'd eaten, but I've only eaten what you have, and you don't seem to be sick. So what can it be?"

Mary continued to study her, dreading the thoughts that were rushing through her mind. "Are your breasts feeling sore and itchy?"

"Yes, that's another strange thing. They feel very sore. Why is that? What kind of food could cause that?"

Mary reached out her arms, took Holly's face between her hands, and looked into her eyes. "It's not anything you've eaten; it's what that bastard spent in you. You're pregnant."

"Pregnant? Does that mean I'm going to have a baby?" Holly exclaimed, a puzzled look filling her eyes.

"That's about the gist of it," Mary said with a hapless shrug.

Holly's mouth gaped as she tried to take in what Mary was telling her. "But how could that have happened?"

"When that bastard rammed his cock in you, he didn't care about using a rubber, so you're now impregnated. You've got a baby growing in your tummy."

Holly gazed at Mary, her eyes wide, weariness and fear darkening her face. "I don't understand any of this. So what happens now?"

Mary allowed herself a smile. "Well, we will just have to take care of you until the baby's born."

"How long will that take?" she asked in all innocence.

"Usually nine months. This is something else I'm going to have to talk to the solicitor about."

* * * *

"I see. Are you sure about this?" Mr Makepiece asked, a pensive frown creasing his forehead.

"Oh, I'm sure all right. She's pregnant," Mary said, her smile turning a little brittle. "And that bastard is going to have to pay for it."

"How can we be sure it's his?"

"She's a virgin—or was until he raped her."

"And she hasn't been with anyone else since then?" he asked, his expression serious.

"Of course not. She's young and knows little or nothing about sex. She can't even understand how she's become pregnant."

"I see," he said, pausing to turn the thoughts over in his mind. "The problem, of course, is proving he's the father."

"If we can prove he raped her, then it will automatically prove he is the father," Mary reasoned.

"Not necessarily, my dear. We have been all through this, and as I advised you, we stand very little to no chance of proving he raped her, so the fact that she is pregnant is irrelevant. I'm sure he will claim that as she came from a brothel, the father could be any one of her many clients."

"My God, you're telling me he's not only going to get away with rape but also he's not going to have to support his own kid?"

"I'm afraid so, unless …" He paused again.

"Unless what?"

"Unless somehow the message gets to him that his wicked actions have resulted in the poor girl becoming

215

pregnant. Maybe your friend Stewart Matthews at the newspaper can hint at it. He seems to have done a good job with the last article as people are starting to ask questions as to who the rapist might be amongst the landed gentry."

"Thanks. That's a great idea. I'll go around and see him right now, Thank you for that piece of advice. I owe you," Mary said, getting up from the chair and hurrying out.

Hmm, a nice freebie would be a great way of repaying me, he thought lustfully as he watched her sultry figure glide smoothly out through the door.

* * * *

Having had a long chat with Stewart Matthews, Mary felt good. She was confident he would write the article in a way that would state the alleged rapist had also by his violent act impregnated the poor defenceless young woman. But her face dropped as she spotted Leon standing on the pavement outside the house.

"It frightened me for a moment to see you standing there."

"I need to talk," he said. There was urgency in his voice.

"You know Michael's not here. He's training."

"No, it's you I've come to talk to. It's about Holly."

"Right, then you had better come in before anybody spots you, if they haven't already."

"The thing is, is Holly still with you?"

"Yes, of course she is. Why?"

"Because I need to talk to you before we talk to Holly."

"This sounds ominous," she said, eyeing him with suspicion.

"I'll explain once we get inside."

"We can't because it is going to impossible to talk with Holly being there. And I don't want to tell her to go out while we talk as she is in a pretty bad state as it is, which is also something I want to talk to you about," she said, tensing her muscles at the thought of what she was going to have to tell him. "I think we are going to have to risk going to a coffee house," she suggested.

"That's OK. Madame Rosita knows that I'm coming to see you. In fact, it is her idea."

Mary's face tightened. "You mean that cow sent you?"

"Yes, with good news hopefully," he said, forcing a smile as they set off for the coffee house.

"So what devilish errand has she sent you on this time?" Mary asked as they sat down at one of the tables. The strong smell of freshly ground coffee hit her nostrils. The place was crowded with a mixture of people from the elite to the crimps, including prostitutes, gamblers, and those just wanting to quietly drink a coffee and read the latest newspapers displayed freely for anyone to peruse, which made Mary smile. She was hoping they were reading news about the rape. She was happy to be there despite the fact that her eyes were beginning to burn from the suffocating clouds of tobacco smoke emitted from the numerous pipes and cigars being smoked by the customers, the women as well as the men.

Leon looked around, hoping they wouldn't be overheard. "I have come," he began in a formal manner, "as the representative of Lord Blamfont and—"

"You, working for that rapist? I thought you said Madame Rosita had told you to come."

"Please keep your voice down. Listen to what I have to say," he said, trying to keep his own voice low. "I have been sent to make you, I mean Holly, an offer for her to forget about making any alleged claims of rape and—"

"Alleged? Are you fucking living on the moon? There is no *alleged* about it. That bastard raped her!" Mary reacted angrily. Her raised voice caused other customers to stop talking, turn, and look in their direction.

"For goodness' sake, Mary, keep your voice down. Everyone is looking at us," Leon cautioned, feeling uncomfortable at the inquisitive eyes.

"As far as I'm concerned, I'd like the whole fucking world to know what an evil bastard that man is," she cursed, meeting Leon's eyes in an unwavering stare.

"Look, Mary, you have no idea what you're up against. The person we are talking about has very powerful friends and—"

"He won't when they know what he's been up to," she cut across him.

"The point is, he is prepared to make a generous offer for it all to go away."

"He ought to be put away," she snapped, not wanting to give up.

"He is prepared to offer her two hundred pounds," he said, ignoring the remark.

"Two hundred fucking pounds? That's it?" she exploded, not attempting to keep her voice down.

"I might be able to persuade him to go to three hundred," Leon offered, hoping that would seal the matter.

Mary tried to remain calm, but anger was in her eyes. "You have no fucking idea, have you? He not only beat and raped her but also made her pregnant."

He could hear the tremor in his own voice as he said, "Pregnant? Are you sure?"

"For fuck's sake, Leon, if I don't know when a girl is up the fucking duff, then nobody does. Yes, Leon, she's fucking pregnant, so you can go back and tell that bastard and Madame Rosita that three hundred pounds is nowhere near enough. She now has a kid to bring up, his kid," she said angrily as she sprang to her feet just as a gentleman from one of the other tables got up and came across.

"Good luck with the fight. I've got my money on you," he said, giving Leon a friendly slap on the back.

"Thank you, sir," Leon responded, slightly embarrassed.

"Fuck me, the word's already beginning to spread, and they haven't even fixed a date yet."

"That's Madame Rosita. She doesn't miss a trick. And it looks like she's already got her clients betting on the outcome.

"But you and Michael don't want the fight to happen," she said, resuming her seat.

218

"No, we don't, but I don't know how we're going to avoid it. As I said, we're up against some very powerful people who don't give a shit about what we feel. They are only interested in making money. We are merely pawns in their game. They see us as gladiators, white against black."

"Then we have to think of something."

"Yes, but I don't know what," he said resignedly as the waitress came over with the coffees.

"Sorry, Leon, I know it's not your problem, but tell that bastard to dig deeper into his pocket, and then we might, just might, come to some sort of deal," Mary added, the waitress giving a fleeting look of disapproval.

Leon drank the hot coffee, the acid taste revitalising his dulled senses.

* * * *

Madame Rosita sat with Lord Blamfont in her lounge, anxiously waiting for Leon to return.

"So how did it go? Everything settled?" she asked cheerfully as soon as Leon walked in.

"No. Far from it. There is an additional problem, and I mean additional. Holly is pregnant."

Madame Rosita and Lord Blamfont exchanged glances, looking horrified. "Did you say the girl is pregnant?" Madame Rosita asked, not sure she had heard right.

"Yes, Madame. Mary told me the girl is pregnant."

"Mary told you. She could just be lying to try to squeeze more money out of us."

"Yes, she's demanding more money, but I do believe her about Holly being pregnant. After all she was—"

"She was what?" Lord Blamfont cut in angrily.

"Sorry, I didn't mean to—"

"Thank you, Leon. Would you now leave us?" Madame Rosita said with a dismissive wave of her hand, looking at Lord Blamfont in silence until Leon had left.

"So what do we do now?" he asked in a dull, flat voice.

219

"Well, first we have to find out for sure the girl is pregnant. But if Mary says she is, you can be pretty damn sure she is."

"And if she is?"

"We'll deal with that when we have to. In the meantime, you do nothing while I go and visit Mary to find out for myself."

* * * *

"I don't have to guess why you're here," Mary said as she let Madame Rosita into her apartment.

"All I want to know is whether that stupid bitch is really pregnant," Madame Rosita said deprecatingly. Mary could see the look of suspicion etched on her face.

Mary suppressed an urge of irritation as she said, "She's pregnant all right. Stopped her periods, morning sickness, a white creamy discharge, and her nipples are becoming sore. What other proof do you need?"

"Where is she?" Madame Rosita asked, her eyes sharp as she surveyed the place.

"She's in the bedroom. She is scared, frightened, still unable to come to terms with what happened and how she got pregnant as a result. She was—and still is for that matter—a young, innocent girl whose innocence was stolen from her by that bastard, who doesn't give a fuck, except whether he might be found out."

"Can I see her?"

"What do you think you're going to do, give her an internal examination? No, but what I am prepared to do is to take her to a doctor and get him to examine her and confirm she is pregnant."

"Can I come with you?"

"No, that would be too much for Holly. And she doesn't deserve you, of all people, being there while she's being examined. You will have to trust the doctor. And if you don't believe him, then you can sue both of us for all I care.

Understand one thing: that bastard is going to have to pay for what he did, and three hundred pounds is nowhere near enough to compensate for what Holly's suffered," she told her. There was a deep underlying sadness in her voice.

"So what do you think would be a sensible offer to put this all behind us?"

"One thousand pounds, so that I can set her up with her own apartment where she can bring up the baby in safe, clean, and comfortable conditions. Unless, of course, he would like to adopt the baby and bring it up as his own, which it is, as it was he who raped her."

"Well. I don't think he'd want to do that."

"No, of course he wouldn't. He's too much of a fucking snob to want to adopt the baby of a scullery maid."

"You have really changed. There's a hardness about you that I haven't noticed before."

Keeping the malice out of her voice was difficult as she said, "It's people like you and him that have made me this way."

"Well, I don't think you're going to be offered anything like a thousand, but—"

Mary gave Madame Rosita a cold, forbidding look. "That's up to him. But I'm not prepared to give up on the girl. I will send you the doctor's report as soon as I have it, but take my word for it, she is up the duff," she said forcefully.

"Very well, but I'm not promising anything," Madame Rosita said, turning on her heel and making for the door.

* * * *

"A thousand pounds!" Lord Blamfont exclaimed, his face reddening with fury at the thought. "Do you think I'm made of money?" he said, looking at Madame Rosita scornfully.

"Well, you seem to spend a lot of it here for a start," Madame Rosita said in a matter-of-fact voice.

"Have you any idea how much I've lost on my investments into the railway companies, which it seems I now have no prospect of any return on those investments? And with the Bank of England putting up interest rates and undercutting the boom, the money has started to flow out of railway companies, leaving them without funding, which means my shares are virtually worthless. Now everyone is reinvesting in bonds."

"Well, you're not the only one to lose out. I invested too, so I'm in the same boat as you, except I haven't got a rape case and a pregnant girl to deal with," she said sardonically.

Chapter 27

A thousand pounds?" Holly exclaimed. "You mean he is going to give me a thousand pounds?" she said, her mouth gaping at the enormity of what Mary was telling her. "How much is a thousand pounds?" Holly asked.

With too many thoughts colliding in her brain, she was unable to understand what a thousand pounds actually meant or looked like, for she had never in the whole of her life had any money and didn't know actually know what a pound was. She'd never even seen the coins her father brought home from work, and she had no idea how many farthings, halfpennies, pennies, or shillings made a pound.

"I would have had to fuck nonstop for a couple of months to earn that sort of money," Mary said jokingly. "And you only had to fuck once," she added, instantly regretting the words the moment she said them. She blushed, her face reddening, as she looked at Holly, whose blue eyes glittered with rage. Her pretty face was wrought with confusion as she fled from the room.

Mary chased after. "Sorry, that was cruel of me. I only meant it as a joke," she said, hastening to comfort Holly as she slumped on the bed, fighting to hold back the tears.

A grimace of pain passed across Holly's face. "I don't understand any of it. You told me we were going to charge him with beating me and raping me. Are we not going to do that any more?"

"The problem is, 'an eye for an eye, a tooth for a tooth' simply means you end up with two blind and toothless people."

Holly looked a picture of puzzled innocence. Mary felt the tension between them. "I don't understand what you're talking about," Holly said. Mary could hear the desolation in her voice.

"What I mean is, we have no chance of getting him to court, let alone proving him guilty. He is of the landed gentry and has powerful friends in high places, which means he would come after us and yours and my life would be ruined."

"So why is he paying me a thousand pounds?"

Mary was feeling unhappy with the way Holly was looking at her. "Look, it's very complicated, but think of it this way. If we had tried to take him to court, we would surely have lost, and it would have cost me a lot of money. This way, you've come out of it a very rich young woman, and you don't have to skivvy to anyone. So although it's been painful, you have to count yourself lucky. I know of many girls who suffered worse than you and got nothing for it," she said, hoping that news would give Holly some hope and comfort.

"It's more than enough to set you up in your own home and take care of the baby," Mary added with an assuring smile. "You will be a very rich girl."

"I don't want my own home. I want to stay with you," Holly said, a shiver of apprehension running up her spine.

"It's early days yet, so you don't need to worry. You will stay here with me and Michael, and we'll take care of things," Mary said, seeing the anxiety in her eyes.

"So what are you two doing hunched up on the bed?" Michael asked as he walked into the bedroom.

"Some good news for a change," Mary said, her face brightening into a smile.

"Well, we could certainly do with some of that," he said, smiling back.

"Holly has been offered a thousand pounds in compensation."

"She doesn't look happy about it," he said, looking at her saddened face.

"She doesn't quite understand it all. I've tried to explain, but it's all too much for her. We'll just have to give her time to come to terms with it," Mary said consolingly.

"Well, another thing we're going to have come to terms with is the fight. I even had men coming up to me as I walked home, slapping me on the back, saying, 'I saw how you beat that Tom Dyer, and my money's on you to beat that blacky.' I asked the man who said that how he knew about the fight, and he told me it's all the talk in the pubs and coffee houses. People are already laying bets everywhere. I don't know how we can stop it now."

"We'll think of something. I know we will. We didn't think we would win with Lord Blamfont, but we did. We need to get a message to Leon so we can talk about it."

"Yes, we must, before things get completely out of hand."

* * * *

"Keep up the good work, Michael," Sir Richard said enthusiastically, having walked down the garden to watch him training. "You've got a big fight coming up, and I've got a lot of money riding on you, so I want you at your best."

"Have you fixed a date yet, sir?" Fisty politely asked.

"Not yet, but I'm aiming for it to be as soon as possible as I don't want your opponent to have too much time to train," he said with a wicked grin as he turned to walk back up to the house.

"I'm sorry, sir, but I don't want to fight Leon," Michael called after him.

Sir Richard stopped in his tracks and spun around, an angry look spreading across his face. "You don't want to fight him? You will fight whoever I tell you to fight. You signed a contract and I own you, so don't start getting any ideas that you have any choice in the matter. The fight is on, and that is all there is to it," he said, turning and walking off in a huff.

"I've got to get out of this somehow," Michael said, slumping to the ground after Sir Richard had disappeared out of sight. Michael was confused, focusing on nothing.

"That's not going to be easy," Fisty said, squatting down beside him. "You heard what he said: he has you under contract. And if I know Sir Richard, if you were to break the contract, he'll have you hauled off to prison. What does Leon think about it?"

"He doesn't want the fight to go ahead either. I'm having a meeting with him to decide what to do. You know what it's like to hurt a man? I mean, really hurt a man? Most times you don't know the man or care about him, but it's not like that with Leon. It's not like we've got a personal grudge against each other. Although we had a squabble, he was the one person who helped me when I needed help the most, for which I will always be thankful."

"Well, you can always run away, but that depends on how far you can run and how far you want to run."

"What do you mean by that?"

"Go to America, which is what I'm thinking of doing."

"You?"

"Yes, I fancy travelling to America or Canada as a missionary helping to spread the Word of the Lord, but I have not decided which is best."

Michael looked at him, a hint of panic in his shocked expression. "Are you serious?"

"Oh yes, I've been thinking about it for a long time, and I've actually decided I will leave after you've had your next fight."

"Do you think we could do it?"

"We?" Fisty asked, not having expected that. "Are you thinking we all will go together?"

"Yes. As you said, this is something you have been thinking about for some time, so you must know how to go about it."

"To a certain extent. Who would you expect to come with you?"

"Mary and Holly. Holly's pregnant. We couldn't leave her behind. And I suppose Leon as I guess he won't be able to stay here either if we all run away."

"It will cost quite a bit of money, unless you want to go steerage."

"Steerage? What's that?"

"From what I've found out, it's the cheapest and most unpleasant way of travelling. I'm told the decks are usually only four to six feet high and contain hard wooden berths built in two layers, taking up most of the floor space with little room for people to move around. The entrance to steerage is by a ladder from a hatchway on the deck. There's almost no ventilation with the only fresh air coming through the hatches, which are only allowed to be open in good weather and which are shut tight during bad weather, which can become quite suffocating."

"Well, I'll tell you something: that sounds a damn sight better than what I travelled in when I came here."

"It's going to take a lot of planning, and it could all go wrong, particularly for you. I'm not under any contract with Sir Richard, so I'm free to do what I like."

"I need to talk it over with Mary and of course Leon," Michael said, getting to his feet, feeling there could be a way out of all this.

* * * *

"Well, now that you've got the problem of that silly bitch out of the way, we can concentrate on the fight. I have to say, I am excited at the interest it's building. We are going to make a lot of money out of this. As I said, what you've paid that stupid girl will pale into insignificance," Madame Rosita said, sitting with Lord Blamfont in her luxurious lounge.

"So do you have any idea on a date?" Lord Blamfont asked.

"The thing is, I don't want to arrange it too quickly as I want Leon to train up. Don't forget, the ruffian has been training for some time and has already had one fight, plus the fact that, as I said, interest is building up, which is going to make it the fight to end all fights. And we will have a champion on our hands."

"Then I suggest we drink to it, and then I will have a fuck to it. And when are you going to find me a new girl?" he asked with a lustful grin.

"I'm working on it, but I can't act on it immediately. I have to be careful after what you did," she told him in a deprecating tone.

"If only Mary was back. She was a great—"

"Fuck. Yes, I know how you felt about her," she said, finishing the sentence for him. "And she may well be back after Leon has knocked the stuffing out of that ruffian she's shacked up with."

"Can't wait for both things to happen," he said, the thought giving rise to the familiar stirrings in his loins.

"I'll tell you what, when we've won the fight, I think we should have a celebratory orgy. What do you think?"

"What a glorious, fantastic idea," he replied. "Everybody wearing masks so they cannot be recognised. Then you will have to find a virgin to be sacrificed at the altar of success," he added, feeling his manhood beginning to stir.

She could sense his impulse. "In the meantime, I think you'd better go and see to your immediate needs," she said, looking at the bulge in his tight breeches.

Chapter 28

Are you serious?" Mary asked after Michael had told her about the idea of emigrating to the United States.

"Yes. Fisty gave me the idea, and it sounds to me the only way Leon and I are going to get out of having to fight each other."

"What does Leon say? Have you spoken to him about it?"

"No. He will be here any minute, but I wanted to tell you first."

"What about me? I don't want to be left here on my own," Holly spoke up, frightened at the thought.

"No, you'll come with us," Michael assured her.

"Do you think Holly will be all right travelling on one of those ships? I saw a baby die on the ship I came across on."

"The ships that go to America are much better than those horrible ones."

"I've heard about the thousands who have left for the promised land, but I haven't heard what it's like out there. Is it any better than it is here?" Mary wondered.

"I don't know, but it seems that's where everybody wants to go to—there or Canada."

Michael was still thinking about the plan as Mary ushered Leon into the room.

"So this is what you're planning?" Leon asked as he stood by the fireplace. There was nowhere else to sit.

"What do you think?" Michael asked.

"Fine for you, but not for me. Slavery may have ended here, but not quite in America, as slavery still continues in many states. I don't want to risk going back there and then find myself being caught and ending up a slave again."

"But you are freeman," Mary said, surprised by what he was saying.

"Like I said, black men are still not safe in America. Maybe one day, but not now."

"So what do you suggest?" Michael asked.

"One of two things: you can make your own way to America and I'll help all I can, or we can all go to Canada, which would be better for me as the British have abolished slavery there," Leon proposed.

"I would like you to come with us, so I don't mind which, as long as we get away from here. Are there Catholics or Protestants in Canada?" Michael asked.

"As far as I was told when I was escaping, there is a mixture, Catholics, Protestants, Methodists, and Quakers."

"That's good, because Fisty wants to come with us. He wants to work as some kind of missionary," Michael told him.

"It's going to take a lot of planning. If any of them get a hint of what we're scheming, then we'll all finish up in jail," Leon cautioned.

"So how do you suggest we go about it?"

"Firstly we must let them think everything is all right and that we are going to fight each other right up to the very night of the fight. With everything going on, with the crowds packed in and the tension building, when the crowds learn we are not there and that there isn't going to be a fight, there will be riot. And then Lord Blamfont, Madam Rosita, and your Sir Richard as the organisers will be in real trouble."

"I like the sound of that. I only wish I could be there to see the crowd turn on Lord Blamfont."

"With luck you won't. You and all of us will be safely on board a ship to Canada or America. We are going need you girls to help for the plan to succeed, but we can't do anything until we know the date of the fight. Then we just have to hope there is a ship sailing on that day."

* * * *

"I have finally set on a date, Friday, the twenty-eighth of April. I have discussed it with Sir Richard, and he is agreeable,"

Madame Rosita told Lord Blamfont as they sat together in her luxurious lounge.

"Excellent. I can't wait."

"And I have another surprise, one which I know will excite you. I have decided to up the stakes by arranging a fight between two females."

"Two females? Now that does sound exciting. You never cease to amaze me. Where did you get the idea for that?" he asked. She could feel the excitement coming off him in waves.

"I remembered reading about two women who had fought each other over the price of a pint of gin and of an Irishwoman and an Englishwoman who had fought over a man they were both trying to offer their services to and decided to visit the area where most of the common prostitutes plied their trade, seeming it was quite normal for them to be fighting over their patches or over a man. So on my way to the docks to find out whether any of the crimps had found a young nubile female I might be interested in, and by chance as I was walking through one of the less salubrious parts of town, I happened to pass the Crown pub in Lime Street, where there was one hell of a commotion going on. As I stood watching, two women suddenly burst out onto the street, determined to beat the shit out of each other, pulling at each other's hair and clothes, and cursing and swearing at one another. It was while watching the two of them that I had the idea of two vampish, aggressive females displaying animalistic passions that would undoubtedly provide sexual titillation for the male audience before the big fight and draw an even bigger crowd. So decided to find out what had caused the fight between the two women."

"So what did cause it?" he asked, still exhilarated.

"I asked around and was told that Ivy, one of the fighters, was Protestant born and bred in Liverpool. She works with her father in the Crown pub he runs in Lime Street, close to the docks, where the Irish community is concentrated and where most of them work, Great Homer Street being the division between the mainly Protestant areas, where clashes are a regular occurrence. Anyway, it appears the fight had broken out between Ivy and a woman called Bridgit, who had dared to walk into the pub with a client. The sight of a Catholic prostitute with a Protestant client brazenly walking into the pub was too much for Ivy, and she charged at Bridgit, ordering both her and her client out.

Bridgit stubbornly refused to budge, and so a fight ensued with both of them going at each other. The word quickly spread, and soon more Catholics charged into the pub, at which time all hell broke loose with furniture, the bar, and windows being smashed. Bridgit, a feisty mix of mammy and sassy Irish Catholic, had immigrated to Liverpool with her family, like Michael and thousands of the others, in the hope of a better life after the potato famine. Unfortunately her father was a lazy, good-for-nothing drunkard who forced her onto the streets as a pickpocket to fund his excessive drinking. She had refused at first, but with the constant beatings, she finally gave in. She soon learned the easiest and most profitable thing to steal was silk handkerchiefs as they had a relative high resale value and could be easily sold on.

The dealers who bought them would display the silk handkerchiefs on poles outside their shops, where many went to buy back the very ones that had been stolen from them. That worked fine and brought in a good deal of money until Bridgit got caught red-handed and was arrested. She was sentenced to twenty-one days' hard labour. It was then that she decided prostitution, as it was not illegal, would be safer and just as profitable, if not more so. The beatings from her father and the constant fights on the streets to defend her patch had toughened her, and she was ready to take on anything or anybody who threatened her."

"So how did you manage to persuade them to agree to fight?" he asked, almost drooling at the mouth.

"I went back to the pub a few days later and asked Bridgit how she would feel about taking on Ivy in a proper controlled fight. The chance to earn big money and the thought of having another go at Ivy made the prospect that much more exciting. Just think, an opening bout playing on the Protestant-Catholic antagonisms is bound to add to the crowd's excitement."

"That it certainly will for sure. But how does the fight with women work? Is it the same as men?"

"Yes, basically the same. I've read up on it, and the way it works is the girls strip to the waist just like the men and—"

"You mean they'll be fighting bare-breasted?" The thought instantly travelled to his groin.

"Yes, which will undoubtedly provide sexual titillation for the male audience to see two female boxers fighting bare-breasted, particularly as it is looked upon with abject horror by the prudish, sexually repressed elite women who are not allowed to show an ankle, let alone anything else."

"Yes, that will definitely cause consternation in certain quarters."

"Yes it will. But from the women's point of view, there is a very good reason why they fight bare-breasted, and that is because of the scarcity of medication and the fact that any upper garment they normally wear would be somewhat dirty, so any blow that were to bruise or break the skin could cause infection in the breasts, which ultimately could become life-threatening."

"Whatever their reason for doing it, baring their tits will really draw the crowd and, as you say, work up the crowd's appetite for the big fight. We are onto a winner," Lord Blamfont said, feeling his body pulsating with anticipation.

"I think we're going to have to build a special stand for the dignitaries, who I'm sure will be even keener to come once they hear about two females fighting topless."

"Build a stand? That will cost money."

Madame Rosita looked at him angrily, the smile falling from her face. "You're unbelievable, you miserly man. Look, if you can't afford it, I can easily find somebody else who can, or I'll do it myself."

"No, no, sorry, you're right. Of course I'll do whatever is required," he hastily assured her.

"Good, so let's get the ball rolling."

* * * *

"It's all set then, Friday, twenty-eight April, so step up the training. I want you as fit as you'll ever be for this fight," Sir Richard told Michael with an air of exulted enthusiasm.

"Look, sir, I'll fight anyone you want, but I don't want to fight Leon. And he doesn't want to fight me either."

"Now you listen to me," Sir Richard barked, looking at him scornfully, the enthusiasm draining from his face. "I've got a lot of money riding on you, as well as my reputation as the sponsor of a champion. You will fight the bloody Negro and beat him to a pulp, so forget any fancy ideas about honour amongst friends or whatever you want to call it. Make no mistake about it: your life depends on you stepping into that ring and giving your all. Anything less and you will wish you never stepped foot in Liverpool."

Michael looked at him squarely, his eyes never wavering, as he said, "Yes, sir," suppressing the anger he felt rising in his chest.

"Very good. Now get on with the training," Sir Richard said, turning and walking back up the garden, his steps widening, showing his annoyance.

"We've just got to get out of this somehow," Michael said as she watched Sir Richard storm off.

"We'll work something out," Fisty offered encouragingly. "But in the meantime, we have to make it look like you're training hard for the fight."

* * * *

"Luckily there is a ship sailing on Friday, the twenty-eighth of April. It is called the *Britannia*, one of the very latest ships, driven by steam, so it is faster and takes less time to cross the Atlantic to America. We can book cabins on it instead of travelling steerage," Mary explained to Michael as soon as he got home from training.

He nodded with a smile. "How did you find all this out?"

"I went down to the docks and asked," she said simply.

"How much is that going to cost?" Michael asked, rubbing his still-sore hands.

"Seventy pounds a person, but that gives us proper berths, meals, and wine, believe it or not."

"That's a lot of money for us to find. With Mary, Holly, and me, that's, er—"

"Two hundred and ten pounds. It's a great ship and has all the other necessary fittings for a passenger ship with accommodation for one hundred and fifteen cabin passengers and two dining saloons on the main deck. It's a cabins-only passenger ship so does not take any steerage," she explained, showing him a brochure.

He briefly glanced at it and looked back up. "I guess we can raise the money between us, and Holly has money to pay for her fare. What time is the sailing?"

"They wouldn't give me a time, but they said it would sail when the passengers and cargo are fully loaded. We have to arrive a good time before the ship sails for checks on our health."

"Our health?"

"Just to make sure we're not carrying any contagious diseases."

"What do we do while we're hanging around waiting to board the ship? Because by then they will have started looking for us."

"I checked on that. As we'll being travelling first class as it were, the shipping company will provide accommodation while we wait to board, so we can hide out there," she assured him.

"Let's just hope it all works out. We'll have to speak to Leon and see if he is happy with the arrangements. And we have to talk to him to find out exactly how we're going to make it work without raising suspicion. It's not going to be easy, that's for sure."

* * * *

Because of bare-knuckle fighting's illegal status, it depended on the word being spread throughout the inns and coffee houses, where the merits of the fighters would be discussed, with people assessing the masculine prowess, valour, physical courage, and fortitude of the two contestants. Bets would be laid on who was thought to have the best chance of winning.

The only news the populace were waiting for now was the venue where the fight was to take place, but everybody guessed it would be the field where the last fight had been held.

Chapter 29

I can't go with you," Leon told them as they gathered together at Mary's apartment to discuss final details for tomorrow.

"Why not? What has made you change your mind at this late stage? Has Madame Rosita got to you?" Michael asked, surprised by the statement.

"No, I just can't take the risk."

"But you're a freeman, and you say you have the papers to prove it."

"So what are you proposing to do? You could put the whole plan into jeopardy," Mary protested.

"Actually, it might help."

"How do you work that out?" Michael said irritably.

"Well, if I'm there, it will help to make things look normal. And hopefully by the time they begin to get suspicious, you will be on the ship and hopefully sailing away."

"But they'll punish you," Mary said worriedly.

"No they won't, because in their eyes I will have done nothing wrong and will have no idea of why you haven't turned up."

"That's when they'll start searching for him," Mary said, still worried about the change in events.

"Your best hope is that the crowd begin to riot, causing so much confusion that it will take time for them to organise a search."

"I hope to God you're right." Michael sighed.

* * * *

The crowd began to gather early for the fight, coming from all directions with the usual hustle, bustle, and confusion of the ordinary people scrambling over the hedges and across ditches in a rush to get in without paying and get a good position as close to the ring as possible, particularly as the word was spreading that there would be two seminaked female fighters on before the main fight.

In a special closed-off area, the rich were also arriving early, either on horseback or in their open carriages, to secure a good position, some with streamers flying, indicating the fighter they were supporting.

A special stand had been erected for the elite to give them a vantage view of the ring, behind which was a large tent where they could dine and drink with their wives or mistresses to their heart's content with Madame Rosita, Lord Blamfont, and Sir Richard Fernwright greeting them royally, revelling in the praise they themselves were receiving for having organised such a great event. In no time large sums of money were being exchanged with wagers placed on not only who would win but also at which round the fight would end.

By the side of the main tent was a smaller tent for both the female and male fighters to relax and to change into their fighting clothes.

It had been arranged that Leon and Michael would meet up at the brothel and be driven in a specially decorated coach to the ground amidst a blaze of trumpets announcing their arrival.

As a precaution, a constant lookout had been set up for any potential raid the police or bluebottles, the derogatory nickname the fancies of bare-knuckle fighting had coined for the men in blue, might be planning, although Lord Blamfont, Madame Rosita, and Sir Richard Fernwright had done their best to make sure it wouldn't happen by inviting the chief of police and the local judges as their guests. Those men were now seated in the tent, being served drinks by the young women from the brothel.

* * * *

Michael, Mary, and Holly with their faces half covered with

hoods made their way to the docks. A feeling of apprehension spread through each of them as they were passed by noisy crowds, shouting, "Come on, the Irish" hoping they would not be recognised.

"I just hope they will let us onto the ship straightaway," Mary said as they arrived at the docks.

"Why wouldn't they?" Michael asked.

"Because, I was told passengers are not allowed to board until the ship is ready to sail."

"So what if they don't?"

"Then there is some sort of lodging house provided where the passengers are allowed to rest and wait, but I hope that won't be necessary. We'll be much safer on board as only those with a valid ticket who have passed the medical examination will be allowed on board."

"Medical examination?" Holly exclaimed. "I'm pregnant. They won't let me on."

"Of course they will. They'll only be checking your health to make sure you are not infected with any contagious diseases, which to me is a great relief, knowing that everyone on the ship will be healthy."

"When we get to the ship, leave the talking to me. I don't want you to be noticed too much," Mary said to Michael.

* * * *

"What you looking at?" Ivy demanded, glaring at Lord Blamfont, who was studying her closely, wondering what she would look like stripped to the waist. "You looking for a quick shag?" she asked, unashamedly meeting his gaze.

"I can give you a better shag than she can," Bridgit spoke up as she came across to join them.

"She'll be in no state to offer you anything by the time I've finished with her," Ivy cut in scathingly.

"Save all that for the ring," Madame Rosita remonstrated as she entered the tent. "Once in the ring, you can knock the shit out of each other. Until then, behave yourselves;

otherwise, I'll send you both packing and you won't earn anything. Now get yourselves ready," she said, turning and brusquely walking away.

"I can't wait to see them at it," Lord Blamfont said, feeling the familiar stirring in his loins as he followed her out.

"You can fuck the winner and the loser if that is what is turning you on," she said haughtily.

* * * *

Michael stared at the ship in awe, thinking it was a lot different from the ship he'd sailed in from Ireland. It seemed to be a mixture of a sailing ship and a steamship as it had three tall masts with full rigging for sails and a very tall red funnel in the middle of the ship. Two huge paddle wheels gulfed either side of the ship.

"I think I'm going to enjoy this once we get to sea," Michael said, still admiring the ship.

"Right, let's see if we can get on board," Mary said as she led Michael and Holly off towards the ship.

"What do you think you're doing? You can't come aboard yet," a steward called out as he hurriedly moved across the deck towards them as they attempted to walk up the gangplank.

"But we were hoping we could board early as this young lady is with child," Mary began to explain.

"Can't help about that. The rules are that no one is allowed to board until they have had a medical check," the steward told her.

"So when can we have a medical check?" Mary asked, irritation beginning to creep into her voice.

"The medical officer isn't here."

"So when will he be here?" she asked, her irritation growing.

"I don't know. He and the captain and most of the crew have gone off to watch the big fight, so I've no idea when they will be back."

"So what time is the ship sailing?" Mary asked. There was an anguished air about her.

"That depends on when they get back. Some of these fights last a long time, so your guess is as good as mine," the steward said with a shrug of his shoulders.

This fight won't last long as there's not going to be a fight, she was longing to tell him, but instead she smiled at him as she said, "So what do we do in the meantime?"

"There is provision for all passengers who have a valid ticket to rest at the lodging house until it is time to board," the steward explained.

"Thank you," Mary said, a worried look clouding her face as she turned and led Michael and Holly away.

"So what do we do now? We can't hang around too much as we'll get spotted, and then we'll have no chance of getting away," Michael said as soon as they were far enough away not to be overheard.

"There is only one thing we can do: go back home and wait until we know when it's time for the passengers to board the ship," Mary suggested.

"But how are we going to know when the ship is ready to sail? And what about Fisty?"

"I will have to stay here. When I know when the ship is ready to sail, I will come and fetch you. And if I see Fisty, I will tell him what is happening, although I hope he will have found out for himself as we have agreed we shouldn't make contact until we are safely at sea. The one good thing we can be sure of is that the delay won't be long as there isn't going to be a fight, so the captain and crew will soon be back, getting the ship ready for sail."

"Yes, I guess that's all we can do. But be careful," Michael said, resigned.

"I will. Don't worry about me. Just make sure nobody sees you."

Chapter 30

Right, you two get yourselves ready. You'll be on in a few moments," Madame Rosita told the two prostitutes as they sat in the changing tent enjoying a glass of gin. "I want a good fight—no fancy stuff, dancing around each other. There's an extra five pounds for both of you if you give the crowd a good show."

"Don't worry, I can't wait to knock the shit out of her," Ivy said, glaring at Bridgit.

"Chance'll be a fine thing. She can't even shag the shit out of a man," Bridgit countered spitefully.

"Good, keep up that hostility for the ring and we will have a good fight. I'll be back soon," Madame Rosita said. Then she turned and walked back out.

* * * *

Leon waited nervously in reception for the moment the coach would draw up to take him and Michael to the fight, knowing full well Michael was not going to turn up. His nervousness increased as he worried about what he was going to say and how long he could keep the coach waiting before troubled started.

* * * *

The crowd let out a great cheer as Ivy and Bridgit made their way out of the tent towards the ring.

The crowd edged forward, all wanting to get a closer view of the women as they bent under the rope and entered the ring.

The crowd erupted with a greater, more appreciative cheer as the two women slipped off their cloaks to reveal they were stripped to the waist, wearing just Holland drawers and white stockings with their hair combed tightly back and tied into a bun. Both women had reasonably good figures with full well-rounded breasts, which seemed to add eroticism to the fact they were about to tear at each other.

Madame Rosita, acting as referee, ducked under the rope and stepped into the ring. She called the two women to the scratch and spoke to them loudly so that most of the crowd could hear. "You will each hold a half-crown in each hand," she said, handing them the half-crowns. "Those are to stop you from scratching each other's eyes out or scratching anywhere else on the body or face. You are allowed to hit and punch with the fist on any part of your opponent's body or face. If you are knocked down, you are allowed thirty seconds to get back on your feet; otherwise you will be counted out. Or else the first to drop the half-crown from either hand will be declared the loser. So go back to your corners and come up to the scratch when I blow the whistle. May the best woman win."

As soon as the whistle blew, Ivy, who appeared to be the most aggressive, was quickest to the scratch. She threw out a right punch to the chest of Bridgit as the latter got to the scratch. It was a powerful punch. Bridgit was surprised by its force and began to move around carefully to avoid another punch like that.

For twenty minutes or so they fought fiercely, the excited crowd cheering them on. Savage as their inclinations were becoming with bloodlust on their faces, both managed to successfully fight the urge to tear, claw, and scratch each other's eyes out by having to hold on to the two half-crowns. They continued punching each other with their fists until blood was running in streams down their swollen faces and breasts.

As the fight intensified, Ivy's nose was broken and Bridgit received a powerful right hook to the jaw which fractured her cheekbones. Bridgit retaliated with a heavy punch to Ivy's body, cracking one of her ribs. Soon they were standing face to face, hammering at each other with punches landing all over their bodies. They were cheered on by the excited crowd. Blood was now beginning to seep from the nipples of their bloated breasts with both of them now trying to prise open each other's fist, the intent being to force the other to drop the half-crown. Bridgit twisted Ivy's wrist to try to force her hand open, but Ivy swung a vicious right to Bridgit's head, which sent her reeling to ground, the half-crown slipping from her hand. In a daze she looked up at Ivy, who was standing over her and holding up the half-crown she'd dropped.

Angrily Bridgit grabbed Ivy's legs and pulled her to the ground. She rolled on top of her and began to beat her about the face. The crowd, now ecstatic at the women's antics, continued to cheer them on, particularly when Ivy started tearing at Bridgit's Holland drawers. At that point the crowd was shouting, "Go on, rip them off. Strip her!"

"Aren't you going to stop it? Ivy's won," Lord Blamfont asked Madame Rosita.

"Why? The crowd are loving it, and those two don't seem to want to stop until they've killed each other. And if you look around, you'll notice that people are placing bets on whether Ivy'll succeed in tearing Bridgit's drawers off. Mind you, with a bit of luck they'll finish up tearing the clothes off each other."

Madame Rosita's instincts were right as Bridgit began to retaliate by tearing at Ivy's drawers. In no time the sound of tearing fabric filled the air with both women frantically trying to rip what shreds of clothing were left on the other. Soon they were both left with nothing covering their bodies. Unabashed, they continued to wrestle on the ground naked, the sight becoming even more sexually arousing, much to the delight of the already excited crowd.

"I told you it was better to let them get on with it. Just listen to the crowd. They'll think they got their money's worth, and what a build-up to the big fight. Things couldn't have gone better," Madame Rosita said, her face beaming with self-satisfaction.

"Yes, I must admit you're one smart lady. This is

something I would never have thought of," Lord Blamfont said by way of a compliment, his eyes still fixed on the two sprawling naked women. "I'd like to fuck both of them as they are right now."

"You're welcome to them, and I don't think you'll get much resistance from them. I think they'll be happy just to lie there and let you do whatever you want."

"So how long are you going to let it continue?"

"Just as long as they keep at it and the crowd are enjoying it. The one thing I have learned from this is that all our future fights will start with a female fight—before Leon's future fights, that is, after he's beaten the ruffian," she told him, the self-satisfied look still glued to her face.

* * * *

"So what's a nice lady like you doing hanging around here? We've been watching you. Looking for business, are we? Well, we can take you to a better place where they would be very interested in a nice-looking bit of stuff like you, and then you wouldn't have to hang out at places like this," one of the crimps said as he and the other members of his gang sidled up to Mary.

Mary hesitated, but only for an instant, as she rounded on them. "Piss off. Go and annoy someone else. I'm waiting for my husband, and I don't think he'll like it to see you lot annoying me. He can cut up pretty rough."

"Oh, listen to her. Has me shaking in me boots."

"We're not frightened of anybody. How much money you got on you?" one of the other crimps asked, moving threateningly closer to her.

She could see the determination in his eyes as she gazed at him distantly, trying to hide the sudden fear she was feeling. "Not enough that would interest you," she said defiantly.

"Well, let's see, shall we?" He snatched her handbag before she had a chance to get a firmer grip on it.

She tried to grab it back, but he smacked her across the

face with the back of his hand. It was a hard blow that made her nose bleed, but with him holding onto her handbag, she had nothing with which to stem the flow. She was forced to use her hand.

"Wow, what about this? What would you be doing with three tickets for the *Britannia*?" he said, pulling the tickets out of the bag and holding them up for his mates to see. "These must be worth a few bob."

"We are sailing on the ship tonight. Like I told you, I am waiting for my husband and daughter to arrive, so you had better give them back to me before he gets here if you want to stay in one piece," she warned them, wishing she could say Michael's name, guessing they would have heard about the fight. But she knew there would be rich pickings here with a ship carrying rich passengers leaving for the United States.

"I'll tell you what we'll do. We'll hold onto these, and when your husband gets here, he can pay us to get them back," he said, tucking the tickets into his coat pocket, before he searched into the bag again, feeling for any money. His face brightened as he felt a number of large coins. His smile stretched wider as his hand clutched a roll of notes. "This really is our lucky day," he said, pulling out the roll and removing the rubber bands. "Five-pound notes. There must be over a hundred pounds here," he added, holding up one the five-pound notes.

"Why don't we just take the money and go?" another of the other crimps spoke up.

"Oh no, I reckon there'll be more rich pickings when her husband turns up. Because if she's carrying this, just think what he might be carrying," the other crimp told him. "We'll just have to hold onto her and keep her out of sight until he turns up."

"Yeah, and maybe we can have a bit of fun with her while we wait," another of the crimps suggested, giving Mary a lecherous sneer.

"No, I don't want him to see her in a distressed state, as

that might cause a problem. If he doesn't pay up, of course we'll sell the tickets and take her to the brothel. But don't worry. I'll let you have some fun with her first to get her in the way of things."

Chapter 31

How long are we going to keep waiting? The horses are getting restless," the coach driver called down to Leon, who was sitting in the coach asking himself the same question.

"Not long now. He should be along in a few minutes. We can't go without him, that's for sure."

"Do you think he has turned chicken and is not going to turn up?" the coach driver hinted.

"I wouldn't have thought so, but you never know."

"No, you don't. I've met all types in my job, so nothing surprises me," the coach driver said. "Maybe he's got confused about where he was supposed to meet us and has made his own way there," he added as an afterthought.

"Possibly. We'll give him a few more moments, and then we'll make our way there."

* * * *

For an hour or more there was still no sign of the fighters. The crowd's jubilation at having watched the two women fighting and ripping the clothes off each other was beginning to diminish, and they were starting to get a little restless, anxious for the big fight to get going.

"Where the blazes are they? What can be holding them up?" Madame Rosita asked Sir Richard as she looked around at the crowd, sensing their restlessness.

"I've no idea. Everything has been planned as agreed for your man to meet up with mine and for them to arrive here together in the coach."

"I think one of you had better go and find out what's going on before we start to have trouble here," Lord Blamfont interjected.

"Yes, I think we need to. Would you mind going to find out, Sir Richard? I don't think it would sensible for me to go."

Sir Richard hesitated, not sure whether that would be the wise thing to do.

"Well, nothing is going to happen if you're going to just stand there and think about it," Lord Blamfont interjected again.

"Why not send Hudson, his second? He can find out what is going on just as well as I. With luck he'll meet them on their way here," he suggested.

"Yes, of course. I'll send Hudson."

* * * *

Holly sat hunched in the chair, watching Michael pacing around the room. He was unable to relax, wondering what was happening.

"Why don't you sit down, Michael? Mary will be here soon. She won't let us down," Holly said, trying to reassure him.

"It's not her I'm worried about. It's if the bastards get a sniff of what we're up to, then all hell could break loose and all our plans will come to nothing," he said, continuing to pace the floor.

"But you and Mary said you had it all worked out, so what can go wrong?" Holly said, her voice beginning to tremble at the thought of what he had just said.

"You're right. Sorry. I was just thinking of what might go wrong. But as you say, we got it all worked out, and Mary is patiently waiting at the docks to come back and tell us when it is safe to board the ship," he said, forcing a smile to his lips to reassure her.

* * * *

"What the fuck are you doing sitting here in the coach all on your own? Where the fuck is Michael?" Hudson asked as soon as he got to the coach and saw Leon sitting there.

"I don't know," Leon answered, not wanting to say any more.

"What do you mean, you don't know? Have you heard from him? Has he chickened out?"

"I told you, I don't know what's happened to him. I've just been sitting here as instructed, waiting for him."

"So what should we do?" Hudson asked, becoming a little nervous.

"We'll wait here a little longer, and if he doesn't turn up, then we'll make our way there on the assumption that's what he's done."

* * * *

The crimps were holding Mary in an old disused shed on the edge of the docks, all of them looking bored and restless as they waited for the husband to turn up.

"When is your shit of a husband going to be turning up?" one the crimps asked, impatience sounding in his voice.

"He'll be here; you don't have to worry about that. What you need to worry about is what he'll do to you lot when he gets here," she told them, her voice unwavering.

"I'm trembling in me boots. You know what? I'm really looking forward to fucking you. The people at the place we'll be taking you to are pleased if I've broken the bitch in. It saves them time and money," one of the crimps said, reaching his hand up to grab her breast.

"In your dreams, crimp," she said, smacking his hand away. "The one who is going to get fucked is you and your mates when my husband gets here. You have no idea who you're messing with."

"You make him sound like some kind of pugilist. Probably can't punch his way out of a paper bag. One punch from any of us and he'll turn and run, that is, of course, if he's still on his feet," he said sarcastically.

"Did any of you go to see the last fight Tom Dyer had?"

"Yeah, he was knocked clean out by some Irish git called Flanagan," one of the other crimps spoke up.

"Isn't he the one fighting the Negro tonight?" another of the crimps spoke up.

"Yeah, I wanted to go to that," another of the crimps said.

"Why didn't you?" Mary asked.

"Cos of the bleeding ship, of course," he snapped. "Hang on a minute, you're not trying to tell us that your old man is the Irish bare-knuckle fighter, are you?" he asked, looking around at the others as he waited for her to answer.

"What do you think? I've been trying to tell you. So now you know what you're up against," she said, her voice sounding more confident.

"Oh shit, maybe we should just let her go and get the hell out of here. I don't fancy getting my head punched in by the likes of him."

"Hang on, you lot, you're all supposing he's going to win the fight. That Negro is one tough son of a bitch, and those blacks are built like brick shithouses. He's most likely to be the one to win, so the Irish git could finish up splattered across the ring. Even if he can get to his feet, he'll be no match for us, a pushover. So I suggest we just wait," the crimp who appeared to be the one giving the orders said.

Chapter 32

"*Why are we waiting? Why are we waiting?*" the crowd were beginning to chant. The chant was quickly spreading around the field with the voices becoming more boisterous and threatening.

"We've got to do something. The crowd are not going to wait much longer," Madame Rosita said, a hint of panic beginning to sound in her voice.

"With no sign of Hudson as yet, I don't know what we can do. What do you think, Sir Richard?" Lord Blamfont asked, turning to him for an answer.

"One of us has to go in the ring and speak to the crowd," he suggested.

"And tell them what?" Madame Rosita challenged.

"Tell them there's been a slight delay, but the fighters will be here soon. At least that will keep them calm for a time while we try to sort out what the devil is going on," he suggested.

"Very well. I think you would be the best person to do that. Would you be so kind?" Madame Rosita pleaded in her best sultry voice.

"I'll do my best," he said, turning and making his way to the ring as the noise from the crowd was becoming deafening.

"My lords and ladies, gentlemen and fancies," he began, holding his hands high to command silence. Slowly the noise lowered to a murmur. "We must apologise for the slight delay, which has been caused by some unforeseen circumstances."

"*Cut the crap. When are they going to be here?*" a group of the crowd angrily shouted out.

"As I was saying, it won't be long now. And you are going to see a fight like no other fight you've seen, so kindly bear with us," he pleaded, ducking back under the rope and hurrying back to the tent.

"That crowd are likely to get very nasty if we're not careful. For God's sake, where are they?" Sir Richard said, breathing a sigh of relief that he was back safely with his peers.

Just then they heard the noise of galloping horses as the coach approached.

"At long last." Madame Rosita sighed. "Now we can get things started," she said, hurrying towards the coach as it came to an abrupt stop, the driver pulling hard on the reins to rein in the horses, which began to snort at their exhausting gallop.

"What the blazes?" Madame Rosita said as she looked into the coach and saw only Leon sitting there. "Where the fuck is he?" she blurted out as the others came running up to the coach.

"I don't know. I sat there waiting, but he never turned up," Leon said, maintaining an innocent expression.

"I should have kept my eye on him. I should have known …"

"You should have known what?" Madame Rosita cut across Sir Richard with an accusing glare.

"When I told him about the fight, he told me he did not want to fight your man."

"Why wouldn't he want to fight Leon?" Lord Blamfont asked, a puzzled look spreading across his face.

"Because he said they were once friends and apparently your Leon had been good to him. And he told me your Leon didn't want to fight him either for the same reasons."

"Well, my man is here ready to fight, so you can't blame him. The point is, where is your man? We have to find him quick. Otherwise we are going to have a riot on our hands," Madame Rosita said, her glare becoming fiercer.

"I suggest we send someone to that whore Mary's home. Which is where he's probably hiding," Lord Blamfont suggested.

"And what if he's not there?" Sir Richard asked.

"Then your guess is as good as mine. He could be anywhere. But I suspect Mary will know where he is, so I suggest we get hold of her and force her one way or another to tell us where he is. I suggest we send Hudson and Leon to go and get her," Lord Blamfont proposed.

"No, Leon must stay here so the public can see that one of the fighters is here. At least that will stave off any unrest. No, I've got a better idea. I'll send Ivy and Bridgit. They've proved they're a match for any woman. And while they're doing that, I suggest you check out whether he may have taken a coach somewhere or the train to Manchester," Madame Rosita told them.

"What about the docks?" Lord Blamfont asked.

"What about the docks?" she retorted.

"He might be trying to get on a ship to somewhere," he answered.

"If he is, he's not going to get very far as there is only one ship in port, the *Britannia*, and the captain of that is here in the tent as one of our guests, so the ship won't be going anywhere without him. So let's stop arguing and find that ruffian as fast as we can," she said, her temper rising.

* * * *

"I'm worried. I don't like the idea of Mary being there all on her own in those docks. There are too many thieves and crooks around. We've got to go and see she's all right," Michael said, beginning to get anxious.

"But she said she will come back as soon as it's OK for us to get on the ship," Holly said apprehensively, trying to reason out whether what he was saying was the right thing to do.

"I know she did, but it's been a long time, and I would have thought the crowd would have started to break up by now and the captain would have been back to his ship. In any event, it can't be long now. So we may as well make our way there," he said resolutely, grabbing his coat and picking up the case containing Holly's money, which was hidden amongst the other belongings they were taking with them.

Holly said nothing, just grabbed her coat and meekly followed him out.

* * * *

The crowd's impatience was building again because nothing seemed to be happening. There was the danger that it would escalate into violence as the supporters of the rival boxers started to hurl abuse at each other, the ones supporting Leon calling Michael and his supporters yellow-bellies.

The bedlam continued with Lord Blamfont stepping into the ring and screaming for calm and promising the fight would soon take place as Michael Flanagan was on his way.

Unfortunately his words did nothing to calm the crowd. In fact, what he'd said only added to their fury, causing the crowd to press forward with those close storming the ring. One of the angry crowd threw a vicious punch at Lord Blamfont that sent him flying to the ground.

As he struggled to his feet, the crowd were now spiralling out of control with fights breaking out all over the field. Women and children were running scared, trying to get clear of the fighting.

Lord Blamfont, his face bloodied, having managed to scramble to his feet, was knocked down again by the charging crowd and trampled on.

"We have to get out of here before they catch up with us, or we'll be killed," Madame Rosita said, her voice shaking with fear.

"Yes, we must tell everybody to get away from here as fast as they can. There's no telling what the crowd will do next. I tell you, when I get my hands on that ruffian, I will skin him alive before I send him to debtors' prison," Sir Richard said, his anger rising in an effort to overcome his fear.

The crowd were now completely out of control with many heading en masse towards the tents and shouting, "We've been tricked. Let's get the get the cheating bastards."

* * * *

Michael looked anxiously around the docks, trying to determine where he expected Mary to be standing. He became increasingly worried when he couldn't see her. "Can you see her anywhere?" he asked Holly.

"No, I can't. Maybe she's on her way to get us. We should have waited," she told him.

"No, we would have seen her. She's still here, maybe having a word with the captain."

"He's gone to the fight, remember," Holly reminded him.

"Yeah, I forgot. So where is she? We'll have to start looking around. She may be resting in the lodging house. Let's go and look there first," he suggested.

The lodging house was full of people waiting to board the ship. Michael's anxiety grew as he looked around but was unable to see Mary anywhere. "I suggest you stay here and take care of the case while I go and look for Mary. She has to be here somewhere," he said to Holly as he hurried over to the woman sitting behind the small reception desk by the entrance.

"Excuse me, can you please keep an eye out for this young lady and her case as I have to find the other person travelling with us on the *Britannia*?" he asked.

"Of course, as long as she doesn't go wandering off," the woman said with a reassuring smile.

"Thank you. I will be back soon," he told her as he hurried off.

* * * *

"I think I saw him wandering around the docks, and then I watched him go to the lodging house. He had a young woman with him, and he was carrying a case," one of the crimps said as he rushed back into the old disused shed on the edge of the docks.

"Are you sure?" the leader of the crimps asked, his eyes rising in excitement.

"Yes, I'm sure it's him. I recognised him from the posters announcing the fight," he said.

"Are you certain? I mean, he should still be at the fight. Did he look beaten up?"

"No, he looked fine. Smartly dressed. Didn't look like he'd even been in a fight."

"So what's been going on? Has he chickened out like a snivelling coward?"

"He's no coward as you'll soon find out," Mary cut in, relieved to know Michael was looking for her.

"If he's not a coward, why wasn't he at the fight? Or could he have won the fight that easily, which is why there are no telltale marks on his face? All a bit strange. And what was he doing with another young woman and a case? So this is what it's all about—you lot are running away, or rather sailing off, together," the leader of the crimps said, turning to look questioningly at Mary.

Mary said nothing.

"The ship, of course. You're all pissing off to America, and he's ..."

At that moment they began to hear the noises of a crowd surging onto the docks. There were groups screaming, shouting, hurling abuse at each other, and fighting using iron bars, heavy sticks, and anything else they could lay their hands on to use as weapons.

Chapter 33

The police had been called and were attempting to take control of the situation, but the rioting was now totally out of control with groups chasing each other out of the field and the fighting spilling out onto the streets in their efforts to get away from the police, who were lashing out with their truncheons at anybody they came in contact with.

Madame Rosita, Sir Richard, Leon, and Hudson, with the help of the police, had managed to get to their coaches and make a hasty retreat before the rioters got to them.

Unfortunately Lord Blamfont had been badly injured as a result of being trampled on. His clothes were in ruins, and his face and body were bloodied, bruised, and caked in mud. He was finally rescued by the police, who carried him bodily to his coach and rushed him to safety. "I'll sue them all" were his last words before lapsing into unconsciousness again.

* * * *

A mob was charging into the dock area, clearly drunk and angry, arguing and fighting amongst themselves. Michael realised he had to hide somewhere in case any of them recognised him, for there were plenty of posters with his face advertising the fight around the area. He spotted a ramshackle shed tucked away in a disused part of the docks and made a run for it.

"Well, well, well, look who's just popped in," the leader of the crimps exclaimed as Michael rushed in.

Michael stopped in his tracks and stared in disbelief at the bunch of crimps staring back at him. His eyes widened in a mixture of surprise and horror as he saw Mary standing there amongst them.

He looked at her squarely, but her eyes didn't waver.

Worry shadowed her lovely features with her nose bloodied and swollen. Michael knew instantly they were in trouble, trapped in a scenario he could never have dreamed of. He had to think carefully before he said or did anything.

"It kinda looks like you chickened out of the fight. Now why would you do that, I wonder?" the leader of the crimps spoke up.

Michael watched him quietly as he struggled for an answer. "Look, I don't know what you're up to, but if you were protecting my friend—"

"Your friend, not your wife?" he cut in, looking from one to the other.

The word *wife* threw him, and he wasn't sure what to answer as he looked across at Mary. "OK, my wife. I didn't think she had told you. As I was saying, if you were protecting my wife from the angry mob that's causing trouble outside, then I thank you, but if you are holding her against her will for some other reason, then—"

"Then what?" the leader challenged, his eyes boring into him.

"Then that changes everything," Michael said, his manner giving no indication of what he was thinking: *Never be afraid of a bully, because if you confront him, you'll find he's really a coward.*

"I'm waiting," the leader said with some irritation.

Michael knew he could handle them. He was fitter and stronger and could take more punishment than anyone of them could, but it was Mary he had to protect. If they were to threaten her, then he could be at a disadvantage. "You let her go. We'll just walk out of here, and there'll be no trouble," he said with more confidence than he felt.

The leader gave an irritated snort. "You've got to be joking. Do you think we've been waiting all this time for you to turn up just to let the two of you walk away?"

Michael had learned from his father that when faced with such odds, a person had three choices: fight, give in, or hold off in the hope of something happening that could narrow the odds in one's own favour. "So what exactly is it you want?" he asked, determined to keep the dialogue going as long as he could while his brain worked desperately to think of a way out of the situation.

"All the money and valuables you've got on you."

Michael didn't answer. He just kept watching, staring at the crimp. He knew the signs. He had been through this before with the other crimps. He could see the determination in this one's eyes and the hatred on his face. "I haven't got any money and neither has she," he said, his whole body bristling with anger and frustration.

"Is that so? Well, for your information, your wife here was carrying a lot of money and three tickets for the *Britannia*. So it seems you were planning to skip the fight and piss off to America before anyone found out about it. But I guess that's what all the rumpus is about outside, crowds of fancies angry they've been cheated out of a fight. What if I were to go out there and tell them you are here?"

"And I will tell them you have been holding me and my wife ransom," Michael said in quiet anger. "And in the mood they sound in, I think they would tear the lot of you apart."

The leader gave him a cold, forbidding look, his jaw clenching at the thought. "You think you're smart."

"A lot smarter than you lot, that's for sure. I could rush to the door and start screaming for help. I wouldn't think much of your chances then. So why don't you be sensible? Give my wife back her money and the tickets and we'll—"

"Not so fast. I know a way out of here through the back, so we'll take your wife. She'll make good money for us. We'll leave you to your own devices as you won't be able to explain why you're hiding here all on your own," the crimp said, staring at Michael, a hard and silent stare like a physical force, like a cold, crushing pressure, his bleak cold eyes unblinking.

A surge of rage coursed through Michael's body. Uncertainty tugged at his sleeve, and his heart was beating fast. The urge to do what he knew had to do and damn the consequences was becoming overpowering. It gave him an exhilarating feeling he had felt once before with the other crimps. He knew this had to be sorted out quickly for time wasn't on his side.

The problem was that it could cost him and Mary their lives, but that was a chance he had to take. The leader was getting cocky and inadvertently dropped his guard, which is what Michael had been waiting for. Acting on pure adrenaline, his heightened awareness making him more aggressive than ever, he shot out a straight right to the face. The leader's lips exploded and his teeth burst out of his mouth before he telescoped to the ground.

One of the other crimps rushed to attack Michael, but he met with the same fate as he was hit with another straight right to the chin, crunching the bones of his jaw, sending him spiralling to the ground. The other crimps, still holding Mary, hesitated, not sure what to do, neither of them brave enough to attack Michael.

"Let her go and give me the money and the tickets or I'll beat the shit out of all of you," Michael yelled at them.

"We haven't got the money. He has," one of the crimps spoke up, pointing at the leader still sprawled on the ground, his face a mass of blood.

"Then let go of her and get the hell away before I do you some serious injuries," he threatened them.

They released their hold on Mary and scampered out the back of the shed. Mary, free from their grip, rushed forward and threw herself into Michael's arms. "Thank God you came looking for me. I shudder to think what would have happened if you hadn't."

"Yes, well, we can talk about that later, but in the meantime we need to think how we're going to get out of here."

"We can go out the way those crimps went," she suggested.

At that moment the fighting was getting louder as it seemed to be coming closer and closer to the shed.

"Yes, you're right, let's go. But I must get our money and

the tickets back," he said, pulling himself away from her and moving swiftly to where the leader was lying, clutching his hands to his face. "Now give me the money and the tickets, or I swear I will beat your face to a pulp," he threatened him.

As the leader lowered his hands to his pockets, the door was suddenly smashed open by bodies being hurled against it. The fighting spilled into the shed with fists and weapons being wielded in all directions. The fighting was so intense that the crowd didn't notice Michael bent over the leader. "You say anything, and I swear you'll never utter another word," Michael swore as he grabbed the money and the tickets.

Mary had pressed herself into a corner on the other side of the shed from where Michael was standing. Michael wiped the blood he had gotten on his hands from the leader's head and face to serve as a disguise and make it look like he was one of the melee. He whacked a couple of the crowd, who went down without any idea of who had hit them as he charged his way across to Mary.

"My God, you're bleeding!" she exclaimed in horror.

"No I'm not, but don't worry about that. We've got to get out of here," he said, frantically looking around at the senseless goings-on, knowing he was directly responsible for it.

"That's him," he heard one of the fighters call out. "Michael Flanagan, the one that was supposed to be fighting tonight!"

"The fighting stopped abruptly, and they all turned to stare at him.

"So what have you got to say for yourself?" one of the fighters asked as they all surged forward, trapping him and Mary in the corner.

"It's a long story," Michael said.

"So tell us. We've got plenty of time. We've lost a lot of money because of you. We bet on you to win."

"I didn't bet on you, but I've still lost my money, which was why I've been fighting, thinking you had chickened out," another of the mob joined in.

"You lost your money not because of me but because of those organising the fight," Michael began to explain, his brain racing to think up a story.

"How do you mean?" one of the men asked.

"They never intended me to win. They wanted me to take a fall, and I refused, which is why I've been forced to hide out here with my wife as I know they're after me."

"Who're those two reeling on the floor?" one the fighters asked.

"They had abducted my wife and were holding her here. I think they were hired to try to force me to fight and take the dive. But as you can see, they weren't very good at their job."

"The bastards!" another of the fighters called out. "I want my money back," he added, giving the gang leader a hard kick in the ribs to vent his feelings.

"So who is responsible for all this? And what can we do to get our money back?" another shouted out.

"Do any of you know Madame Rosita's brothel?" Michael asked.

"Yeah, I know where it is," one of the fighters said. He hesitated, looking at Mary, a faint feeling of recognition flashing through his mind as her features seemed vaguely familiar.

"Well, she is the principal organiser, along with Lord Blamfont." Michael said, taking pleasure in telling them.

"Lord Blamfont, did you say?"

"Yes. Do you know him?

"That son of a bitch had me and me family thrown out of our cottage back in Ireland," another of the fighters with a strong Irish accent called out, which made Michael smile.

"He did the same to me and my family," Michael told him. "So you'll be doing us both a favour if you get to him. He deserves all he gets for what he's done to so many of us. So go to it, my friends, and get your revenge and your money back," Michael said, urging them on.

The crowd, now united in a common cause, turned and hurried out.

"What made you think of that?" Mary asked, looking at him in amazement.

"I don't know. It was the first thing that came into my head."

"Well, it sure as hell worked."

Chapter 34

"I hold you responsible," Madame Rosita said, looking up at Sir Richard as she lay stretched out on the chaise lounge completely exhausted, her mind in a whirl, trying to figure out why it had gone so badly wrong.

"Are you sure you knew nothing about that little shit not turning up?" Madame Rosita challenged, turning her head to Leon.

"No, Madame, I had no idea. And I still don't know what his plan was. Has anyone found out where he is?" Leon asked, hoping to turn attention away from himself.

"No, but we've got people out looking for him. It won't be long before he's found, and then he'll be made to fight on pain of death," Sir Richard said vehemently.

"You can't make a man fight if he doesn't want to," Leon said in a conciliatory tone.

"That depends on the choices," Sir Richard retorted, the venom still thick in his voice. "He has no choices. Either he will fight or I will have him sent to debtors' prison until he repays every single penny I have spent and lost on him."

"And you can add the money I've lost to that," Madame Rosita cut in.

Suddenly there were howls of hysterical screaming coming from the reception area that made Madame Rosita sit up. "What the devil's going on?"

"I'll go and have a look," Leon volunteered, but before

he could even make it to the door, a group of the crowd from the docks burst in, forcing him to step back as they charged forward into the lounge, almost tripping over the chaise lounge Madame Rosita was sitting on.

"That must be her," one the maddened crowd shouted out.

"You owe us," another shouted as they gathered threateningly around her.

"Who the hell are you, and what do you think you are doing barging in here? I'll call the police," she retaliated, a mixture of shock and fear spreading across her face.

Leon stepped forward as another of the crowd went to grab her. Leon forcibly shoved him away.

They all stopped and went quiet as they stared at Leon.

"The Negro, the one who was supposed to be fighting the Irishman," another spoke up.

"Except he wouldn't have been fighting for very long, would he? Cos our boy was being forced to take a dive."

Madame Rosita looked around at all of them and then up at Sir Richard. "What the hell are they talking about?"

"Don't look so innocent. We know what you were up to. He told us all about it," another of the crowd told her.

"He? You mean you've been talking to him? You know where he is?" Sir Richard exclaimed, excitement, for the moment, overcoming his fear.

"Yeah, we just left him and made our way here when he told us why he was refusing to fight," the same man explained.

"So where is the lying, cheating bastard now?" Sir Richard asked.

"He's not the lying, cheating bastard. You are. And we want our money back," another of the crowd spoke up.

"Money back? I don't owe you anything," Madame Rosita said angrily. "It is not my fault he chickened out, the miserable coward. It has cost me a fortune; I've lost thousands," she said. There was genuine grief in her expression at being reminded of the huge loss she had suffered.

"As have I," Sir Richard said, wanting her to know she

was not the only one who had suffered losses. Then his expression brightened as an idea sprang to mind.

"I'll tell you what, you want your money back and so do we. You take us to where he is hiding, and if you help us keep a hold on him, we'll pay you each a half-crown."

"Make it a crown and you've got a deal," one of the crowd called out.

"Very well, a crown each. But you must help us hold him until we can secure him somewhere safe," Sir Richard insisted.

"What are you going to do with him then?" another of the crowd asked.

"Rearrange the fight, of course."

"What, and force him to take a dive?" another asked.

"No, he's told you a lie. It was always going to be a straight fight to the bitter end," Sir Richard explained.

"Right. You're on. Let's go and get him," the one who seemed to have taken on the role of team leader said.

"What are you going to do with him when they find him?" Madame Rosita asked as soon as the crowd had gone.

"That's simple. I will have him arrested and held in the debtors' prison until the day of the fight, then I will pay for his release. But if he still refuses to fight, he will stay there and rot, which I don't think he will be keen to do. I will also pay for his keep and send in food as I don't want him coming out of there in a weak condition. I'll also have Fisty committed too so that he can keep the ruffian training and fit. The sooner we arrange the fight, the sooner I can get them out of there."

* * * *

Fisty made his way along the docks towards the *Britannia*, hoping to spot Michael, but he dared not risk lingering. He continued on his way as per the agreement that they would not meet up until they were all safely on board the ship.

"You can't board yet. The medical examiner is not here, nor is the captain. You'll have to wait with the others in the lodging house," the steward told him.

"So when will they be here?" Fisty asked, not wanting to mix with anyone until he was safely on board.

"I don't know. They went to see the fight, but something seems to have happened there. We had a drunken angry mob roaming the docks and fighting amongst themselves, which seemed to have been some kind of spillover from the fight," the steward said with a hapless shrug of his shoulders.

Fisty reluctantly turned away, knowing that Michael's not turning up was the obvious cause of the trouble, but he hadn't expected it to spill out onto the streets and the docks.

The lodging house was crowded. As he weaved his way around, he spotted Michael, Mary, and Holly huddled in a corner, obviously trying to keep themselves away from prying eyes.

Michael's eyes lit up as he saw Fisty hurry towards them. "I thought you would be waiting until Mary came to tell you it was safe to board the ship," Fisty said, surprised to see them all together.

"I got worried about Mary, and a good thing I did, because she was being held by a gang. They had stolen her money and the tickets and were waiting for me to turn up so they could rob me."

"Looks like you managed to sort them out."

"Not quite. A mob of drunken and angry fancies came onto the docks wanting to smash each other's heads in. They burst into the shed where we were being held, and they scared off the crimps, but then they recognised me and accused me of chickening out on the fight. I quickly made up a story that the fight was fixed for me to take a dive, and that was the reason I had refused to fight. It seemed to do the trick. They've all charged off to Madame Rosita's to get their money back."

"Well, all we're waiting for is the captain and the medical examiner to return, which shouldn't be long as there's been no fight, so I guess we'll just have to wait here until then," Fisty advised them.

Just then they heard the rumbling noise of a crowd outside the lodge. The next moment the crowd burst in with the receptionist leaping up from behind her desk and rushing towards them. "You can't come in here," she protested, but they just swept past her.

"We're looking for Michael Flanagan," one of them called out.

"What are we going to do?" Mary whispered to Michael.

"I don't think there is much we can do. There are too many of them. I suggest you and Holly get out of here quickly. They're not after you two. Don't worry about me and Fisty; we'll sort this lot out," Michael told her.

* * * *

Debtors' prison allowed a varied amount of freedom, even permitting the prisoners to buy extra freedoms where they could go out and visit their family and friends provided they returned to the prison by the time prescribed, a practice known as "liberty of the rules". Failure to keep to the rules was met with instant punishment and all privileges taken away.

Kirkdale prison was a privately run institution that had separate areas for its two classes of prisoners, the masters' side and the commoners' side. On the masters' side the prisoners had to pay rent of around ten shillings a week and were expected to feed and clothe themselves. They were allowed to furnish their rooms with little extras to make the cells a little more comfortable. The rooms had two beds, which could be shared with a fellow prisoner, which fortunately in Michael's case was Fisty. They also had the luxury of a bar where they could buy alcohol; a chandler's shop where they could buy candles, soap, and a little food; a coffee shop; a steakhouse; a tailor's shop; and a barbershop. They could even hire prisoners from the commoners' side to act as their servants. The problem was, of course, that paying for all these luxuries very often put them further into debt, which in turn made it increasingly more difficult to clear their initial liability.

Michael, however, was lucky in that Sir Richard was picking up the bill so that he could be well fed and continue training to prepare for the big fight while locked up.

* * * *

"The thing is, you have to block as many of the incoming punches as you can, but don't hold yourself tense. Allow the momentum of blocking the punch to manoeuvre you into a position to be able to punch back even harder. How the blow hits you will dictate how you counterpunch, but you have to be prepared to take the force of the punch if you are to be able to use it to your advantage. It's a skill that most fighters never manage to master or even understand. It requires that you have the strength to absorb the punches and convert them into energy so you can use that energy to power your own punches. That's what we are going to be concentrating on today," Fisty explained to Michael as they set out to train in the prison exercise yard with all the prisoners who were allowed out looking on or with those confined to their cells staring in amusement from their small iron-barred windows at the antics of the two men sparring.

Mary was also allowed to visit Michael every day and bring him food and a change of clothes, but as much as that made life a little more bearable, the fact that he was being held there in an effort to force him to fight Leon was gnawing at her.

Unbeknown to Michael, Leon too was being forced into intense training by Madame Rosita and Lord Blamfont with the threat they would report him as an escaped slave if he didn't do as he was told.

* * * *

Madame Rosita was aware of the success of having had two female fighters as warm-up for the main fight. The sight of two vampish, aggressive women, their bare-breasted, sweaty, and bloodied bodies providing an exciting display of animalistic passion, was something the crowd really enjoyed.

Madame Rosita knew it would draw the crowd again, but she wondered where she would be able to find another two females who could match the performance of Bridgit and Ivy.

On her usual walk to the fish market, which she had to do now that Leon was in serious training and not allowed to leave the premises, she was alerted by a sudden piercing scream appearing to come from a female, which immediately began to draw a crowd.

"Go on, Polly, give it to her," she heard one the crowd shout out, which was followed by a general acclamation: "Yeah, go on, Polly. Pitch into the bitch."

"What's the fight about?" Madame Rosita asked the man standing next to her.

"Usual thing, jealousy. You see, Ned over there, who owns the fish stall, is Polly's fancy man, and he lets her have free fish for services rendered, if you understand what I mean?"

"I get the picture," Madame Rosita said knowledgeably.

"Well, she came down this morning expecting to get her fish and found another woman being giving the same amount of free fish she usually got, so she went for her."

Madame continued to watch as the bitterness between the two females escalated with them beginning to tear at each other. She reckoned that if they were prepared to fight over a man and some miserly fish, then it wouldn't be difficult to persuade them to fight over some real money. She knew at that moment she had found her next two female fighters. All she had to do was find out who the other woman was.

Chapter 35

Word of the big fight was spreading like wildfire around the pubs and coffee houses with bets already being waged on who they thought was going to win. Trade around the fishmongers' stalls was booming with not only the regular customers but also other people, on hearing about the whores fighting over the fish, coming to the fish stall to learn more about the story. This excited the fishmonger so much that he had a poster made with a sketch of the two women raising their fists at each other, advertising the fight.

Even in the Crown pub in Lime Street there was a great interest developing in the fight, particularly with Ivy, who was, encouraged by her father, willing to put up a purse to challenge the winner in order to determine the best woman fighter in Liverpool.

The story of two fighters, one white and the other a freed black American slave, being forced to fight each other was taking on an international flavour, spreading around the pubs and coffee houses with large sums of money being staked on whether a black fighter was better than a white fighter.

All the news and rumours spreading about the fight began to worry Lord Blamfont and Sir Richard, particularly as Madame Rosita had decided to arrange a lavish private prefight party, inviting those in authority and in charge of the police so that they could be bribed with either money or sex, or if necessary both, to persuade them to turn a blind eye to the upcoming event.

The party was a great success with plenty of food and drink, the women ready to avail themselves to the specially invited guests, offering any form of sexual activity they might be tempted by, with Madame Rosita carefully watching all that was going on and making a special note of the men's particular desires and preferences for future reference should any of them renege on their promises.

* * * *

With so much publicity, the crowds were arriving in their droves from all over, either by train or by whatever means of transport they could muster. The elite arrived in their coaches and carriages. It wasn't long before the field was thronging with a mass of people.

In the staked-out ten-foot square ring there were jugglers, acrobats, and fire-eaters keeping the crowd entertained.

"This is going to be a big success. We are going to recover all the money we lost and make a lot more in the process," Madame Rosita said, dressed in her finery as she, Lord Blamfont, and Sir Richard looked on at the crowd still pouring in. Some were trying to scramble over hedges, trying to get in without paying the one shilling entry charge, and others were climbing up trees around the edge of the field to find a good vantage point without having to pay.

Michael, having been released from the debtors' prison, was now confined with Leon in a tent from which there was little chance of escape. It was being guarded by four men who had orders to restrain and cuff them if either tried to make a run for it.

Leon and Michael sat hunched, listening to the noise of the crowd, staring at each other like two gladiators in Roman times, knowing that at some point they were going to be called into the arena to fight each other and that only one of them would survive.

"We are victims of our own situations. At some point the anger dies or at least is tempered by the realisation that however hard we try and whatever we manage to accomplish, the feeling remains. And that's when a sense of worthlessness can take over and leave us with a feeling of emptiness as we're unable to do anything to heal the numbness. But it is in these moments of despair that we must find our true selves. Soon we are going to be put to the test, not for us but for the benefit of others, and it is at that moment we are both going to have to make a choice," Leon said, sensing a profound moment.

"And what choice is that?"

"I don't know. All I can say is that we must choose carefully because the choice we make today will determine what we are tomorrow."

"I remember my mother saying to me one day, 'You are free to make whatever choice you like, but you will never be free from the consequences once you've made it,'" Michael reflected with a smile.

"That is true. Every choice we make has an end result. You'll know we've made the right choice when we lose that sense of worthlessness."

* * * *

Meanwhile, while the champagne was flowing in the hospitality tent for men of special importance, with the women making sure all their needs were being catered for, Madame Rosita was busy preparing Polly and the other young woman, who she had discovered was another prostitute who went by the name of Daisie.

They were both of average height with reasonably good figures and large busts, which pleased Madame Rosita, knowing that it would delight the crowd.

"Now this is the way it's going to work. You will be announced, and when you come out, you walk to the ring, strip off your blouses, and toss them into the ring. Two of my girls will be acting as your seconds and bottle girls. We are going to do away with the half-crown bit, so I want you to really go at each other. No fancy stuff."

"Don't worry. I can't wait to rip the tits off that fucking whore," Polly cut in, her face contorted in anger.

"She won't get a chance when I get at her. If she's got any fucking sense, she'll give in now and save herself a lot of punishment," Daisie retorted with the same measure of antagonism.

"Good. That's the spirit. May the best woman win," Madame Rosita said, before turning and walking out with a broad, satisfied smile on her face.

* * * *

A great cheer went up as Polly and Daisie, with their hair tied up in bundle behind the head, made their way to the ring. An even bigger cheer went up as they stripped off their blouses and tossed them into the ring.

"You got a great pair of tits. I'd love to have a fumble at those," one of the crowd nearest to the ring shouted out at Daisie, whose high and proud breasts were tipped with pink nipples.

"I might even let you when I've finished with that bitch," Daisie shouted back, tucking her hands under her breasts and pushing them up, causing the whole crowd to cheer her.

"She won't have any tits left to fumble by the time I've finished with her," Polly shouted out.

"In that case, can I have a fumble of yours?" the man shouted back.

"In your dreams, creep," Polly answered him.

"Right. You two come up to the scratch," Sir Richard, who was acting as referee, called to them.

Both came up to the scratch, glaring at each other.

"You know the rules: there is no set length of time for any round, and the fight will end when either of you is knocked down or thrown to the ground. Once floored, you have thirty seconds to come back up to the scratch. If you can't, then you are declared the loser. You are not allowed to take a break, and you will be instantly disqualified if you fall without having taken a blow. Is that understood?"

"Yes, understood, although I doubt it will get through her dumb head," Polly said acrimoniously.

"You won't have a head, dumb or otherwise, by the time I've finished with you," Daisie retorted with equal hostility.

"You start fighting as soon as I step out of the ring and

blow the whistle," Sir Richard instructed them.

Polly and Daisie squared up to each other, the intensity building between them as they waited for the moment when Sir Richard stepped out of the ring.

As the whistle went, Polly landed the first blow full in the face, surprising Daisie, sending her reeling back against the rope, but she quickly bounced off it and swung a vicious right-hander at Polly, which missed. The fight quickly erupted with both women fiercely going at each other tooth and nail, punching with their bare fists, with the crowd cheering them on, until blood was streaming down their faces and bodies.

As Daisie went to throw one of her vicious swinging rights, Polly shot out a straight left and caught Daisie in the left eye, causing it to swell above and below, reducing her ability to see clearly. Spotting the advantage, Polly began to lay into Daisie with a series of punches to the head and body, her breasts swelling with the number of blows she was receiving, much to the delight of the crowd.

Daisie, brazen with fury, in an effort to defend herself, began to claw and scratch Polly, tearing at her face and body, the blood from the deep long red claw marks dripping down over her bruised breasts to her waist.

Polly retaliated by lunging at Daisie, grabbing her around the waist, and hurling her face down to the ground. As Polly attempted the fling herself onto Daisie's prostrate body, Daisie spun over onto her back and raised her foot, catching Polly full in the stomach, taking the wind out of her.

As Polly lay breathless, Daisie grabbed her hair, jerked her head back, and started pulling at it with large chunks coming away in her hands.

Polly then grabbed Daisie's skirt and started ripping at it, revealing her underwear, much to the delight of the crowd, which made Daisie change her tactics and start to tear at Polly's skirt.

Soon they were tearing at each other's clothes in such a frenzied rage that it wasn't long before they had almost ripped the clothes off each other.

Both tiring in their efforts, they struggled to their feet with blood streaming down over their bruised and battered near-naked bodies. They started throwing punches at each other, although with much less force than before.

Suddenly, having drawn every ounce of strength from her body, Polly threw a punch which caught Daisie full in the mouth, splitting her lip and sending a few teeth flying before she collapsed to ground and stayed there.

Sir Richard immediately stepped into the ring and declared Polly the winner, which was met with a boisterous cheer from the crowd.

"I don't think anyone would fancy fumbling with those tits the state they're in," one of the crowd remarked as Polly held her hands up in victory.

"Well, they can't say we don't give them value for money. That was one hell of a fight," Madame Rosita said to Lord Blamfont, who was standing beside her.

"Yes, we should arrange some more of them," he agreed, having clearly enjoyed the sight of two near-naked women tearing at each other. "Pity, really. I was beginning to fancy that Daisie until she got so badly damaged."

"I'm surprised you still don't want to fuck her. After all, you do seem to get excited at seeing a girl being humiliated and made to suffer," she said scornfully.

He looked at her, angry at the remark, but steeled himself. "I'd better go and see the two of them are ready," he said, knowing this was not the time to fall out as the big fight was yet to come and so much was at stake.

"Yes, you do that while I check on how our guests are doing and what they thought about the female fight," she told him, turning and making her way to the VIP tent.

Madame Rosita was hoping to see all her guests were happy and being looked after, having enjoyed the females fighting, but when she entered, it seemed all reservations and social niceties had been drowned in champagne. In the middle of the tent were a group of the men standing in a circle and looking excitedly at Maisie, who was down on all fours, her dress pushed up around her waist. She was naked from the waist down, the top of her dress having been pulled down and the corset partly undone, revealing her breasts. One man was taking her from behind while another stood in front with his manhood inserted between her bright-red-painted lips.

Madame Rosita stood there watching for a while, smiling to herself and thinking, *At least I've got them where I want them if there is to be any trouble.*

* * * *

The crowd, many of whom were well imbibed with alcohol they had brought with them or had bought from the stalls set up around the field, were now beginning to get impatient for the big fight. They started to call out with the calling spreading around the whole area of the field.

"They're as ready as they'll ever be, so we'd better get them on before there's a riot," Sir Richard said as he came and joined Madame Rosita and Lord Blamfont.

"Yes, I agree. You lead your man out, and then I'll lead mine out," Madame Rosita suggested.

"I don't think there'll ever be another fight like it," Sir Richard said, his excitement at the prospect growing.

"And may the best man win," she added as they walked off.

Chapter 36

A tumultuous cheer went up as Michael and Leon were led to the ring by Madame Rosita and Sir Richard, accompanied by Fisty as Michael's second and Hudson as Leon's second, each fighter also having a bottleman.

"You know the rules, so I don't need to repeat them," Sam Bicket said as they came up to the scratch. Bicket had been chosen by Sir Richard because the latter wanted to ensure an impartial person would referee the fight, although he knew Bicket would be more favourable towards his man because he was paying him.

"When I step out the ring and blow the whistle, you come up to the scratch and start fighting. Are you ready?" Sam asked as he prepared to step out of the ring.

The two fighters nodded. To the surprise of everyone, Leon gave Michael a brief hug as the crowd pressed forward. Sam made his way to the ropes, ducked under, turned to face the ring, put the whistle to his mouth, and blew.

The two knew each other's style so well that every move produced the exact countermove, with the result that the two of them moved in synchronised fashion with one waiting for the other to throw the first punch.

The problem was that neither of them wanted to throw the first punch and were giving little impression of aggression, which was beginning to irritate the crowd, who had expected they would have laid into each other right from the start.

"Go on, you two. Get into it or I'll disqualify both of you," Sam called out.

"Don't do that. We'll have a riot on our hands," Sir Richard told him as he rushed over in panic.

"We came here to see a fight, not a dance," one of the crowd heckled.

"Yeah, why don't you two kiss and make up and let the girls back on?" another of the crowd shouted out.

"Yeah, I'd sooner see them fighting with their tits out than you two prancing around like a couple of fairies," another angry member of the crowd called out.

Michael and Leon looked at each other, not sure what to do, but they knew they had to do something. Still, neither wanted to throw the first punch.

Michael had a better jab and better overall boxing skills, but Leon was a warrior and he had equal power in both hands.

Eventually Michael threw the first punch with a straight left to the face, but it was jab with little power in it. Leon retaliated with a flurry of hooks and jabs to Leon's arms with restrained force. They began to exchange blows as a shiver of delight spread around the crowd.

Leon swung a hard punch to Michael's solar plexus, which brought him to his knees, but he quickly collected himself. He straightened up, looking surprised at Leon for having hit so hard, and countered with a solid right to Leon's head, which sent him back several paces, his eye beginning to swell badly and his nose starting to bleed. They both now began to pace around, parrying and lunging at each other with single blows that were no longer restrained.

They had been fighting for over thirty minutes, and although both fighters were showing signs of bruising on their bodies and Leon's eye still swelling up, there was a pulsating pressure building up amidst the crowd, who were expecting a more merciless aggressive fight from the two belligerents.

Leon could sense this. He lunged at Michael, taking him into a hold, with Sam Bicket shouting, "Break!"

Leon whispered, "One of us now has to make the choice we talked about. Land me a hard punch, and I'll go down."

"No, you have too much to lose. I'll go down."

"You have as much to lose as I do."

"Break," Sam shouted again.

"Yeah, get on with it, you two. Anyone would think you

were lovers, the way you're prancing around each other," another of the crowd shouted out.

They broke away and began exchanging punches, mainly to the body to avoid damaging their faces too much. A murmur of hostility was building in the crowd, who were not happy with the way the fight was going.

"I've seen better fights in our pub," another of the crowd bellowed.

There was now a deafening clamour of jeers and shouts erupting from the crowd, which was beginning to worry Madame Rosita, Sir Richard, and Lord Blamfont as they looked on at what was happening.

Michael charged at Leon with a flurry of blows before letting him grapple him into a hold.

"Break," shouted Sam.

"I'll go down. Sir Richard won't want to have anything to do with me after I've lost, and we can set off for the United States. As the winner, you will be loved by Madame Rosita," Michael whispered to Leon.

"Break! I said, break," Sam shouted again.

As they broke, Leon swung a powerful overhand right to Michael's jaw, and he went down.

"Get up, you lazy bugger, and fight. He only stroked your chin," someone else called out, joined by the rest of the crowd, who began to chant, "Get up, you lazy bugger. Get up, you lazy bugger."

But Michael just lay there, not moving. Sam rushed across, bent over Michael, and said, "You have thirty seconds to get to your feet."

The crowd waited patiently with those at the ringside keeping a careful eye on the action. The tension that was building up amongst the crowd as Sam counted Michael out and raised Leon's arm as the winner.

At that moment someone hurled a bottle into the ring. It caught Leon on the forehead, causing a gash to open.

Suddenly the rest of the crowd followed and started hurling anything they could get their hands on into the ring.

Simultaneously they were shouting, "*Fix, fix.*"

"Yeah, a right bloody fix. The Irishman told us he was being forced to take a dive, which is why he refused to fight last time, so he was telling the truth," the man who had confronted Michael at the docks the last time said. "Yeah, definitely a fix. *Fix, fix, fix,*" he began shouting with the others, joining in until it was reverberating all around the field.

In no time a riot broke out and spread across the field with the crowd now fighting each other over whether the bets should be paid. They were arguing amongst themselves whether the fight had been fixed and Michael had taken a dive.

Madame Rosita stared in horror as the fighting moved closer and closer to the stands, causing the people there to panic and try to get away. The movement made the not so robustly constructed stand begin to shake. Together with the pressure of the rioting crowd surging forward, it wasn't long before the supports started to wobble and give way. Soon the whole structure collapsed, dropping some twenty feet to the ground, trapping many underneath.

The sounds of the rioting and the screams coming from the collapsed stand alerted those in the VIP tent, many still in the throes of various sexual activities, who began to panic, adding to the chaos.

Leon and Fisty pulled Michael to his feet to the jeers of those in the crowd who were now fighting amongst themselves. They managed to carry him out, doing their best to avoid the missiles that were still being hurled into the ring.

"Let's get the hell away from here before we get lynched. That mob is capable of anything," Sam said. "I've got my buggy just up there. I told them it was a fucking mad idea right at the start, so fuck them," he added, clearly scared out of his wits.

"You're right, a fucking mad idea. So let's get the hell out of here as fast as we can," Hudson agreed as he came to join them.

"There she is! She's the one who's responsible for this, the cheating bitch," one of the rioters called out as he spotted

Madame Rosita coming out of the tent.

"And him," another of the rioters shouted as he spotted Lord Blamfont coming out behind her.

"Let's get 'em," somebody else yelled out.

"Get back in the tent," Lord Blamfont said as he stood staring in terror at the advancing rioters.

As the rioters charged into the tent, they were amazed at what they saw: several women in various stages of undress, as well as some of the men with their breeches around their ankles. But what surprised them even more was the exotic display on the luxuriously laid-out tables of oysters, lobsters, large joints of beef, venison, wild boar, and stuffed pig, together with a glittering array of silverware, crystal stemware, and large bottles of champagne.

"Fuck me. Have you ever seen anything like this?" one the rioters exclaimed amidst the screams from the women.

"So this is what you've been enjoying while we've been watching a fight that was fixed from the start—so that you lot could fill your bellies with the like of this," the leading rioter said with an expansive sweep of his arm.

"No, you don't understand," Madame Rosita began to protest.

"Oh, we understand all right," the man behind him spoke up. "You've been having fun at our expense. Now it's our turn to have fun at your expense," the leading rioter said.

The leading rioter went straight for Madame Rosita. Helped by some of the others, he started tearing at her expensive clothes. The rest of the rioters charged forward, some going for the women with others going straight for the food. It wasn't long before Madame Rosita was divested of most of her clothes and had been hoisted onto one of the tables, where they were about to take turns raping her, her protests blending with the screams of the women as they tried to fend off the men. Suddenly a gun went off and blew a large hole in the top of the tent.

Everything stopped and all went quiet as they everyone turned and looked in horror at a police sergeant standing there holding a pistol, still pointed upwards, together with about ten constables standing behind him, their truncheons drawn.

"You are all under arrest. I expect you all to come quietly. Those that don't will be handcuffed," he announced, lowering the pistol and pointing it around at the crowd.

"Incredible. We spent a fortune bribing the police and the authorities for this not to happen," Madame Rosita whispered to Lord Blamfont while trying to cover her undressed body with anything she could grab hold of.

"This would not have happened if you had not fixed the fight," one of the senior police officers, who was there as their guest, told her.

"The fight was not fixed. I had nothing to do with what happened in the ring," she strongly protested.

"And neither did I," Lord Blamfont asserted.

"Well, I will see what I can do, but don't hold out too much hope. I think things have gone too far for me to be able to do anything," he told them. Then he moved to speak to the sergeant.

"I'm ruined. This has cost me a fortune," Madame Rosita said in anguish.

"It's cost me just as much," Lord Blamfont sharply reminded her.

* * * *

"What the hell do we do from here?" Leon asked as soon as they had gotten safely away.

"Well, I'm going to collect Mary and Holly and see if there's a boat leaving," Michael told him.

"That's providing Sir Richard doesn't try to stop you," Fisty said.

"I don't think he'll have any interest in a loser. And anyway, I reckon he's got bigger problems to deal with now," Michael said with a hint of satisfaction. "And you'll be all right with Madame as you're the winner."

"I just hope you're right. But the way the crowd were

behaving, I'm not sure how she's going to react," Leon said.

"Why don't you come with us?" Michael suggested.

"No, I told you I can't risk going back to America."

"Sorry, I forgot," Michael said, embracing Leon. "Then it's goodbye. You've been a good friend, and I am going to miss you. Sadly we may never see each other again, but I will always remember you."

"And I will never forget you. Now go before anyone catches up with you," Leon told him, breaking the embrace.

Chapter 37

For the North Atlantic routes, the Cunard Shipping Company had built four sisters ships, the *Britannia*, the *Acadia*, the *Caledonia*, and the *Columbia*. They were wooden-structured paddle steamers, two hundred and seven feet in length with a beam of thirty-four feet.

The massive wheels, driven by steam engines, that took up over seventy feet of the length of the ship produced the equivalent horsepower of more than four hundred, *horsepower* being a term adopted by Scottish engineer James Watt to compare the output of steam engines with the power of draft horses. Each ship burned around thirty-eight tons of coal per day in order to maintain a speed of around eight and a half knots.

The ships had two decks, the upper deck having the officers' cabins, galleys, bakery, and cow-house, and the main deck featuring two dining saloons and accommodation for one hundred and fifteen cabin passengers, together with all the necessary trimmings for a paying-passenger ship. The long sea voyage lasted roughly two months depending on the weather conditions.

Given that the craft had the barest of medical and sanitary conditions, it became a breeding ground for all kinds of diseases, causing serious weakness and sickness amongst the passengers, particularly as there was rarely a doctor on board, which made giving birth on board the ship painful and dangerous for both the mother and the newborn, the mother having to rely on a so-called midwife, a woman who had experience bearing several children herself to help the mother through rigours of giving birth.

There were, of course, no such things as anaesthetics or an understanding of antisepsis, which meant there was a great danger of infection. The only medication available was opium, normally used as a sleeping draft known as laudanum.

In all their anxiety to get away, Mary had not given much thought to Holly's pregnancy. And suddenly here she was some two weeks past her due date going into labour, about to give birth.

Rather than let anyone else offer to help, Mary did all she could to help in the birth, but it soon became evident that Holly's baby was stuck in the birth canal and would have to be drawn out.

Reluctantly Mary searched for the woman who had announced herself to everyone as a midwife, hoping her services would be called upon to earn some extra money. She boasted she had a Pinard horn, a type of stethoscope, hollow, shaped like an ordinary horn, made of wood or metal, its purpose being to listen to the heart and determine the position of the foetus. She also had a pair of Simpson forceps, the most commonly used amongst the various types of forceps. It had an elongated cephalic curve, specially designed for women whose vaginas had not been stretched by previous births. It had the appearance of a rather gruesome gadget that seemed more a medieval torture instrument than a medical one.

After many painful attempts, the midwife managed to eventually hook the baby out - a boy - but it was stillborn.

Holly, however, seemed to survive the ordeal pretty well, but by the next day she became feverish. By the following day she was in agony with peritonitis, and by the next morning she was completely delirious. Sadly she passed away later that day.

Both Holly and the baby were sewn up in sailcloth, and the two bundles were then carried onto the deck to lie in one of the deckhouses prior to burial.

Mary, Michael, and Fisty attended the burial, which was carried out in the early hours of the morning so as not to disturb the other passengers. The burial service was performed by the captain, who read the service as the bodies were lowered gently down into their watery graves in the deep blue Atlantic sea.

As they watched the bodies disappear beneath the waves, Fisty offered up a prayer: "We therefore commit the earthly remains of Holly and her child to the deep, looking for the general resurrection in the last day, and the life of the world to come, through our Lord Jesus Christ, at whose Second Coming in glorious majesty to judge the world, the sea shall give up her dead, and the corruptible bodies of those who sleep in Him shall be changed and made like unto His glorious body, according to the mighty working whereby He is able to subdue all things unto Himself. Amen."

The death of Holly was very hard for Mary and Michael to take. They blamed themselves, thinking that if they had not persuaded her to come with them, she would still be alive and be the proud mother of a beautiful bouncing baby boy.

Part III
New York,
United States of America

Greater Awakenings

Chapter 38

The Dutch built a town on the southern tip of Manhattan Island which they had named New Amsterdam. It had developed into a flourishing market, trading in the buying and selling of animal skins. It was a relatively small town in the mid-seventeenth century with only about one thousand five hundred inhabitants. However, the city at that time, like most cities, was expanding in a fast and haphazard way. The English took over the colony in 1664 during the Second Anglo-Dutch War and changed the name to New York to honour the Duke of York, later to become James II of England.

At that time New York was becoming the main entry point for immigrants from many European countries. These people were coming to the United States to make a better life for themselves and their families, with over three hundred and seventy thousand arriving in 1850 alone, earning New York the title of metropolitan city of the New World.

But wages, if these immigrants were lucky enough to find work, were very low, which meant they could only afford the most basic of accommodation—tenements as they were called. And there were few, if any, laws protecting the residents of tenements. Unscrupulous landlords took full advantage of this by allowing the buildings to become overcrowded, cramped, and squalid.

As a result, prostitution was becoming a pervasive part of immigration life, particularly on the Lower East Side, with Allen Street standing out as the most notorious area, where many of the prostitutes lived in the small tenements, plying their trade in broad daylight by leaning out of the windows and calling down to passers-by below. Others, less fortunate, were forced to walk the streets with their paramour pimps, who waited around nearby corners, ready to grab the proceeds of their concubines with little being done by the police to deal with the ever-increasing problem as the police themselves were often customers of the prostitutes, although they would occasionally arrest a streetwalker as a vagrant or disorderly person. But the elite brothels were never disturbed, protected by corrupt politicians and big businessmen who formed underground clubs that protected the owners of the brothels.

* * * *

It was a cold, misty morning when the ship sailed into the mouth of the Hudson River, heading for the Port of New York.

Henry Hudson was an English explorer who, in 1609, set out on a voyage, funded by the Dutch East India Company, to search for an ice-free passage to Asia. The voyage took him to the New World, where he discovered the body of water that would later be named after him.

* * * *

On arrival at the Port of New York, no one was allowed to disembark until the health inspectors came aboard and rudimentarily examined the immigrants. If anyone was found to be infected with a contagious disease, the inspectors would hoist up a yellow flag and immediately take everyone off the ship and send them to the Marine Hospital on Staten Island for treatment, where everyone was thoroughly checked again. Those found to be disease-free were then allowed to continue to Castle Clinton in Battery Park, where they were processed and permitted to enter the United States as there were no strict laws at that time on who could and could not enter the United States.

As Michael, Mary, and Fisty emerged from the hospital, Fisty fell to his knees, kissed the ground, and then raised his face and arms to the sky. "I thank Thee, Lord, for our safe deliverance upon this new land. I will do my best to treat it with kindness. Amen."

"So what are your plans now?" Michael asked, watching Fisty get back up on his feet.

"God saved me from ruination for a purpose, and I know now more than ever that I have to fulfil that purpose. He has given me the strength and guidance I need to stay and help the sick and the dying. You go your way. I pray you find peace and happiness," Fisty said with an air of solemnity. "It is a great sadness that Holly is no longer with us, but I know she will always be in our hearts. We have been on an incredible journey, and God has guided us through it, so embrace the new beginnings in the hope that there are far better things ahead than what we have left behind. Just think: yesterday is history, today we are blessed with a new presence, and tomorrow is the beginning of a new life. So work hard, be happy, and enjoy what is to come."

"Amen to that. We can never forget Holly and what she suffered. And we will certainly miss you," Michael said, embracing Fisty warmly.

"Well, you'll know where to find me. I rather feel I shall be here for a long time," Fisty said in his solemn tone.

"So where are we going?" Michael asked, turning to Mary.

"You have money. I suggest you look for somewhere well away from this squalid and disease-ridden area," Fisty advised them.

"Yes, you're right. We shall look around and find a nice boarding house well away from here, particularly after what happened to Holly," she told him.

"Then be on your way, and may God go with you," Fisty said, giving Mary a hug before turning and heading off back to the Marine Hospital.

Michael was surprised when he and Mary set off, giving Castle Clinton one last look before turning away and making their way across the New York Harbor docks. Michael was surprised to see shifty characters and con artists operating in the same way as the crimps did on the Liverpool docks, offering to "help" their fellow countrymen, knowing they would be confused and frightened at the mere prospect of arriving in a new country and therefore relieved to be met by fellow Irishmen telling them they knew of a good place where they could stay, a boarding house run by friends with good meals and comfortable rooms at very affordable rates.

"I've got to warn these people. It's just like the Liverpool docks. They're out to con them," Michael said, putting his case down and about to rush over to a group, but Mary managed to restrain him.

"No, don't get involved. There are too many of them. You can't take them all on, and we'll only finish up in trouble. The last thing we need is to get arrested on our first day in the country, so let's get away from here," she said, pulling at his arm.

"So where are we going?" Michael asked as soon as they were clear of the docks.

"As Fisty advised us, we'll try to find some lodgings well away from here," she said, setting off with a determined stride.

* * * *

After walking around for several hours looking for a suitable place, they eventually turned into West 39th Street, where Mary spotted a square brick building that had a fan-shaped window above the front door, on top of which was a wooden sign with "Parlour House" painted on it.

"That looks clean and worth a try," Mary said, crossing the street to have a closer look. "What do you think?" she asked, turning to Michael.

"Better than anything we've seen so far," he told her.

"Then let's enquire," she said, approaching the front door and pulling the door chime.

The door was opened by a woman wearing a brightly coloured dress decorated with sequins, the bodice cut low over the bosom. Under the bell-shaped knee-length ruffled skirt and at the hems, colourfully hued petticoats could be seen, her legs covered in silk lace stockings. Her hair was dyed a bright red.

"Yes?" she said curtly, looking at then suspiciously.

"We saw you have a sign saying parlour house and wondered whether you have any vacancies?" Mary told her.

"No, sorry, I haven't," the woman said, about to close the door.

"Do you know of anywhere around that might?" Mary asked, pushing her hand hard against the door to prevent her from closing it.

"Why this area?" the woman asked, looking at them capriciously.

"We want to be in a nice clean area well away from some of the places we've seen, like Allen Street, which is full of prostitutes."

The woman continued studying them. "Yes, well, they're the dregs of the trade who finish up there. You just come off the boat?"

"Yes. Even though we had a cabin, the journey was horrendous, something I never, ever wish to go through again."

"You had a cabin?" the woman cut in, her face lightening a little, seeming to be impressed they had had a cabin. "Well, maybe I might have a room. Are you going to be looking for work too?"

"Yes, once we've settled."

"As it happens, I am looking for a maid and someone to take care of security, which looks like your man is fit and strong enough for," the woman said, giving Michael the once-over.

"Oh, he's fit and strong enough. Used to be a bare-knuckle fighter."

"But not any more," Michael cut in. "I've had enough of that."

"Right, you had better come in," the woman invited, opening the door wide enough to let them in.

She led them into the drawing room, and they looked around the room admiringly, surprised at the decor. The walls were painted in chartreuse green, and the ceiling was painted in white with Lafever-style plaster cornices and an imposing

Brigitte chandelier hanging from the centre of the ceiling. The windows had trim draperies with ebullient fringes and drops. The floor was covered with matching white thick-piled carpet.

The room itself was elaborately furnished in rococo revival style with two sofas, two armchairs, and four side chairs with silk-upholstered tufted seats and backs in matching chartreuse green. The occasional tables were topped with oil lamps and porcelain pieces. A mirror-backed étagère stood in one corner with an arrangement of shelves displaying a variety of small porcelain objects. All in all it was a harmonious combination that clearly had a female element to its design, in total contrast to the plain-looking, unassuming front of the house.

The woman smiled as she studied their reaction to the room. "You seem impressed by the decor," she said appreciatively.

"Yes, very impressive," Mary said, already beginning to understand why it was called a parlour house.

"What exactly is it you would want us to do?" Mary asked pointedly.

"As I said, it would be working as a maid and your husband taking care of security, for which you will be given free accommodation and a small wage."

"Why the need for security?" Mary asked, her hunches becoming stronger.

"As you can see there are some very valuable things in this house, and what with all the comings and goings, one can never be too careful," she explained in a slightly dismissive manner.

"Yes, I can see there are some very valuable things in this room. Is this a brothel or a bordello as you might refer to it?" Mary asked, surprising herself by the bluntness of her question.

The woman's brow furrowed as she eyed Mary suspiciously. "What makes you say that?"

"I recognise the trappings," Mary said, looking at her squarely.

It was a long moment before the woman spoke, still eyeing them with suspicion. "How would you recognise a bordello unless you worked in one?"

"I did, back in Liverpool. A rather upmarket establishment that catered for the elite."

"As a prostitute?" the woman asked, surprised by her frankness.

"Yes, as a prostitute," Mary answered honestly.

"Is that what you want to do here? We could do with—"

"No, I'm not interested in working as a prostitute, but I would be interested in helping you in any other way as I have the experience. My name is Mary, and my partner's name is Michael. He also worked as a bodyguard at the brothel, so he too has the experience."

"I see," she said with a certain amount of detachment. "Let me show you to the room where you can stay, at least for tonight while I think about things. By the way, my name is Betty Talbot. I married an Irishman, but he turned out to be a useless drunkard gambler who drank and gambled himself into oblivion. I have no idea where he is now, not that I care," Betty told them.

"I always say, being single is better than being lied to and cheated on by a man who has no respect for women," Mary told her.

"But you've got a man, so you're not single," Betty countered her.

"I just happen to be one of the lucky ones," Mary said, giving Michael an adoring look.

"I've seen too many women lose their senses while waiting for a man to come to his. Some women choose to follow men, but I've chosen to follow my dream of being rich and independent of any man," Betty said ruefully.

"Is it possible we can have a meal or buy some food off you as we haven't eaten for some time?" Mary asked, a little embarrassed by the conversation.

"It will only be a sandwich or something. I'll see what I can do," Betty said as she led them up the stairs to the fourth floor, where she opened the door to the first room.

"It's not large, but it's adequate," she said, inviting them to enter, closing the door as soon as they were inside.

The room was rather small, but it was clean and reasonably well-furnished with a double bed, a double wardrobe opposite the bed, and a handbasin unit against the other wall with a small round mirror fixed above it. The walls were covered with the same chartreuse green patterned with flowers. The floor had a matching-colour carpet.

"Why did you tell her all about us working in the brothel?" Michael asked angrily as soon as the door was closed.

"Why? Are you ashamed of what we did?"

"Well, I …"

"Look, I knew this was brothel by the way she was dressed and the way the place is furnished. I'm surprised you didn't; all the trappings are here. Didn't you notice the porcelain statues of naked men and women in poses of performing various sexual acts?"

"No I didn't."

"Anyway, don't worry. I think she is going to offer us work."

"You're not thinking of going back to—"

"No I'm not, but I think there could be a great opportunity for us here. It gives us a place to stay and a chance to earn money. Just think, we've only just arrived in this country and we've already been offered work and accommodation. How lucky can that be?"

"Yes, but …"

"We have no idea what the work situation is here, and it could be months before you're able to find a job. While we are here, we won't have to have to spend any of the money we've saved," she said calmly in a matter-of-fact voice.

He nodded slowly as he thought about what she had said. "Yes, I suppose you're right. You have a way of thinking things out."

"Yes I have, and I've got a feeling something good is

going to come out of this. It seems as though we were guided to this place," she said with a smile, giving him a kiss on the cheek after seeing the forlorn look on his face.

* * * *

"I hope you find the room comfortable," Betty Talbot said with a smile as she stepped into their room carrying a tray with a pot of coffee, two cups, and a plate of sandwiches. "Sorry, but it's all I could manage, having to carry it up four floors."

"You should have called me. I would happily have come down to get it," Mary told her, hurriedly taking the tray from her.

"Well, I hope that is something you will be willing to do as I've been thinking about the job offer. And since you mentioned your previous experience in such an establishment, I thought I ought to explain how this house operates. We like to think of it as a gentlemen's club catering for the so-called upper middle class. We make sure their identities are never known to others inside or outside the house. As well as servicing clients who know about the house and the services we offer, the girls can recruit their own customers as long as they are respectable and from the well-to-do bracket. There are set charges for the various services the girls specialise in, and the house takes 50 per cent. The girls get a 50 per cent share in the profits from the sale of liquor. We also rent out rooms to adulterous couples for short periods or overnight. So if you're still interested, then I would want you to help me with the running of the place and whatever needs doing. And your husband Michael—"

"We are not married, but we are very close and love each other," Mary hastily corrected her.

"Not a problem. Anyway, I thought Michael, as he already has the experience and looks fit enough, could take care of security."

"Oh, he's fit enough all right. As I said, he used to be a bare-knuckle fighter," Mary assured her.

"Even better, as we do occasionally have problems. This will be your room, and you will each be paid fifty dollars a week. There is a small kitchen in the basement where I have a cook who makes canapés for the guests. You can use the kitchen to make your own meals when she is not using it, providing you keep it clean and tidy. So how does all that sound?"

Mary looked at Michael for his reaction, and he nodded acquiescently.

"Thank you, Mrs Talbot. I think we find that quite acceptable," Mary said with a gracious smile.

"Good. Well, now you two get a good night's rest. I suggest you stay in your room and take no notice of what is going on. Come down for breakfast early, and we'll start to organise your duties," Betty said, turning and walking out with a satisfied smile on her face.

* * * *

They both felt better after a good night's rest and a wholesome breakfast of hot cakes, bread, sausage, and fried potatoes, ready to face whatever plans Betty Talbot had for them.

"Right, I hope you both slept well," Betty said, starting to clear the plates away.

"Let me do that," Mary offered, springing to her feet. "We had a good night's rest. We were so tired, we fell asleep in no time and never heard a thing."

"Good," Betty said, relieved as she watched Mary start to clear away the dishes. "I try to make this place as a social gathering for men, providing a club atmosphere in luxury surroundings to create a feeling they are entering a special sexual-orientated world in which they become immersed in an erotic and sensual ambiance where they can patronise the services of one of the girls or just enjoy the companionship, not necessarily involving sex. And that's where your duties will be, Mary, to make sure our clients relax and enjoy the fine selection of our wines and spirits, which is a very lucrative part of the business. I will pay you an extra 10 per cent on all the liquor you sell."

"That's very generous of you," Mary said appreciatively.

"You will need to work hard to earn it, and you will have to wear fine enticing dresses. We have a tailoress who works part time who, I'm sure, can knock out something that will fit your shapely body and make you look every bit the part."

Betty then turned to Michael. "Your duties, which you said you've already had experience with, will be security to sort out any trouble and remove those who are causing the trouble. Most men, in our case gentlemen, seek and are provided with exactly what they require: impersonal sex with a girl who knows how to please them and whom they feel comfortable with. The problem is that occasionally we get a client we consider undesirable who has to be removed without disturbing the relaxed atmosphere and the smooth running of the place. This requires a certain amount of delicacy as well as strength, for the one thing we have to avoid at all costs is the police being called in. For the most part they turn a blind eye to the more respectable places like ours, as long as we keep them happy, if you know what I mean. Indeed, many of the top law enforcement officers and government officials, you will discover, are some of our best clients."

"I think I can handle that," Michael assured her.

"Good. We'll have to find you some fine clothes as well. Now that's been sorted out, you can start work tonight."

Chapter 39

Things started quietly with Mary applying her seductive skills to the waiting gentlemen, encouraging them to buy the most expensive drinks, mainly champagne, so as to greatly increase her earnings, which she could add to even more if she were keen to take up the many offers to provide additional services the men kept proposing. But she was happy to keep herself solely for Michael.

Michael was also doing well, doing the same as Leon had taught him in the brothel in Liverpool. He stood by the main entrance, politely welcoming the guests, taking their coats and hats, and ushering them to the lounge for Mary to take care of them.

It worked well. Betty was pleased with them. Their presence improved the reputation of the establishment, and its clientele increased, which in itself created another problem. Betty needed more women to satisfy the demand, but not just any women. They had to be of a certain standard. The only place to find them was the gambling saloons, theatres, and opera houses where many actresses and courtesans circulated, using their bodies, wits, and skills in seeking to attract a wealthy patron, even if he was with his wife, into a sexual relationship for financial gain. Betty especially wanted those who had the aptitude to engage in a variety of topics ranging from art to music and politics.

Betty decided she would talk to some of her most elite clients who she knew frequented these places and ask them to look out for suitable women, particularly foreign, as that would add an extra aura of eroticism to the place.

The idea worked well. Soon she had two new recruits, one a twenty-year-old Frenchwoman whose name was Nicolette and the other a Norwegian woman whose name was

Helene.

Helene was blonde with light skin, blue eyes, and a slender body with all the curves in the right places. She was the only child, her mother having died from puerperal fever three days after giving birth. Her father became an alcoholic and a reckless gambler. As soon as she was old enough, Helene got a job as a servant girl to help buy food and pay the rent on their tiny tenement flat. With her father's increasing need for money to pay off his gambling debts, he tried force her at the tender age of twelve into prostitution. She refused at first, but the beatings became more violent as she continued to refuse. Her father even raped her to show her what customers would expect of her. Unable to bear the brutality being constantly inflicted upon her, she gave in and went out on the streets.

With her father eagerly grabbing all the money she was earning and forcing her to stay longer on the streets in order to pay off his mounting debts, Helene decided she had to get free of her uncaring, brutal father. One night while he slept slumped in a chair after a boozy night spending her hard-earned money, she decided to run away.

Being free from her father was one thing, but finding somewhere to live and finding work to be able to rent a place was another. Every house displaying a vacancy sign refused her a room unless she could pay a week's rent up front plus a deposit, which she couldn't do, because in her eagerness to get away from her father, she was frightened to search his pockets for fear of waking him up.

They all think I'm a prostitute, and they're right: I am a prostitute. I was earning good money. I should find a few good customers, and then I can then afford to pay up front for a room, she told herself as she began to walk the streets. It was by chance she came upon a man who looked reasonably respectable and wealthy. The man, immediately struck by her youth and beauty, offered to find her somewhere nice and clean to live. It was her first experience of a pimp, who took all the money she earned and kept a tight control on her, beating her just like her father had if she didn't bring in enough money.

She knew she had to get free, be her own person, make her own decisions, and keep whatever money she earned for herself. She was determined to get out from under the clutches of this man.

Helene managed to escape while her pimp was busy grooming another young woman he'd found in the same way he had found her.

Having managed to keep and hide some of the money she earned, she moved to Boston, then finally to New York. She was still young and smart enough to attract the better class of client, who, she quickly discovered, were to be found at the gambling saloons, theatres, and opera houses.

Nicolette, on the other hand, was born into a luxury life in Paris. She beautiful and polished and as elegant as a ballet dancer. The daughter of Claude Marechal, a member of the National Assembly, she enjoyed all the privileges her father's position provided, that is until Louis Napoléon, nephew of Napoléon Bonaparte, staged the coup in order to stay in office and implement his reform programs, which resulted in Claude, along with other protesters such as Victor Hugo, being forced into exile. Claude Marechal chose to escape to the United States. He landed in New York, where he put his knowledge of French fashion into practice and opened a fashion house on Broadway. With Nicolette elegantly modelling his latest creations, it wasn't long before her poised demeanour was soon being displayed on the cover of *Godey's Lady's Book* displaying the latest in French couture. She gathered the attention of male admirers, which resulted in a string of prominent lovers, much to the chagrin of her father, who branded her immoral, a prostitute, and promptly disowned her.

* * * *

Betty was pleased with these two women as their names and sexy foreign accents, she knew, would be well sought after.

The only problem was that Nicolette insisted she be allowed to keep contact with some of her regular clients and her lover, a man a few years younger who didn't mind her being a prostitute. Indeed he encouraged it as it brought in money to pay for food and the rent on her expensive and lavishly furnished apartment, and it gave him money to spend. In return, she demanded strict fidelity from him.

Betty, keen not to lose Nicolette, agreed, warning her that having a lover could ruin her career, not to mention the parlour's profits. Betty suggested Nicolette bring her clients to the parlour, and she would just charge for the room and any extras the house supplied.

The two young women quickly settled into the routine. Things ran smoothly with both women in demand, the men loving how they talked dirty in their own language while they applied their special skills to satisfy the customers' various and peculiar desires, particularly Nicolette, who fulfilled her clients' dreams with her special French flair.

Mary proved a great asset, keeping the clients happy, making sure they were never without a drink. It started an idea in her head as she noted a couple of the men exchanging postcards of seminaked women.

"I have an idea," she announced to Betty the following morning while they were having breakfast. "I saw two men exchanging postcards of seminaked women."

"They do that all the time. French postcards, they call them. So what of it?" Betty said, taking a sip of her coffee.

"Well, I just thought that if our clients are so interested in them, why don't we make some of our own? Michael was telling me of the new camera that's been invented. I think it's called a daguerreotype or something like that. Anyway, he tells me the images are good. Just think, we can photograph the girls we have, sell the photos, and make ourselves a nice profit. We can also sell them in other places like the gambling houses, theatres, and opera houses."

Betty thought for a moment as she slowly replaced her cup on its saucer. "That's a brilliant idea. Maybe we can be a little more daring with the poses," she said excitedly.

"Would you like me to arrange it? We will have to buy a camera. I think it costs around six dollars."

"No problem, we can easily afford that. But what about someone who knows how to use the thing and is discreet and able to work with the girls who will be doing the posing, displaying all they've got?" Betty worried.

"I think Michael could do it. He sounded really excited about what this camera can do."

"Then I leave it with you and Michael. We'll work out some form of extra payment for both of you."

The postcards proved a great success. News of the naughty postcards began to spread all over the city with many other prostitutes offering to be photographed as a way of showing new customers what they had to offer.

It was so successful that Betty decided to display the pictures of her girls on the walls of the parlour and in the bedrooms, where the more explicit pictures were displayed to help stimulate the clients.

The reputation of the postcards began to spread well beyond New York to other towns and cities with the result that many people were writing to the parlour house wanting to know how much the photos cost and where they could purchase them. Soon a system was developed where customers could send a banknote in the value of five dollars for a set of five photos, which would then be sent to them through the postal service.

Incredibly a mail service quickly developed, with demand for the photos coming from all over the United States and beyond, making Betty's parlour one of the most well-known and sought-after brothels in New York, with clients particularly demanding the services of Nicolette and Helene, both featuring in a series of sexy poses in a postcard set.

Money was now pouring in with both Mary and Michael adding greatly to their earnings, enabling them to open a bank account with the Chartered Albany City Savings Institution.

Things couldn't be better, and all seemed to be going

extremely well, until something dreadful was to happen to change all that.

Chapter 40

When Nicolette didn't turn up at her usual time, with a client already waiting, Betty became worried and sent Michael to her apartment to find out if she was all right.

Michael gently tapped on the door of the apartment, expecting Nicolette to say "Qui est-ce" in her sexy French accent, but he heard nothing, so he banged harder. There was still no response, so he thumped the door even harder, knowing that if there was someone inside, they couldn't help hearing it. He waited, but there was still no response.

He tried the door handle, but the door was locked. He felt something was wrong. Nicolette seemed in very good health and had never missed a day at the parlour. Michael hesitated, trying to decide whether to force the door. It wasn't a particularly sturdy door. He knew that with a few hard kicks he could break it open. As he braced himself to kick the door in, it suddenly flung open, and a man rushed past him and charged down the staircase.

Michael stared at the open door and called out Nicolette's name, but there was no answer. He hurried in and stopped in his tracks, staring in horror at the sight that confronted him.

Nicolette was lying on the floor, a pool of blood on the carpet beneath her body, with what appeared to be several stab wounds to her back. A knife, the long blade covered in blood, lay nearby, along with several torn-up postcards of her posing naked on a chaise lounge, which Michael recognised as ones he had taken.

Michael knelt down by the body and felt for a pulse. Her body was still warm, but there was no pulse.

"That man must have killed her," he muttered to himself. "I wonder who he was. What do I do? Go back and tell Betty, or go to the police?" he muttered to himself.

"You must go to the police," Mary said, standing behind him. "Otherwise they'll think you killed her."

He looked up, surprised, as he saw Mary standing there. "What made you decide to come?"

"I thought I'd better come and see if she was ill as you seemed to be taking a long time."

"I couldn't get in at first. And then as I was about to kick the door in, a man charged out, nearly knocking me over."

"You mean you saw the murderer?"

"I guess I must have. She couldn't have been dead long; the body's still warm."

* * * *

Most of the important newspapers like the *New York Times*, the *New York Journal of Commerce,* the *New York Herald,* and the *New York Tribune* were mostly interested in reporting on the international and financial markets, tailored to the city's elite businessmen. However, with competition for circulation growing because of the cheaper papers like the Sun, the Courier, and the Enquirer, these papers seized on the story because sex was a topic rarely open to discussion in polite society. They all plastered the story on their front pages, and the papers flew off the newsstands.

Playing up the sexual details, they were still lacking positive facts, so they turned to blatant speculation as to who could have murdered Nicolette.

Michael had given his account of events to the police, and the police decided the most likely suspect was Nicolette's young lover, but the problem was that nobody knew much about him or even his name as Nicolette never talked much about him. As a consequence, the police decided that since the newspapers were connecting the murder with the brothel, they had better release the whole story and ask for the newspapers' help in finding her killer.

The story was suddenly propelled to the front pages of all the national newspapers. This changed the nature of crime reportingas well as the public's role in it.

The killer, Nicolette's boyfriend, a German who went by the name of Freddie, was eventually caught and arrested.

Thousands of people crowded the second floor of the city hall, where the trial was to be heard, in the hope of getting a good view of the alleged murderer of an infamous prostitute.

On the second day of the trial, the mob broke the railings in the courtroom as the accused was brought into court, forcing the courtroom to be cleared.

Michael, of course, was the chief witness for the prosecution with the circumstantial evidence leaving little doubt of Freddie's guilt. Over five days, the all-white male jury heard testimony from Mary, Betty, and Helene. The prosecution also produced the bloodied knife and the torn-up postcards, which caused an excited hush amongst the court and the jury.

But what surprised the court more was when Freddie, with an outburst of anger, suddenly shouted, "Please don't show those postcards around! They're disgusting, displaying her naked body for everybody to see. I didn't mind her working as a prostitute, but I told her I would leave if she didn't stop posing for those dirty pictures. She told me that she would do what she wanted to do. She said she was no longer in love with me and told me to get out. I was angry and picked up the knife I had been using to cut up the postcards and stabbed her with it, telling her she was a slut who deserved to die."

The court was stunned into silence as he slammed his fist down heavily on the bar of the witness box, with the prosecuting counsel saying before he sat down, "I rest my case, Your Honour."

The judge then looked at counsellor for the defence. "I have nothing further to add, Your Honour," he answered.

The jury took just fifteen minutes to find Freddie guilty of fatally stabbing Nicolette. He was sentenced to death by hanging.

Unfortunately the newspapers' coverage of the trial with the links to prostitution and whorehouses, together with the postcards, attracted the attention of a group calling itself the

New York Female Moral Reform Society, which had started around 1840 with the fundamental purpose of preventing prostitution and of encouraging sexual abstinence before marriage.

Soon it broadened its name to the American Female Moral Reform Society and was now attempting new strategies by lobbying politicians to try to make male solicitation of prostitutes a crime, adding the selling and the sending of explicit photographs of naked females through the mail, labelling them pornographic, unfit for persons of refinement to look upon, saying they should be deemed a criminal offence.

This group also discovered a pocket book that was in circulation called The Gentleman's Directory, which described in graphic detail the various parlour houses and what special services were on offer, making special mention of Betty's parlour, where clients could obtain sets of the naughty pictures featuring Nicolette and Helene.

The American Female Moral Reform Society, on learning where the photographs were being produced, stormed the parlour house, terrorising the place and smashing all the photographic equipment, before praying for deliverance of the prostitutes and their clients and, at the same time, threatening to publish the names of the men visiting the brothel in their monthly journal.

The public's fascination with the story gave the newspapers another excuse to expand on it, heralding prostitution as the inevitable result of a decline in society's morality with innocent lives going astray, even portraying Nicolette as someone who did not fit the concept of a common prostitute's sorrowful existence, those who practised their trade on a casual basis, describing her as working in a well-situated house near the top of the profession's hierarchy, leading an independent life, a life she had readily chosen for herself over more conventional options.

The massive amount of reporting by the newspapers caused people to begin to voice their moralistic concerns in the pulpits, depicting prostitutes as innocent victims caught up in a corrupt society and the brothels as places of evil, a modern-day Gomorrah.

IN EVERY ORGANISED SOCIETY, THERE IS ALWAYS SOMETHING UGLY GOING ON UNDERNEATH, one of the leading newspapers splashed across its front page.

This developing attitude caused many of the politicians and rich clientele to avoid visiting the parlour houses for fear that their names would appear in the society's journal and subsequently in the newspapers.

Their actions sent shock waves through the parlour houses. The politicians who not only frequented the places but also were taking substantial bribes to turn a blind eye were also reeling. Both knew they had to do something, and quickly, because on the one side the politicians would lose their perks, and on the other side the parlour houses would be in danger of losing their girls.

The Society of St Tammany, which was also called the Columbian Order, had been founded around 1789. The organisation had taken its name from Tamamend, a legendary Native American chief in the North-East of the United States who was said to have had friendly dealings with William Penn in the 1680s. William Penn was the son of Sir William Penn, an English nobleman, writer, and early Quaker, founder of the English North American colony that was to become Pennsylvania.

He was an early advocate of democracy and religious freedom, well known for his good relations and successful treaties with the Lenape Natives. It was also under his influence that the city of Philadelphia began to develop.

The principal aim of the Society was to make sure the poor families, notably the Irish, were taken care of and given shelter, coal, and food during the hard winters, as well as helping them find them work. As a result, the new arrivals to New York, already poor and struggling to survive, became intensely loyal to the Society of St Tammany.

The Tammany Society was organised with titles and

rituals based on Native American lore, the leader being known as the "Grand Sachem", and the club's headquarters known as "the wigwam". It wasn't long before the Society turned into a powerful organisation and became a major influence in New York politics, engaging in flagrant election fraud by employing neighbourhood thugs from the gangs of New York to make sure the vote went Tammany's way.

In 1828, the leaders of Tammany threw their support behind Andrew Jackson in his bid for a second term as president.

He defeated John Quincy Adams in a landslide victory, and Tammany Hall was rewarded with what became known as the "spoils system" with the pick the top federal jobs.

Unfortunately it was the very same top officials who appointed officers to directly run and profit from alcohol sales, gambling, prostitution, and the drug trade, making them often indistinguishable from organised criminals, often using the same gangs of thugs to extort political contributions and harass potential rivals.

The authorities, in an attempt to make it look as though they were now taking action, ordered notices to be posted to the front doors of the parlour houses which stated:

> The landlords, tenants, and occupiers of all houses of ill fame situated in and about the neighbourhood are hereby notified that all houses of the above description will now become the particular objects of the vigilance of the police, until they are supressed.

Mary and Michael were also caught up in the aftermath as their earnings were cut back, upsetting Mary's plans to open her own parlour house. She had been very careful with her and Michael's money and had saved enough for them to buy a suitable property, but all that had to go on hold as so many other things were beginning to happen.

Chapter 41

In 1863, in the midst of the American Civil War, Congress passed a conscription law making all men between the age of twenty and forty-five years eligible for military service.

By the end of the first day of the Conscription Act, over a thousand names had been selected. That night as the men drifted to the bars and taverns, they scrutinised the list of names to see if they, their sons, or their brothers were on it. As the drinks flowed, the crowds began to get angry, mainly the Irish, who had found their dream of living a good and better life, living in overcrowded slums, who were now being forced to fight for something they knew little or cared about. They had no understanding that New York businesses had a vested interest in maintaining the Southern system of slavery.

In the government's attempt to enforce the draft, violent protests broke out that ignited the most destructive civil disturbance in the city's history.

As the wealthy responded to the riots, there were renewed calls for reform with the immigrants and poor struggling to find a more effective and peaceful way to express their grievances. Realising there were political opportunities to be exploited from such groups, the new boss of Tammany Hall, William H. Tweed, who had started his political career as a volunteer fireman, decided to favour the Irish immigrants by utilising the immense resources at his disposal that only he had the power to provide, thus helping him to grow significantly in power.

The problem was that many political bodies and people like William Tweed used the laws to suit their own purposes. They awarded contracts to friends and relatives, as well as to illegal gambling dens and parlour houses, with the profits from these unlawful enterprises greatly enhancing the personal bank accounts of these corrupt officials.

Michael, to his horror, had found his name on the conscription list, but he discovered that by paying the sum of three hundred dollars, as all the elite were doing, he could get himself exempted from the draft.

Because of this, and because he was the key witness in the murder trial and also took care of security at Betty's parlour house, Michael came to the attention of William Tweed, who regularly searched after people he could employ under the state budget as so-called representatives and political advisers, who would meet with the newly arrived Irish immigrants at the docks and help them to find accommodation and generally get acclimatised to their new surroundings. These advisers would also help the new Irish immigrants gain citizenship so as to make sure that when the time came, they would vote for the political candidates nominated by Tammany Hall.

Michael wasn't sure how to react to the invitation, particularly when he discovered a gangster like John Morrissey, the leader of a gang called the Dead Rabbits, one of the most feared gangs of New York.

Strangely, the Dead Rabbits was not made up of ruffians but mainly consisted of self-employed small businessmen wearing smart suits. Because of his close association with William Tweed, John Morrissey was allowed to open a gambling house without any police interference.

John Morrissey was an Irishman born in Templemore, County Tipperary, in 1831. He was a fervent supporter of the Irish Catholics, particularly as the city was a very divided and contentious place with many anti-immigrant nativists.

One of these nativists was William Poole, commonly known as Bill the Butcher, anti-Irish and a virulent enforcer of the Native American Party, which was also known as the Know-Nothing Party, so called because its members reputedly answered any questions by saying, "I know nothing." The Native American Party believed that the overwhelming immigration of Irish Catholic immigrants was a threat to American values and that the Irish were controlled in what they thought and what they did by the Pope in Rome, an instrument of the Devil. The party called the Catholic churches "the whorehouses of Babylon".

All seemed to be going well with Betty's parlour. She managed to keep going because of the illicit patronage from Tammany Hall. Helene was now the favourite, still featuring in the photographs, although circulation was on a much smaller scale, going undercover because of the public outcry.

Mary was kept busy with a constant flow of young girls, some as young as ten, which was still the legal age for consent, being brought in by the mothers, who were fearful of their daughters having to walk the streets with the increasing level of violence, but Betty was adamant that her girls had to be of a certain standard, at least sixteen and virgins.

What Betty didn't realise was that some of the very young girls and their mothers were actually controlled and being pimped by some of the gangs of New York that inhabited Five Points, an all-pervading area of corruption, a slum consisting of countless brothels and saloons, a hot pot for crime, violence, alcoholism, drug abuse, and disease. The residents were made up of immigrants from around the world as well as hundreds of freed African American slaves.

The gangs were always looking for safer places for their girls to work. The fact they had been rejected by Betty because they were too young and not of the quality she demanded infuriated Jason, the leader of one of the gangs known as the Backstreet Boys.

Jason decided to take revenge by attacking Betty's parlour, storming in with his gang and running riot, terrifying everybody. They proceeded to smash up the place, picking up small tables and chairs and hurling them through the windows, helping themselves to the vast amount of liquor on display, smashing the empty bottles against the richly furnished walls, and abusing the girls by attempting to rip off the scanty clothes and rape them.

Fortunately Michael was on his way back, having just completed an errand for Tammany Hall, and rushed in amidst the chaos, not able to believe what was happening. He grabbed the first man nearest to him, who was now completely drunk and trying to force his attention on one the girls, and with one powerful punch sent him unconscious to the floor.

"Make another move and I'll slit her throat," Jason called out, who had taken hold of Mary and was wielding a knife at her throat.

Michael froze and everything inside him turned cold as he stared at Jason, a thick-set man with broad shoulders standing the same height as Michael, his hair cropped. But his most striking feature was a scar that ran from just below the lobe of his left ear to the middle of his cheek.

Michael knew he was no match for the gang. As he beheld the petrified look on Mary's face, he knew he had to do or say something quick.

"I have just come from the boss at Tammany Hall, and a few of his friends are due here any minute to enjoy a quiet drink. If they find you lot here and they see the damage you've caused, you won't make it back to Five Points in one piece. And even if you do, they'll come after you," he said, knowing it was a bluff, but he felt certain the mention of Tweed's name would be enough to evoke fear in them, for everyone was well aware that if you crossed the boss, you did so at your peril.

Jason, still holding onto Mary with the knife at her throat, glared at Michael, not sure what to do, while one of his gang dragged Betty into the room, her expensive clothes in tatters. "Look what I found," he announced, waving a bottle of cognac.

"Betty is a close associate of the boss, so you're even in bigger trouble now. And if you hurt her any more, you're a dead man. My advice to you is to get the hell out of here before they get here," Michael said, his voice firm and definite.

Jason slowly lowered the knife. "OK, we've done what we set out to do," he said as he turned to Betty. "So next time we offer a nice young girl, you take her and there won't be any trouble. I'm sure the boss and his associates would appreciate a nice, ripe young virgin."

315

He then turned to face Michael. "You think you're so brave hiding behind the boss, but I bet you're not so brave on your own. I reckon I could wipe the floor with you, with one hand tied behind my back."

"Well, anytime you want to chance your luck, just let me know," Michael said challengingly.

"That I'll do. You can be sure of it," Jason responded, signalling his gang to leave.

After the gang had left, they all set about tidying the place up as best they could.

"That was very brave of you," Mary said, still shaking from the effect of having a knife at her throat as she wrapped her arms around Michael.

"Yes, you were very brave. They could have attacked you, and you would not have stood a chance against that drunken, out-of-control mob," Betty told him.

"It was all I could think of to say, and thank God it had the right effect."

"Well, thank William Tweed is all I can say," Betty added.

"Do you think Jason will take you up on the challenge?" Mary asked, a look of concern clouding her face.

"No, he's all mouth and trousers as long as he's got his gang around him, but like all of them, he is a coward when he's on his own. No, we won't hear any more from him."

But Michael could not have been more wrong as word of the challenge soon quickly spread around Five Points. Like all gang leaders who make such a challenge, Jason would have to follow it through or lose face.

Chapter 42

News of the prospect of a bare-knuckle fight quickly began to spread far afield beyond Five Points, especially when rumours spread that the man Jason had challenged had been a bare-knuckle fighter back in England. It soon attracted the interest of the elite, who were always looking for excitement, anything that was worth a bet. In no time, money was being wagered on which man they thought would be the winner.

John Morrissey was an ex-pugilist himself who had had many bare-knuckle fights in his time, winning his first professional fight in 1852, against George Thompson. With the money he earned, he decided it was time to look for bigger opportunities, so his made his way to New York, where he became the US boxing champion by defeating Yankee Sullivan in thirty-seven rounds. Sullivan dominated the match for most of the early rounds with Morrissey holding his own, not willing to quit, although his face had become distorted and unrecognisable. In the thirty-seventh round, a little more than an hour into the fight, a riot suddenly broke out when Sullivan hit Morrissey while he was on his knees. The crowd started jumping into the ring, and after the chaos had been quelled, the referee disqualified Sullivan and awarded the fight and the US championship to Morrissey.

In a later fight, Morrissey defeated John Benicia Boy Heenan at Long Point, Canada, before a crowd of two thousand, pocketing a four-thousand-dollar purse and another thousand dollars on a side bet. After the Heenan bout, Morrissey, still a champion, retired from the ring, but he never lost his interest in the game. When word reached him about the possibility of a grudge bare-knuckle fight, particularly between one of the gangs of New York and an Irish Catholic immigrant, he was more than interested.

John Morrissey was already the owner of several successful saloons and gambling houses, helped by his close connections with William Tweed as well as his bribing of the police to stay away, earning him a vast fortune. Still, ever ambitious, he was always thinking of other ways to keep his clients and their wives or mistresses happy. It was while he was on a trip to Saratoga Springs that the idea came to him.

The area originally known as Serachtague, "place of swift water", was sacred to the Mohawks and other Native Americans. They believed the naturally carbonated water had been stirred by the god Manitou, endowing it with healing properties.

Over time, the extraordinary and sensational claims regarding the benefits of Saratoga mineral water multiplied to include the belief that it could cure kidney and liver disorders, rheumatism, diabetes, heartburn, scrofula, dyspepsia, cancer, malaria, and hangovers. This kept the visitors coming to enjoy these benefits the waters supposedly offered.

Interestingly, Saratoga was the spot where Lieutenant General John Burgoyne made his ill-judged attempt to invade from Canada by charging down the Hudson Valley towards New York in an endeavour to cut off the rebellious New England forces.

Finding himself surrounded, Burgoyne fought two small battles at Saratoga to break out, but he became trapped by the superior US forces and was forced to surrender his entire army of sixty-two thousand men on 17 October 1777.

It is said that the Battle of Saratoga was the most crucial and decisive battle during the American Revolutionary War, often coined as the turning point in the conflict, the victory boosting the spirit and morale of the Americans, which also gave inducement to the French to secure an alliance with the Americans to provide military and financial support to oust the British. Burgoyne obtained permission from General Washington to return to England, where he came under sharp criticism for his actions and was never allowed to hold an active command again.

The village soon became a town and gradually evolved into the city of Saratoga Springs, with the waters still the main attraction. By the mid-1800s, the city was becoming the summer home of many wealthy Americans and internationals, as well as a hotbed for both tourism and gambling. Even the Civil War was of little concern to the wealthy who sought refuge from the heat of cities like New York and Boston, and so Saratoga Springs continued to grow.

Morrissey saw it as the perfect place to set up a gambling house. It was conveniently near the new train station and full of well-heeled tourists with little to spend their money on, who needed something more to fill the evenings apart from the few restaurants.

Soon the gambling house was up and operating during the evening and night.

With the success of the gambling house, John Morrissey quickly realised the potential of the area and purchased the Saratoga Race Course, used for harness racing, so that his clients would be able to gamble at the racecourse during the day and gamble in the casinos at night.

It was a financial success. He purchased the ninety-four-acre site across the street from the trotting grounds with the idea of building a brand-new racecourse and converting the original dirt course into a training track.

It was the perfect place to stage the fight and make a lot of money in the process. Morrissey knew bare-knuckle fighting was illegal, but with his connections to William Tweed and Tammany Hall, he felt confident he could make it happen.

All he needed was to get to Michael before anyone else and offer to sponsor him. He knew of Michael, of course, through his work at Tammany Hall and was impressed with his stature and apparent fearlessness. He was even more impressed when he found out he was an ex-pugilist like himself.

Michael was surprised by the offer that Morrissey was willing to sponsor him and put up a purse of five thousand dollars to go to the winner.

When the news reached Jason, he got excited at the thought of winning five thousand dollars and sent a note to Morrissey to say he was more than ready for the fight.

"Are you seriously going to go ahead with this?" Mary asked, looking at Michael, concern clouding her face.

"I don't think I have much choice," he said with a despondent shrug. "If I don't, everyone will think I'm a coward."

"Who fucking cares what people think? I know you're not a coward," Mary said reassuringly. "I don't want you to be a hero. All I want is for you to be an ordinary guy who cares for me."

"I don't want to be a hero either, but that Jason and the rest of the gangs will think I am a coward, and who knows what they would do then. Mr Morrissey is letting me use one of the stables at his racecourse to train in. If only Fisty were around. I could really do with him now." Michael exhaled contemplatively.

"If he's still in New York, we should be able to find him," Mary suggested, accepting the inevitable, that Michael had little choice but to go ahead with the fight.

* * * *

Mary, not sure of what Fisty's religion actually was, could not be certain of where to start looking. She knew he wasn't Irish, so that ruled out contacting the Catholic churches. It was now a matter at looking at what other churches there were.

The first church Mary visited was St James Church, a small parish church established in 1810 as a summer chapel for New Yorkers with country homes north of the city. Situated on Hamilton Square, it was a simple building with clapboard siding and a quaint belfry. The priest told her Owen Fitzgerald was a parishioner, but he tended to do God's work in his own way, caring for the immigrants, spending most of his time at the hospital and the docks.

Mary suddenly felt silly. *Stupid me, that's the first place I should have looked. He told us when we parted that was where he was going to work,* she reflected as she made her way to the docks.

Strangely Fisty was not surprised to see her when she confronted him outside the hospital.

"I guess you've come to talk to me about the fight," he said with a knowing smile. "It's the talk of the docks. Everyone's speculating on it."

"Yes, Michael needs your help," she told him.

"Give Michael my blessing, but I can't ignore the plight of these people. Just look around; they are desperate for help," he said with a wide sweeping gesture of his arms.

"We'll happily pay you for your time," she said, hoping it would encourage him.

"Jesus says if you have Him, you have everything and that anything extra is a blessing. So on that basis I will accept it as a blessing, a blessing for those I will be able to help with that money," he said with an air of reverence. "Tell Michael I can start whenever he wants."

Fisty had not lost much of his stockiness, and his face was still covered with a silver-grey beard, matching the colour of his curly mopped hair.

He had not lost his touch either. Soon he had Michael in shape with the racecourse being the perfect training ground, having him racing against the horses to strengthen his legs, doing press-ups to strengthen his arms, and soaking his hands daily in the mixture of brine, green vitriol, copper, whisky, gunpowder, and horseradish to make them hard as iron again.

On learning his opponent was in intensive training, Jason began to realise things were becoming serious. If he were to stand any chance of winning, he had to get himself fit as well, as this time he was going to be in a fight without any weapons or his mates to back him up should he get into difficulty.

With all the rumours spreading about the approaching fight, giving it all the promise of being one of the greatest sporting events of the year, John Morrissey knew he was onto a winner and wanted to maximise on it in every way he could. He had the small stand where the crowds who could afford the entry fee would watch the harness racing, but he calculated it would not be enough to hold the expected crowd for this event.

As the publicity grew, the police were even more of a worry. He decided to draw the boss, William Tweed, into the event, offering him a nice backhander if he would use his powerful influence to get the police to keep clear of the event.

William Tweed explained to the chief of police that the fighters were not going to hurt each other. It would be more like a match where they would score points, as was done in fencing, but without the swords. It was simply to be an exhibition of the noble art of boxing.

Whether the chief of police believed him, which of course he didn't, was of no consequence as the bribe was enough to convince him not to intervene.

With the hostilities between the Irish and native-born Americans at a peak, fights were breaking out on a daily basis between supporters of the two men as talk of their respective merits filled the working-class saloons. John Morrissey knew he now had to fix a date for the fight.

The result of the massive social transformation was a powerful resurgence of anti-immigrant sentiment with immigrants being accused of undercutting the wages of American native workers. The sentiment was particularly strong against the Irish, whom they accused of having established a foothold in urban politics, which caused the native-born politicians to depict the Irish as a threat to US democracy.

Finally, both Michael and Jason signed the articles of

agreement, which stated the fight would take place in a twenty-four-foot roped-off ring at the Saratoga Race Course according to the London rules as laid down in the fistiana. Each man would be attended by a second and a bottleman, and the combatants would toss a coin for choice of corner. Two umpires would be chosen by the backers to watch the progress of the fight and take exception to any breach of the rules. A referee would be chosen by the umpires, and his decision would be final and binding on all parties. The date was fixed and the fight was on.

Chapter 43

They came by train, by stagecoach, by carriage, by cart, on horseback, or on foot to see the fight, converging on the racecourse in their thousands.

John Morrissey was in his element as he surveyed the crowd, which he estimated to be around five thousand, each paying a dollar entry fee, on top of which he would increase his takings by way of his gambling houses and the betting booths he'd set up on the grounds.

It was without a doubt going to be the most successful event he had organised with the biggest crowd in attendance he had ever drawn.

Mary and Betty had been given seats in the stand alongside the wealthy men, their mistresses or their wives enjoying the occasion, sipping their glasses of champagne, while around the grounds the working class were enjoying knocking back mugs of beer with many of them already in a state of drunkenness. The Irish and the Native Americans beginning to square up to each other.

Suddenly a great cheer went up from the nativists as Jason emerged from his tent behind the stand, waving to the crowd as he approached the ring and throwing his hat in. Michael emerged a few minutes later to rousing cheers from the Irish immigrants as he reached the ring and tossed his hat in. Both stripped to the waist and tied their colours to their corner: red, white, and blue for Jason and emerald green with white spots for Michael. Then John Morrissey tied the stake money, a banker's note for five thousand dollars, in a leather pouch to one of the neutral stakes.

Both men were impressive and almost equal in stature. It looked like it would be an even fight that could go some thirty rounds.

"This is going to be the fight to end all fights," John Morrissey said to William Tweed, who was standing beside him, elegantly dressed, his incipient paunch bulging out over the top of his waistband and his famous ten-pointed five-carat diamond brooch pinned to the front of his silk shirt.

"Yes, I reckon you're right. And I hope our man wins. The honour and reputation of Tammany Hall is at stake here," William Tweed said mordantly.

"Yes, and mine too and the future of the racecourse. I don't mind who wins as long as it is a good fight and the public feel they've got their money's worth. Then we can arrange a return fight and make even more money."

"Hmm, an interesting thought," William Tweed acknowledged, his mind already calculating how much he would personally make out of the deal.

"Just remember all I've taught you, the same as before. Let him come at you. He's a scraper with no finesse who will just swing wild punches in the hope of catching you with one of them. Keep your distance and let him tire himself out. Then you can pick him off at your will," Fisty told Michael as he sat him on the bottleman's knee, a black man he had chosen by the name of LeRoy, which pleased Michael.

"Go for the kill and knock the shit out that Irishman. The whole of Five Points is behind you," William Poole told Jason, giving him a heavy slap on the back as he sat on the bottleman's knee. "Your win will be a kick in the teeth to all Irishmen who think they can come over here and take over our country, as well as Morrissey, William Tweed, and all who suck up to them. Just remember, he's got a preacher training him, praying for a miracle that God lands a punch for him," he added with a chuckle.

John Morrissey blew the whistle for the combatants to come up to the scratch. Jason got there first, determined to show he was eager to get on with fight.

"I'm going to beat you to a pulp," Jason snarled as he and Michael squared up to each other.

Michael said nothing, just stared him out as Tom Casey,

325

appointed by Morrissey to referee the match, reminded them of the rules.

"You have been told the rules," he began. "But just to remind you, a knockdown will be the end the round, followed by a thirty-second rest and an additional eight seconds to come back up to the scratch. Butting, gouging, hitting below the waist, and kicking is not allowed, and either one of you attempting that will be disqualified. So when the whistle goes, come up to the scratch and start fighting," he said finally as both fighters returned to their corners.

The whistle blew and Jason rushed across to the scratch, his head down. He started throwing wild punches as he attempted to land a heavy blow anywhere on Michael, to the great boisterous cheers of his supporters.

Michael smartly sidestepped and backed away across the ring, not throwing any punches, just making sure he stayed a safe distance from the wild swinging punches. The more Jason was missing with his punches, the more he was becoming angry. He shouted out, "Stand still, you Irish pig, and fight like a man."

Michael said nothing and kept moving back, well away from the punches Jason was continuing to try to land on him. The punches lost most of their power in their aimlessness.

The Irish crowd began to jeer at Michael, thinking he was scared of Jason, frightened to get into a slugging match with him, but he ignored them, knowing exactly what he was doing. No jeering was going to make him move until he was ready. Once Jason had begun to slow and not swing so wildly, Michael knew it would only take one good solid punch to put him down. As long as he kept dodging Jason's flurry of punches, the moment would present itself.

It came quicker than he or anyone could have expected. As Jason appeared to be flagging his head down with his arms flailing wildly, Michael moved in with a series of jabs to his head and body, following up with a powerful right cross to the jaw, causing Jason's leg to buckle. He folded to the floor. His second and his bottleman rushed in and dragged him bodily to his corner. They propped him up on the bottleman's knee, trying to revive him as quickly as they could within the thirty seconds allowed.

Jason was in a bad way. His face was swollen, one eye was almost completely closed, and his body was badly bruised.

"Come on, you lousy coward," his supporters began to shout. "Get back in the ring and do what you promised you'd do."

Jason wasn't hearing them, and no matter what his second tried to do, there was no way he was going to come up to the scratch.

After the thirty seconds had elapsed and the referee had counted the added eight seconds, Jason was still on the knee of the bottleman, but before the referee could declare Michael the winner, Jason's supporters stormed the ring in the hope of giving Jason a chance to recover while the organisers tried to restore order.

But the Irish was having none of it as they too stormed the ring to protect their victor. In the confusion, with hundreds of people pushing, shoving, and punching and hurling missiles at each other, the situation was quickly spiralling out of control with both corners trying to protect their fighter.

It was the one thing John Morrissey was fearful of, particularly as the fighting was now spilling out all over the grounds with rival factions using whatever they could get their hands on to attack their opponents.

The elite in the stand were now in a panic, adding to the confusion as they tried to flee the brawls that were ebbing ever closer to the stand. Mary and Betty were lucky and managed to get away when one of the parlour house clients offered them a lift in his carriage.

Fisty and LeRoy managed to get Michael away, with the crowd more intent on wrecking everything in their path, including the beer tents, from which they stole and consumed what alcohol they could grab, while the Native Americans were storming the betting stalls, demanding their money back, claiming the fight was a fix.

Jason was dragged away to safety by his gang.

Fisty, LeRoy, and Michael got to the stables and hid themselves amongst the horses. Unfortunately they had been spotted, and a large mob of nativists, mainly from the Bowery Boys gang, armed with metal bars, pickaxes, crowbars, and wooden clubs, quickly massed in front of the stables. "Come out, you cowards, or we'll burn the stables down," one of the gang members shouted out.

"What the hell do we do now?" Michael asked, fear beginning to show on his face.

"Let me talk to them," Fisty suggested. "They just might listen to me."

"And they might beat you up as well," LeRoy said fearfully.

"But I have the Lord on my side," Fisty said with a confident smile. "You two stay back while I speak to them."

Fisty slowly opened the stable door and stepped out. The crowd suddenly went silent as though stunned that someone would have the nerve to dare face them unarmed.

"I have long understood that in any contest, someone has to win and someone has to lose. It goes with the territory. It is part of the risk. And pain is part of the bargain when you find you or the one you gambled on has lost. As long as anger, paranoia, and misinformation drive the unhinged souls amongst you who feel justified in turning to violence as a remedy for their disgruntled feelings, there is no hope for any of us," Fisty said solemnly.

"What a load of rubbish. The fight was fixed, and your Irish git in there was part of the fix. So bring him out and let us deal with him, and then we'll let you go," the man at the front wielding a crowbar, who appeared to be the leader, told him.

"In God's name, I urge you to turn and walk away," Fisty pleaded.

"You mean in the Pope's name—and he doesn't tell us what to do. That's the trouble with you Catholics. You think the Pope is all-powerful. Well, he ain't as far as we're concerned, so get out of our way or we'll take you down as well," the man threatened.

"I'll take down the first man that moves," Fisty challenged.

The first man did move, and Fisty felled him with a single blow, which stunned the mob into silence.

Another man moved forward, and Fisty felled him too, but then the mob surged forward and Fisty was beaten to the ground. The mob then set about breaking down the stable door using their axes and iron bars, the yelling and the noise of splintering wood frightening the horses. It didn't take long for the door to give way.

Michael and LeRoy were discovered hiding in a corner as the terrified horses bolted through the open door.

What excited the mob more was the sight of LeRoy, a black man. They hated blacks more than they hated the Irish.

"Right, let's lynch the nigger," one of the gang called out.

LeRoy was grabbed and hauled outside. "Come on, let's string him up," another of the gang urged them on, the excitement growing.

Fisty, struggling to his feet, saw what was happening as a group of the mob grabbed a rope hanging with an assortment of horses' harness and threw it over a heavy branch of a nearby tree.

"If you do that, you will all rot in hell," Fisty shouted at them.

They all turned and stared at him.

"All that crap about hell and damnation means nothing to us," one of the mob retorted.

"Well, it should, for it is His pleasure that keeps us all from being swallowed up in everlasting destruction. So I urge you to think carefully on what you are about to do. His wrath will burn like fire if He looks upon you as deserving of nothing else but to be cast in hell," Fisty told them with as much as solemnity as he could.

"I don't care about all that crap. The nigger's guilty of aiding and abetting in the fixing of a fight and should hang for it," the leader spoke up.

"Yes, lynch the bastard," the gang shouted in chorus as they rushed forward and grabbed hold of LeRoy.

Fisty and Michael rushed forward to try to free LeRoy, but they were relentlessly beaten until they were badly bruised, bloodied, and rendered unconscious. Fortunately they didn't witness LeRoy being strung up and left to dangle, his legs flailing until the final kick, which signalled his death.

The rioters were spilling out onto the streets, frightening the local residents. The police, although slow in reacting because of their deal with William Tweed, were now forced to intervene.

When they reached areas where the rioting was happening, they were violently beaten back by the members of the various gangs of New York, who were streaming through the streets and surprisingly working together, angry at the defeat of one of the leaders of the Five Points gangs, hell-bent on revenge.

On top of all this, there were thousands in the saloons across the city awaiting word of the outcome of the fight. When the news came that the fight had been fixed, fighting began to break out between rival groups who only minutes earlier had been laughing, joking, and sharing drinks with each other.

The newly invented telegraph lines were tapping out the result of the fight as soon as it was known to deliver it to the multitudes by way of railway stations and newspaper offices across the nation, as far as the system reached, quickly followed by news of the riots.

Barkeepers were working overtime, keeping the glasses filled of the Irish, who were packing the saloons and celebrating their hero, but not for long as the rumble of thundering footsteps could be heard approaching.

One of the drinkers rushed to the door. "It's the native gangs from Five Points. They're heading this way," he called out. "We'd all better get the hell away from here."

"No, we stand and fight the bastards. This is our part of

the city, and none of the likes of them are going to shift us," Paddy, one of the other drinkers, spoke up, raising his pot of ale to demonstrate his defiance.

"Paddy's right, we're as good as them anytime. So let the bastards come, and we'll show them what for," another of the drinkers called out.

There was a general shout of approval.

"Please," the landlord shouted out. "Not in here. They'll wreck the place."

"Nah, don't you worry, the bastards won't get in the door," another of the drinkers shouted out.

The thunderous noise of the approaching crowd was getting louder, together with the sound of street signs being torn down and trash cans being kicked and overturned as they came closer to the saloon, shouting, "Down with the Irish Catholics and lovers of niggers, taking all our jobs on the docks."

The angry gangs charged at the heavy wooden door, but it was solid oak and wouldn't budge.

"Let's burn it down," one of the gang shouted.

"Yeah, burn it down and them with it," a chorus of them shouted out.

One of them lit an oil-soaked rag and placed it against the door. The dry varnished wood soon took hold of the flames as someone else lit another oiled-soaked rag and placed it up against the wooden-framed window. In no time the saloon was engulfed in flames.

"Let's burn all their saloons," someone else in the crowd cried out.

"Yes, burn, burn, burn," the gangs echoed as they moved on to find the next Irish saloon.

Squads of police and militia were being hurriedly despatched to the reported troubled areas, but their numbers were too small to have any real effect as more buildings were being set on fire and shops looted.

Columns of smoke were beginning to appear over the city skyline. The volunteer fire services started racing to the fires to see who would get there first, but when another fire service arrived, instead of cooperating to extinguish the blaze, they would face each other off and fight for who would have control of the building and be able to claim the insurance money and the spoils, completely ignoring the fire, letting it burn itself out. The situation repeated itself as more and more fires broke out around the city.

Word had also gotten around that Michael worked at a whorehouse called Betty's Parlour, and a gang called the Whyos, one of the most dominant gangs of New York, which had started as a loose collection of petty thugs, pickpockets, and murderers, had graduated to more high-class crimes like counterfeiting, prostitution, and racketeering, took notice.

Betty and Mary had made it safely back. All seemed well, although they could hear sounds of the rioting. Suddenly the sounds seemed to be coming closer. Betty hesitantly peered out the window and was horrified to see an angry mob heading straight for the house.

"Upstairs, everyone. They're coming for us. We can't risk staying down here," she shouted to everyone.

The women started to scream in panic. "Shut up, you idiots, and get yourselves up to the attic now," Betty yelled at them. Luckily because of the rioting there were no clients around.

The Whyos quickly bashed the door down and poured in, smashing anything in their way in the process.

"Where are the fucking bitches?" one of the Whyos called out.

"Search the house! They've got to be here somewhere," another of them called out.

Rampaging through the house, they eventually found the women all huddled up together in the attic.

"Bring the whores down and we'll teach them a lesson not to have an Irish bastard who cheats at fighting working for them," the one who appeared to be the leader told them.

They dragged Betty and the working women down to the lounge.

"Right. Strip them. We may as well have some fun in the bargain. And there's plenty of booze if any of you fancy a drink," the man leading the Whyos said.

Full of booze and lust, several of the Whyos started to tear at the women's clothes, ignoring their screams of protest. One of the women was completely stripped, dragged across the room, bent over a table, and held down and as one of the Whyos prepared himself to penetrate her. Then there was a sudden sound as several of the Dead Rabbits gang members rushed in.

"This is our territory," the leader of the Whyos shouted out.

Not any more, it ain't," the leader of the Dead Rabbits countered. In that instant the women were forgotten as a fight ensued. The place was eventually wrecked, both sides using furniture and anything else they could grab as weapons.

The Whyos, clearly outnumbered and suffering a heavy beating from the Dead Rabbits, decided to make a retreat while most of them were still on their feet.

After they had fled, Betty, adjusting her torn dress as best she could, thanked the Dead Rabbits and told them they could drink what they liked. She added that the girls would be happy to reward them for saving their lives.

Chapter 44

The repercussions started as soon as the riot was over with accusations flying around Tammany Hall. People were demanding to know who was responsible for allowing an illegal bare-knuckle fight to take place, who the organisers were, and who the main ones to financially benefit from it were. There was little mention about the lynching.

The finger of suspicion pointed straight at William Tweed as everyone knew he was the only one with the power to allow such an event to take place. The suspicions grew stronger when rumours spread that William Tweed was demanding a large sum of money from John Morrissey in recompense for the money he had wagered but had never gotten his winnings because the gambling houses refused to pay out, believing he was part of the fix.

In no time John Morrissey and William Tweed were at war, accusing each other of being the one responsible. Tweed threatened Morrissey that Tammany Hall would no longer turn a blind eye to his illegal gambling houses.

In return, Morrissey threatened to expose the corruption, and the kickbacks and payoffs William Tweed received from contractors and his other nefarious deals with businessmen.

As the newspapers reported on the riot and the notoriety of the feud, it marked the beginning of the end for William Tweed and Tammany Hall.

* * * *

Michael had slowly and painfully recovered from the beating under the careful nursing of Mary and Betty, who at considerable expense quickly repaired and refurbished the parlour and had it back open for business in no time.

Fisty was cared for at the Marine Hospital, where he too made a slow recovery, but the lynching of LeRoy affected him greatly. He was unable to comprehend how a so-called civilised society could behave in such an inhuman manner.

And things would never be the same at the parlour houses with the wealthy clients now wary of the newspapers exposing the large bribes being paid to William Tweed, the police, and other members of Tammany Hall.

Reform groups like the Society for the Prevention of Vice and the Society for the Prevention of Crime, and its successor the Committee of Fourteen, patronised by wealthy New Yorkers including Andrew Carnegie and John Rockefeller Jr., began to target brothels and pressured for reforms and laws aimed at curbing vice.

Fed up with the rampant corruption and the total disregard for the lynching at Tammany Hall, John Morrissey ended his association and turned his attention to his gambling enterprises and his dream to build a new racecourse on the land he'd purchased on the other side of Union Avenue.

He had struck up a friendship with Cornelius Commodore Vanderbilt, the shipping and railroad tycoon, a sportsman and gambler who was a frequent visitor to his establishments. The two men got along well. Vanderbilt gave Morrissey valuable tips on the stock market and what shares to buy.

Morrissey's empire was growing fast with more people visiting his gambling houses. He realised he needed stronger security against the cheaters, con artists, hustlers, thieves, prostitutes, and thugs who managed to sneak in, hoping to make a killing. He decided that Michael was the perfect man for the job, having proved himself a tough fighter.

Michael was flattered to be offered the job, but he told Morrissey he would only accept if Mary was offered a job as well.

That pleased Morrissey because he was also wanting someone to supervise the waitresses in the restaurants and those who served the drinks in the gambling houses.

Much to Betty's regret, they accepted the offer, which

also included a fully furnished apartment all to themselves.

Morrissey moved Michael around his various enterprises whenever he got news of impending trouble.

As Michael moved around the tables, he was met with different reactions, some people acknowledging him for his prowess and slipping him a tip, and others from Five Points resenting him for beating one of their own. The latter shouted obscenities as he walked past.

He was in no doubt that if there were any trouble, it would be a situation he would have to handle with care, as the wrong word or wrong move could easily provoke a fight.

Everything was going along well. Michael and Mary were both earning well, but Michael was getting restless and was constantly looking around for something else that would spark in him an interest. The opportunity came while he was taking a walk along Broadway, where he chanced to hear the sounds of a group of violins playing.

Fascinated, he stood listening, recognising some of the music they were playing, particularly Michael O'Rourke's *Amilie*. It made him smile as he began to mimic the bow movements on his pretend violin.

"I see you play the violin?" a voice spoke up from behind him.

Michael turned to look at the man who had spoken, an expression of sadness spreading across his face, causing him to lower his eyes in embarrassment. "I started to learn, but that was a long time ago."

"Well, it's all a question of practice. We all keep on learning. If you played once, you can play again. Would you like to come inside and meet the others?" the man invited.

"Others?" Michael asked, surprised.

"We are a group of amateur musicians. We've formed a quartet, and we perform at various functions, which helps to pay the bills and to rent this room so we have somewhere to practise. I was on my way in, so come in and meet the others. My name is Henry Delaney. I'm the first violinist. Unfortunately we lost our second violinist recently, so we are anxiously looking for someone to replace him," Henry told him, offering his hand.

"I don't think there would be much point. I've forgotten all I learned."

"No, it didn't look like you had. I was watching you, and your movements were cantabile, smooth and flowing with a sense that you know that particular piece well," the man said in a knowledgeable manner.

"That's because that was one of the first pieces of music Mrs Talbot taught me to play."

"She taught you well, so please come and join us? We're all Irish, by the way," he added, recognising Michael's accent and again offering his hand to shake.

"I'm Michael Flanagan," he said, taking Henry's hand and shaking it warmly.

"Wow, you have very strong hands," he reacted, feeling Michael grip his hand firmly. "Unlike any musician's I know. We tend to keep our hands supple at all times."

"Mine were supple once, until I took up bare-knuckle fighting."

"Bare-knuckle fighting? What a contrast. How did that come about?"

"It's a long story, a situation forced on me," he said, a sense of guilt nagging at him.

"I remember my parents telling me once that we learn something from everyone who passes through our lives. Some stories are painful, some are painless, but all are priceless, because the pain you feel today can be the strength you feel for tomorrow. For there is always the chance to change every situation encountered giving the opportunity," Henry said, surprising Michael with his profundity.

"I'm not sure what you're saying, but I would like to come and meet the others."

The chamber was relatively small and barely furnished with a scattering of chairs and a small table. The chairs were arranged in a circle, where the other two members were seated with their music stands placed in front of them.

They stopped playing as Henry walked in with Michael. "This is Michael Flanagan," Henry announced to everyone. "He used to play the violin."

"Used to?" the cellists spoke up.

"Those are his words, but I'm sure he still can play. He hasn't played for a long time. It's like riding a bicycle. Once you get back on, you find you can still ride it," Henry explained, before turning to Michael. "I have a spare violin. Would like to try it out?"

"I don't know. I told you, I haven't played for years," Michael pleaded, his jaw clenching at the thought.

"Well, there is only one way you're going to find out," Henry said, taking a violin and bow out of one of the cases stacked against the wall.

The whole group watched as Michael took hold of the violin and the bow. They were surprised as he instinctively felt the tension of the hairs and then carefully turned the screw at the end of the bow to tighten the hair, finally sliding his pinkie finger between the stick and the hairs to check the tension. He then tucked the violin under his chin, took up the perfect hand positions, and began practising the open strings, G, D, A and E, from the top to the bottom string.

"Well, for someone who hasn't played for years, you don't seem to have lost your touch," Henry said appreciatively, turning to the group. "I watched him outside miming to Michael O'Rourke's *Amilie*, so why don't we play a section of that and see how Michael manages?"

Michael struggled with the piece, his hands not as supple as they needed to be.

"Obviously your hands are not supple enough to be able to feel the string vibrate as you play the note. I assume you are pressing too hard on the fingerboard, your left arm and shoulder tending to get tense while doing vibrato," Henry said. "But never mind. With a few more practices you'll soon get rid of that," Henry said encouragingly.

* * * *

"What's all this about this about you and the violin?" John Morrissey asked, as word had gotten to him, causing him to become worried that people would think his head of security was a sissy and chance their luck elsewhere.

"I've joined a small amateur string quartet. I used to play the violin when I was young, back in Ireland," Michael told him.

"Are they any good?"

"They are, but I'm having to learn all over again."

"You'll soon catch up. You're a determined man. But you've given me an idea. Since we've upgraded the casino, we are attracting a higher-class and more sophisticated clientele, and I think it would give a more relaxing atmosphere to have soft music playing in the background. And it would give the women something to listen to while their husbands are at the tables."

"Are you suggesting the string quartet I'm playing with?"

"Yes, sounds a good idea to me."

"But I can't do security and play the violin at the same time."

"No, of course not, but you will always be at hand should trouble
break out."

"Well, if you're happy with that, then I will have a word with them and see how they feel," Michael said, excited about the thought.

Chapter 45

Mary was proud of Michael, amazed at his versatility with the violin, not really having taken much notice when he had told her he had been taught to play the instrument as a young boy. But she was a little worried when she remembered him telling her that he had a fight with someone who had called him a sissy for playing the violin.

"Do you think they'll call you a sissy?" she found herself asking as they left the apartment for the first night the quartet were going to be playing at the gambling house.

"I'm no different just because I play the violin," Michael said, his impassive face and exasperation hardening his words. "No one can take away from me who I am and what I am as a person. One man tried that once and came to regret it," he said, the thought stirring up his childhood memories.

"Yes, you told me about it, which is why I asked the question."

"Well, let's just hope I don't have to prove myself again."

The idea was a great success, and the quartet proved popular, particularly amongst the women, who were fascinated that a strongman like Michael could play the violin. It pleased the men too as they could relax at the tables in the knowledge that their wives or mistresses were not sitting around getting bored.

John Morrissey was also pleased as it was attracting a better class of clientele, which is what he had hoped for. To him it was money well spent. As for the quartet, they were now earning more money than they ever had.

* * * *

Ironically, it wasn't long before Michael's words were to come back to haunt him. Jason had not forgotten the beaten he took and needed to prove to the Whyos that he could still wipe the floor with Michael given the chance. When the rumours spread that Michael had gone soft and was now playing the violin, Jason felt this was his chance to get his revenge.

It was late in the evening in the clubhouse, as John Morrissey had renamed it. It was crowded with every gaming table occupied. John looked around pleasurably, his mind happily counting the dollars the punters were losing at the tables. The women sat at the small dining tables in the lounge sipping their champagne as they listened to the quartet playing Antonin Dvorak's *Serenade for Strings* in E major.

"Look at him, the sissy, fiddling away," Jason's loud voice boomed out across the clubhouse. His mouth curled back in a malicious grin, revealing a row of rotten teeth.

Everyone turned and stared in his direction as he continued shouting. "Bet you're not so handy with your fists now."

The quartet stopped playing, and Michael looked across hard at Jason, who felt Michael's malevolent stare course through his body. It was a long moment before Michael spoke. "I have no desire to fight with you or anybody else. Just go quietly and there will be no trouble."

"Trouble? Who's going to make trouble? What are going to do, whip me with your fiddlestick?"

"No. I've done with fighting," Michael said coolly, his manner giving no indication of what he was thinking. "They say the memory of a beating gets worse with time, so go away, lick your wounds, and stop being a nuisance to everyone."

"All I want is a chance to get revenge for that beating and knock the shit out of you, sissy boy," Jason replied, flushed with outrage, the lust for revenge and his unyielding hatred clearly showing on his face, the anger dripping from him like sweat. "We can have it out either in here or outside on the racecourse. Which would be better? I'd be happy to punch you to the ground like you did me, but as everyone knows, that was a fluke. This time I won't be so careless and make the same mistake," he challenged.

The atmosphere was heavy with suppressed violence. One wrong word or move was all that was needed for the place to erupt into violence.

"Look, no one wants a fight," Michael said as he carefully placed his violin back in its case and got up, his body bristling with frustration. "It is by choice and not by chance that we change our circumstance. I have chosen to change mine, and you should change yours, for violence only achieves more violence," Michael surprised himself saying, remembering that Fisty had once said it to him.

"That's all bollocks. The only thing people understand are these," Jason said, holding up his clenched fists.

Michael remembered his father saying the same thing when he persuaded him to give up the violin and learn to fight, but now Michael had determined he would not be a victim of circumstance but would do the things he wanted towards a better and happier life. "It doesn't matter how much you try to provoke me, I am not going to fight you," he said without anger, in a quiet, dignified manner.

Jason gave him a cold, forbidding look, worried Michael hadn't taken the bait and was getting the better of him. He had not provoked Michael in the way he had hoped, and his gang members were looking at him, wondering what his next move was going to be.

Tension was building as everything had stopped at the tables and the men were now beginning to take bets on whether the fight would take place and who would win.

Jason was beginning to the think his foe had taken the bait, but Michael was getting the better of him.

"If we don't do something quickly, a fight could break out, and that would be disastrous. There's only one way to settle this," John Morrissey said as he stepped onto the small stage. "Go outside and settle it. Give him a good hiding like you did last time, and that will be the end of the matter."

Michael turned and looked at him. "Some people don't

like to be beaten and never forget when they are. So how many times do I have to beat him for him to forget?" Michael said, a growing tension in his voice.

"He is not going to go away until you do. Another good hiding and he's finished. The gang will then walk away from him," John Morrissey said in an attempt to encourage Michael, knowing another fight, even untimed like tonight, would draw a crowd and earn him extra money.

"No, I'm not having you fighting any more," Mary said firmly, her eyes cold and disapproving as she rushed up onto the little stage.

"Now he's got his fancy woman telling him what to do. Only a man who plays a fiddle would allow a whore to tell him what to do!" Jason jibed.

A hot rage was beginning to possess Michael at Jason's calling Mary a whore; he knew he had to control his emotions. But before he could say anything, the crowded clubhouse began chanting, "*Fight ... Fight ... Fight.*"

The other three of the quartet looked up at Michael sympathetically but said nothing.

The chanting from the crowd was becoming incessant as the excitement grew. Even the women joined in, equally excited at the prospects of a fight.

"I don't think I've got a choice," Michael said to Mary.

The muscles tightened in her neck. "Of course you've got a choice. Say no and let's get out of here," she said angrily. "What is it you once told me? The best fight is the one you don't have to, and this is one you don't have to."

He clamped his top lip between his teeth. "The truth of the matter is, if we tried to leave, we'd never get out of here in one piece because they would be waiting for us. And I wouldn't be able to protect you. There will be too many of them for me to handle. So the best thing is to deal with him alone and finish it once and for all. As Fisty always told me, never start a fight, but never lose one either," Michael said with an air of resignation.

Michael then turned to look across at Jason. "OK, you got your wish, but understand this: whoever wins, let it be the end of the matter."

"It sure as hell will be the end of the matter—the end of you, that's for sure," Jason snorted in a sarcastic tone.

"So if everyone would make their way to the training round, I think we have a fight on our hands," Morrissey announced, relieved there wasn't going to be any fighting in the clubhouse.

On hearing this, the whole clientele moved as one, getting to their feet, rushing out of the clubhouse, and heading for the old racecourse, which was now used as a training ground for the horses, to ensure a good position. Their wives and mistresses quickly followed behind, eager to see the fight.

"What am I going to wear? I can't fight dressed like this," Michael asked, dressed as he was in a tuxedo.

"I'll go back to the apartment and get the clothes you wore at the last fight. I never threw them away after I'd washed the blood off them," Mary told him.

"You can definitely throw them away after this," he said as he watched her hurry off.

* * * *

The crowd was getting larger all the time as news spread about the fight. It worried John Morrissey as there was no time to warn and bribe the police and he could no longer ask Tammany Hall or William Tweed for help, so it was a risk he was going to have to take. He would argue it wasn't an organised fight; it just happened and he had no control over it.

He was right about Tammany Hall and William Tweed. When they heard about the fight, the first thing William Tweed did in his bitter resentment of John Morrissey for having turned against him was to inform the chief of police.

There was no time for a proper ring to be erected, so the crowd at the front squared off to form a human ring.

Jason was the first out, his gang mates forcing a path through the thronging crowd, some slapping him on the back as he made his way through. Once in the ring, he stripped to the waist and called out, "I'm ready, so where's the fiddler? Tell him to bring his fiddle as he's going to need it."

The crowd laughed, all getting excited they were about to see a hard-fought bare-knuckle fight to the finish.

"Look at that crowd, just baying for a fight. You don't have to do it and I don't want you to do it," Mary pleaded as they stood watching Michael now stripped to the waist, wearing the tight-fitting knee-length breeches and canvas boots.

"If you don't fight him, there'll be a riot and they'll start wrecking the place. I can't let that happen," John Morrissey said, a hint of panic in his shocked expression.

"So who am I fighting for? You? Me? Who?"

"For both of us—you for your reputation and me because I employ you, which will end if you don't go out there and deal with it," Morrissey said, the ruthless lines of experience around his eyes showing that he sensed Michael's indecision.

"That's unfair. Michael didn't ask for any of this," Mary protested, her face flushed with outrage. "You're a hard man."

"Life has made me that way," John Morrissey retorted, meeting her gaze head-on.

"This won't stop him or others like him," Michael said, feeling his whole future was at stake.

The crowd was getting impatient and started calling out. "Come on, Michael, show us what you're made of."

"Nah, he's too cowardly to try a second time," Jason shouted over them. "There you are. Listen to them," he said in Michael's direction. "Do you want to be thought a coward?"

"He's no coward," Mary fumed, her eyes glistening as she glared back at him.

"I know that, but just listen to them. They're beginning to think you are," John Morrissey said as the crowd continued with their banter.

"Right, let's get it over and done with," Michael said,

anger getting the better of him.

The ranting changed into a great cheer as the crowd spotted Michael heading their way. Suddenly all kinds of bets were being placed with all sorts of odds on offer.

With John Morrissey carving a way through the crowd, Michael made it to the ring.

"Right, we don't have a referee, so I trust you both to play by the rules."

"I don't care about any rules; let's just get on with it," Jason said aggressively, squaring up to Michael.

"OK, as soon as I step out of the ring, you two set to it."

As Morrissey pushed his way out through the crowd forming the ring, Jason immediately started throwing punches, wild punches that were doing more damage to the air than to Michael, who was still light on his feet, managing to keep a safe distance from being hit. But as Michael backed towards them, Jason's supporters shoved him forward, causing him to take a heavy punch on the jaw, dazing him. As he stepped back, the supporters shoved him forward again, resulting in Michael taking another heavy punch.

Dazed but careful not to step back, Michael raised his arms to protect himself as Jason threw a series of punches to his head and body. "I'm going to finish you for good," Jason cursed as he continued the flurry of punches.

They were wild punches without direction, so they were not as effective as they should have been. For this reason, Michael let him continue, knowing it would tire him and slow him down. But Jason seemed to be much fitter this time as though he had trained for this fight. He didn't seem to be tiring, and his punches were beginning to have an effect. They were hurting. Michael knew he had to back away before Jason did too much damage. Michael's nose was already swelling and bleeding.

He pulled away and sidestepped at the same time and went into the attack, forcing Jason to back away towards Michael's supporters, who moved forward and shoved Jason forward, allowing Michael to catch him full in the face with a straight left, causing his nose to bleed.

This made Jason angry. He rushed at Michael, grabbing him around the waist and wrestling him to the ground. Rolling on top of Michael, Jason began to pummel his face.

Michael's face was starting to swell, and the blood from his nose was spattering over his face.

This was not the kind of fight Michael was used to, nor was it what he had trained for. While trying to defend himself against the merciless continuing blows, he was trying to think of the best way to get out of the situation, which he knew he had to do quickly, before his face became pulp.

Michael's accepting that Jason was not playing by any rules forced one of his arms free. He raised it up and punched Jason on the back of the neck. It stunned Jason into temporary immobility. Michael was able to push him off and get to his feet. He looked down at Jason, knowing he had only thirty seconds to get to his feet, but again Jason wasn't playing by the rules. As Michael started to walk away the winner, Jason grabbed him around the ankles and tripped him. Michael fell heavily onto his already swollen, bruised face and was stunned enough for Jason to roll onto his back and begin pummelling him again, only this time on the back of the head, forcing Michael's face hard into the ground.

Michael placed his hands firmly on the ground and, with herculean effort, raised his body up, twisted, and threw Jason onto his back. Michael once again sprang to his feet, aware he was not going to win this fight wrestling the man.

Jason once again tried a leg sweep to try to knock Michael off his feet, but Michael managed to move away in time. Jason, realising Michael was not going to wrestle him, scooped up some of the dirt with his hand and, as he got to his feet, threw it in Michael's face, temporarily blinding him. As Michael raised his hand to wipe the dirt from his eyes, Jason swung a vicious right hand to the stomach, causing Michael to lower his hands as he doubled up. With Michael's guard down, Jason swung another hard right to the jaw. Michael's legs buckled. As he fell to his knees, Jason moved in for the kill, but before he could deliver the coup de grâce, some of Michael's supporters rushed forward and dragged Jason away as he shouted, "You can't hit a man when he's down."

This provoked Jason's supporters to surge forward. They broke up the human-formed ring to drag Michael's supporters off Jason. Soon the supporters were fighting each other. The fighting quickly spread through the crowd, who now started fighting amongst themselves, to the horror of John Morrissey and others standing a safe distance away. In the melee that followed, several were knocked to the ground and were trampled on, and some who remained standing were pushed and jostled, the women starting to scream as they hurried back to the clubhouse.

Adding to the horror was the sudden arrival of the police in large numbers, who simply charged into the crowd, hitting out at anyone within reach, whatever their social rank.

As John, Mary, and the others looked on, the chief constable appeared. "You're really in trouble this time," he said to John Morrissey with a wry smile.

"I don't know anything about this. I came out when I heard the commotion and was about to stop it when …" John Morrissey said, meeting the chief constable's malevolent stare with a look of total innocence.

"That is not what I've been told," the chief constable replied with a sarcastic scoff.

"Yes, and I bet I know who told you. And he'll bring you down just as he will be brought down, so you had better be careful which side you choose," John cautiously warned him.

"You're right in one respect, but this was not just the work of William Tweed. He had no choice but to act as he did with the political reformists demanding changes."

"In that case I'm happy to join with them to bring Tweed and his corrupt regime down."

"That's as it may be, but I'm still going to have to arrest you," the chief constable reminded him.

"That's up to you. But do you really want me to spell out in court all the bribes I've given you over the last few years?"

John challenged.

The chief constable's eyebrows furrowed and his lips pressed together as he consciously thought of the consequences.

"Depends on how much faith you have in the law," John Morrissey continued. "It's not the same for everyone, as we would like to believe. You and I know different. So you had better decide whose side you think the law would be on in this case. As you saw it, I was standing here, not having had anything to do with the fighting," John Morrissey said, not confirming or denying anything.

The fighting by now had fizzled out with the police having succeeded in breaking it up. Now people were walking or limping away, many with blood-spattered head wounds.

"I suggest you put it down to a fight between a couple of the New York gangs that got out of control and you rushed here in good time to put a stop to it. That will look good on your record, and no more will need to be said," John Morrissey suggested.

Michael luckily had been pulled to safety by some of his supporters all the way back to the clubhouse. He was in a bad state, his face swollen with one eye almost closed, his lip cut, his body covered in bruises. "He would have killed you if we hadn't stepped in when we did," one of the helpers told him.

"I know. I've never had to fight like that before," Michael said, every word hurting as he spoke it.

"That's the only way those gangs know how to fight, and they're prepared to fight to the death if they have to. They don't care who gets killed," the helper continued.

Mary came hurrying in, horrified at the sight of Michael, and rushed to his side. "My darling, you're really hurt. I was weak. I should have stopped you."

"No, there was no choice. It had to end here. And if he thinks he's won, then fine, I don't care," he said, forcing a smile to his cut lip. "I'll soon recover, and then we can think of what we want to do."

"How do you mean?" she asked, worry shadowing her

lovely features.

"I've had enough of this place. How would like to come with me back to Ireland?" he surprised her by saying.

"But you said it was a horrible place with everyone starving and dying."

"Yes, it was then, but I've been told things have changed since. I want to go back to where my parents died and lay some kind of memorial to them and all the others that perished during that dreadful time. And then if you are not happy, we can always come back."

"That is a lovely thing you want to do, and I'm happy to go with you. And who knows, you might find a string quartet over there that you can play with," Mary said approvingly.

"Now that is a very exciting idea. I might even find Mrs Talbot."

"Who's she?"

"The teacher I told you about, who encouraged me to play the violin."

"Oh yes, I forgot."

"I would kiss you if my lips weren't so sore," he said, forcing another smile, a little broader this time.

"I'll try to kiss them better," she said, leaning forward and gently brushing his lips with her own.

Chapter 46

Michael was in the reception of the clubhouse, his mind going over how he was going to tell John Morrissey they were leaving, when he heard a voice call out in an anguished tone, "Thank God I've found you."

The voice was immediately recognisable. Michael broke into a smile as he turned around, but the smile slipped from his face as he stared at Leon standing there. He looked in a terrible state, his clothes dishevelled and stained, his face strained.

"Leon," Michael said, not sure what else to say, gladdened, but stunned by his sudden appearance and the condition he was in.

"Michael, I need your help," Leon said. "Can we please go somewhere and talk?"

"Sure, let's go to my and Mary's place," Michael invited.

Leon gave a cursory look around and followed Michael to his place.

Mary leapt to her feet as though she was looking at a ghost as Michael walked in with Leon.

"Leon," she exclaimed, "where the hell did you come from?"

"Let him sit down. I think he could do with a drink—and maybe a good meal as well judging by the look of him," Michael said as he guided Leon to a chair.

"Sorry to surprise you like this. I have been searching for you since I arrived in New York, but now I'm on the run."

"On the run? Why, what have you done?" Mary asked anxiously, not giving him a chance to explain.

"That's the point: I've done nothing wrong. Just being black is enough. I'd had enough of Liverpool and decided I would like to come out here and join you."

"We're delighted to see you. So what's the problem?" Mary asked, always having had a soft spot for Leon.

"Slave catchers and the Ku Klux Klan."

"Slave catchers and the Ku Klux Klan?" she repeated in astonishment.

It was after Robert E. Lee's surrender that the Ku Klux Klan came into being when six young ex-Confederates met in a law office in December 1865 to form a secret body. It was from that beginning in the little town of Pulaski, Tennessee, that the body began to grow as word quickly spread about a new organisation whose policy was to protect the rights of slave owners travelling the countryside, North as well as South, to recover runaway slaves and punish them before selling them back to their owners," Leon explained.

"Yes, a lynch mob here hung a black American and nothing was done about it. The perpetrators were allowed to walk free," Mary said, her eyes full of meaning.

"Yes, some people I was hiding with told me about the lynching of LeRoy, who they said acted for you as a bottleman in one of your fights," Leon told them, looking at Michael as he spoke.

"Yes he did, and it cost him his life," Michael said, fighting to control the tremor in his voice.

"Lynchings are still taking place all over America, particularly the South," Leon said as an awful stillness took hold of him.

"I don't understand. Slavery has been abolished," Mary exclaimed.

"Yes, that's what everybody believes. But do you know anything about the Fugitive Slave Act?" Leon asked.

"No, what's that about?" Michael asked.

"To abolish slavery, wasn't it?" Mary cut in.

"Not exactly, because the Act effectively compelled citizens to assist in the capture of runaway slaves."

"But you're not a runaway slave," Mary interrupted

again, trying to cut through the emotions that were beginning to cloud her mind.

"In order to ensure the statute was enforced, the Act placed control over whether you were a freed slave or not in the hands of the federal commissioners. These agents are paid more for returning a suspected slave than for freeing him. The Act also denies slaves the right to a jury trial and increases the penalty for interfering with the rendition process to one thousand dollars and six months in jail."

"You said the Act *was* enforced, which suggests it is no longer enforced?" Michael queried.

"It was repealed in 1864, but the Southern States refused to accept it, and it hasn't stopped the illegal slave catchers from doing their work. You may remember me mentioning Eugene Trompson, the owner of the plantation in South Carolina where I was enslaved?" Leon said.

"Yes, I remember you telling me about you and your father fighting for him," Michael said.

"Well, Eugene Trompson died, and his son now runs the plantation. He apparently spotted me when he was last in New York on business. It seems New York does a lot of business with the South as the cotton kingdom, but it is also trading in tobacco and sugar from Louisiana, filling the warehouses along the waterfront with all the products of slave labour. Even the New York banks are helping to finance the crops as well as planters' acquisition of land and slaves. The insurance companies offer policies that compensate owners on the death or disappearance of a slave."

"How is it you know so much about this? And where does Eugene Trompson's son fit into all this?" Mary asked, becoming even more puzzled.

"Well, like you, I thought slavery had been abolished, which is why I felt it safe to come back. Apparently after having spotted me, Trompson's son immediately reported me to the commissioners as one of his runaway slaves and paid some slave catchers, members of the Ku Klux Klan who freely roam the streets, to kidnap me and take me back to the plantation."

"But he can't do that. It's illegal. And you've got a paper stating you are a freeman."

"I had, but someone stole it, which means I can't prove a thing. So if the slave catchers get hold of me and put me in front of the commissioner, he'll adjudge me a runaway slave, hold me in Ludlow Street jail, and order me to be returned to the plantation."

"So what can we do about it?" Michael asked, anxious to help. "Although I'm not quite sure what we can do as we are planning to leave for Ireland."

"Could I come with you?"

"Of course you can. At least no one can touch you there," Michael said with an air of certainty.

"The words of the Declaration of Independence were proposed to embrace the whole of the American people, but it seems the enslaved African race were not intended to be included," Leon said despairingly.

"Then the sooner we leave, the better," Michael said.

Chapter 47

The Saratoga racetrack was packed as it was the last day of the four-day meeting with the Travers Stakes race, the highlight of the meeting.

"Maybe we should come back tomorrow when this is all over," Mary suggested, looking at the crowd packing the stand and the others spread all along the rails surrounding the track.

"No, we have to start packing today. We'll find Mr Morrissey and explain the urgency. He'll understand," Michael said assuredly as he headed to the clubhouse with the others following.

It was then that they encountered four men dressed in a variety of costumes which featured animal horns and fake facial hair, the men's faces blackened with polka dots. Each had a reflective silver badge with a star at the centre and Runaway Slave Patrol, Georgetown County, South Carolina, embossed around the edges pinned to a black flowing robe. Each of them carried a heavy wooden stick or club. These men had appeared from out of the shadows and confronted them.

"And where do you think you're going?" one of the Klan asked, a note of menace in his voice.

"We are on our way to see Mr Morrissey, whom we work for," Michael told them.

"You might, but the nigger as sure as hell doesn't," the Klansman who appeared be the leader said.

"What is it you want?" Michael asked, knowing full well what they wanted.

"The nigger," the lead Klansman answered, waving his heavy wooden stick in Leon's direction. "We've come to return him to his owner, Mr Trompson."

"You can't do that. He is a freeman," Mary protested.

"Then he can show us his paper," he demanded, holding

out his hand.

"My paper was stolen from me," Leon told him.

"Yeah, that's what they all say. Mr Trompson insists he's a runaway slave," the lead Klansman said in a derisive tone. "And we're here to take him back."

"You have no right to do that. Slavery has been abolished," Michael persisted.

"Maybe here, but down South things are different. The slaves are needed back to repair the damage you Unionists did to our land and plantations, and the Thirteenth Amendment to the Constitution provides that neither slavery nor involuntary servitude, except as a punishment for crime whereof the party shall have been duly convicted, shall exist within the United States, or any place subject to their jurisdiction, but nigger boy here will be convicted of assaulting Mr Trompson's father, resulting in his untimely death."

"That is absolute rubbish," Leon exclaimed.

"Well, you'll get your chance to prove that," the lead Klansman said, his eyes cold and disapproving.

"What are we going to do?" Leon whispered nervously.

"There is only one thing we can do. I'm not going to stand here and let them take you," Michael whispered back, feeling rage rising in his chest.

"We're outnumbered, and they've got sticks," Leon whispered apprehensively.

Michael allowed a slight bitter smile to cross his face. "But we've got fists which have proved their worth many times. They're bullies. Once we get in close, they won't stand a chance. As my dad taught me, get them before they get you," Michael said under his breath.

"Stand well back," he said to Mary. In that instant both he and Leon charged, catching the four Klansmen by surprise. Before they had a chance to raise the clubs and sticks, the lead Klansman was caught by Michael with a vicious right cross to the chin, sending him reeling backwards. The one standing beside him was also caught with a straight left to the face by

Leon, splitting his nose with blood beginning to spurt from the wound.

The other two Klansmen waded in, swinging their clubs wildly in an effort to force Michael and Leon back, but their aim was erratic, allowing Michael to duck under the wild swings and land a heavy blow to the stomach of one of them, causing the man to double up, which gave Michael the opportunity to deliver a right upper cut to the chin, which knocked the man senseless. He dropped the club as he collapsed in a heap.

Before Leon had a chance to deal with the other man, he decided the better part of valour was to turn and run, leaving the odds very much in Michael and Leon's favour.

As the lead Klansman recovered enough to scramble to his feet, still clutching his stick, Michael went for him, delivering a heavy blow to the side of his head, sending him back down, knowing it was going to take him a long time to recover this time.

The other Klansman looked down at his fallen leader in dismay, his face reddened with anger. "OK, you've got the better of us this time, but this is not over. We'll be back. That you can be sure of."

Without anyone realising it, a crowd had begun to gather on hearing the commotion, although they were not sure what it was all about. Then suddenly a policeman barged his way through the crowd.

"What the blazes is going on here?" he demanded, waving his baton in no particular direction but simply as a sign of his authority.

"These men were trying to take my friend away, accusing him of being a runaway slave," Michael explained.

"And is he?" the policeman asked, snorting contemptuously.

"No I'm not," Leon asserted.

"Have you got your paper?"

"He doesn't need a paper. All slaves are free now," Mary said, her face flushed with outrage.

"Well, that's what you think, young lady, but the plantation owners are demanding the return of their property, and we have a duty to …"

He didn't get a chance to finish the sentence as the crowd began to close in on him with one of them saying, "We fought the South to end slavery, and your duty is to arrest these bastard so-called slave catchers."

The policeman looked around at the threatening crowd, trying to make his mind up as to what he should do next. The atmosphere was heavy. The people could sense his indecision. He felt trouble looming if he didn't say or do the right thing. "Right, you three are under arrest for violating the Constitution," he said, hauling the Klan leader to his feet, knowing he would release them once he had gotten them away from the hostile crowd and out of the racecourse.

"You two put up one hell of a fight," John Morrissey said as he joined them.

"You mean you watched us and didn't come to help?" Michael said, surprised.

"I wanted see how you would handle it. We would have come to your aid had it been necessary," John Morrissey assured Michael and Leon. "Thank heavens I've got someone like you working for me."

"As a matter of fact, that was something I was coming to talk to you about. I'm afraid we are going to be leaving much sooner than we planned as a result of what has been happening to Leon, like just now."

"Yes, I can understand that, and I'm truly sorry you're leaving. I wish there was some way I could dissuade you," John Morrissey said, saddened by the news. "What made you want to go back to Ireland?"

"It's something Michael has been thinking about for some time," Mary told him.

"I don't know where I'm going to find anyone to fill your places," he said with a long, drawn-out sigh.

"We would have given you more time if it hadn't been for Leon's problem."

"I see," he said, trying to understand. "But those things are now against the law."

"As far as they are concerned," he said, speaking of the Klan, "there are no laws, just force and fear," Leon told him. John could see there was an anguished air about him.

Morrissey's eyebrows furrowed and his lips pressed together as the scene came back to him with appalling vividness of Jason and his gang invading the clubhouse and the consequences that followed.

"No," he found himself saying. "You're right. I can't risk having anyone else coming here threatening to wreck the place," he said, his voice low and strained.

"Don't worry. There is no reason for them to come here. And we intend to leave as soon as we can," Mary said soothingly in an attempt to reassure him.

"No, there isn't. And Leon will be a lot safer in Ireland."

"Well, if you ever come back, there will always be a place for you here," John Morrissey promised Michael.

"Who knows, I may well take you up on that," Michael assured him as he took his hand and shook it warmly, not knowing whether he would ever see John Morrissey or the United States again.

Turpitude

Sin is as old as time itself, for it is said that the fall of humankind began when Eve tempted Adam to eat the fruit from the tree of the knowledge of good and evil, which God had forbidden.

It is believed the Fall brought sin into the world, causing all humans to be born into original sin.

Therefore, throughout the ages, there have been a number of factors that have contributed to sin, such as poverty, gender and ethnic biases, social unrest, and military conflict.

Since the beginnings of time, serfdom in all its forms was accepted and recognised as a natural way for society to conduct itself. With the progressive advances in technology, people were beginning to find ways to travel, explore new-found territories, and expand their influence over larger and larger areas. The first form of transport was, of course, the animal, which people had learned to domesticate.

The earliest form of travelling on water was achieved by making a boat by hollowing out the inside of a large tree trunk.

The Egyptians were the first to invent a sailing boat, by binding bundles of papyrus reeds together to form square sails. Progressively they began to construct stronger vessels, using linen to make the sails, that could travel greater distances across the seas.

This new-found form of transport gave rise to mass immigration of the underprivileged living in poverty and desperately wanting to find a better land, free from want and serfdom, but without realising it, they instead found themselves being enslaved by the people of the new land where their boat had landed, with the men being forced to work the land and the women forced to become concubines. Slavery progressively increased as boats got bigger and became ships, able to carry more people, resulting in the pirates capturing more and more people, providing the Egyptians with a surplus of slaves, which they quickly learned they could sell to other countries they were trading with.

Slave markets began to spring up, producing a new source of revenue. With wars breaking out, the captured prisoners, both civil and military, were forced into slavery and sold at the markets to the highest bidders.

The practice of buying and selling slaves, particularly females being forced into prostitution with brothels being established at the ports, provided another lucrative component to a developing sex industry.

Even though sex trafficking is technically illegal in every country in the world, the law is rarely enforced owing to a number of factors, including corruption in law enforcement and a lack of international coordination in investigating and prosecuting sex trafficking criminals.

Whether they are women forced into prostitution or men forced to work in agriculture or construction, or whether they are children in sweatshops or girls forced into marriages they have no say over, their lives controlled, giving them no choice but to do as they're told, slaves exist in the world today.

Slavery did not end with abolition in the nineteenth century as we all would like to believe. For all its good intentions, all abolition did was to change its form so people could continue to enslave millions of other people in every country in the world.

With the advent of the internet, a superhighway uniquely suited to both the promotion of and increase in the scope sex trafficking and sexploitation, the situation has worsened. It therefore should come as no surprise that since the invention of photography, pornography in all its forms has pervaded the internet with the number of pornographic websites continuing to explode to more than double the number of websites devoted to any of the other highest categories within the United States, which seems to be the capital of pornography.

About The Author

John Sealey has spent his entire working life in the film and television industry, beginning his career in the cutting rooms, becoming a film editor, and working on many international feature films and many major filmed television series. John decided to widen his scope and move into production, becoming an assistant director, then moving into production management, becoming a production manager, production supervisor, associate producer, and finally producer/director working with many of the major US and British studios.

John has also written and directed many commercials, documentaries, and feature films. John now concentrates his creative mind on writing novels. This is his eighth novel.

John is a freeman of the City of London.

Printed in Great Britain
by Amazon